THIEVES First printing. July 22, 2020.

ISBN: 978-1-7329215-4-2 (Hardcover)
ISBN: 978-1-7329215-2-8 (Paperback)

Creative Force Publishing
cfpublishingllc@gmail.com

Cover by: Damonza.com

THIEVES

A STOLEN TIME NOVEL

LYN SOUTH

*For my Head Boy with the
Ravenclaw lanyard.*

CHAPTER 1

THIS IS the last heist I'll ever pull. After this, I'll have enough money to do as I damn well please. I'll never be hungry or homeless again. I'll pick my favorite year, go off-grid, and disappear into time itself. I'll be free.

As soon as I get out of this cramped, stinky bathroom, I'll be free.

My only escape route is closed. *Merde.*

A mere six feet from my hiding place, the Grand Duke of Tuscany pens a letter at his desk. Peering through the crack in the door allows a glimpse of the Duke as he works. His feathered quill bobs in staccato rhythm with each furiously scribbled stroke, but my attention is drawn to the closed door to his right.

I can't leave without the diamond. I've planned too long, risked too much, to abandon my prize. I had only been in the Grand Duke's bedroom for a few minutes when my search was interrupted by his early arrival home. By a rough estimate, I've been hiding for thirty minutes. I'm forced to wait until the duke leaves the room or retires for the night before finishing my search for the jewel.

Patience is not a quality I possess.

The bells of the nearby church tower ring midnight. It doesn't faze the master of this house. Cosimo de' Medici sits in a linen nightshirt, his coat discarded next to the chair. Close at hand are dusty, unpacked saddlebags. A decanter on his right has dispensed three glasses of expensive Italian brandy since he sat down to work.

His bony shoulder blades strain against the opaque fabric of his shirt, and he looks like an overgrown schoolboy in his father's clothes. More to the point: He looks settled into work that could burn further into the night than his half-spent candle will bear. I bite my lip to suppress another, louder, curse. Fagin chides me for being vulgar, but I find it a useful means of self-expression.

The maids empty the chamber pot — a cream-colored ceramic piece adorned with the five red balls of the family's coat of arms — and the acrid smell of aged piss hangs in the air. It doesn't bother me; as an indentured servant on the merchant ships of New Orleans, I'd smelled worse. The bigger problem? There's nowhere to hide if the duke relieves himself before going to bed. I have one small advantage: Sneaking into the villa dressed as a servant boy allows more stealth and anonymity than the seventeenth century gown I wore earlier in the evening.

"Clémence Arseneau, where the hell are you?" Commander Jackson Carter says. I don't know why he's whispering. The Comm-Link all Observers wear sits down inside the ear canal, so only the person wearing the thing can hear its broadcast. The unit includes an integrated microphone that allows hands-free voice-activation and volume control.

Damn. I turned the volume down earlier, because I was sick of hearing him talk. I give the computer a command. "Increase audio volume twenty-five percent."

I know I'm late to the extraction point. The other thieves made it on time, I'm sure. They all resist the urge to stray outside the strict boundaries of our fortune-hunting mission rules. Incentives for mercenaries to stay on the straight-and-narrow lie in the penalties for taking a cut of the Benefactors' plunder: A life sentence to a prison planet or a slow, painful execution.

Fearing imprisonment or death is no excuse for the absence of imagination and having the courage of profiteering convictions.

"Arseneau, acknowledge," Carter says, his voice tinged with irritation. I know what he'll say when we're face-to-face because I've heard it dozens of times—I put the mission and the team in danger with my side jobs. I disrupted the legendary clockwork precision of his plan by going off on my own. Again. Blah. Blah. Blah.

My mentor, Fagin, has said that I'll regret ignoring rules, but I don't believe in regrets. They're a waste of time and energy.

My tongue sweeps over parched lips. "I'm trapped," I whisper.

A beat. I imagine him peering at his display screen to see where I am. "In the toilet? Again?" Carter asks. "You have twenty minutes to get your ass back to the ship or you'll be walking home."

He thinks he's hilarious.

He knows I'm stuck in the loo because he can see everything I see. I could turn off the LensCam contact lenses—another piece of required equipment—without removing them, but there would be questions. They're designed to broadcast the minute they're inserted; the operations team, back on the ship, uses them to record everything Observers see. Turning them off without authorization comes with a hefty fine -- up to twenty-five percent of the commission for the entire job.

There are ways to manipulate the LensCam; all it takes is a little help from a friend. When I need to keep mission commanders from poking their noses in where they don't belong, Nico Garcia—my co-pilot and partner-in-crime—manipulates the LensCam feed with a recorded video of the physical environment, running on a loop, so the commander continues to see the physical environment, and not whatever shenanigans I'm getting up to in real time. Once I can get out of the toilet, Nico can interrupt the LensCam broadcast with our custom-made footage, and I can finish this job.

There's a noise from the bedroom. The duke shifts in his chair, stretching his Condor-like arms out to each side. He pushes back from the desk, and the chair makes a jarring noise as it scrapes across the stone tile. I creep backward, out of view as he passes the door, and hold my breath. Papers rustle as his frantic hands rummage through something I can't see.

I creep back to the door for another look. The duke crouches over the bags on the floor, his body positioned so that his face, with its hooked nose and deep-set eyes, are in profile. He retrieves a small, square leather box with a looped closure from the bag.

He opens the case and I glimpse its contents: an enormous, yellow-tinted stone. Gently removing it from the case, he holds it up for inspection. The jewel sparkles, refracting the candlelight at dozens of interesting angles. It's so breathtaking, my palms itch at the thought of holding it.

This is it. The Florentine Diamond. The jewel worth more than all the other jobs I've ever done combined. This is the payday I've waited for.

This legendary stone, so coveted by royalty and thieves alike for nearly five hundred years, disappeared in the mid-twentieth century. For this part of its long and storied journey, in the year of our Lord Sixteen Hundred and Fifteen, the de Medici duke has reclaimed it from the stone cutter hired to finish it.

It looks odd, this lemon-shaped thing with its 126 facets in a double-rose cut. The stories say it's at least 137 carats of unrivaled worth. I breathe a little prayer that the seams of my small pouch can hold its eight-pound weight.

There's a knock at the door. Startled, the duke tucks the diamond into its case, and slips it into the top draw of his desk and locks it. He drops the key, threaded with a black silk cord, around his neck.

"What do you want?" the duke says through the bedroom door, not bothering to open it.

"Your wife. She calls you," a man answers.

"I am busy."

"She is most insistent, Your Grace. She says you must come at once."

The duke sucks air through his teeth. "Anon. I come, anon."

He strides over to the desk and, though he locked the drawer moments ago, tugs on the handle. Satisfied the drawer is secure, he throws a robe over his nightshirt and rushes from the room, pulling the bedchamber door closed behind him.

I listen for the last echoes of his footsteps to fade at the far end of the corridor and I am at the desk in a wink. I drop to my knees and retrieve the lock pick tools tucked inside my waistband. The lock is intricate, with three ornately scrolled openings, two of which are likely false keyholes.

Choosing the center keyhole in the cluster, I slip the pick into the top of the hole. Two pins move when I poke them, but the sound isn't right, which means the lock mechanism isn't released. I move to the keyhole on the right and slip the pick inside. This is the one. I feel and hear the difference as the pick slides over the pins, moving them in sequence to release the lock.

Just another few seconds.

Almost there.

Almost.

There is the sound of heavy footsteps moving up the corridor at a fast clip. It could be the duke.

Scrambling back to the water closet, I barely make it into hiding before the duke bursts through the door and closes it behind him. He tugs on the drawer handle and sighs, relieved. Still locked.

I tick off the time that has passed since the final warning from Carter. Twelve minutes left. Maybe thirteen.

A quick review of my options doesn't produce any perfect solutions for escape. I could wait for him to fall asleep, but time isn't on my side. Any distraction I create would only draw him closer to where I'm hiding.

I could feign an overpowering sexual desire for him — one so strong that I had no choice but to disguise myself as a boy and hide until the opportune moment to seduce him — but it would be hard to explain my presence to his satisfaction.

I curse myself for not bringing tranquilizers with me. It would've been easy to add a sedative to the glass of brandy on his desk and be fairly certain he'd drink it. The duke loves his brandy.

I met the duke at a dinner party hosted by a rich Marchesa; her family's jewels were the deepest desire of a disinherited progeny living in 2533. The duke undressed me with his eyes more than once during the evening and, since I flirted back, I could make seduction believable, then knock him unconscious the moment his back is turned.

I'm out of time. If I don't get out now, I'll be left behind. Taking a deep breath, I steel myself to make an impassioned entrance into the bedchamber and profess an unquenchable fire in my loins for this scrawny, chicken-legged man.

There is a groan followed by a heavy thud.

I sneak into the room and see the lower half of the duke's motionless body sprawled on the floor, his upper half obscured by the canopy bed. Moving carefully to peer around the foot of the bed, I nudge the duke's foot with my toe.

Is he breathing? A loud snore, then a snort, answers the question.

The duke must be deeply inebriated because he doesn't stir when I remove the desk drawer key from his neck. This is awesome. Now, I don't have to seduce this scrawny bag of bones.

Within moments, I have the desk unlocked and the diamond out of its case. It's as heavy as I thought it would be. Into my small bag it goes. I slip the cord around my neck, tuck the pouch into my shirt, and sneak into the hallway.

Just as I did during dozens of hologram rehearsals, I walk on tiptoe to avoid clacking the heels of my shoes against the tiles in the marble hallway. As I move through the darkened corridor, I pause to ensure the small sitting room between me and the North staircase leading down to the first floor is empty.

Every landmark along my escape route is where the hologram blueprints said it would be. I make a mental note to find a creative way to thank the hologram programmers for their precision. There's only one torch in the stairwell, so I feel my way along the wood-paneled walls as I go down the stairs. The first-floor landing opens to the main hall which boasts five columned archways on each side of the room. The house is asleep. The best plan to get out the front door at the far end of the foyer without waking anyone is to skirt the north wall until reaching the ornate entry door.

In a trice, I'm outside in the cool night air. The house faces west toward Florence, our ship is nestled in the fruit orchards to the North. I make a quick right turn and follow the outline the villa toward the upper terrace wall.

If I am the luckiest I have ever been in my life, I might make it to the extraction point with seconds to spare.

"Carter," I whisper into the CommLink. "I'm on my way."

Nothing.

"Carter."

More silence. My heart skips a beat. *Did they really leave me?*

Instead of Commander Carter's condescending tone, I'm relieved to hear the Spanish-accented voice of our ship's co-pilot. "Five minutes, Dodger," Nico says. I like Nico because he's smart, doesn't pry, and sometimes laughs at my jokes. He's the only one I allow, other than Fagin, to use my nickname.

He's also the only one sharing my bed. He has an ass that could stop time itself if the temporal gods had a mind to marvel at perfection.

"Don't make me come after you," Nico says.

"You'd like that, wouldn't you?" I ask, volleying the banter back to him.

"As a matter of fact, I would."

Moving briskly through the door in the stone wall that surrounds the terraced villa, I make my way toward the first of several fruit tree orchards. There is one hundred meters of exposed ground between me and the relative safety of the trees.

"Intruders! Intruders in the garden!" A man shouts.

I turn to see three of the duke's guards running toward me. I break into a dead run. My heart pounds in my ears as I race through the grove, dodging low-hanging branches and weaving in and out through rose bushes and ornamental sculptures.

"Four minutes," Nico says.

I'm back out in the open, headed toward the next section of the orchard. A quick cut left, and I duck into a path lined with tall boxwoods which temporarily shields me from the soldiers' view. Their shouts continue, calling others to the chase.

They're not far behind. I run another mental time check based on the remaining distance to the ship.

It will be damn close.

At the end of the pathway, I spot the darkened outline of the Marchesa's house in the distance beyond the orchards. Our Time-ships are chameleons. No matter what time period or the terrain, the ship's hologram program projects a three-dimensional image that camouflages the sleek hull. It can also hover—cloaked—ten feet off the ground, keeping locals from bumping into it.

The LensCams detects the faint outline of our ship, a robin's egg-blue aura glowing at the grove's perimeter, unseen by the naked eye.

"Left the lights on for you," Nico says. "Two minutes."

My legs pump harder, faster than I have ever run; my lungs heave with labored breath. I'm getting light-headed. There's more shouting behind me.

"Open the door." My voice wheezes with the effort to speak.

There's a moment's hesitation between my command and the response before the door slides open and I tumble inside. The palace guards are so close, it will be mere seconds before they topple into the ship after me.

One of the other mercenaries shouts, "We've got her. Go!"

The three men outside skid to a halt, their shoes scuffing the dirt up in small clouds around their feet. Their mouths hang open in disbelief. From their perspective, it looks as though trees have opened to reveal a strange world. They can see the blinking lights on the console panels and hear the sounds of our ship coming to life.

One guard drops to his knees and cries, "God save us."

The others backpedal, arms wind-milling as they trip over each other to escape, leaving their companion to scramble after them.

The door slides shut and a high-pitched whirring sound mellows into a deep hum as the ship launches. I wish I could see the faces of the palace guards as they try to answer why they returned from the chase with no prisoner. Would they be able to speak of the strange world inside the trees? I bet they never tell a soul what they've seen and only speak of it to each other in hushed, drunken voices.

Still gasping for breath, I push myself up to sit against the wall. Before I'm able to make a joke and ask if I'm on time, Carter's voice booms over the speakers. "Arseneau. Get your ass up here. Now."

CHAPTER 2

THERE ARE technical explanations for the mechanics of time travel, but I don't care what they are. Let scientists and academics discuss warp drives, harnessing the unpredictable power of wormholes and dark matter, and manipulating the fabric of space and time. I want to eat pomegranates while watching the pyramids at Giza being built, infiltrate Catherine the Great's royal court, and play muse to Vincent van Gogh as he paints just for me.

If there's a universal complaint among time thieves—aside from minor seasickness ripping through time can produce—it's the pieces of shit we're forced to travel in. Living in the shadows to avoid capture for illegal time travel means the state-of-the-art Timeships are reserved for government sanctioned time travel missions. We make do with antiquated ships that afford little privacy other than the cramped crew quarters. Even worse, the meal replacement bars from the replicators—nutritionally complete and filling—are shit.

As I enter the cockpit, I'm not worried about another recitation of The Sins of Clémence Arseneau According to Jackson Carter. I enjoy banter with mission commanders because it's so easy to outwit most of them. It's the thought of a public ass-chewing that bothers me because I hate people knowing my business.

Nico glances at Carter, then shoots me a warning look as he pulls a set of headphones over his ears. It's likely that he's heard the preamble to the lecture that's coming. Quiet and focused, he's already engaged in the business of getting us home to 2533.

Elna and Umbari, a pair of petty thief sisters, settle into side-by-side jump seats toward the front of the main cabin. They haven't bothered to change out of their mission clothes—Seventeenth Century ball gowns—preferring, instead, to treat my dressing-down as if it's an evening's entertainment at the cinema.

If bookmakers at casinos took gossip-mongering bets, I'd win a fortune betting on the sisters to spread my business all over the base within minutes of the ship docking.

Carter doesn't look at me. Laser-focused on his task, I'm left staring at the back of his curly blond head as he operates the ship's three-dimensional augmented reality control screens. The navigator, seated behind Nico, casts a furtive glance at me before shaking his head and returning to work.

"Eh-hem," I clear my throat. Carter keeps working. I try counting to ten to keep my impatience in check, but only make it to three. "Carter?"

"Commander," he replies, still not turning around. "Use the title. It's there for a reason."

The hairs on the back of my neck prick at the thought of showing him any deference. "It's been a long day. Say your piece so I can change my clothes."

Carter moves from the pilot seat to perch on the edge of the instrument console. He studies me for a moment before speaking. "How many missions have you completed, Arseneau?"

Finding myself at a loss for words doesn't happen often, but this opening salvo isn't the firefight I expected. He notes my surprise and cocks his head to the side.

"How many?" he asks again.

"Enough that I lost count long ago."

"I don't think that's true. You're the kind who remembers every conquest in great detail. Mind like a steal trap, yours." He leans forward to tap my forehead, and I take a step back. "Recruited by Fagin Delacroix at ten years old. At eighteen, you became the youngest person to get a mercenary contract. Even if you followed the one-week recovery and debrief time between jumps, which I'm sure you've ignored the way you dismiss every other rule, you've completed a minimum of fifty-one missions in the two years since you got your contract."

How does he know so much? Fagin had my records sealed.

My age allows me to play four or five years younger than I am, and being mistaken as an adolescent has opened more than a few doors on difficult missions. People underestimate kids all the time and I use it to my advantage. I can also look older through makeup and clothing. Like our Timeships, I'm a chameleon.

Whatever Carter thinks he knows about me—where I come from, what I've done—he can kiss my ass if he thinks I'm going to confirm anything so he can feel vindicated.

"Doesn't matter how old I am. What matters is that I get the job done for my clients."

"An answer for everything." He leans back and crosses his arms over his chest. "I'll bet you have a mark on your bedpost for every commander you've served and driven half-mad with your bullshit side jobs."

"I don't serve anyone unless they pay me." My blood pressure rises, but I won't give him the satisfaction of watching me crack under pressure. "I'm sure you already know the answer to your trivial question, *commander*, so why don't you tell me?"

"Ten commanders in two years."

"Your point?"

"Do you know my mission count?"

"I don't care about your mission count."

"Over six hundred profitable missions in twenty-four-and-a-half years. More than any other living person. I'm in the records book. Got a special commendation and everything."

"Congratulations. I'm sure your clients don't mind that you accept their accolades with one hand while skimming a little off the top."

"My point is that I've commanded hot-shot asshole thieves like you longer than you've been alive. If you think you're something special, someone the Benefactors can't live without, you're dead wrong. There's always someone better ready to step into your shoes if you lose a step."

"No one is better than me." I tap a button on a wall panel console. The floor behind me slides open, providing access to the ladder leading to wardrobe storage on the lower deck. I need to get out of this damn costume. "If anyone is expendable, I'd say it's the old man ready for the rocking chair."

Carter's gloating tone changes. His voice is colder than steel. "Don't get snotty with me, kid. Screw with my retirement and I'll have your guts for garters."

"I don't think my guts come in your size, commander." I give him a tart smile and a dismissive head-to-toe glance. "I don't give a single fuck about your opinion or your retirement."

"Maybe not. But your bullshit jeopardizes our livelihood. Mercenaries are only able to work for Benefactors under the cover of legitimate missions. Teams who cut return windows too close, too often, are begging for the government to poke its nose into the mission records, and that's bad for business. Not to mention your recklessness could cost someone their life. You don't want that on your conscience."

"No one has ever gotten hurt because of how I do my job. You can save the concern for my conscience."

Carter takes a breath. Exhales. His expression softens a little. "Did you know the Benefactors asked me to train you? They wanted me to guide you, help develop the discipline your current handler has failed to instill in you." There's a slight edge to his voice that helps me read his expression better. It's not softer. It's not kinder. It's patronizing.

"You didn't want that plumb job? Your loss, because I'm amazing."

"Fuck, no, I didn't want that job. I told the Benefactors that you and Fagin Delacroix, the two-bit grifter who thinks she's the shit, are beyond help. You're both detrimental to their operation."

My hands clench into fists at my side; my fingernails dig into my palms. Still feeling the after-effects of racing to get to the ship, I have to work to keep my breathing steady. "Fagin could outplay you any day of the week and twice on Sunday. She's the best Thief Master in the business. She made me the one who lays the Benefactors' golden eggs. They have to know I'm the only merc out there with the guts to do whatever it takes to get them what they want."

The cool, calculating look returns to Carter's eyes. He purses his lips into a thin hard line. He pauses a moment, then says, "So bloody arrogant. So convinced you're irreplaceable."

The stone nestled in its pouch, still tucked inside my shirt, could wipe that smirk off his face, but I have orders. No one but Fagin and my client can know about the diamond, or I won't be paid.

"The six-month waiting list for the privilege of employing me says I am." I flash a satisfied grin. "If you're delusional enough to think there will be some sort of comeuppance for me because I've almost tainted your perfect mission record, you'll be disappointed."

Behind me, one of the girls emits a low gasp. The navigator, trapped in his seat because there's nowhere else to go, steals a sideways glance at the commander before burying his nose in his work again. Nico's shoulders quiver, giving me the impression that he's working hard to stifle his laughter. The only sign of emotion from Carter is a slight tremor at the corner of his right eye.

"One of these days," he says, "you'll find yourself in tight spot with no way out. Be careful of the bridges you burn, girl. You might need me someday."

CHAPTER 3

THERE ARE three types of time travelers: First are the Observers, tedious little analytical researchers tasked with cultural intelligence gathering for no other purpose than simply knowing things. Second are the Restorers, highly specialized experts in science, anthropology, and social structure who focus on fixing planet-threatening climate shifts, eradicating poverty and, in general, working to ensure humans don't go extinct out of stupidity. Third are the Mercenaries who, for the right price, will steal your grandfather's fortune out from under him.

Two of these groups are sanctioned by the Global Temporal Congress—the GTC—as time travelers for the advancement and protection of humankind. It doesn't take a Hawking to figure out which of us fall outside legal boundaries. Give me a straightforward thief any day of the week. The smarmy politicians who take bribes to overlook our existence while publicly condemning the "mercenary scourge" are the real crooks. The greedy ridiculously easy to buy. But aren't we all? Corruption is simply a matter of degrees.

The adrenaline from the Florentine Diamond job waned halfway through the time leap home. I'm tired. Hungry. Cross. Before collapsing in bed tonight, there's my fee to collect for carrying this rock across nine hundred years.

La Taverne de l'Fagin is filled with people. It's always crowded because the food is good and the apartment rents are reasonable. The ambience is old world New Orleans French Quarter; a slow and easy respite from the crushing pace of twenty-sixth century life. It's four storeys high with iron lace balconies overlooking a gallery of pub tables below. At Fagin's the liquor is top-shelf, and the clientele notoriously tight-lipped. Here, anyone wanting an unsavory job done can usually find a willing merc to take it on.

Assignments of the murder-for-hire variety are a different animal. Fagin hates the trouble that comes with contract killing. If it's an assassin's skills you seek, she'll send you packing in a hurry.

I spot Nico as I come in the door. He's settled himself at a corner table by the kitchen. He raises an empty glass to me — his usual invitation to buy me a drink. As much as I'd love to drag him up to my apartment for post-mission cavorting, someone else has caught my eye, so I wave him off for now.

A skinny fair-haired girl, no more than nine or ten, sits on a wooden bench just to the right of the red-carpeted grand staircase. Her fingers repeatedly smooth the skirt of doll with a fine porcelain face. The child is dressed in the uniform issued to all new arrivals: a light blue jumpsuit that zips up the front. Her legs are short, so the cuff of each leg is doubled up on itself several times.

I sit on the other end of the bench. Not too close, though; I don't want to frighten her. I recognize the look in her eyes all too well. It's the wide-eyed stare of someone plucked from a time long passed and dropped into the fantastically strange Twenty-Sixth century. This time is both amazing and overwhelming.

We sit in silence, playing a sideways game of peek-a-boo. When I catch her looking at me, she looks away. When she catches me out, I do the same.

"Comment ça va?" I ask, leaning toward her, so she can hear me over the buzz of patrons eating and drinking at nearby tables.

Her brow furrows. I knew it was a long shot that she might speak French. I ask again, this time in English. "How are you?"

She shrugs as she averts her eyes and hugs the toy closer. I decide to try a different tactic.

"Your doll is very beautiful."

I'm paid for the compliment with a shy smile. I slide a bit closer to her.

"When I was a girl, I wished for a fine doll like this one. But where your doll is golden-haired and wears a green silk gown, the one I wanted was raven-haired and wore a crimson dress." She's watching me out of the corner of her eye, so I pause and give a small sigh for dramatic effect before continuing. "She was a rare beauty, this doll, with rouged porcelain cheeks, and a soft body that just begged to be cuddled. I wanted her more than anything in the whole world."

"Did you ever get your doll?" she asks, concern coloring her blue-gray eyes.

"No," I say. "My family had no money for luxuries like dolls and toys."

The child nods in solemn understanding. "I was poor, too. My mommy and daddy died. Miss Fagin bought my doll so I wouldn't be so lonely." She bows her head.

I knew it. My mentor has a type for those she recruits: young kids —usually girls—orphans between eight and twelve years old. Any older, they're hard to train and they soon go their own way. Any younger and they don't understand what's expected of them.

Fagin's crews are a collection of broken souls. She chooses those with the weight of the world on their young shoulders—extreme poverty, homelessness, and trauma—because life can only get better from there.

Glancing around the nearby tables, ensuring no one can eaves-drop, I give this little one a glimpse of my sorrow. "I'm an orphan, too. My papa died when I was eight years old. My maman died soon after. I know how it feels to lose your world," I pause, then lay a hand gently on her small one. She lets me keep it there. "Fagin gives us a family so we never have to be alone."

She nods. Her shoulders slump and she wipes tears away with the back of her tiny hand.

"Does she have a name?" I ask, gesturing to the doll.

"Miss Fagin said her name is Isabella and I must take very good care of her."

"She is well-named. In French, Belle means beautiful. My name is Clémence. What's yours?"

"Anna," she replies.

"Enchanté, Anna."

She purses her lips and her eyes narrow slightly, which makes me laugh. "It's French. It means, I am pleased to meet you."

"I don't know how to speak that way," she replies.

"I can teach you, if you like."

Another noncommittal shrug. "Nobody talks like that where I'm from."

"And where is that, ma chere?"

"Chicago."

"That's in America, yes?"

Again, she furrows her eyebrows. "It used to be. I don't know where it is now." She pauses, lifts her nose in the air and inhales. Anna leans forward to look around me. I follow her gaze right to the food at a nearby table.

"Hungry?"

She nods, wide-eyed, and I hear her stomach rumble.

"Wait here. I'll be right back."

Moments later, I return with two bowls of hot, savory stew and thick slices of crusty bread with butter. She digs in without hesitation. We sit with the bowls nestled on our laps, napkins tucked under our chins like bibs.

"You dress like a boy," Anna says, talking with her mouth full. She nods at my clothes.

Back on the ship, I changed into my usual post-mission mono-chrome uniform: black T-shirt, leather trousers, and hunting boots. A small messenger bag containing the carefully wrapped Florentine Diamond is slung across my body.

"These clothes are very comfortable. Sometimes I have to wear long gowns when I work, much like Isabella's. Those clothes are a bitschhh... um, are very hard to move or run in." *Fagin will kill me if I teach this kid to swear.* "On my last job, I was disguised as a boy."

"Did you have to run a lot?"

"Yep. I was chased by three men, and I didn't want them to catch me."

"Were you faster than they were?" Anna peeks up at me through thick, dark eyelashes and smiles.

"I was faster," I whisper back, returning her conspiratorial grin. "They didn't stand a chance."

She giggles, a deliciously light-hearted sound. "I'm faster than a lot of boys, too," she says. "They don't believe it until I beat them. Some of them get mad."

"If you work with Fagin, you must be fast and smart and strong. I can help you with that, too."

"I'm sure there are many things Clémence can teach you, Anna," a woman's voice says from above us. It's Fagin gazing down on us over the bannister from several steps up the grand staircase. "She's one of my best students."

Fagin has a runner's build; long, lithe, and strong. Her move-ments are so graceful -- as she descends the remaining stairs, it seems she floats on air.

"I expected you upstairs twenty minutes ago," Fagin says. To other observers, her comment might seem casual, almost aloof, but I've known her since I was Anna's age. The comment—delivered with rigid posture and a steely gaze—is anything but casual.

"She was hungry," I say by way of explanation.

"Diondra is her induction guide. She was supposed to get the child something to eat." She shifts her attention to the girl. "It looks as though you were deposited on this bench instead, eh, my sweet?"

Anna's eyes instantly go wide. The spoon she holds slips and clanks against her bowl. "I don't want to get her in trouble, Miss Fagin. She said she'd be right back."

"Don't worry about that." Fagin gestures toward some teenage girls a few feet away. Two of them jump up from their table. "Go sit with Nelle and Angeline. When you've finished your dinner, they'll take you to your room. I'll say goodnight in a little while."

Fagin turns to the girls and gives them more direction as Anna clutches my hand.

"You'll be fine, ma petit," I reassure her with a kiss on the forehead. "We take care of each other here. They'll get you settled."

Anna swallows hard and gives the two new girls a thorough once-over before releasing my hand. One girl carries her bowl to the table, the other picks up the small valise deposited next to the bench. Anna tucks her doll into the crook of her arm. "I want Clémence to say good night to me, too."

"Of course," I say, "I'll come as soon as I can."

Satisfied, Anna joins the other girls at the table. Fagin loops her arm through mine and guides me up the staircase.

"Where did you find her?" I ask, as we pick our way through clusters of people congregating on the second mezzanine. Some are socializing, others are making deals in hushed voices. Fagin's suite is at the far end of the hall.

"Chicago. 1932. Anna's father was a banker. During the early years of the Great Depression, as that time was called, he drank himself to death. Anna's mother died of influenza a few months later. The poor thing had been in an orphanage for over a year when I saw her pick a man's pocket with such skill and confidence that she reminded me of you, Dodger." She gives me a sideways glance and chuckles.

We didn't coin our nicknames. Fagin's father—an aficionado of nineteenth-century English literature, and the man who taught Fagin everything she knows about high-class thievery—decided that our relationship fit the mold of Charles Dickens' characters: Jack Dawkins, a light-fingered and stylish young pickpocket—called the Artful Dodger by his most intimate friends—and Fagin, the ringleader of a juvenile gang of thieves who bring him stolen goods to fence in exchange for food and shelter.

When I retire, I'll read that book and see if he was right about Fagin and me.

A smirk lifts one corner of Fagin's mouth, "Let's hope she doesn't inherent your penchant for completely disregarding rules."

We enter her office, a spacious room filled with ornate French provincial furniture, crystal chandeliers, antique bookcases stuffed with first-edition books, and a large fireplace with an eighteenth-century carved mantle. The room is Old World elegance from floor to ceiling. The only concessions to modern contrivances are the computer monitor on the desk and the personal teleport pad in one corner.

"You see the irony in reprimanding a thief for disregarding rules, don't you? If CVs were required for this job, 'must ignore rules and laws' would be a top requirement."

I drop into an eggplant-colored chair nearest the fireplace, which casts a warm glow over the room as the fire blazes. A decanter of port sits on the side table, so I pour a glass. There is an explosion of summer berries and a hint of chocolate when it hits the back of my tongue. When I retire, I'll buy a bottle of port for every room in my house.

"Have you forgotten something?" Fagin asks. Raising an expectant eyebrow, she extends her hand.

"No, but I was hoping that you might." Smiling ruefully, I collect the leather pouch from the bottom of the messenger bag, and deposit it gently on her desk before returning to my chair.

She picks up it up, estimating its weight by juggling it from one hand to the other. "Hmpf. Seven or eight pounds, I'd wager." She reaches inside. She pulls the diamond from the bag. Her lips part in surprise. "Oh, my."

I watch as she examines it, smiling in wonder to herself. Finally, she puts the jewel carefully into a box that she locks with a key. The box goes into her desk drawer, which also gets locked.

"Worth ignoring the rules for, isn't it?"

"The rules are there for our protection, Clémence. Without a code of conduct, it would be chaos out there. We'd lose the Benefactors' protection and the full weight of GTC law would fall on us." She pauses as I pour a second glass of port. "I don't remember inviting you to help yourself."

"Given that you interrupted my dinner, the least you can do is buy me a drink," I reply, raising my glass to her and draining it as quickly as the first.

"You were late to the extraction point."

"Why are you worrying? I always get myself out of trouble."

"Not this time."

I groan, thumping the glass down on the table harder than intended. "Carter reported me, didn't he? Does he ever grow weary of hearing himself talk? You should have heard him scolding me like I was a child. He was ridiculous," I laugh.

"This is not a laughing matter. The Benefactors are furious with you."

"I'm sure you can calm them down." I say, waving my glass at her. When I realize the glass is still empty, I grab the decanter and pour another drink. "Everyone respects and fears you, Fagin, because they know you have GTC leaders in your pocket."

"Not all of them." She pulls a sheet of cream-colored paper from a manila folder, and places it on the desk. She gestures for me to have a look.

My steps are wobbly as I shuffle over to the desk and lift the paper to the light. The handwriting looks blurred. God, why can't anything be simple? I push it back toward her on the desk. "Read for me."

"Being a cheap drunk is unattractive. You should give it up." She doesn't read the paper because she has memorized its contents. "You're grounded." She moves to the front of the desk and takes the glass of liquor from me.

"Grounded?" I repeat, stupidly, not understanding what sort of probation is implied.

"No regular missions until you prove yourself capable of following a commander's orders, including making it to extraction points on time. Too many missed time jumps and the government gets suspicious that their machine isn't so well-oiled."

I feel dizzy, so I steady myself on the desk. "How long am I grounded?"

"Until further notice. Angering them earned you the wrong kind of attention. They think your arrogance puts their interests at risk. Until this blows over, we both have to play by their rules." The look on her face is serious, and she holds both of my shoulders firmly, forcing me to stay eye-to-eye with her. "I have orders, too. If we don't do as they say, everything blows up in our faces."

The public view the Benefactors—a powerful cabal rumored to consist of anonymous billionaires and corporatists—as modern day Robin Hoods. If the people knew they hire mercenaries to steal riches from the past to fill their own coffers, their reputation as altruists would be destroyed.

Or maybe not. The public is quite forgiving if you tell a good story, and the Benefactors-as-philanthropists narrative had reached mythic proportions generations ago.

"They're angry at me. I get it. Why'd they get you involved in all this?"

"Because you work for me. I'm expected to lead a specialized training mission designed to test you. Failure means execution or time on a prison planet. Neither option is particularly appealing, if you ask me."

I shudder at the mention of prison planets. As overpopulation increased on Earth, businesses with vast resources moved off-world to pad their profit margins by maximizing cheap alien labor on other planets. One of the first to move were privatized prisons owned by the Benefactors; they didn't want prison scum on the same planet they had rehabilitated into their private paradise.

Rumors of extreme guard cruelty pushing half of inmates into insanity earned the facilities reputations as Pits of Despair. One of my first clients—a twitchy hulk of an old man bent on changing an ancestor's will to gain control of the family business—was a retired Mars prison guard. Curious, one day, I asked him about the rumors. He shoved me against the nearest wall, his eyes haunted and wild, and almost crushed my windpipe with his forearm. "Never ask again," he had snarled.

The lightbulb that exploded over my head as I struggled to breathe was this: The rumors didn't come close to the harrowing truth about the prisons.

I press my fist against my chest, trying to quell the simmering rage; it feels like a hot branding iron lodged inside me. My dreams of never again owing anyone my fealty now feel as fragile as spun sugar. "They can't do this to us."

"They can," Fagin says. "It's late. Go say goodnight to Anna. We'll talk more tomorrow. I'll send you a note telling where to meet me. We have a lot of work to do."

"My fee will be in the bank by morning?" A plan to take the money and run is already forming. I could send word to Nico to join me. Fagin, too, if I can convince her we could disappear and never be found.

"Not quite."

"Meaning?"

"The Benefactors will pay out on the de' Medici job after we complete this assignment."

"Shit." Whether it's too much liquor with too little food or the time lag catching up with me, I'm suddenly tired down to my bones. All I want is my bed.

"Yeah. Shit," Fagin nods. "They've frozen my assets, too. From now on we play the Benefactors' game."

CHAPTER 4

THE SIMULATION CENTER is sparsely populated; it's just me and a janitor in the foyer styled in a late twentieth-century industrial complex motif. The ceiling is open and cavernous, supported by exposed steel beams and corrugated steel duct work, which makes the janitor's mop bucket sound like thunder as he rolls it across the concrete floor. There's nothing warm or welcoming about this space —even the chairs lining the hallways outside the individual simulation studios are uninviting with their black plastic seats and stainless-steel frames.

Yawning, I pull a crumpled piece of paper from my jacket pocket and read the instructions again. *Sim Studio number eight. Five am. Don't be late.*

When Fagin draws a line for me to toe, she schedules meetings at ungodly hours. It's Saturday, so there are no trainee classes scheduled and the weekend receptionist won't be on duty for at least another hour. I haven't had breakfast because eating too early in the morning makes me nauseous.

A mission I don't want. Pre-dawn training on a weekend. No breakfast.

Merde.

Following the room number placards posted on the heather gray walls outside each room leads me down a long corridor to a sharp right turn, up a stairwell and finally through a set of double doors. Sim Studio Eight is tucked into an alcove.

I press my thumb on the Comm Panel's bio-metric pad and the door slides open. Inside, the walls are a seamless surface that gleams like iridescence opals. The ceiling and floor are made of the same material. The room feels like an enormous blank canvas waiting for an artist to fill it with color and texture.

Fagin is nowhere in sight.

"Computer," I say, activating the voice controls. "What time is it?

"Four fifty-nine and forty-eight seconds," the computer answers in a tranquil feminine tone.

"Where is Fagin Delacroix?"

Strangely, the computer doesn't answer this question about my mentor. Instead, the lights flicker and there's a low hum like a beehive buzzing inside the walls. The artificial intelligence hologram program springs to life.

I find myself standing on a dirt path on an overcast day. A stone building facade faces me. Light, steady raindrops saturate my hair.

"Must you make everything so realistic?" It's a rhetorical question, but the computer answers anyway.

"The simulation experience is designed to prepare time travelers for their missions through true-to-life interactions. The Simulation Center's holographic programs create artificial environments that are as realistic to human senses as their tangible counterparts, this includes humanoid figures, and—"

"Yes, I know. Shut up," I cut in. The computer's droning voice instantly stops.

As annoyed as I am with Fagin's absence, it still astonishes me that everything in our simulations—from the dirt beneath my feet to the scent of the trees mixed with the rain— feels authentic. Even the food produced in the sim rooms is tastier than the meal replacement bars on the Timeships.

Both exterior doors to the building are locked, so I'm left standing exposed to the elements. This part of the realism is not astonishing or delightful. It's wet and cold and I'm still hungry.

Turning in a slow circle, I study my surroundings: The building stands along the banks of a river. There's a grand multi-story stone building with a series of tall, narrow windows on both the first and second floors. A large entrance stands to my left and a short pier leads to the waterway.

The door opens and a man with a pug-dog face peers out at me.

"You are welcome to His Grace's house, young mistress," he says. He's dressed in a white ruffled shirt, oatmeal-colored doublet, and knee-length breeches in the same linen as the doublet. "The Mother of the Maids is in residence, and will escort you to your chamber in the Maiden's Tower anon. Until she arrives, the cooks will see to your comfort with bread and ale in one of the lesser rooms."

His skin has the tone and texture of human skin. The cadence of his breathing is slow and steady. His voice is human, not tinny and automated, and it's unnervingly familiar.

The Sim Room door swooshes open and Fagin enters. "Computer, pause program," she says. The manservant freezes in place and the rain stops; the drizzle is suspended in mid-air creating a perpetual mist.

"His accent," I say, trying to keep my voice from breaking. Rain drips from my hair, down my forehead and into my eyes. I'd brush the wetness away, but I can't tear my gaze away from the man. "He's English."

"Computer," Fagin says, "Load Greenwich Palace program. The royal apartments of Lady Anne Boleyn."

The scenery transforms into a lavishly appointed chamber boasting high ceilings, wood-paneled walls hung with red velvet tapestries, and expensive furniture. Fagin crosses the room to sit at a round table adorned with a lace tablecloth and bowls of fresh fruit.

"He's English," she says, "because we're traveling to the year 1532 to join the court of King Henry the Eighth. The Benefactors who devised this mission have a particular interest in Tudor history."

"Fagin, you know what happened to my family. You gave me your word. You said I would never have to go to England." My voice sounds shrill and panicked, even to my ears. "You promised."

She doesn't budge. Doesn't say a word. Her silence drives the inevitability of my predicament deep into my core. Anger wells in the pit of my stomach, intensifying into bone-deep anguish, a pain so fierce it makes me feel hot and cold at the same time.

Steadying myself on the edge of the French-style writing desk, keeps me from collapsing in a heap on the floor. I notice a riding crop nestled among a small stack of books. A destructive urge takes hold of me.

The wood cane shaft feels well balanced. It's thicker toward the silver handle end, becoming slenderer as it tapers down to the leather tongue on the other. I like the heft of it in my hand. It will do.

A guttural moan rumbles up from my belly, erupting into a howl that propels me forward, swinging the crop in my hand with all the force I can muster.

I thrash through the papers on the desk, sending them flying; the feathered quills and ink pots crash to the floor. It's soon apparent that using only the crop as the weapon of my rage isn't close to being enough.

My hands tear through the books and fragile artefact replicas on every table in the room. I overturn tall iron candleholders and every piece of furniture that yields to me. Fagin watches, but doesn't interfere.

My arms grow heavy from the exertion. My heart is heavier still. Slumping into a corner by a tall bookcase, I let the sadness take me and the tears come in great heaving sobs. Fagin kneels by my side, sitting with me in the pain until I look at her, pleading. "Don't make me do this."

There's sympathy in her eyes, and cold reality, too. "There's nothing to be done, pet," she says. "It's submission to the Benefactors or punishment." She pauses, then addresses the computer. "Reset program elements to original state."

Within seconds, the room returns to perfection as though my tirade never happened. Fagin pulls me to my feet and holds my shoulders.

"They murdered my papa. They forced Maman and me onto a ship to the American colonies that sank from beneath us," I say, my voice still trembling. "You can't—"

"We must show the Benefactors they can trust you."

She turns to walk around the room and I follow, considering her words as I inspect items the hologram has restored on her command. A tantrum isn't nearly as satisfying when things don't stay broken.

On a desk by the fireplace, there are jewels displayed on a silver tray lined with black velvet, including a pearl choker with three teardrop pearls at the bottom of a gold letter "B."

Fagin puts one arm around my shoulder, holding me close like she did when I was as a child. She places her other hand on mine and, together, we run our fingers run over the smooth surface of the pearls. "We'll bring back treasures of such rare and exceptional value, it will prove our worth to them beyond any doubt," she says, her voice a whisper. "We will rob the English blind, darling girl. That can be your revenge."

Touching the pearls stirs unsettling memories of the day my papa died. He was a sailor on a merchant ship that spent long months at sea on trading journeys and, on one particular trip, promised to bring fine pearls home for Maman. No gifts he brought home to us were more loved than his presence.

It was always a joyous occasion when he sailed back into Halifax. On those days, Maman and I dressed in our finest clothes. I wore blue ribbons in my hair and Maman wore a fancy beaded headband. We didn't look rich to anyone else, but we felt like we were.

On my eighth birthday, Papa returned home from a long voyage down the maritime coast to Boston town. I saw him up in the rigging of the *Anna Maria* but, from where I stood, he couldn't see me wave to him. I always thought him so brawny and handsome. Quick, too. Papa could climb down the ropes as nimbly as a squirrel scampers down a tree.

He helped the crew unload the cargo from below deck, and I felt a surge of pride that he could throw a hundred-pound sack of grain down to the longshoremen on the dock like it was filled with air. No one was as strong as my Papa.

"Ho there!" he shouted to Maman and me when he finally spotted us. "How many kisses have my girls for me?"

That was my signal to run to him as fast as my legs would carry me. We met in the middle of the gangplank where I would jump into his arms and smother his face with kisses and happy tears.

"Did you bring my present, Papa?" I asked, excitement bubbling out of me like the first time I tasted pure sugar cane.

He carried me in the crook one arm and slung his rucksack over the other shoulder. I knew my long-promised birthday gift—my beautiful porcelain doll—was in that bag somewhere. We strolled over to Maman who smiled and threw her arms open wide.

"Let me kiss Maman before we talk of presents, little dove." He kissed her long and deep, and she held him tight.

After a few moments, the celebratory mood turned somber. Maman talked of her worry for our village, and the anger over English occupation. There were fights in the town square where red-faced soldiers shouted insults and commanded townspeople to bow to the king or everyone would be forced out of Acadia forever. Maman would quickly turn me away when these things happened, but I still heard them. I remember them all.

Papa's face clouded like a storm at sea. That's what we called it when Papa was cross: stormy sea moods. He saw me watching them and put on a brave smile.

"Mariette, hush," he said to Maman in a low voice. "We mustn't frighten the child. After supper, I'll speak with the minister to ask for news." His eyes brightened and our jester returned. "We have a grand ball to attend in honor of a very special birthday. And, if Maman is good," he winked at me, then grinned at us both, "maybe I will give her the pearls I stole from a pirate's chest just for her."

I squealed in delight and skipped happily over to Beau, the Boulonnais workhorse we borrowed from our neighbors for trips into town. Papa mounted first, then Maman boosted me up to sit behind him. Finally, she swung up behind me with the aid of Papa's strong arm. When I was small, I would drift off sitting between the two of them as the rhythmic walking of the horse rocked me to sleep. On this day, with the birthday excitement and the continued serious conversations in hushed tones, I stayed awake until our village came into view.

Maman gasped, and I could feel her heart pounding against my back through her clothes. Her panic frightened me. Papa spurred the horse forward as quickly as the animal could manage with the burden of three people to carry. I heard anguished screams and smelled smoke before I saw the fires.

English soldiers went door-to-door, flushing families from their homes, then setting the buildings aflame. Women wept as they ran with their little ones; the soldiers quickly rounded them up like sheep toward buckboard wagons waiting to take them away. Anyone who dared to fight back was beaten into the ground.

When we drew close enough to see our house, Papa shouted at a torch-brandishing soldier standing on the doorstep. He dismounted the horse and ran with a fury I had never seen. He tackled the man to the ground.

Maman clutched me tightly and yelled, "Louis! No!" She slid from Beau's back, me in her arms, and the horse neighed as he backed away from the flames and chaos.

Two soldiers ran to rescue their comrade. The torch, still burning, lay in the dirt within arm's reach of both Papa and the soldier as they rolled on the ground throwing punches at each other. Another soldier pulled Papa off of his friend. Papa swung his arms, and his enormous fist smashed into the face of the man who'd grabbed him. Blood spurted from the soldier's mouth.

A loud bang echoed from behind us.

I looked backwards and saw an officer, his arm outstretched and his musket smoking from the fired shot.

Maman screamed.

I watched Papa fall. A pinpoint red stain bloomed on the back of his shirt. He didn't move. After that everything blurred together.

A torch was thrown into our house.

Maman lay crying on Papa's body until soldiers pried her from him and dragged us both to a nearby wagon.

The soldiers took the rucksack, with my doll and Mama's pearls inside, and threw it into our burning home.

The last thing I remember about that day is watching my Papa's lifeless body get smaller and smaller as the wagons took us away. I was eight years old when I learned the meaning of rage.

I pull my fingers away from Fagin's hand, away from the pearls. *There aren't enough jewels in the world to pay this blood debt.*

Fagin's plan is meant to rally me to the mission. More to the point, it's meant to guarantee my obedience with promises of imperfect vengeance. Fagin is right about one important fact: The threat of imprisonment or death is a powerful motivator. If we fled, we wouldn't last a day on our own before either the Benefactors or the GTC caught up to us.

We move back to the round table in the Sim Room's reproduction of Lady Anne Boleyn's chambers at Greenwich Palace. Fagin drones on about the mission plans based on the Benefactors' acquisitions list, which I have yet to see. She likes to be methodical and organized, which means searching through mountains of Tudor simulation programs pieced together from hundreds of time jumps to the era.

· · ·

After hours of searching, we find enough nuggets to create a rudimentary plan. As Fagin reads mission summary aloud, I stand to stretch my back and legs and wander over to the table of holographic jewels. Looking at the necklace with the initial 'B.' I pick it up and secure it around my neck.

"What's our cover story? It's no easy task to gain entry to a royal inner circle unless you have connections." I gaze at myself in the silver looking glass on the table. The necklace is exquisite.

Fagin looks up from the reports. "Current plan is to assimilate into the French court of King Francois the First," Fagin says. "I am the wealthy widow of his favorite wine merchant, delivering a shipment of rare and expensive Port to the king."

"Who am I in this scenario?"

"You're my ward."

"An orphan?" I give her a sideways glance. "Why not pretend you're my mother?" People have commented on our familial resemblance since Fagin took me in, so it wouldn't be a stretch to claim we're related. The suggestion that we could be parent and child elicits a response that's equal parts mock horror and genuine admonishment.

"Watch it, kid." She shoots me a look. "I can still pass as your sister. Don't be a brat."

Fagin is a beautiful woman. Aside from being tall and lean, she has clear skin and auburn hair swept back into an elegant chignon. While she looks young, no one knows her real age. Not even me. She could be old enough to be my grandmother.

"Why France?" I ask, continuing to admire the look of the pearl choker on my neck. "If we're infiltrating the English court, wouldn't it be better to start in England?"

"This is why." Fagin taps the touch screen on a handheld computer interface. A large hologram schematic of a historical timeline—a bright red line with blue labels for the key dates of Henry the Eighth's reign—hovers above the table. She uses two hands to stretch the timeline, exploding a few months in late 1532 into a larger view.

"King Henry, his lady, and nearly the whole of English court journey to France. The purpose of the trip is to secure the French king's support of Anne as Henry's legitimate queen, after he set aside his first queen, Catherine of Aragon. They arrive in Calais on 11 October 1532."

She launches a separate timeline that spans Anne Boleyn's childhood. "Lady Anne is more French than English in many ways, having spent a great deal of time in France when she was a young girl. She would likely welcome a young courtier from Francis's court as one of her ladies-in-waiting."

"If she loves all things French, she may have some redeeming qualities." I return to the looking glass and pile my black hair on top of my head, then turn my head from side-to-side, getting a sense of how well this jewelry fits me. Would Lady Anne miss this pretty bauble if I relieved her of it?

"Let me put a finer point on this for you." Fagin turns and notices I'm wearing the pearls. She gives me a wry smile, like she can see the gears turning in my head. "They suit you. Remember, my dear, the light field creating that necklace will dissipate the moment the simulation ends. The real thing is waiting for you in 1532."

There's more than just a necklace waiting for me.

I decide to change the subject. "You were going to put a finer point on something for me," I say, removing the holographic pearls and placing them back on the velvet-lined tray.

Fagin puts her hands on her hips. "This is the most complex job we've ever had, with the highest possible stakes. Once the King and Lady Anne arrive in France, we have little more than a month to get into their good graces and secure an invitation to return to England with them." She pauses for a moment and her smile broadens. "What do you think?"

"I'll only need two weeks to get us to England."

CHAPTER 5

THERE'S one thing that never loses its shine, no matter how shitty the circumstances: the crazy shot of adrenaline that blasts through my system as I walk a tightrope between pulling off the perfect heist and getting caught. Even training sessions can be a gas if I'm in the right mindset. When I channel that crazy energy—the lightning-in-a-bottle surge—it's better than sex. There is the risk that if I stay in the vermin's court for too long, my rage might suffocate me faster than death by vacuum after being blown out of an airlock.

There's a familiar twitch in my fingers and as the hologram scene at Greenwich Palace springs to life around me, excitement vibrates in every muscle in my body.

Here we go.

Courtiers mill around the great hall awaiting the king's arrival. The room is decorated with flowers and banners bearing the Tudor rose entwined with Lady Anne Boleyn's falcon emblem. There are tables laden rich food, and the wine is flowing. Most well-wishers chat and laugh as though this is a normal party, while others whisper in huddles, casting furtive looks at passersby who might mistake gossip for treason.

This is an extraordinary day for the king. He has overthrown his first queen for a new lady, and everyone holds their collective breath to see what this new order will bring. Having just returned from a triumphal visit to France, today represents the first day of Lady Anne Boleyn's ascendance to power.

The trumpets sound. People make way for the royal processional. From the depths of a curtsey, I sneak a glance as the king and his pretender queen pass. The hundreds of diamonds Anne wears — they drip from her ears and neck and are embedded in the embroidery of her white linen gown — are only half as incandescent in reflecting the candlelight as her face.

While she is radiant from the joy of her triumph, the King doesn't gaze at her. Instead, he surveys the room with raptor-like eyes, searching for signs of disrespect in the sea of human faces.

It's a good thing King Henry doesn't look directly at me or he would see my rage. The Duke of Suffolk stands within arm's reach of me. A brief fantasy plays in my head: Snatch his dagger from its sheath, rush the king and his lady, and drive the shaft into his heart, then hers.

Henry mounts the dais. Anne follows, taking her place in a chair next to the monarch's chair of estate. According to our plan, the optimal window for obtaining the first item on the Benefactors' acquisition list is the next thirty minutes, as the entire court is occupied with this nonsense. I walk through the room, chatting with Anne's ladies-in-waiting—*God, do they ever stop talking?*—so they can attest to my presence in the great hall during the reception. A steward offers pewter goblets filled with wine, and I accept a cup so he will move on to the courtiers chatting near the windows overlooking the gardens.

Music and dancing begin and the reception line to greet the royal couple still stretches half way across the room. No one notices when I slip out of the room. Columned archways frame the perimeters of the hallway, offshoots to different parts of the palace. They offer adequate cover where I can observe the corridor as I make my way to the king's chambers.

When I reach the top of the staircase leading to the king's apartment, I find both sentries slumped against the wall with their legs splayed out in front of them. I watch them for a moment. The only movement is the gentle rise and fall of their chests as they breathe. A few steps closer and I find half-drunk cups of wine beside each man, the remnants of Fagin's sedative-laced Madeira spilled on the floor where the cups have dropped.

If I'm lucky, they'll be out for a couple of hours. The door to the king's chambers is locked, but it doesn't slow me down. In less than a minute, I've picked the lock and slipped into the room.

There's no moon in the sky, and no light filters through the leaded glass windows. There's a dim glow from the banked embers in the fireplace—the servants haven't yet stoked them into flame before the king retires for the night. The room is in deep shadow; I won't find what I'm looking for without some help.

Reaching into a pocket hidden in the folds of my gown, I grope for the small pair of night-vision glasses that will help me search the room.

They're gone.

Patting down the three other hidden pockets produces the same result: nothing. Perhaps I dropped them. Retracing my steps back to the great hall would be risky and time-consuming. I could search for a candle, but I'd need to find a matchstick to light from the fireplace embers. Unless the clouds in the night sky part, allowing moonlight in, I'm out of light source options.

My kingdom for a damn flashlight.

There are shouts outside in the corridor. The unconscious men have been discovered, and the general alarm sounds. The door to the privy chamber bursts open and four guards, armed with daggers, rush toward me.

. . .

"Computer, stop program and reset." Fagin says from the shadows. "Lights to one hundred percent." On command, the snarling guards disappear in mid-stride and fluorescent lights come up to full power.

"I swear I had those glasses in my pocket when we started," I say, pre-empting the lecture I know is coming. I don't need a litany of all the things I'm doing wrong. Fagin, however, is hell-bent on giving a lecture.

"Are you sure?" she asks, dangling the missing glasses on two outstretched fingers. "You left them in the loo during the last break." She levels a steady gaze at me, brows knitted together in frustration. "Where is your head? You've made every stupid mistake a first-year recruit wouldn't make after a month of training."

"It's nothing." I shake my head to clear it. It doesn't help at all. I have to move. Standing still, even for a few minutes, drives me crazy. "Let's go again." I spin away from Fagin and head for the door, but don't get very far.

She grips my arm, pulls me around to face her. "We can't afford distractions. It's neither an understatement nor a cliché to point out that mistakes will get us both killed." There's an edge to her voice that surprises me; Fagin doesn't get easily rattled. She also doesn't usually lay hands on me like this. One raised eyebrow from me, and she releases my arm, but her expression remains tense. "How many times must I remind you what's at stake?"

A ringtone interrupts us—a shrill whistle that reminds me of a demented exotic bird. Fagin shifts from one foot to the other, and a muscle in her jaw twitches. It doesn't look like she's done reminding me of the stakes. The newcomer is insistent and the tone sounds again.

"Computer, open door," she says.

The door to the Sim Room swooshes open and Nico pokes his head inside.

"Looks like I'm in the right place," he says with a big grin. When neither Fagin nor I return the greeting, he frowns. "Unless, I'm not."

He pauses, then jabs a thumb toward the hallway behind him. "I could leave and come back later, if you like."

"Stay," Fagin replies tersely. "Maybe you can get her to focus so we can get through this training simulation."

Nico's smile falters. He shuffles his feet as he moves hesitantly toward me and scratches the back of his head. "Bad day?" he asks with a desperate expression that says his morning plans didn't include being thrown between two fighting women.

"Nothing I can't handle," I say, trying to sound nonchalant.

Fagin rolls her eyes. If she weren't here, I'd push Nico down on the nearest table and straddle him. *God, I could use the release after the morning I've had.* A shiver runs up the back of my neck at the mental image of looking down into his face, feeling his hips nestled between my thighs. "Didn't expect to see you here."

"I didn't expect to *be* here." He points at me and sits on the edge of the table where he had just been flat on his back in my brief daydream. "You're my next assignment."

His proximity, the way he sits with his legs slightly apart, the scent of shaving cream and soap lingering on his skin: All of it serves as a distraction I'd willingly give myself over to if I could get rid of Fagin for half an hour.

"You're our co-pilot?" I ask.

"Your pilot, actually," he replies, looking like he can't quite believe it himself. "I was promoted this morning."

Fagin's brow wrinkles. "I didn't realize you were eligible for promotion."

"I wasn't. This came out of nowhere, but hey, I'm not going to refuse the gift. It comes with a hefty pay raise." The thousand-watt smile returns. "Guess you're stuck with me."

Relief washes over me and I allow myself a smile. Our work partnership—Nico's and mine—is like a blade honed on a whetstone: sharp, smooth, and polished.

I bury the smile, but not fast enough. Fagin notes my reaction with narrowed eyes and a darting glance from me to Nico who, wisely, keeps a straight face. While fraternization between Observers isn't forbidden, Nico and I agreed to keep our physical relationship private to avoid the policy restriction that significant others can't be assigned to the same mission in case the something goes pear-shaped.

"We'll get you up to speed over lunch," Fagin says, turning to him. She pauses a moment to throw a quick glance in my direction. "Unless, there's something the two of you need to tell me."

We shake our heads, feigning confusion over her question, but I'm not sure she buys the denials. She pulls up the lunch menu from the catering hologram and orders sandwiches.

An hour later, Nico knows everything we do about the English mission, minus my personal family history. I'm not sure how to tell him, or if I even want to tell him.

"I thought the Benefactors loved their favorite thief's renegade ways," Nico says with a smirk between bites of his roast beef-and-swiss sandwich. "Why punish the goose when she's delivering golden eggs?"

"Maybe to keep her from flying into a window because she's too focused on her own reflection," Fagin says.

"More like revenge," I shoot back. "Carter called in a big marker that someone important owed him because he hates me."

"Maybe." Nico nods, considering the options. "But they've always given you leeway because you're, well...you. Taking their best mercenary out of the game just to teach her a lesson doesn't make sense."

Fagin sighs. I can tell she's eager to get back to business. "If we're done discussing Dodger's behavioral issues, shall we take a look at the first item on the acquisition list?"

Fagin taps the augmented reality screen. A string of intricately carved wood beads hovers in midair in the middle of the round table.

"King Henry the Eighth's rosary. These prayer beads are carved out of boxwood and bear the Royal Arms of England, along with..."

Fagin highlights several tiny letters carved into the rosary. "Abbreviations for the king and Katherine of Aragon: He8 and Ka." She pauses and taps the three-dimensional panel again. A holographic video of the king and Lady Anne replaces the rosary. This ghostly image of the real king and his second wife—not a theatrical performance or historical reenactment, but real video from an Observer's LensCam—shows the couple at church. "Historical holograms tell us that the protestant reformation emerged during King Henry's reign, and it began as a way to get what he wanted."

"Lady Anne," Nico says, cocking his head to one side as he studies the hologram version of the woman. "The king abandoned religion for love."

"It wasn't just a romantic consideration," Fagin replies. The image switches to a tight shot of Henry, all pious and solemn-looking; the very image of spiritual devotion as he lowers himself onto the kneeler. "Henry wanted a son. When wife number one failed to produce an heir, he sought alternatives, and Anne was determined to be more than just the king's maîtresse-en-titre—"

"The king's official mistress," I say, translating.

"Exactly," Fagin nods. "Being the king's flavor-of-the-month, as her sister, Mary, had been, was far less than she would accept."

"It seems stupid to pay a fortune for a relic that has no real significance if the king renounced Catholicism," I say.

Fagin chuckles. "Dear girl, if you've learned anything, by now, it's that an item is worth precisely what a fanatical collector is willing to pay for it."

"Yes." Nico draws the word out, waggling a finger in the air as though he's a great authority on the subject of odd ducks and their collecting habits. "People will pay a lot of money for silly things. In the twentieth century, hordes of consumers collected tiny stuffed toy animals under the delusion they would later be worth small fortunes if the funny tags weren't removed." He waggles his finger in circular motions around his temple. "Crazy."

"Rumor has it," Fagin says, "King Henry remained a practicing

Catholic in private, and he held this rosary on his death bed. Observers have never been inside the King's bedchamber during his final days, so this is all conjecture. Our Benefactor is a Tudor aficionado. Anything owned by Henry, his father, or his children is of particular interest."

"Ours is not to reason why," Nico says, in a sing-song voice, "ours is but to steal and spy." He raises his eyebrows in satisfaction as I belly-laugh. Fagin rolls her eyes. "I need to steal a sense of humor for Fagin because *that* was clever."

"We should ask for a different pilot before it's too late." I poke him in the ribs as I head toward a bookshelf to peruse the ancient book holograms. "With jokes like that, we'd be tempted to boot you from the ship before we're halfway to England."

Nico responds by tossing a pomander made of tiny, perfect rose-buds at me.

"Even if you were serious about that request, which I know you're not," Fagin says in a wry tone, "ours is an exclusive team. It's just the three of us. Nobody else. It's also highly classified. Any gossip gets out and we'll wind up in prison."

This bit of news gets my attention. I'm used to secrecy; merce-naries are accustomed to keeping well-paying clients' secrets. It's the size of our team that comes as a shock. "That's unusual. We usually go in teams of at least five or six."

"Not this time," Fagin replies. I could be imagining things, but her hands look shaky as she thumbs through a reference book. "It's just the three of us from here on out."

CHAPTER 6

IT TAKES three attempts to get my apartment door's retinal scanner working, and two more to position my right hand on the biometrics pad so it opens. I'm so exhausted that the simple act of laying my hand flat inside the scanner outline is a Herculean task. The marathon planning sessions and Sim Lab exercises are mentally and physically taxing, but it's the constant conflict with Fagin that makes me bone-weary more than all the rest of it combined.

Once inside, I notice it's darker and hotter than normal. *I haven't touched the window tint in weeks*, and I had adjusted the enviro controls before leaving this morning. It should be a comfortable sixty-nine degrees Fahrenheit in here. Instead, the lounge feels as hot as the salt pan of the Namib desert during the dry season.

Damn system must be glitching.

"Computer, report enviro control malfunction to the mainte-nance department. Priority level one. It's too damn hot in here. And why didn't you turn on the lights when I entered?"

The computer doesn't answer. What the hell is it with the tech-nology today?

"Computer, lighten the window tint in the main lounge by one-hundred percent," I feel my way along the wall. There's a full moon, so a little natural light should keep me from running into the solid oak provincial furniture. The computer doesn't answer. The windows remain dark. "Technology sucks," I say, muttering as I work my way around the furniture.

There's a shallow intake of breath on the sofa behind me. It's so quiet, most people would miss it. Hell, I'm trained in advanced observation skills and I almost missed it.

My fingertips find the bulge on my right calf beneath my leather pants; the blade is almost free from its sheath when a bright light snaps on, temporarily blinding me.

"Apologies, my dear," a smooth masculine voice says. "Overhead light to sixty percent."

In the millisecond it takes for the computer to obey, the blade is in my hand. Even if I were close enough to the intruder to chance a stabbing lunge, my depth perception is skewed from the spotlight's assault. White spots float across my eyes.

"What you're considering would be unwise," he says. I may not see him clearly, but he can clearly see my knife.

Cutting someone in my apartment, likely justifiable under the circumstances in the Lawkeepers' eyes, would generate massive bureaucratic red tape; I'd be buried in paperwork and administrative hearings until the next millennium. Still, I'm not dropping my weapon.

As my eyes adjust, I note that he's two or three inches taller than my own five-foot, seven-inch frame, and his physique is nothing extraordinary. He's wiry, but not overly muscular. He has big hands for a skinny guy, and I wonder if they're strong enough to tear someone limb-from-limb if their owner had half a mind to do it.

He bypassed my apartment's security protocols. He must have also disabled the intruder alert notifications and reprogrammed the voice controls to respond only to him. He's not a garden-variety thief looking to get one over on the Dodger; if he were, he would've been long gone before I got home. Which means he wants something that can't be hauled out in a duffel bag.

Some mercs use enhanced security features in their private quarters: double or triple authentication on entry pads including biometrics or retinal scans and keypads for complicated passcodes. Security cameras. Panic rooms with exits to escape tunnels for those who are exceptionally paranoid—or hated. Rabid security measures are a matter of self-preservation because there are mercenaries who don't buy into the philosophy that a gang of thieves should be found family. It's a pity there really isn't much honor among thieves.

My mind flits to the trouble I had getting in the door. *Note to self: Reprogram the biometric scanner to make it harder to hack.*

Aside from standing uninvited in the middle of my apartment, the man hasn't made a move against me. Still, a barrage of quick offense tactics to gain leverage and neutralize him race through my brain.

Sand from the Zen garden on the occasional table in his eyes. Knife hand strike to side of throat. Drive the knife into his carotid artery.

"I know it's highly unorthodox to surprise you like this, but we can't be interrupted in the course of our conversation. I hope you don't mind that I adjusted the climate controls. I prefer balmy temperatures."

"Not at all," I say, deadpanning the response. "I enjoy it when total strangers break into my home, mess with the heat, and ambush me in the dark."

"Your blade suggests otherwise." He sits on my sofa and snaps his fingers. A hulking goon, holding one of my lace bras looped around his index finger, emerges from my bedroom. Another man, drinking from my damn coffee cup, emerges from the kitchen to my left.

"Put the knife down, Mademoiselle Arseneau. Don't be foolish enough to follow through on what will surely be a tragic choice on your part."

Rivulets of sweat dribble down the back of my neck. I'm not sure whether it's from the heat in the room or the adrenaline. Likely, a little of both. The knife rotates in my palm once, twice, three times. It's a physical tic when I'm nervous or backed into a corner. The goons each take a step toward me, but the man sitting on my sofa holds up a hand. They stop.

"Who the fuck are you and why are you in my apartment?" I ask.

"Language, mademoiselle," he says with a straight face. "Unless you are very unlucky, we'll never meet again. I don't see the point in telling you anything beyond what you need to know for this conversation."

"Doesn't seem fair that know my name, but I don't know yours."

"Sit down. We have business, you and I," he says with a tone of impatient authority that brooks no argument. He settles into my Louis the Fourteenth settee—once owned by Louis himself—and stretches his arms along the top of the gilded bronze wood frame. The man tips his head toward the chair to his right, the one that matches the settee, and keeps his gaze on me.

I choose to sit on the hand-painted floral-and-gilt wood coffee table directly in front of him. Still gripping the knife, I allow it to rest lightly on my thigh. Perhaps I can muster up a little intimidation of my own. His men slip their hands into their coat pockets and move closer to us.

Again, he holds up a hand and they stop.

He rubs the fingers of his right hand together as his brows furrow slightly, a look of interest on his face. "If you put the knife away, you won't be harmed. You have my word. I'm here to talk, not fight. As a show of good faith, I'll tell my men to move back." He glances at the man on his right, then the one on his left. They each take several steps backward, eyes still trained on me.

Reluctantly, I sheath the knife.

"You have quite the collection," he says. "Priceless antique furniture and rare Greek, Roman, and early twentieth-century Americana relics. Very impressive. One wonders how you acquired such an expensive luxury apartment, complete with rare treasures, all to yourself. Most time travelers make do with much more meager accommodations."

"Being the best at what I do comes with certain privileges.

Privacy being the most important, and at the moment, you're invading mine. What is it to you if people buy me gifts in appreciation of my skills and hard work?"

"I apologize for the intrusion," he says. "There are powerful individuals who have a keen interest in your continued success. That's why I'm here."

"Are you from the GTC? If you have questions about my recent missions, you can talk to Fagin Delacroix. Her office is one level down, directly below my apartment."

"I'm not with the government."

From humble public houses to the crustiest upper crust salons, people have speculated for eons about the Benefactors. Everyone has a favorite theory about which famous luminaries may inhabit the secretive and rarefied stratosphere of these most powerful of power brokers.

Extreme wealth is a given; only the insanely rich could afford to finance time travel ventures. It's not for me to judge what billionaires do with their money; let them manage their own affairs and account for their own souls. As long as some of their freedom spills into my pockets, I don't care.

Except when one of them is sitting, menacing and uninvited, in my apartment. That, I care about a great deal.

"I've never met an honest-to-God Benefactor before. Funny, I thought you'd be better-looking," I say, taking a chance that my guess is the correct one.

"Zero for two. I'm not a Benefactor, either. Call me..." He rubs his chin, apparently contemplating how to communicate exactly how influential he is without giving away anything of real value. "A consigliere."

"A what?"

"An advisor. A fixer. Someone who assists powerful, influential people to achieve their strategic objectives."

"So you work for the Benefactors."

His palms turn upward and he offers a noncommittal shrug.

"Powerful, influential people. We'll keep it at that. The most important part of our conversation is what I'm about to say to you now.
Listen very carefully." He leans forward, placing his forearms on his
knees as he bores craters into my soul with beady gray eyes. "The
mission you're undertaking is of critical importance to my employers.
Failure would be detrimental to your future."

"Sounds like a threat to me."

"It's only a threat if you don't deliver. Consider this a friendly
piece of advice: Swallow your anger. No one cares if you fucking
choke on it. Get your head on straight and follow every order given
without question, complaint, or attitude from now until the minute
you return to base."

A stark realization hits me squarely between the eyes. The air
feels like it's been sucked out of the room and I can't breathe in the
vacuum left in its place. "Is... is Fagin reporting on me?"

"Of course she is. It's one of the tasks my employers require of
her."

Merde. She should have told me.

The Consigliere ignores my discomfort. "You must secure each
item on the acquisition list, no matter how difficult it may be. If you
come up short by even one artifact, you will pay dearly for it."

"What if we refuse to play along? We're resourceful, Fagin and
me. Surviving exile wouldn't be a problem." The lie sticks in my
throat. Truth is, aside from time traveling, I haven't ventured much
beyond the borders of the surrounding towns near our base. Why
visit mundane locales when the whole of human history is your play-
ground? The bigger problem of exile would be surviving on the run
from both government forces and the Benefactors.

"Exile would be the least of your worries, my dear. Should you
fail, the Benefactors won't stop with a slap on the wrist."

Heaviness squeezes my chest like a vise. *If exile is a minor reper-
cussion for disappointing the Benefactors...*

The Consigliere motions to one of his men. The asshole holding
my bra approaches and hands him a small, square, black box. A quick

shot of adrenaline pulses through my body; I almost pull my knife again. Until I catch a glimpse of the phaser cradled in the body-guard's shoulder holster.

I've seen the damage phasers cause; a merc who stole from a Benefactor was cut down by one in Fagin's tavern last year. The weapon burned a wound into his chest that started as the size of a walnut. It grew to the size of an avocado pit, the edges of the surrounding flesh glowing crimson before turning to gray ash. He was dead before he hit the floor.

The Consigliere tosses the black box into my lap.

"What's this?" I ask, opening it. Inside is a data chip in a small plastic bag.

"Research so riveting, you'll stay up all night studying every detail."

"You should leave the training to Fagin."

He stands, walks around to the back of the settee. The goons flank him on either side. They look like a pair of muscled bookends as they stand with their arms crossed over their chests. "Trust me, Mademoiselle Arseneau," the Consigliere says, "The information on that chip is quite illuminating and, if knowledge truly is power," he pauses, a grin tugs at one corner of his mouth. "then you're about to become one of the most powerful women in history."

"Bullshit."

His eyes narrow. "Obey without question. Without complaint or attitude." The reminder is as pointed and sharp as my knife. "Get your shit together or it will go very badly for you."

The doorbell rings, and the Consigliere tilts his chin up as though he's about to sniff the air like a dog. "My cue to leave."

The door opens. Nico registers the Consigliere's presence a split-second before the two collide in the doorway.

"Commander   Garcia,"   the   Consigliere   nods   in acknowledgement.

Nico's eyes widen in surprise, and he pushes past the Consigliere. He notes the two large goons and gives me another quick look. I nod in return, a signal that I'm okay. "Have we met?" he asks the Consigliere.

"No. I'm glad you're here, though. Perhaps you can get Mademoiselle Arseneau to focus on the mission. Get her back on track, eh?" He winks and gives Nico a solid clap on the shoulder. Before leaving, the Consigliere gives me another pointed direction: "Watch the hologram files I gave you. I promise you'll find them...enlightening." He pauses. "Computer, return domestic controls to Clémence Arseneau. Authentication code: QE1." He bows to me before the goons follow him out and the door closes behind them.

I rush to the door and slam the manual lock controls. The solid thunk of a deadbolt makes me feel better. "Computer," I say, "get maintenance up here tomorrow to reprogram security protocols and add authentication layers."

"Message to maintenance department sent," the computer replies.

"Hello to you, too," Nico says. "You okay?" His eyes narrow in concern and he takes my hands in his. "Who was that guy and why was he giving commands to your computer?"

"He works for the Benefactors. He was in my apartment when I got home."

"A Consigliere broke into your apartment?" Nico breathes out a low whistle and takes a slow step back. "What the hell did you do, Dodger?"

"Nothing. I didn't do anything."

"Something happened. Whatever it was, it must've been big. These people don't screw around, and the fact that you're still breathing means his visit was a just a warning."

"I handled it fine," I say, jerking my hand from his, irritated that his tone has turned annoyingly paternalistic. Truth is, I don't know what kind of deep shit I'm in or how much deeper it could get. I'm more spooked over the entire situation than annoyed at Nico for giving voice to my fears.

I head to the kitchen to order wine from the replicator. Nico follows, snuggling up behind me as I open the cupboard to grab two glasses.

"I'm sorry," Nico says, nuzzling my ear as he rubs my shoulders. "I didn't mean to imply...look, these people are deadly. I want to know what's going on so I can protect you. That's all."

The day's tension coils inside me like a boa constrictor, squeezing its way through my body. He kneads his fingers over one stubborn knot that runs the length of my neck until it melts beneath the heat and pressure of his hand.

"I know it's been a hell of a day, but you can't stay this tightly wound or you'll explode."

"I'll forgive you if you keep doing *that*," I say, letting my head roll forward.

One by one, the lumps soften until everything feels warmer, looser. Still, this relaxation is only skin-deep. My mind can't let go of the agitation gnawing at my nerves, the frenetic anxious throbbing that won't quit.

I need action. Need a roaring bonfire, not smoldering embers. By the time Nico moves to my neck, I know exactly the kind of release my body needs.

"Kiss me," I say in an urgent whisper.

"Are you sure? You've had a rough day. I don't want to take advantage—"

"Yes, damn it, I'm sure."

I pull him to me. His mouth is hot and savage on my skin as his lips blaze a trail from my earlobe, down my neck to the top of my shoulder. He retreats to my ear, sending sparks through my insides like a flint igniting tinder.

"Yeah. That's it." My breath quickens.

He braces himself against the cabinet with one hand and cups my breast with the other. He works slow, beautiful magic on my neck with his mouth.

I flip myself around to face him. He lets out a slow breath and runs one hand straight down the front of my body from my breasts to the apex of the mound between my thighs. His mouth hovers over mine, the promise of a kiss lingers in the air. He cracks a small smile, teasing me with a light brush of his lips against mine.

"Now. Please," I say.

My frantic tugging at his clothes and a deep, wild kiss convince him the undercurrent of slow and sensual is now a racing, fervent craving for some man-handling.

He holds me by the shoulders, searches my eyes for agreement. I nod and he launches himself into removing his clothes, and mine, at a speed I haven't seen since our first fumbling attempt at sex over a year ago.

Amid a torrent of kisses, he cups my ass in both hands, and lifts me until my toes skim the floor. The leading edge of the counter top—the porcelain tile cool against my flushed skin—supports most of my weight.

I wrap one arm around his neck and plant my other hand against the counter for balance. He thrusts upward, taking me with skilled precision. We careen off of each other in frenzied, undulating waves.

Hard.

Fast.

He pulls me in tighter, controlling the roll of my hips with both hands. His buries his face into my neck, panting. My breath matches his, and I nip his earlobe. His hands grasp my hips harder, fingers digging into my skin with urgent need.

His release comes seconds after my own and we're left gasping, slumped against the counter. When he looks at me, a moment later, I see the worry in his eyes.

"I'm okay," I reply, cutting off the question before he can ask. My breath calms into soft fluttering breaths.

He smiles. "Don't get me wrong, that was great. I'm concerned—"

"Really, I'm okay."

He frowns, then rests his forehead against mine. "Are you ever going to let me in there?"

"What?" I say. "You were just in—"

He places his palm on my chest. Gentle, yet firm. "You know what I mean."

Damn. This isn't a conversation I want to have right now. Or ever, really. So, I do what I usually do: change the subject. "What if the Consigliere, or his goons, comes back tonight?"

"Not likely," he says. He doesn't look happy that I've changed topics, but doesn't press the point. "He knows he made an impression."

My stomach grows queasy over the possibility the goons could reappear at my bed side. A throw pillow—usually stuffed into the corner of the settee occupied by the interloper—lay discarded on the floor. It's disconcerting how one small thing out of place can make the entire apartment feel less safe.

"You can stay, if you like," I say.

"You sure? We both have early mornings tomorrow. I have to be at the docks by seven o'clock to review the ship we've been assigned. Don't you have another training session with Fagin?"

"I'm positive," I say, picking up the pillow and tossing it back into the chair. I throw a breezy smile on my face, hoping it covers my apprehension. "Fagin can wait. Besides, I want to ravish you again later."

He glances at the door, then back at me. "I'll double-check the lock."

I smile—a genuinely grateful smile—and head for the bedroom. Nico also checks the window locks, then crawls under the covers with me and snuggles up to my back. Within minutes, he's snoring softly. I'm not so lucky.

. . .

After twelve hours in the Sim Center with Fagin and another vigorous tussle with Nico, I should be passed out. As exhausted as I am, my brain is still wired and restless. I could lay here tossing and turning all night as I ruminate on the shit-show my life has become or move to the living room and ruminate there. Since Nico has groggily asked if I'm okay twice in the last hour, I opt for the latter. No need for both of us to lose a night's sleep.

The Consigliere's black box sits on the coffee table. I pop the microchip into the Comm Panel on the wall and slip a pair of head-phones over my ears to avoid disturbing Nico. The retina screen displays the program catalogue.

"Computer, project all programs beginning with Tudor ER1."

There's a soft buzz as the hologram projectors emerge from the ceiling and walls. The three-dimensional image flickers to life on the coffee table, and I sit cross-legged on the settee to watch.

A red-headed teenage girl dressed in Tudor clothing stands near a funeral bier. Her face is sorrowful and even a bit fearful. There are two other women and a young boy standing with her. They're all wearing mourning clothes. On the platform is a bloated mass of flesh. It almost looks human.

The Observer's narration begins.

King Henry the Eighth has lain in state in his presence chambers for ten days since his death on the twenty-eighth of January, 1547. After his wife and children—including his heir, Edward—say final goodbyes, the king's funeral cortege will make its way from White Hall to Windsor Castle for internment, stopping for the night at Syon Abbey.

In his last days, the king commanded one of his attendants, Sir Anthony Denny, to summon Archbishop Cranmer to his side. By the time the archbishop arrived, the King, while still conscious, had lost the ability to speak. Recording H8, one-five-two documents the last exchange between the archbishop and the king.

. . .

The scene changes to a dimly lit royal bedchamber. The Grooms of the Stool stand nearby, ready to perform any task required of them. King Henry lays on his deathbed as the Archbishop Cranmer leans on the edge of the mattress, tears in his eyes.

Cranmer moves closer to the king, speaking into his ear. "Your majesty," he says, "give me some sign that you die in the faith of Christ."

The room is silent and tense as Cranmer waits for an answer. There is nothing verbal, so he slips his hand into the king's and speaks louder and with more urgency. "Your majesty, please give me a sign that you die in the faith of Christ."

A beat.

Two beats.

"There," Cranmer says in a hushed voice, "the king doth wring his hand in mind as much as he has the strength to do."

"That is surely a sign of his hearty assent, Your Eminence." Sir Anthony lets slip a sigh of relief. He nods at something the king holds between his interlaced fingers."

I stop in mid-bite of another spoonful of my dinner, which has gone cold from neglect. "Computer, where did this file come from? I thought video of Henry on his deathbed didn't exist.

"Unknown," the computer answers. "I have no record of this information in my database."

How did the Benefactors get someone inside the king's chambers on the day he died? "Okay. Show me what's in his hand. Increase magnification fifty percent."

The program zooms in, but it's not quite enough to see the object the king holds in his hands. "Increase magnification another twenty percent."

The king's wood sculpted rosary beads—the one on the acquisition list—emerges into sharp focus. "This better not be why I'm missing a night's sleep," I mutter out loud. "We already suspected he had the rosary on his deathbed."

The recording jumps to the king's funeral service. All but his son, King Edward the Fourth, are in attendance. The Observer picks up the narration.

Even after Henry's break from the Holy See of Rome, the Requiem Mass is performed in Latin according to the faith the king practiced in his early years with Queen Katherine of Aragon, further evidence that Henry held to the old ways, in his deepest conscience, to his final days on earth. This practice of Catholicism would later be completely rejected by his most influential progeny during her reign as England's queen.

The focus of the remaining footage is the young girl with the red hair: Elizabeth, the king's daughter with Lady Anne Boleyn. There are the years she spent in the household of her step-mother, the Dowager Queen Katherine, that end in rumors that she slept with her step-father, Thomas Seymour.

There's the short-lived time in the court of her beloved half-brother, Edward, until his untimely death from tuberculosis at age fifteen. Next is the rise and fall of Lady Jane Grey before the ascension of Elizabeth's sister, more infamously known as Bloody Mary for her zealous persecution of non-Catholics. The program summaries Mary's death and Elizabeth's coronation.

I don't know what the hell I'm supposed to be looking for. Nothing strikes the dimmest chord or gives insight into why the Consigliere proclaimed viewing the file would make me the most powerful woman in history.

More highlights from Elizabeth's reign pass before my eyes in a few hours' time. She survives excommunication from the Catholic church, smallpox and the rebellion of her much-loved cousin, Mary Stuart, the Queen of the Scots. She rages against the pain of heartbreak inflicted by her secret lover, Robert Dudley, by marrying England itself.

She conquers the seas with her royal navy against the entire Spanish Armada and the battles, political plotting, and misogyny within her own court.

This woman is a force of nature and I would love her for the strength and grit and humor but for one annoying fact: She is my enemy.

Just before dawn, the final simulation plays, Elizabeth's funeral. The narrator offers a summary of the queen's life.

Elizabeth the First of England impacted the world by making her country one of the first superpowers in history. While the first clumsy attempts at claiming new worlds in the name of the English crown met with failure—footnote to Observers: refer to the holographic programs documenting the journeys of Sir Walter Scott and Sir Humphrey Gilbert for detailed explanations—ultimately, England colonized much of the North American continent.

Without Elizabeth on the throne in the sixteenth century, England wouldn't have ventured into the New World—including French Acadia, which would later become Canada and parts of the former United States. In the late sixteenth century, England would also colonize India, Africa, and...

"Computer, pause." I'm breathless, and not at all sure I've understood the Observer's conclusions. I have to hear it again. "Rewind program twenty-five seconds."

The simulation rewinds in a blur of motion and sound, then plays again.

. . .

Without Elizabeth on the throne in the sixteenth century, England wouldn't have ventured into the New World—including French Acadia, which would later become Canada and parts of the former United States. In the late sixteenth century, England would also colonize India, Africa, and...

"Computer, pause program." The three-dimensional Elizabeth freezes in place, sitting still as a stone as an artist captures her likeness on canvas. She is serene and authoritative. And powerful.

I lean as far forward as I can, and peer right into Elizabeth's eyes; they're so real that I'm almost surprised when I don't feel her breath on my face. Moments ago, where I first saw a hero, I now see something that forces bile up into my throat. I get as far as the waste bin in the bathroom before I'm sick.

When I stagger back into the lounge, the holographic queen is still frozen in suspended animation, looking more like a tyrant with every passing second. The longer I stare, the more I want her to move and speak like a real-life human so I can scream in her face about what her greed has cost me.

Instead of screaming I let slip a long, slow breath and a curse. "Son of a bitch."

CHAPTER 7

IT'S MORNING. The sun is hot on my face and I'm sweating. I pull the corner of the quilt up to mop my forehead and realize that I never made it back to bed last night. *I must have fallen asleep on the settee watching the hologram files.*

"Nico?"

No answer. I check the bathroom to see if he's in the shower. It's empty. The sheets and pillows still bear his imprint, but they're cool. He must've left early, but not before covering me as I lay on the sofa.

So sweet.

I pad into the kitchen to make coffee and notice the blinking light on the Comm Panel next to the replicator. A message from Nico. *Had to go. Stop by the docks later. I have something to show you.*

My eyelids feel like they're scraping sandpaper when I blink; lack of sleep sucks every bit of moisture from my eyes. There's a distant ache building in my temples and it's gaining momentum. Gonna be a lovely day in the Sim Center, as shitty as I'm feeling.

Damn. What time is it?

Eight o'clock. I'm already thirty minutes late. I run through the shower, dress, and order a chocolate chip muffin from the Replicator to go with my coffee before running out the door.

Our training sessions have settled into a distinct pattern and today is no different: Fagin is sullen and stressed out. I'm sullen and stressed out. She scolds. We squabble. We make very little headway working through the simulations.

Training ends early when Fagin gets a call that drains the color from her cheeks. Without a word, she bolts from the Sim Lab in a state of near-panic. An hour later, when there's still no word about when she'll be back, I head to the ship docks in search of Nico.

The docks are crowded and busy, a typical Saturday morning. It's a circus of constant activity. Mechanics and crew members fuss over maintenance issues and travel schedules outside the shipping office in the West corner of the hangar; Restorers teams load scientific equipment into the cargo bay of a large climate restoration ship.

Other structures in the shipyard store military cargo ships and sleek luxury passenger vessels, all headed to different bases on Earth or to the Moon or Martian colonies. The security for those buildings is tight, but access to Timeships is tighter still, strictly controlled by the government and the Benefactors' privatized corporate security. Neither the skills of these security forces, nor their resolve to protect their masters' assets, are to be taken lightly.

The last time overconfident thieves attempted to hijack a Timeship, the reward for their ill-conceived venture was a one-way ticket to a prison planet. The imbeciles spent the rest of their lives in one of the most dangerous jobs in existence: working as human canaries in the artificially oxygenated mineral mines on Mars where life expectancy is measured in weeks, not months or years.

At the far end of a row of time travel vessels, I find Nico. It's amusing to watch him balance on tiptoes, his upper body wedged inside the rectangular opening of the aft nacelle of a small ship marked with the hull number VSC-1024. His feet reposition every few seconds as he struggles to gain more leverage to reach whatever it is he's trying to reach. Soft grunts punctuate his exertions, echoing briefly inside the fiberglass casing of his narrow workspace.

The ship is different from the utilitarian vessels we're used to. It's larger and the skin of the hull is a color I've never seen on a ship before: a pearlescent white that seems to shimmer and reflect a rainbow of colors depending on how the light strikes it.

I stand for a moment watching Nico's continued gymnastics within the nacelle until an awkward bump of his elbow sends a wrench clattering to the concrete floor. He doesn't seem to notice. Instead of retrieving it, Nico wedges his upper body farther into the carcass of the ship's power supply. His grunting segues into pleas to the ship to cooperate with his efforts.

"Dropped something," I say, picking the wrench up and placing it back in its place.

Nico startles and backs out of the opening, swearing loudly in Spanish as he scrapes the back of his head on the metal frame. He emerges, sweating and flushed from being buried almost to his waist in his work. He rubs his crown and frowns at me. "Stop sneaking up on me."

I smirk and playfully tug on his mop of curly black hair, tipping his head down and forward so I can assess the damage. "Didn't even break the skin. Don't be such a baby."

"You okay?" He studies me with wary eyes. "I cleaned the trash can in the bathroom. Eat something that disagreed with you or was it something else?"

"Just nerves, I guess," I say, not sure whether to tell him about the Elizabethan hologram files. I'm not sure what to make of them myself. Maybe I should just keep it to myself for now. "Fagin and I are still fighting."

"Training wasn't any better today?"

"Nope. She's been distracted and cross all day. Got a call halfway through our session and she sprinted out of the Sim Room like her hair was on fire."

"What d'you think happened?"

"No idea. She didn't say a word." Fagin's not one to tell everything she knows, but given our current situation, her secrets are scaring the hell out of me.

"So you're here to annoy me instead, is that it?" He gathers his tools, including the wayward spanner, and drops them into a toolbox, which he hauls up the walkway and into the ship's main cabin.

I follow him inside. "You're the one who left me a note. You have something to show me?"

As soon as we cross the threshold, he sweeps his arms open wide, gesturing to the opulent furnishings of the main cabin. The luxurious upgrade of the ship's interior stops me in my tracks.

Instead of the dull, scratched Formica worktables and cabinetry of our typical transports, there's expensive looking hardwood—cherry, I think—that gleams with a high-gloss shine. The cabin lights are intact and seem to work and I can stand in the middle of the aisle between two rows of luxury seating facing forward toward the cockpit with at least two feet of space between my outstretched hands and either wall. A rich, earthy fragrance hangs in the air, a mix of new leather and lanolin-polished wood.

"Holy Mother of—"

"I know," Nico says, interrupting. He leans a forearm against a row of sleek cabinets above a pair of crew seats and beams a huge smile. "Not our typical junk ride, is it?"

"It sure as hell isn't." My fingers run across the tops of the high-backed seats -- the fine grain leather is butter-smooth. I push the back of the seat until it swivels around and opens up to me, then sink down into the chair. The seat cushion is five inches thick and molds itself to my backside like the perfect pair of jeans. "My bed isn't this comfortable," I sigh. "Which big shot gets to travel around in this baby?"

"You," Nico says.

"If you're joking to get back at me for startling you earlier—"

"There are two things I never joke about, Dodger." His face turns solemn for a moment, and he places a hand over his heart in an earnest gesture. "The beauty of an expensive ship and how to make

the perfect paella." He breaks into a wide grin again and his eyes
sparkle. "This is our ship. We could christen her Redemption in your
honor."

"Smart ass,'" I say, giving him a smile. "Who the hell gave us a
ship like this? Are they insane?"

"My Mami always said, 'Never look a gift horse in the mouth.'
C'mon, I'll show you around."

He guides me through every inch of the ship. There's a small ready
room in the aft section behind the main cabin. It boasts the same
hardwood and leather furnishings as the main cabin, complete with
modernized replicators that dispenses gourmet food like Boeuf Bour-
guignon and fois gras with truffles, not those disgusting meal bars.

There are four private cabins, each appointed with feather-soft
beds and state-of-the-art technology, including personal replicators
for late-night snacks. On the lower deck, cargo bays are filled with
empty crates ready to store the historical relics we bring back. Empty
wardrobe rooms, ready to be filled with Renaissance clothing, are
marked with each of our names.

"What do you know about the Benefactors?" I say as I follow
Nico back to the main deck.

He settles into the Commander's chair and flips through pre-
departure checklists. "You know as much as I do. They hire us to steal
things and they pay us well. They're anonymous because when
you're sponsoring illegal time travel, you want to avoid the authorities
as much as possible. They also break into apartments on occasion to
get a target's attention."

"You know people who move in those circles. Haven't you
heard gossip about the Benefactors that's not common knowledge?"

"After the visit from the Brute Squad last night, I can see why
you're curious. In all the time I've known you, the only thing you've
ever been concerned with is when the Benefactor payment will hit
your bank account."

"Not this time. Something feels...off," I say, fiddling with a lever on the console.

Nico's brow furrows and he hisses through his teeth at me. "Don't touch anything in Betty's cockpit unless I say it's okay," he says, smacking my hand away from the controls.

"Betty?" I laugh. "You named the ship's AI program after a girl?"

"Pilots naming ships after beautiful women is a time-honored tradition, and no woman was more beautiful than Betty Grable. She was the sexiest pin-up girl alive when I was a pilot during the war." Nico strokes the sleek curve of ship's command console with his fingertips. "She is the most sophisticated artificial intelligence set-up I've ever seen. Watch this. Betty, display Château d'Amboise, the royal residence of Francis the First of France. Year: 1532."

"Image onscreen now," Betty replies, her voice is soft, seductive. Nico ignores my raised eyebrow.

A small three-dimensional holographic model of rolling green fields and an enormous palace hovers on the display pad above the cockpit console.

Nico continues. "The old ships have two-dimensional maps, not these kinds of holographic images where—"

"We have holographic images everywhere. That's not new technology."

"Think so, huh?" He leans back in the chair and cocks his head to the side. "Betty, magnify image of the people walking toward the palace."

"Magnifying image by a factor of one thousand, honey," Betty replies.

Honey? I mouth at him and snicker.

"I am programmed to emulate the soothing tone Commander Garcia prefers. Your commentary is rude and unprofessional." Betty replies with what I swear is a hint of resentment. If I didn't know better, I'd say its feelings are hurt. "Nico, honey, shall I lock this human out of systems access?"

"Did the computer just scold me?" Artificial intelligence got a lot snarkier after programmers included personality infusion as part of the customization package.

"You could be a little nicer," Nico sniffs. "I've programmed your access to all non-engineering systems at priority level one. You also have back-up emergency access to critical ships' systems in the event I'm incapacitated." Then, to the computer, "Betty, I expect you to be nice to Dodger. Don't give her any lip."

"If you say so...*Doll*," Betty replies, the resentment slides into grudging obedience and the emphasis on the term of endearment was —I'm sure—meant to further stake a claim on Nico.

The image swirls creating contrails of green and blue—the mingling of the earth and sky of a late summer afternoon—as Betty manipulates the image to magnify the young couple. A canopy of bright green leaves sways gently with the breeze as the pair, dressed in French Renaissance clothes, pass beneath them. Their mouths move wordlessly as they stroll through the meadow.

"When I get the sound working, we should be able to hear their conversation," Nico says, studying my reaction. He chuckles under his breath when my mouth drops open in confusion.

"Why would a navigational program include human representations in the hologram?"

"Because it's not just a navigational program," he replies. "What we're watching are real French people taking a lovely afternoon stroll in the year Fifteen Thirty-Two."

We watch as the man pulls his companion into an embrace, then turns her around and walks her backwards, claiming her mouth with bruising until she's backed into a tree. He pulls the long skirt up to her knees and slips his hand beneath it. Her mouth opens in what I assume is a moan.

"Got popcorn?" I ask. "This is getting good."

When the man lowers his britches, Nico leans forward and, with awkward throat clearing, zooms the camera out to a respectful distance that blurs the action.

"You don't like watching?" I tease.

He gives me a double-take, frowning at my ear-to-ear grin. "What if Fagin walks in while we're watching Renaissance porn." He taps the controls and the scene changes to a clergyman leading a daily mass in the royal chapel.

"Yes, this is much better," I say, giggling.

He slaps the enviro controls and a blast of frigid air shoots out of the overhead vents. "Damn cabin is always overheating," he says. He gestures at the hologram with a flat hand. "Focus, please. This is bleeding-edge technology. No one has ever before watched live-action footage from hundreds of years ago as it's actually happening."

"That's real time?"

"Real people. In France. Right now."

A beat. "Bullshit."

"Not bullshit. Look at this." Nico cycles through several other images. The cooks in the kitchen preparing the king's meal; the queen of France, and her ladies playing a game of cards; finally, King Francois meeting with his advisors.

"I've heard about this technology," Nico says, "but I've never seen it in action. Observer missions used to record events they witness and bring them back to study. Now we can observe real people in our target environment even before we get there. The Benefactors must've spent billions on this ship."

"The Benefactors or the military." I peer at the scene playing now: King Francois, deep in conversation with his noblemen. The reality of what I'm watching sinks in and its power is astounding.

Conscious now, of the significance of what he thought was just a cool feature of the new ship, Nico lowers his voice. "It's all been conjecture; whispers of experimental technology that was still in testing. Someone figured out how to transmit live action between a target environment's year and ours."

Nico's eyes narrow. He gets up, stretches, and glances around the cabin before thumbing through some papers on a clipboard. He gives me a sideways glance full of meaning before his eyes flit to the corner above my head; my eyes follow his to the corner, too. The cameras.

They're watching us.

"Maybe the Benefactors want you to understand how good your life could be if you behave yourself." He pauses, then asks, "You hungry?"

"Starving," I say, playing along as I follow him to the shuttle door. Right now, I'm not sure I could choke chocolate down past the lump in the back of my throat.

"Me, too," he replies, grasping my hand and giving it a squeeze." Betty, lock up for me, huh?"

"Sure thing, Hot Stuff," Betty replies.

Once we're on the out of the hangar, Nico pulls me aside. "In the last twelve hours, we got a state-of-the-art Timeship and the Benefactors fired a warning shot over the bow at you with the consigliere visit. How did you get on their radar like this? It's gotta be more than being late to extraction points a few times."

"How the hell should I know? Maybe we're overthinking this. There are some expensive artifacts we're bringing back. Maybe they want the fastest, most technologically advanced ship for this job."

"We steal priceless artifacts on every mission. They wouldn't give us the first ship to broadcast live action feeds from the other side of the time vortex without a damn good reason. Why us? Why now?"

"Maybe all the junkers are assigned to other missions." Even as I say the words, I don't believe them.

"They could have given this luxury liner to a sanctioned Observer mission instead of us," Nico replies. "We need to tread very carefully. Do you understand?" He looks me dead in the eyes and there's no mistaking the seriousness in his face.

The Consigliere's warning to get my shit together rings in my head.

"I'm gonna look for a way to encrypt or distort the data feed, on demand, so we can have private conversations when we need to. Your job," he plants a finger softly in my chest as he holds my gaze, "is to stay under their radar. As far as they're concerned, the Consigliere's visit scared you straight."

I take a steadying breath, an attempt to squelch the panic jacking up my heart rate. I put my hand on his chest. His heart is hammering as fast as mine. "I'll try."

"Gotta do more than try, babe. One warning is probably all we'll get. And they're watching us."

CHAPTER 8

FOR WEEKS, Queen Elizabeth fills my nightmares in bizarre snippets reflecting the milestones of my life: Elizabeth is there when Papa is murdered. She herds hundreds of Acadie refugees, including Maman and me, onto a doomed ship sailing for the American colonies. Elizabeth sells me into indentured bondage to the captain of a merchant vessel in New Orleans.

Like grainy, imperfect spools of film from an ancient newsreel, pockmarked with dark spots and blurs, her image runs on a loop through my head while I'm awake. Her shadow is in every face I see; her voice is the echo thrumming beneath every conversation. She's a ghost that has destroyed my life in a million ways.

This morning, as Fagin and I worked through more mission details, I could have sworn I caught a glimpse of her watching me from the shadows—smug satisfaction blazing in her steely eyes.

The center of the room is clear of furniture, leaving space enough for multi-character holographic recordings, queued up from the Observer's Renaissance archives. A series of French court vignettes, circa 1532, rotate in the sequence Fagin designed to complete our initial entry into Calais. Par for the course in this mission, Fagin and I find ourselves on opposite sides of the initial rules of engagement.

We've been arguing strategy all morning, and Fagin dives into her usual modus operandi when faced with an intransigent opponent: She attacks with a barrage of words, intending to overwhelm me with the sheer volume of information. It doesn't take long before my attention wanders.

Fagin discusses the rhythm of French court life: the hierarchy of the nobility, who we must befriend to get close to the king in the shortest time possible, the criticality of getting the all-important invitation to meet King Henry and Lady Anne. On and on and on she talks, until her words run together into a jumble. Meanwhile, I can't tear my thoughts away from Elizabeth.

CRACK!

The sound jolts me out of my daydream and propels me over the armrest of my chair and onto my feet. "What the hell was *that?*" I gasp, trying to steady my pulse to a rhythm slower than light speed.

Fagin leans forward and places both palms on the thick leather-bound portfolio she used to pound the wood table and glares at me. "Now that you're back in the present," she says, not bothering to smooth the irritation in her voice, "recite back everything I said in the last two minutes."

"You're kidding," I say, feeling more wounded at being treated as though I need a nursemaid than feeling guilty at being called out. "We've discussed mission strategy options backwards and forwards and sideways for six weeks. If we're not ready to decide—"

"Recite the last thirty seconds back to me. I'll settle for that much," she says. "This isn't a game. They have called me into three meetings with Consiglieres because of your attitude. What must I do to get through this thick skull of yours?" She thumps her knuckles against the middle of my forehead; an attention-getter is what she called it when I was a child and had lost focus or misbehaved during training.

There's silence. The kind of quiet where the undercurrent in the air is charged with anger and frustration. For Fagin, the saying "don't get mad, get even," isn't a cliché. It's a mantra. A way of life.

It's been a long time since I was on her shit list—my attempt, at fifteen, to run away and marry an eighteenth-century pirate springs to mind—but the throbbing behind my eyes and across the front of my head reminds me it's an unpleasant place to be.

She doesn't move. Doesn't break eye contact. Her gaze is hard and cold, and a quiver shoots down my spine that chills me as thoroughly as if I had just broken into a fevered sweat. I blink and look away. "I understand the danger we're in."

"I remain unconvinced until you show me otherwise." She still doesn't break eye contact.

"We're going about this all wrong," I say. Rather than trying to recount the finger points of Fagin's lecture—and, let's face it, I don't remember a thing she said—I change tactics. I nod at the life-sized holographic image of an auburn-haired beauty with a long nose and pouting lips. "Eleanor of Austria, King Francois' second wife, won't get us into the retinue accompanying him to Calais. The Boleyn girls attended his first wife, Queen Claude, and adored Lady Anne. While this fact isn't lost on Eleanor, the queen is also a staunch Catholic and history says she'll never legitimize Anne by meeting with her."

"Eleanor can get us access to her husband," Fagin says in a tone that expects full agreement. "It would make sense to get close to the King by getting close to her."

"There's another way."

"Enlighten me." Fagin settles into a high-backed wood chair and spreads her arms open in a gesture of invitation. "If the queen isn't the entry point to the French court, who is?"

I smile. "Computer, display Anne de Pisseleu d'Heilly as she was in 1532." Eleanor disappears, replaced by a golden-haired woman with a pointed chin and dark eyes. "This is Frankie's maîtresse-en-titre."

"Frankie?" Fagin snorts out a laugh. It's the first laugh I've heard from her in weeks. "And how does his attachment to his official mistress benefit us?"

"The French have a saying: A court without women is like a garden without flowers. Francois will be eager to display the most beautiful women in France in front of Henry, including his mistress. There will be more courtiers attending him at Calais than we can count. Make friends with his favorite mistress, and we'll be in the King's line of sight. A little flirtation here, a little flattery there, et voilà, we'll get an invitation to Calais."

"That's clever," Fagin says, grudgingly. "But we have to play this carefully. Making friends with the king's mistress could be disastrous."

"Not true. Francois rarely speaks to his wife. Anne wields more power in the French court than just about anyone. Trust me. This will work."

"Trust you? You've been more of a pain in the ass since we got this assignment than when I first found you, and that's saying something."

"Are you seriously throwing that in my face?" I groan and slip into my rendition of Fagin's throaty voice and, for added emphasis, throw up my hands in a frenzied motion to mirror her usual exasperation with the memory of those early days. "I was a little monster for the first six months. Mouthy. Disrespectful. Constantly trying to run away even though there was nowhere for me to go."

"You were a beast," she interrupts, slamming a book into the middle of the table, causing a slight flicker in the hologram image as the book lands with a thud. "The only reason I didn't take you straight back to picking pockets on the wharves of New Orleans was your pure, raw talent. You were the most gifted thief I'd ever met before you'd had a single day of training."

Fagin had considered throwing me back into that cesspool.

This confession strikes a surreal dissonant chord, tinny and out of tune with the rhythm of our relationship since she saved me. She taught me how to get what I want from people and make it think it was their idea to give it to me. She has been my protector, and the only family I have left.

The more her words sink in, the more they feel like a knife being drawn torturously down my chest until my nerves and muscles, my very heart, lay exposed and raw.

How could she have thought of abandoning me?

"I think I'm handling this entire shit show extremely well." I swallow the lie along with the lump of emotion stuck in my craw; it leaves a trail of bile that burns down my throat, all the way to my belly. "What you're asking me to do is—"

"Save our lives. That's what I'm asking you to do, Dodger." Fagin says.

"You know the Benefactors sent goons to threaten me into submission, right?"

"I know." She looks like she hasn't slept in years. Her face is drawn and dark circles mottle the skin below her eyes. "If we play our parts, we'll come out of this in one piece."

"Reporting my every move to the Benefactors is playing your part?"

"Yes." She looks me square in the eyes. Her tone is matter-of-fact, like her choice to be an informant is what any sane person would do in her position instead of what it is: a solid blow to the foundation of our relationship. She doesn't explain her answer further; instead, she pivots back to the argument at hand. "Convince me why King Francois's mistress is the better in-road to Calais than his wife."

Prying a rationale out of Fagin for her choices when she gives definitive one-word answers is akin to prying a coin from a miser's grip. *She knows better than to think I'll let this go forever. For now, this battle will have to wait.* "Neither of these men will risk being seen as having less fortune, fewer servants and courtiers, than the other," I say. "Henry, alone, brings a contingent of two thousand people to Calais. We can expect Francois to do no less."

The skin between her eyes crinkles. "Go on."

"Our cover stories place us as wealthy, influential women, so the most important courtiers—including the king's mistress—should be keen to meet us."

"My cover story includes wealth and influence. You, my dear, are my ward."

"Semantics," I say, waving a dismissive hand. "You won't dress me in rags and refuse to let me attend the king's festival, right?"

She chuckles under her breath, a small concession. I'll take it. Even in our toughest times, if I can get her to laugh a little, I can get her agreement to a plan, too.

"Francis won't spend more than a single night away from the mistress; where he goes, she goes. As long as we make ourselves indispensable to her, we'll get an invitation to the ball. This meeting is as much about one-upmanship as Henry's goals of gaining acceptance of Anne."

"And once we're in Calais?" she asks.

"I introduce myself to Mary Boleyn. The critical path to England goes straight through Lady Anne's sister. She slept with both Francois and Henry, so she knows the inner workings of both courts."

"I'll admit it's not the worst plan I've heard. I need to watch the research holograms again to see if there's anything we missed. Some angle we haven't spotted."

"You don't trust me?" It stings to even have to ask the question. Whatever else happens, their damage to my partnership with Fagin can't be a casualty of war.

"I trust your skills," she says in a resolute tone. I can hear the "but" coming from a mile away. "It's the attitude I don't trust. Your anger controls you. That's dangerous."

"You've never had an issue with how I work before. You love that I'm unconventional, that I take risks no one else does and always come out on top."

"Your unconventional ass attracted the wrong attention from the wrong people, and here we are." Fagin flings both arms out to the side and lets them fall with an exasperated slap against her chair. "Every mistake you make in training, every tantrum or mood swing is weighed against you, and your talent may not be enough to balance the scales."

"Why can't they send us somewhere else? To some other time?" I hate the pleading tone in my voice. It makes me sound like a five-year-old whining about bedtime. "This can't be the only way to prove my worth to them."

"Not happening, kid. This is your only chance to right this ship."

A faint buzzing grows steadily louder in the background. Fagin crosses over to her desk and taps the display screen on her tablet computer several times. I can't see what she's reading, but her brow furrows and she closes her eyes. She exhales a short, sharp breath. "You ready for this?"

Shaking my head and suddenly, feeling quite small and vulnerable, I answer. "Does it matter?"

There's a shaky laugh -- the polar opposite of the chuckles I finessed from her today. "I guess it doesn't. Nico says that the Timeship is ready and we have our departure window. We leave at dawn tomorrow."

CHAPTER 9

MORNING PEOPLE ANNOY the hell out of me. Chipper, bright-eyed people who spring from bed fully loaded and excited to tackle a new day are freaks of nature who get a buzz out of beating the rest of us to the productivity punch. Early birds don't really get the worm; they just wake everyone else up. Overachievers, every damn one of them.

I need coffee.

It's a little before four o'clock in the morning. Dawn is an hour away and, for some perverted reason, the Benefactors scheduled our time jump nearly four hours before any reasonable person should be expected to work. The ground crew swarms around the outside of the shuttle like worker bees, running diagnostic tests and prepping for launch.

Stepping into the ship, I hear someone whistling a happy tune deep in the bowels of the cargo hold. The trilling notes echo up through the opening in the floor, as Nico ascends the ladder into the main cabin.

He looks me over head-to-toe and I'm suddenly self-conscious about my untucked shirt, untied boots, and disheveled hair bound up in a loose elastic band, which allows half of its volume to hang past my shoulders on the right side of my head.

"You look like hammered shit." He walks past me to the galley and gives a command to the replicator. "Sixteen ounces of Garcia's French Roast and chicory root coffee blend. Mix with fifty percent organic whole milk. Brew at precisely one hundred-forty degrees Fahrenheit."

A muted orange glow radiates from the replicator as it produces a glass mug filled with steaming, aromatic coffee. He offers the cup to me, and it's the most perfect Café au Lait I've ever tasted. My personal replicator comes close to reproducing the brew I remember from childhood, but Nico's blend beats every other twenty-sixth-century knockoff in existence. He orders the same brew for himself.

"Mm. Coffee and chicory," I say. The heat from the mug warms my hands as the drink warms my insides, making the ship's cabin a little less frigid. The cold isn't quite at the stage where you can see your breath hanging in a frothy cloud in front of your face, but with the hangar bay air drifting through the open door, it's close.

"After our last mission to New Orleans," he says. "I'll never drink it any other way if I can help it." His morning-person eyes are clear and alert, and he looks annoyingly put-together: his dark curls are tamed with hair product, and a pressed khaki shirt is tucked into his blue jeans. He takes a swig from his own mug and beams a big smile.

"Cooks in French Louisiana's great houses made coffee this way for a century before the American Civil War. When I was a child—"

Nico's eyebrows raise, and he leans forward onto the balls of his feet, like he's anticipating a revelatory tidbit from my past.

Fagin's words ring in my ears. *Giving people your past gives them power over you.* I wave away his interest with a dismissive hand. "Doesn't matter. I could do with a beignet or three."

Nico smiles and commands the replicator again. "Six beignets. Extra powdered sugar."

Memories are weird, imperfect things; the oldest recollections—the fossils buried deep in the sub-conscious—are the weirdest and most imperfect of all. Colored by the passing of years, all it takes to unearth unexpected relics, sometimes at the most inopportune moment, is a trigger. Like the sight of something familiar, or a word or situation that conjures powerful feelings, frozen in time. A song that throws you backward and slams you heart-first into a long-forgotten moment.

Smell is a powerful trigger. The smell of sweet fried dough takes me back to a Louisiana plantation and Marie-Thérèse, the Acadian cook who found my starved, half-clothed body cowering behind the hydrangeas in the garden.

She hid me, fed and clothed me for a month. She tucked me into bed with her own children. I was ten years old and had been an orphan since I was eight. It was the first time in two years I had felt any sense of safety or security. The aroma and taste of the light-as-air pastry reminds me of her; it feels like she's standing beside me.

Nico is talking, but I only know this because his lips are moving. His voice is muffled by the thoughts racing through my head. I catch his last few words. "Well, are you?"

"Huh?" I ask, forcing myself fully back to the present.

"I asked if you're happy. You were smiling, but I couldn't tell if it was a happy smile or something else."

Pushing the last wisps of Marie-Thérèse away, I put on a sarcastic mask to hide behind. "Even with coffee, it's too damn early to be chipper. Whoever scheduled departure for this ungodly hour should be drawn and quartered, then boiled in his own pudding and buried with a stake of holly through his heart."

"Bitching already? Not a very auspicious beginning to the journey, Clémence." Fagin stands on the threshold, a small leather backpack slung across her shoulder. A frown crinkles the skin between her eyes. She drops the backpack onto the floor next to one of the leather crew seats. Then she says to Nico, her voice sharp as a blade,

"Get moving on pre-flight. And turn the heat up in here. It's freezing."

"On it," he says.

Nico and I exchange looks. He orders a Cafe au Lait for Fagin, too, which she accepts without comment. Maybe the caffeine will help dislodge the stick up her ass.

Nico and the ground crew work through pre-departure checklists with surgical precision. Given the consequences of miscalculating time jump coordinates—no one wants to wind up in the wrong place or time or inside a stone wall—attention to detail is required. Nico sits at the pilot's console working through his checklist; a symphony of colors light up the cockpit in oranges, yellows, greens, and blues. They pulse and glow with each rhythmic move of his hands across the Betty's virtual reality screens.

On Nico's left, laminated printouts of the pre-flight checklists and pilot's manual—holdovers from Nico's Spanish Air Force pilot days that he insists on keeping in paper form—are attached to the bottom of the command console by a metal ring. "Belt and suspenders," he had said to me, when I questioned him about it on our first mission together. "Never know when you might need to bypass computer gadgetry and fly by the seat of your pants."

I'm not sure these Timeships can be manually flown. The print-outs are likely a security blanket for him. Most time transplants—those of us plucked from other times to live and work in the twenty-sixth century—have a touchstone of some sort. Something that grounds us and helps with homesickness because integration as a time traveler is a one-way deal. Once you join the team, you can't go home unless your memories are wiped.

A female voice comes over the intercom, the Time Jump Ground Control Director—T-Jump, for short—runs down the steps of her checklist with Nico. "Commence final pre-flight check," she says, her tone all business. "Flight crew affirm mission with go or no-go confirmation."

"Roger, T-Jump. Commencing final pre-flight check," Nico says. "Begin navigation systems checks."

"Launch sequence trajectory data confirmed loaded to command module," she says, "Three cycle flight load: mission base launch, navigation to portal entry, and time vortex jump. Navigation aligned with current enviro conditions and portal threshold magnetic energy data signature."

"Launch trajectory data locked in, T-Jump," he says, his fingers dancing across the screens. "Navigation controls are go."

Fagin frowns at her data pad while nursing her coffee; she doesn't look at me as she reads, and after receiving the second grunt as an answer to a question, I abandon all communication attempts until she's in a better mood which, I hope, will happen sometime before the end of the century.

Burying myself in my own mission prep—reviewing historical and mission plan briefs using portable holo-programs—doesn't distract me from the ships' final systems checks. I'm not interested in hearing the never-ending recitation of technical jargon, but time travel quality control requires checklists to be broadcast over the ship's intercom system so the crew hears the process.

All systems are functioning as expected. Replicators and emergency dehydrated meals, enough to sustain a crew of four people for ninety days, are loaded. Medical supplies including computer-guided medical and surgical operation procedure controls are operational. Emergency egress plans, in the event a launch or landing is aborted, are a go.

One by one, every system gets a thorough check. The pre-flight checklists usually take an hour, about the time required to calm my pre-flight nerves. With Nico at the helm, I find myself more relaxed than usual. I'm beginning to settle in, get my head in the game. Though this is his first official mission as the primary pilot, hearing Nico's calm, steady tone over the speakers is reassuring.

"Last two systems on the checklist, T-Jump, let's finish this up so we can get on our way," Nico says.

"Roger," T-Jump says, "Initiating check of ship's exterior camouflage program."

Watching an intelligent man who is incredibly good at his job strokes every erogenous zone in my body. Nico's smooth, quiet confidence makes a girl want to strip his clothes off and T-Jump him into bed.

"Sorry I'm late," a feminine voice says, scattering my thoughts faster than a fan clearing the fog from a smoky room.

Fagin and I look up from our work and gape at the new arrival.

"I didn't get my orders until super late last night, so packing was a nightmare," she speaks in a rapid-fire cadence that makes it hard to catch everything gushing out of her mouth. The squeaky timbre of her voice reminds me of someone who has sucked helium out of a balloon, and the effects have worn half-way off. "I had to find someone to cat-sit while I'm gone, and Nero is seriously picky about who he lets take care of him. Then I couldn't find my new hiking boots, and I think it's because my roomie borrowed them. She has real boundary issues, that one, let me tell you."

She actually put air quotes around "borrowed."

"Excuse me?" Fagin interrupts in an impatient tone bordering on livid. "Who are you and what are you doing on my ship?"

The woman, a brunette of average build who doesn't look much older than me—twenty-two or twenty-three, tops—beams a sweet-as-honey smile, and hands Fagin a manila folder. Fagin hesitates and looks askance at the newcomer as she takes it.

"Lieutenant Becca Trevor." Fagin reads the name on the front of the folder aloud, then gives the woman, still beaming her sickening-sweet smile, a blank look and a one-shouldered shrug.

Trevor flips open the front cover of the folder and points at the top sheet of paper inside. "Read my CV and the copy of my official orders. I'm sure you'll understand. Everything you need to know is there." She's still smiling.

"I'm not reading anything," Fagin says. "Tell me who you are and what the hell you're doing on my ship."

Lieutenant Trevor's smile withers into a quirky twitch at the corner of her mouth. She cocks her head to the side as she considers Fagin with a long, hard glare. "So much for the breezy and friendly approach." She snatches the papers from Fagin's hands and shuffles through them. Finding the one she's looking for, she offers it to Fagin. "Read it."

Fagin doesn't accept the offering, preferring, instead, to return Trevor's a hard glare. The lieutenant blinks once, then tossed the stack onto the table. Fagin smooths the paper in front of her and silently reads. The color drains from her face; her countenance freezes into stone. An expressionless face can speak volumes about inner turmoil. Right now, Fagin's face says she's terrified.

"Understand?" Becca Trevor asks. Her smile returns and it looks forced and creepy.

When Fagin looks up from the page, irritation is replaced with utter deference to the new girl. "Lieutenant Trevor is our official liaison with the Benefactors," she says, quietly, to me. "Starting now, all mission orders come through her." She gives Trevor a curt nod. "Happy to have you on the team, lieutenant."

My mouth falls open, and when Fagin gives me a dark look, I cover it with a fake yawn.

"Thank you, Fagin. I'm sure we'll get on famously," Becca Trevor says in an overly chummy tone. Her use of my mentor's nickname, rather than an appropriately formal form of address, makes me want to chuck her out the garbage chute even before we launch. "Don't bother getting up, I'll introduce myself to Commander Garcia."

She disappears into the cockpit and chatters away to Nico about late mission assignments, packing woes, and her roommate's lack of boundaries.

"Benefactor liaison, huh?" I whisper. "Babysitter and stool pigeon are more like it."

"Babysitter, stool pigeon, and co-pilot, actually."

"She's... she's what?"

Before Fagin can answer, Nico shoots out of the cockpit, an alarmed look crinkling the faint worry lines in his forehead. "Fagin. A few words, please?"

"Which words would you like, Commander Garcia? Mandatory co-pilot? Or perhaps tough luck, kid, suck it up?"

"I know everyone with GTC pilot credentials, but I've never heard of her," Nico says. "I don't even know if she can tell the difference between the toilet compartment and an escape pod, let alone if she knows how to fly. Am I just supposed to take her word for it? This is bullshit. She could get us all killed if she doesn't know what she's doing."

"Her CV is somewhere here." I point at the layer of printouts lying on the table between Fagin and me. "Apparently, her file tells us everything we need to know."

"Sweet Jesus, have you heard her voice?" He says in a loud whisper, a panicked look widens his eyes.

"Have a problem with your new co-pilot? Take it up with the Benefactors and mission control when we get home," Fagin says. "I have no leverage here." She sneaks an upward glance at the camera above my head before leveling her gaze on Nico. Then on me. "I'm sure you both understand."

Of course. The Benefactors are watching.

"I'm sure you'll find a way to keep us safe, Commander." Fagin's words are a genuine, heartfelt vote of confidence in Nico's command abilities. "In fact, now more than ever, we're counting on it."

Nico sucks air between his teeth, then says in a low voice, "You're not giving me much to work with, Fagin."

"I know."

T-Jump's voice booms over the intercom; the volume is much louder than before, causing the three of us to jump. "Garcia, acknowledge. Ready to finish pre-flight?"

"Sorry!" Becca Trevor calls out from the cockpit. "I was trying to find some music, but I think I did something wrong. How do you turn it down?"

Nico curses softly. He looks ready to spit fire. "Don't touch anything. Don't breathe on anything. And, for God's sake, stop talking until we're airborne."

He settles into his seat to complete the pre-flight checklists. His new co-pilot has taken to singing softly to herself.

"Cabin crew, prepare for lift-off," Nico says, his voice broadcasting at a more comfortable volume. "T-Jump, initiating take-off sequence, phase one."

"Copy that," comes the reply.

I lift my window shade because watching the launch never gets old. The light inside the hangar is dull and gray, creating dappled shadows against the concrete walls as the ship glides toward the launch queue.

"Open hangar doors," T-Jump commands, and the doors groan open, pre-dawn light streaming into the structure through the ever-widening gap. We hover for a few minutes as Nico and the command crew work through the final launch sequences. When T-Jump is satisfied the launch window is fully open—with no impediments or show-stoppers—she gives the command, "Commence launch sequence. Proceed to time vortex portal and hold there."

"Launch sequence, phase two. Acknowledged," Nico says, and we accelerate through the open hangar doors. The pre-dawn sky is an ombre of dusky purple, orange and yellow.

Within minutes, we've streaked across green pastures filled with livestock, tall prairie grasses, a patchwork of farmland and, finally, the dark black-blue waters of Lake Powell.

Past the Northern shore of the lake, the shuttle slows. We hover in place, waiting for clearance to time jump. The ship is smooth and balanced and there's no bone-shaking shudder that rattles my teeth—

a nerve-wracking experience common on the dilapidated buckets of bolts mercenaries often use.

From my crew seat, I see a sliver of the open cavern ahead of us. The entrance is enormous, making it feel as it always does at the start of a time jump: like the mountain is about to swallow us whole and spit us out in another time.

That's an accurate, if inelegant, layman's description of how this method of time travel works. From what I've been told, it's different on other planets. Interstellar time jumps use temporarily stabilized wormholes, which is dangerous because no one knows when one of those things might collapse. This cavern, and others on Earth like it, is built to harness and focus dark matter and energy coursing through the mineral and gemstone deposits embedded in the cavern walls. When a time jump sequence initiates, a fissure in the fabric of time and space opens and allows us to slip through the cracks between our world and other times, other places.

Dark matter is some serious shit.

"Awaiting clearance for phase two launch, T-Jump," Nico says.

"How does it look from your end, Nico?" T-Jump replies.

"Instruments show all green. No showstoppers. Looks like we're ready to rock, so to speak."

A snort comes over the speakers. "Rock on, brother. Not into the rocks, if you please. I don't want to write that report."

"Copy that, T-Jump," Nico says, laughing.

"We're clear on this end. It's all yours, Nico. We'll keep the lights on for you guys. Come home safe, crew."

"Thanks, T-Jump. See you on the other side."

"Commence launch phase two on my mark."

"Acknowledged."

"Launch in three, two, one. Mark."

Through my window, I watch the cavern walls refract prisms of light in long streaks of kaleidoscopic color as we blast through the tunnel. There's a deep hum building, like a wind turbine ratcheting up to a higher speed.

Flashes of light drift by my window in slow, lazy waves, like a ripple on pond water when a stone is tossed into it. The closer we get to the time jump in the vortex, the faster the ripples travel. There's an enormous burst of light and color as we slip the bounds of the twenty-sixth century, then a darkness so deep, it's hard to believe that moments ago, we were surfing a rainbow of brilliant light waves.

There's a nauseous feeling bubbling in my belly, but biometric filters prevent the sometimes-fatal side effects that were once a dangerous byproduct of time travel.

"Betty," Nico's voice is calm and steady in the dark. "On re-entry, initiate exterior camouflage program."

"Affirmative, honey," Betty answers. "Re-entry in ten seconds."

At the end of the countdown, we emerge from the vortex into a vibrant blue sky. "Camouflage initiated and fully intact," Betty says.

Fagin and I move to the cockpit. Fagin speaks first. "Confirm date and location coordinates."

Nico swipes two screens out of the way and pulls up a holographic image of our destination. "Date and location coordinates: 47.5532° N, 1.0105° E, which puts us right in the middle of France's Loire Valley. The date is…" He air-taps a screen to his right. "First of August, Fifteen Hundred Thirty-Two."

"The location of our first base of operations should be in the computer," Fagin says.

"Got 'em right here." Nico pulls the coordinates up and a three-dimensional image of a gray stone manor house, surrounded by lush gardens. "Pretty fancy joint."

"Things will move fast after we land. We have a lot to do before contact with the locals." She pats Nico on the shoulder. "First order of business is to set up security systems."

"Yes, ma'am," Nico replies. Then he smiles at me. "Welcome to France."

CHAPTER 10

I'VE HEARD it said that wine colonized the world, and humans were merely the vehicle for its migration. Since the advent of the oldest known winery in Armenia, cultivated in 4,000 BC, wine production has done more to promote good international and interplanetary relations than all the adventurers, politicians and kings who ever lived. Without the humble grape, civilization would be, well... less civilized.

I may be exaggerating, but probably not much.

As I prowl the perimeter of the chateau's salon, watching the Vicomte d'Auvergne and his wife cast snide, sideways glances at Fagin as they judge the quality of the drink, I wonder if there's a problem that can't be resolved over a collegial glass of exceptional wine. My predicament with this mission answers that question with a resounding "yes."

I take a deep breath. I hoped once I was in Papa's and Mama's ancestral homeland, I would feel a new connection to them. Something that would give me strength, or at least ease my restlessness as this heinous mission begins. We've been in Paris for twenty-four hours. I'm still as jumpy as a puppet on a string.

That's an apt job description for a time thief: The Benefactors' bitch. Must perform for their demented pleasure.

The Vicomte is tall and regal with a patrician nose, useful when judging aromatic properties of fine wines. He wears a fussy ruffled shirt beneath a satin burgundy jerkin with matching short breeches. His beard and mustache are cropped close, and his arched eyebrows give him a devilish appearance.

His wife is resplendent in a green silk kirtle embroidered with tiny perfect yellow flowers. Her ivory shift is visible through the slashes in the embroidered sleeves, and the low-cut square neckline shows off an ample bosom. She is as vapid as she is beautiful, demonstrated by her inability to say anything original—preferring, instead, to parrot her husband.

She makes me want to scream.

The Vicomte raises a glass to his nose. His eyes close and a deep inhale follows. His expression suggests he's lost in the aroma, and wondering if the drink will fulfill the bouquet's promise when it hits his tongue.

He sips, swirls the drink around his mouth. There's a contented sigh as he swallows and beams another satisfied smile. "Exquisite. I have never tasted its equal," he says. "There is a hint of something I cannot quite place." He pauses for a second sip, another swirl of wine in his mouth. "Is it...wood smoke?"

"Yes. Wood smoke," his wife agrees.

"I love the new Translator upgrade." Nico's voice is soft as a feather in my ear, courtesy of a CommLink set at a comfortable volume. "The speed and accuracy of the translation are so amazing, I bet it could translate the Vicomte's French thoughts to English before he opens his mouth." A beat. "You're discussing the wine, right?"

Fagin's eyelashes flutter and she glances in my direction. I note the almost imperceptible widening of her eyes that indicates irritation. She makes a discreet motion of drawing the tip of her index finger across her throat. Fagin hates idle chatter on missions. It's one of her rules: If you're not directly involved in a conversation, shut your damn mouth so others aren't distracted from theirs.

I cast a glance at the miniature surveillance camera installed in the ceiling, then turn to gaze out the windows overlooking the lush gardens. Nico can see everything from the command center in the ship. An abundance of rose bushes, and rows of waist-high boxwoods, extend to the oak-lined alee leading to the main road. At the far end of the lane, there's a sharp right turn in the road that meanders south toward Paris.

"Fagin wants radio silence," I say in a low voice.

The CommLinks we wear are the most sophisticated communication devices ever designed. The microphones pick up the slightest whisper, and Betty runs noise gates that distinguish between the user's voice, at any decibel level, and other ambient noises in the room to cancel out distractions. Coupled with a number of creative techniques for discreet conversation in surveillance settings—simple things like turning away from bystanders or using a wine glass to conceal the mouth when speaking—it's relatively easy to carry on conversations with team members on the ship with minimal risk of eavesdropping locals.

Still, depending on the mission's time period, communication in the wild can be super tricky. On one of my first jobs, in 1217 France, we searched for the bodily remains of Saint Edmund; a holy relics collector wanted his bones for his private collection. I was overheard talking to the Timeship by a small group of powerful, superstitious men. Turns out that talking to yourself within earshot of ignorance can be misinterpreted as muttering witchcraft spells under your breath. I narrowly escaped burning at the stake—with Edmund's right femur safely stowed in my bag—thanks to Nico's technical wizardry and a talking goat.

"I saw her," Nico says, sniffing in clear indignation. "She doesn't need to be snippy." The CommLink goes silent.

If Fagin registers his displeasure, she gives no sign. Her focus remains on the potential buyer. "I have connections with influential courtiers who introduced me to the merchants importing wine from Portugal, Spain, and the island of Madeira," Fagin says, a coy smile on her lips. "This vintage is an extremely rare Madeira. Let me assure you, Monsieur le Vicomte, this," she taps the decanter on the table for emphasis, "can't be found anywhere else unless you come to me."

"Indeed?" he asks. "If I negotiate with you, then I would have exclusive purchase privileges? A common wine anyone can buy doesn't interest me. It would displease me to discover that our arrangement leaves room for other buyers."

"Yes," the Parrot says, "we would be displeased."

"If we agree on terms, you will hold the exclusive contract. You should know our wine commands a premium price. Our winemakers have keen instincts for all vineyard matters—from the health of the vines to preparing the casks that hold this liquid gold." She raises her glass to her nose and sniffs. The Vicomte and his wife follow suit. "They are the only winemakers in the world capable of producing the same wine year after year."

More accurately, the Replicator is the only winemaker capable of producing the perfect wine, year after year, no matter what.

The Vicomte's eyebrows fly right to the top of his forehead. "Do you mean there are no variations in your wine from one season to the next? You must forgive me, Madame, but my sensibilities tell me this is quite impossible to achieve," he says with a smirk that I'd love just one shot at wiping clean off his face.

"Yes, quite impossible—" the Parrot begins, but, mercifully, Fagin derails her.

"I have proof."

"Please don't misunderstand," the Vicomte replies. "My faith in you as an accomplished woman is not in doubt. I do suspect that someone has taken advantage of your natural naiveté, a trait I'm afraid all women share, and convinced you that such a remarkable feat is attainable." His laugh is thin and reedy and insulting.

Fagin gives me a quick wink—our agreed-upon signal because she'd known the Vicomte would require proof. Five wine bottles are displayed on an ornately carved side table where the trio are gathered. I do this two more times for a total of five new bottles and set crystal decanters on the table as well.

The last two bottles show less age and dust than the others. Fagin opens each one, ensuring the nobles watch every move as she decants the wine, then she sets the bottles where their labels are visible at all times. I bring two clean glasses for each decanter, and uncover a small tray of sliced bread and bring it to the table.

"The wine needs to breathe, but it's important for you to watch as I decant them so you can verify you're not drinking from one bottle. Even in their current state, your discriminating palates should discern the veracity of my claim." Fagin disarms him with a flattering gaze. She gestures to the first decanter. "First, the Fifteen-Aught-Seven vintage."

"Twenty-five years old?" he asks, as he leans toward the table to read the dust-smudged label. He runs his thumb across the delicate paper until he's able to read the faded ink stamp.

Fagin spreads her hands open in a gesture of invitation. "The first of several rare and precious vintages before you today."

The Vicomte gives Fagin the same look he might give a clueless child. Simple, weak-minded female, he might be thinking. She's been duped into believing a fairytale about her wine.

"We'll see about that." The Vicomte pours a small amount of the deep ruby liquid into two glasses and hands one to his wife. They sniff. Then sip and swirl and swallow.

"Please, cleanse your palates before the next drink," Fagin says, handing them each small pieces of bread. She notes the pair's dubious expressions, and explains. "It ensures your mouth is a fresh canvas for the wine to paint upon."

Still doubtful, they each nibble a small amount of bread before proceeding to the next carafe.

"Now, the Fifteen-Twelve," Fagin announces with a flourish, and provides two generous pours of the next decanter. *God, I love watching her work. So damn smooth.*

The Vicomte raises his glass, leveling a steady gaze on the implacable Fagin. Again, the couple sniffs. Sip and swirl. Swallow. Confusion clouds the Vicomte's eyes as realization dawns, but he's not ready to admit the truth on his own taste buds. His wife's expression doesn't change as she samples the first three bottles; she seems clueless about what she is experiencing.

The ritual continues for each bottle, the vintage presented in five-year increments: A Seventeen, a Twenty-Two, and a Twenty-Seven.

"How can this be?" The Vicomte says, dumbfounded. He pulls a handkerchief out to mop his brow and my fingers twitch in response.

As a young pickpocket, I learned how to spot quality merchandise. This handkerchief is superior quality. It's silk, likely Italian since Francois is several years away from establishing a silk monopoly in Lyon. I could get a pretty penny for it back home since it's a status symbol in this time. Only nobles can afford such expensive things.

No embroidery or monogram. I wouldn't have to spend hours with a needle picking out the threads. My palms itch.

"Have I proven my wine is what I say, Monsieur le Vicomte?" Fagin asks, even though she can see the answer in his face.

"It's quite remarkable," he says, stumbling over his words. "There is no discernable difference between the old bottles and the new."

"With the first shipment, ten bottles of each vintage—fifty bottles in all—you would become the envy of Paris overnight."

At this, the Parrot's eyes sparkle like greedy little diamonds. "The envy of Paris," she says in a whisper.

"If you wish to sell this unique wine for profit, I'm sure we can agree on terms," Fagin says.

"Perhaps. You will find me a merciless negotiator, Madame," he says in all seriousness, as Fagin retrieves the contract and a quill.

If you're as good at negotiating as you are at hiding greed, you'll be begging Fagin to pay you instead of the other way around. For a moment, I wonder if the new translator program can indeed read minds because Fagin flashes me a smile behind the Vicomte's back that radiates her joy of a victorious hunt. She has her prey caught in a thicket, and he'll not escape.

"I think you'll find, sir, that my desires run to more important currency than money."

"Currency more important than money?" It's his turn to parrot; his tone is equal parts aghast and curious.

"Certainly." Fagin returns with the paper and sets it down on the table. "I have made my fortune in imports and exports of various kinds, and I find myself an independent woman of means. What I want is—"

"A suitable husband," the Vicomte says, with a thrust of his index finger into the air. He's button-busting proud that he guessed Fagin's ulterior motive before she revealed it. "Of course, the Vicomtess and I could introduce you to eligible and wealthy bachelors in Paris. We know everyone of importance in the city."

"Yes," the Parrot says, nodding, "we know everyone."

"No, Your Grace." Fagin says, with a demure hand raised in front of her chest, a gesture of both deference and resistance. "I want to provide the wine for the English king's visit in two months."

The Vicomte's eyes widen and his mouth pulls into a small circle. "How do you know about that? The visit is a state secret."

"Sir, there are no secrets at court," Fagin laughs. "I have my sources."

"Even so, Madame, I am not at liberty to discuss the king's business."

"I know what will take place in Calais, and how important this visit is to both sides. King Henry wants heads of state throughout the continent to accept his new lady as queen. He is merely starting with the friendliest ally he can think of: our king."

"Madame, your intimate knowledge of the circumstances is as extraordinary as your wine." He seems to be weighing his words like a merchant at his scales. "Why do you think I can help you?"

"Because you are landlord of The Staple Inn, the venue for the festivities. Here is my proposal," Fagin says, rubbing a finger around the opening of the decanter. "I will sell you my wine for twenty percent below value, enough drink for the banquet and some for your own personal use."

"What do you expect from this arrangement?" The look in the eyes of the Vicomte and his wife suggests they're already envisioning their elevated status within Paris society after the banquet as the purveyors of our unique wine.

"An introduction to Lady Anne Boleyn."

"The maîtresse-en-titre?" The Parrot changes its tune. Before, she was unquestioningly docile. Her tone now is assertive and filled with abject contempt for the English king's lady. "That is what she is. Regardless of her new title and stature, she is a common whore. Wicked and—"

"Powerful," Fagin finishes the sentence. "She will be England's queen. I could have offered this opportunity to any of your peers, but you own the venue where the English court will be received. We could have gone to England, but I thought we could come to an amicable agreement so both of our desires could be satisfied: We get an introduction to the English court and you elevate your status in both French and English societies."

"We accept your terms, Madame," the Vicomtess says, her eyes shining with ambition.

Her husband wrings his hands. "Marguerite, ma cher, we should discuss this before we commit to a course of action."

"Quiet, Henri," she says. She holds herself differently than a moment ago; she looks assertive, in command. It's becoming clear who the power in this power couple is. "We shall accept Madame Delacroix's generous offer." She turns back to Fagin. "Would delivery on Tuesday next be convenient for you?"

Sensing an end to the negotiation, Nico's voice pipes through the CommLink. "I'll order more Madeira from the Replicator. I'm going to need some help. Wine-making isn't easy, you know."

As they leave, I put myself in the Vicomte's way. He leans in to catch a sneaky peek down the front of my dress. I bend slightly forward to distract him with a better look. Then I sideswipe him.

"Pardon, mademoiselle," he says, extending a hand, a half-hearted attempt to steady me that turns into a grope.

"My apologies, monsieur. I am clumsy sometimes." I bat my eyelashes as I slip the handkerchief from his sleeve.

He didn't feel a thing.

CHAPTER 11

"WHAT IF WE don't have enough?" I ask Nico, trailing behind him as he counts the oak casks filled with Miracle Madeira, the name the Vicomtesse has given to our replicator wine.

"Please, stop talking. I'm trying to count," Nico says, as he waves a portable scanner across the wine casks loaded, pyramid-style, onto wooden pallets. "Instead of nagging me, go talk sense into the lady who is drinking her way through France with our wine before the English even get here."

Miracle Madeira has catapulted the Vicomtess d'Auvergne, and her husband, into instant notoriety in Paris, and they've been hitting the party circuit hard. Their continual demands for more personal-use wine have put a strain on our replicator's production capacity, and it's impacting the supply for the banquet. Fagin's negotiation skills secured our contract as wine merchants for The Staple Inn, but none of us expected threats to cancel the agreement if our partners' demands for free wine weren't met.

Charged with managing the ship and ensuring the health and security of all our technology, it's rare that Nico leaves the confines of the Timeship. We couldn't allow locals to ferry the wine from the ship to its ultimate destination, so we paid a handsome sum to rent space in The Staple Inn's private wine cellars so we could teleport the casks directly into the building.

Good thing the Benefactors have deep pockets. I can't imagine how much my occupation of the time-out corner is costing them, but it's got to be billions of dollars by now. This whole situation still doesn't make sense, but our primary concern is keeping the mission from going off the rails as the Vicomte and his wife act like teenagers whose parents are out of town for the weekend.

"What if we run out of wine? The replicator is barely keeping up with generating the supply we need and the banquet is only a few days away."

"Clémence," he pleads with an exasperated sigh "Please?"

"Okay. I'll shut up."

He shoots me an *I'll believe it when I see it* side-eye glance. In return, I mime the universal gesture of locking my lips with an imaginary key, then tossing the key over my shoulder.

He works methodically, moving from one stack of five barrels to the next, all the way to the end of the line. Ten pyramids in all. He taps the scanner's data pad, and then scratches the back of his head as he reads. He gives me a quick glance.

"Do we have enough?" I ask, again.

"Each cask holds fifteen-hundred liters, give or take. If each goblet holds...oh, let's be generous here... we'll say twelve ounces, that's three hundred-fifty-four milliliters. If each guest has two or three cups apiece, and we expect about four hundred people at the feast, it should be enough."

"Four hundred? The hologram histories say there are several thousand people, from both sides, descending on Calais."

"We only have to serve the courtiers attending the party. Besides, we could serve limited quantities to keep everyone's interest piqued, or serve Madeira to the highest ranking nobles and cheap stuff to everyone else." Nico pauses, giving me a strange look; it's an unexpected deep gaze into my eyes, followed by a quick glance at my lips.

"Common things are never as desirable as those that are exceptionally rare."

"Sweet talker," I say, kissing him full on the mouth.

"Is it working?" Nico asks.

"Always." I tease him with a quick nip on his ear.

"If we get the Vicomtess to cool it with free wine demands," he says, "we have enough Miracle Madeira to get through the evening."

"If we don't?"

"Then, we serve the good stuff until everyone is good and drunk, then let the landlords fill in with their house wine. No one will notice the difference by then."

Nico hunches over a cask on the bottom row to inspect a spigot pounded into the lower crescent of the barrel lid. Holding a cup below the valve, he flips a small lever on top allowing a stream of ruby liquid to fill the cup.

He swirls the cup beneath his nose. I fold my arms across my chest and give him a curious look and a half-snort of a laugh.

"What?" he says, perplexed by my reaction.

"Were you a sommelier in a past life? Isn't the whole point of the replicator to produce the same quality and taste in every single barrel?"

"The replicator makes the same wine every time. But, once produced, it's as vulnerable to degradation as any other wine. Oxygen is the biggest enemy." He gestures broadly toward the ceiling and the walls of the room as though we might, at any moment, catch errant puffs of oxygen targeting the wine like phantom missiles. "If air gets into the casks, we only have about three days before the drink starts to oxidize and turn to vinegar. We need to pull random samples, daily, to see if the wine is starting to turn."

"Who do you think will have time to babysit the booze?"

"I'd assign our dear lieutenant to that detail, but it'd be just our luck she'd get smashed and start blabbing to anyone who would listen about time travel or, worse yet, talk about robbing the English king. Let's avoid that if we can. I'll pop down here and take the samples."

Nico bends down to inspect the fit of the seal around the barrel's spigot to ensure as little air as possible finds its way inside.

I consider the outcomes of both scenarios, weighing which one would be worse: Becca's tales of traveling through time might earn her an exorcism or land her in London's Bethlem Asylum, the oldest known hospital for the mentally ill. It would be problematic to return home without her, but it wouldn't put the mission in irredeemable jeopardy unless she gave one of the monarchs a private tour of our Timeship.

The outcome of the second scenario, Becca spouting off about robbing the King would be disastrous. At the very least, our operation would be blown wide open and we'd be forced to abort. While the threat of what the Benefactors would do to Fagin and me for failing to complete the mission was more than a little problematic, I reckoned we could shift the blame to Trevor.

The worst that could happen is that Becca's mouth could land all of us in prison and end with each of us swinging at the end of a hangman's noose. A shiver runs up my spine. The Benefactors don't risk exposure by rescuing mercenaries. It's a rule.

"Let's avoid that. You know what they say about loose lips and ships. We can't give Trevor room to sink us." Realizing that I haven't seen her all day, anxiety gnaws at me. The thought of an unsupervised Becca is unnerving. "Now that you mention it. Where is Trevor?"

"She's on the ship replicating the last batch of wine for today."

"Really?" I say, unable to keep from sounding surprised. "Didn't we just talk about this?"

Nico halts his barrel inspection and straightens up to his full height. "Relax. All she has to do is push a button to start the replication process, push it again to stop it, then move the hose I rigged up from the full barrel to the next empty one, and..." his voice trails off. "You're right, we should get back."

"We should talk to Fagin about managing Trevor on gala night. We don't need her traipsing into our carefully laid plans, unannounced, and wrecking months of work." I cringe at the mental movie running through my head of a tipsy Trevor spilling every bean we've got to the whole assembly.

"Got a plan for that, too," he grins wickedly. "I'll ask her to perform a critical quality control check of the last bottle of Madeira, then slip an undetectable sedative into her glass. The only damage control we'll have is her hangover the next morning."

"You're sexy when you're sly," I say, kissing him deeply in appreciation for his cleverness. "Think we should tell Fagin?"

"Definitely not. The less she knows, the more plausible deniability she has.

Nico grabs his coat from a chair shoved up against one wall—a knee-length, onyx-colored number embroidered with intricate gold fleur-de-lis designs. After years of missions where the clothing can be as adventurous as the job at hand, I've adjusted to wearing everything from linen togas to miniskirts. For Nico, accustomed to the easy fit of civilian attire, adjusting to the restrictive fit, elaborate styling, and the weight of costume drama clothing, proves to be more challenging than calculating how much wine we need for the banquet.

He gets one arm into the coat, but the other coat sleeve hangs up on the sword he wears on his left hip. The result is Nico chasing his errant sleeve in small, backward-stumbling circles of flailing arms and flapping fabric.

He shoots me a pleading look. I stop his Whirling Dervish spin and free the garment from its entrapment between the scabbard and the hilt of the sword. He gives me a grateful nod as I hold the coat's collar so he can slip his arm inside.

"You didn't answer my question," I smooth a bit of his puckering collar that refuses to lie flat. "We lost our ticket to England when Anne de Pisseleu canceled her invitation to the French court. We don't have guaranteed introductions to anyone attending the gala, let alone the royals. Our options to get to England are fading fast."

"After all this time together, you still doubt me," he teases, wagging a finger. He ambles toward a stack of boxes tucked into one corner, tapping the portable scanner's data pad a few times before slipping it into a hidden pocket in his clothes.

He cuts a striking figure as he moves. His pantaloons and doublet are cut from black velvet cloth. In contrast to his pants, the upper garment is close fitting, showing off his strong shoulders and trim waist to good effect. His stockings are snowy white and I can trace the outline of his toned calves.

The black slip-on shoes are less impressive, the shine of the fabric is dulled by a fine, musty coat of dirt that collected as he moved around the cellar. The smell of wine and damp earth mingles with his natural scent, and it goes right to my head.

I could sneak into his quarters later, but with Trevor on board, the ship feels like a prison and conjugal visits probably aren't a good idea with the Benefactors watching every move.

"Here's what I'm thinking," Nico says, "Position yourself as not just the ward of Miracle Madeira's purveyor, but a writer—a poet worthy of elevation in both the French and English courts—and you'll get Lady Mary's and Lady Anne's patronage. It's a two-for-one package: Fagin brings the wine, you bring the entertainment."

"Not the worst idea in the world. The Boleyns do love all things French," I say, allowing the concept to settle in my brain.

Nico steps onto the teleport pad and, smiling, extends his hand. "If it doesn't work, we'll figure out Plan B. There's more than one way to crack this nut."

I slip my hand into his warm grip and step onto the teleport pad next to him. "Have a little faith, Dodger. We'll get through this and be home before you know it."

He flashes a mega-watt smile and the sincerity and sweetness in his eyes reassures me. We may be jumping each other on the regular, but it's the solid bedrock of loyalty and friendship, the easy cama-raderie we've developed over years of partnership that seems to be turning me and him into an "us."

In the split instant before the teleport whisks us back to the ship, I realize a new problem: this apparent shift from casual sex to something more serious invades the space where my vengeance lives, making it weaker, less urgent in the context of this thing with Nico.

The trajectory of my life has never propelled me anywhere close to 'happy ending' territory. Yet, Nico's touch makes me want to believe I can be happy in love. From what I've seen, love and vengeance are mutually exclusive pursuits.

There are dark impulses brewing inside my rage, and it feels like I'm being pushed down a path that's impossible to avoid. What if I can, somehow, prevent the carnage that King Henry and Anne Boleyn's offspring will wreak on the world and my family?

What if I don't? What version of happy can I live with?

Our first days in Calais are a whirlwind of exhaustive, frenetic activity, and at the center of it all is Becca Trevor, scrutinizing everything from the details of the strategic mission operation plan to the culinary choices on the dinner menu. She's worse than the Benefactors' babysitter-snitch; she's a fucking micromanager.

In the past thirty minutes, the lieutenant has tripped through the The Staple Inn's salon five times. She has commanded the servants assigned to manage our wardrobe trunks with all the finesse and touchy-feely empowerment of a rabid wild boar on one of King Henry's hunts. Except for a small figure kneeling at the fireplace— a young scullery maid intent on fanning a recalcitrant spark into flame —there isn't another maid or footman in sight. The lieutenant has alienated everyone at the inn willing, or able, to dispose of the trunks by unleashing a barrage of verbal abuse at everyone within shouting distance.

On her sixth trip through the salon, she stops abruptly, then strides over to servant girl and stands with her arms folded across her chest. I've caught glimpses of the cunning and devious bent in Trevor's personality. This demeanor is something else entirely. I recognize the aggression set in her posture, and my nerves—already jangled by Nico— are set even more on edge.

"Marie," Trevor says to the maid through an artificial smile that surely hides clenched teeth. "Isn't it cold in here? You're not trying to freeze us all to death, are you?"

The raven-haired housemaid, little more than twelve or thirteen years old, cowers in the veiled rebuke. I feel the indignity of the insults hurled at this child as keenly as a branding iron on my skin. An image rips through my memory. My old master, Captain Bartholomew, boxing my tiny eight-year-old frame into a corner. "Stupid, good-for-nothing girl," he says, his voice snarling like a vicious dog. "How many times must I show you how to build a proper fire in the grate?"

His hands balled into fists and he pummeled me into submission, blackening my eyes and splitting my lip as he screamed insults about the disobedient and wild spirit that possessed me.

"Mademoiselle," I say, looping my arm through Becca's, trying to sound nonchalant. "A word, please?"

"Clémence," she says. "Whatever it is, I'm sure it will keep until I've finished helping the maid build a proper fire."

She gasps when I dig my fingernails into her flesh. "Now," I say, dragging her into a small anteroom behind the salon and shutting the heavy wooden door.

"Stop it," I say.

"What? I was being nice. That fire should have been lit half an hour ago. These people need a strong-handed supervisor."

Nope. Not having this passive aggressive shit. Even with the Consigliere's warning to not put a toe out of line echoing in my head, I can't let this pass. "Being nice, my ass. You're supervising them toward revolt all day. Keep it up, and I'll lock you in closet for the duration of this mission."

"Are you challenging my authority to lead?"

"I don't care what your orders say. Fagin is the one in charge. You can save the posturing for the daily reports to your bosses."

"No, honey," she says, in the fake sweet tone that makes me want to vomit. "Fagin answers to me. All of you do. The Consigliere warned you what would happen if you complain about your duties or hesitate to obey orders."

My mouth goes dry. I hate that she knows so much. I open my mouth to argue, but the realization that the moment I do, those goons will be waiting for me when I get home makes the words stick in my throat.

"What's this?" Trevor moves in close, I can smell the ale from breakfast on her breath. Her eyes are wide in surprise. "Nothing else to say?"

I shake my head, take a slow step back. She advances another step, and I realize she's backing me into one corner of the room. "Come on. Where's that infamous Arseneau back chat? You act so big and bad only when there's no one around to challenge you, but really you're just a child playing dress-up in mommy's clothes." Her tone is a whining taunt, and a startling realization slaps me in the face.

I side-step Trevor as she moves forward another half pace. "Why are you goading me? It's like you're waiting for me to fail."

"Stop gaping, Clémence," she snaps. "It's melodramatic and if your face freezes that way, I will have zero pity for you." Her expressing changes to an unnerving smile as her eyes go narrow and cold. Her chin dips toward her chest as she speaks. "Why would I want you to fail? It's my job to ensure you complete the Benefactors' tasks. If I'm a bitch, it's in the service of my employers' best interests. Slack discipline means shit results. Fight me and you fight them. I'm sure we both agree that would be a mistake of legendary magnitude."

It looks like she's one loose screw away from being completely unhinged. This is crazy. *She* is crazy. Another realization slaps me. *What if there are cameras already planted in these rooms? What if the Benefactors are watching right now?*

My eyes flit up to the high corners of the salon ceiling, then around at the furnishings, including the flower vases and bookshelves. No surveillance equipment immediately visible, but it doesn't mean it's not there. *I'll get Nico to run a tech sweep later.*

I lick my lips, trying to ease the cotton-mouth dryness, but it persists. "Something's not right with you or this whole mission. I don't know what it is, but I'm going to find out."

"It's quite simple," she says with a sigh that punctuates her boredom with our conversation. "Get your head out of your ass. Do exactly as you're told. Complete this mission to my exact specifications. Before you consider your next move, heed this tiny piece of advice: Think twice before fucking with me again. Or you'll find out how creative I can be in making your life more of a living hell."

CHAPTER 12

SALT HITS the back of my throat in a blast of chilled air rolling in from the bay. I have a complicated relationship with the sea; it has given freedom with one hand and stolen precious people from me with the other. I love the wild tang of brine on my tongue and the expanse of a wide-open horizon as I gaze out from the bow of a powerful ship. I love the comforting memories of Papa bounding down the gangplank, ready to sweep Maman and me up in his arms.

Flashbacks of Maman and me huddling together for warmth in a single bunk as our prison-ship sailed toward the American colonies terrorizes me. Even worse than those melancholy memories are those of the horror-filled screams of passengers as that same ship sank from beneath us in a storm. Before journey's end, the waves dragged Maman down and I was orphaned.

After Maman's death, irony and some fickle deity conspired to sell me into indentured servitude on a merchant ship, of all things. For two years, I endured life at sea with the brutal Captain Bartholomew and relived the horrific memories of losing Maman every time angry storm waves swelled beneath the hull.

When I'm on a mission, I bury these recollections; the numbness that comes from stuffing them deep enough so they're not open and raw is a relief. Far from being immobilized, this detachment usually allows me to get jobs done. Focus hasn't been my strong suit of late.

It occurs to me that stuffing all this rage wasn't the best idea. It's also possible that I'm full of shit and the hours I've spent scouting around this dock waiting for King Henry's ship to make port have given me far too much time to navel-gaze.

"Nothing," I say to Nico through the CommLink. "No sign of The Swallow."

"Patience, Dodger," Nico says, his voice warm and reassuring in my ear. "We have a few more minutes. They should be here soon."

October 11, 1532. Ten o'clock in the morning. That's the moment Lady Anne Boleyn's most ardent effort to sway French support for her impending marriage, and elevation to England's queen, begins. It's also the moment my personal nightmare kicks into high gear. I'm not sure what feelings will assault me the moment I lay eyes on the living, breathing Lady Anne. The acid in my stomach is already building, forcing its way up my throat in a long, slow burn.

"Where's Fagin?" I ask.

"With the Vicomte and his wife at The Staple Inn. She's letting them sample the Miracle Madeira again. They're nervous that the first batches we served them were flukes."

"I'm sure she loves that."

"Gotta keep them happy until after the banquet. While we're waiting on the Tudors, mosey over to that ship on your left so I can record some data for the historical holograms through your LensCams."

"Mosey? I've never moseyed anywhere in my life." I say, walking toward the ship. The deck hands are busy moving large barrels into a block and tackle rigging, and shouting directions to the men waiting on the dock. It sounds like they're speaking a Scandinavian language, possibly Flemish. "I may stroll or amble or even sashay, occasionally, but "mosey"? Never."

"That's what I love about you, Dodger. You never miss an opportunity to be a smartass."

"I did yesterday. Trevor reminded me, for the millionth time, that she owns me on this mission. I had to chew the inside of my cheeks to keep from putting her out of my misery."

"Don't worry. I've taken steps to neutralize our dear lieutenant when we need to get her out of our hair."

"Did you roofie her morning coffee? Please tell me she's blissfully unconscious, and drooling on her pillow."

"No. That's reserved for the banquet." He pauses. "Hey, turn to your left and watch the guys looking at the hull of that small merchant ship. I want to see what they're doing."

"You mean the one with the buxom woman as the figurehead?"

"That's the one."

"I always thought you might be a boob man."

If it's possible to hear someone blushing, I'm certain Nico's complexion is screaming bright red. "Jesus, just... get eyes on the bow of the ship, please?"

Swinging to my left, I set my gaze on four men, sitting on crude plank swings lowered over the railing. They inspect the apex of the bow just above the keel line. "Got it?"

"Yep. Zooming in now. Thanks."

"Are you going to leave me hanging like those guys dangling from the ship?" I ask, trying not to let my eyes wander away while he's recording.

"Hanging?"

"What'd you do to Becca?"

A gust of wind blows more sea spray in my face. The chill seeps through every inch of my navy blue wool cloak from my shoulders to my ankles, and makes me yearn for a balaclava instead of this silly, stylish felt hat that might melt down around my ears before I can get out of the weather. With a cloak edge in each fist, I close my arms over my chest, hoping that gathering the fabric close to my body will provide a more insulation against the cold.

"I filtered our broadcast transmissions, both audio and visual, so we are the only ones who sees what she sees. Nothing she records is getting to the Benefactors back home unless I clear it first. I reconfig-ured the relay circuits in the main transmitters. I can turn the filters on and off at will."

"Won't the Benefactors catch on when they don't see trans-missions?"

"Not if I'm careful how, and when, I use this newfound power. They won't suspect it's anything more than bugs in brand-new soft-ware." He pauses. "Hey, check the harbor. It's a few minutes after ten o'clock. The ship should come into view any minute."

On cue, a dark blot has appeared on the horizon, and grows larger by the moment. "Looks like a ship out there. Is it the king?"

"Must be. According to the dock master's ledgers, the next merchant ship doesn't arrive until close to noon. Get ready. Things will move pretty fast from here on."

Twenty minutes later, the ship passes the Rysbank Tower on the right side of the bay, and maneuvers into one of the jetties on the far end of the dock near the tall, fortified city wall. Deck hands and dock workers swarm the ship, securing the lines and unloading trunks and crates and barrels from the cargo holds.

It takes half an hour before anyone recognizable disembarks and makes their way down the pier.

"It's them," I say, striding toward my next observation point, the corner of a nearby building, which gives me a perfect angle for watching the weary travelers navigate toward their transports to the Exchequer, their lodgings during their stay.

Even after dozens of Sim Lab training interactions with realistic, lifelike human reproductions, watching Lady Anne Boleyn—recently elevated to Her Grace, the Marquise of Pembroke—stroll down the pier makes my stomach churn.

Stay calm. Focus.

"The historical holograms don't lie," I say. "She's not a great beauty, but she has some X-factor qualities going on."

Even with her wide mouth, hooked nose, and the noticeable oatmeal pie-looking wart on the side of her face, praises that history has lavished on Lady Anne Boleyn are not without merit. More noticeable than her trim, stylish figure and smallish breasts is her regal bearing: she carries herself like she knows she's supposed to be at the top of the royal food chain. Her eyes brim with confidence and the promise that she could seduce the whole of France if necessary.

A closer inspection of the female entourage trailing behind her—including Henry's first Boleyn mistress, Anne's sister, Mary—I'm left with very little concrete evidence why this king would choose her over the dozens of beautiful women who surround him.

King Henry is tall, broad-shouldered, and good-looking. He is not, yet, the bloated behemoth his later portraits depict. If Lady Anne's magnetism is the biggest weapon in her enchantment arsenal, the king's position and power are his brand of aphrodisiac.

"Remember, Fagin said stick as close as you can, but don't engage," Nico says. "We're in surveillance mode."

"That's because Fagin's worried I might snap Lady Anne like a twig if she's not around to stop me."

There's an awkward pause, and I can almost see Nico's brow, furrowed in confusion, as he clears his throat. "Why the hell would she think that? We're thieves, not assassins."

Merde. "My family has never been fond of the English," I say, trying to cover the gaffe with a thick layer of nonchalant understatement. "Never mind. It's...complicated."

As the royal couple climb into their coach, I untie my mare from the hitching post where I left her. The palfrey is small enough that I don't require a boost to mount her, but riding side-saddle is literally a pain in the ass. Negotiating this side-saddle contraption in a costume that feels like it weighs more than I do should earn me a medal of some sort. As I settle into the stiff leather of the seat, the whale bones sewn into the stays poke me in the ribs.

Merde.

It's a damn good thing my horse—a chestnut-colored filly called M'lady—is gentle. I stroke her neck and nudge her forward.

My discomfort aside, the journey back to the inn is uneventful. Calais is English territory, for the moment, and the streets are filled with townspeople going about their business. As we pass through the Lantern Gate, the principal entrance to the town, there are no crowds lining the street to welcome their king. Could be that the commoners aren't aware that the king and his lady have arrived. It's also likely they're absent in protest. Anne Boleyn is a woman loathed from the English countryside to the Vatican.

No one would ever rain on Anne's parade, so to speak, because they wouldn't throw one for her in the first place.

"Spotted Mary Boleyn, yet?" Nico says.

Turning in the saddle, I crane my neck to scan the caravan trailing behind me. There are dozens of conveyances: horses with single riders, open-air wagons, and people on foot. Behind a cadre of the king's men—privy counselors and noble lords—I spot several coaches creaking along, bobbing and dipping with each small rut in the road.

"She's probably in one of those closed coaches behind us. I don't see her in any of the open wagons."

I hear him moving around the ship's cockpit. "There's a message from Fagin. She wants you back at the ship."

"Did she say anything else?"

"Nope. She's being tight-lipped."

A drop of water splashes against my cheek. Soon there's a steady drizzle of cold rain, the kind mixed with sleet that will sting if its velocity picks up.

"Dodger, you've got about five minutes before the skies open up on you." Nico says. "Some serious weather is moving in fast from the ocean. Get your ass back here."

"On my way."

. . .

The ride back to my ship is long enough to allow me to ruminate on the problem of Fagin. She used to share the reasoning behind her directives, so I understood the goal of each step of the plan and how it got us to the big payoff for the job. I get that we're reduced to a shitty one-way shorthand—courtesy of Becca Trevor's meddling—where Fagin gives orders and I'm supposed to obey. I can see the anger and frustration in her eyes over being as hog-tied as I am.

Since this mission began, there have been times she looks at me with an emotion—if my intuition is right—I've never before seen in her: true despair. I've seen Fagin put on a great show of pretend anguish over the years; her tears are the perfect distraction so a young, nimble-fingered protégé can pick a pocket, or slip into a room, unseen, to pilfer whatever needs pilfering.

When this is all over, I'll sit her down, a bottle of Miracle Madeira between us, and make her spill everything she can't tell me now about Trevor and the Benefactors. Nobody fucks with Fagin on my watch and gets away with it. One way or another, I'll get my Fagin back.

CHAPTER 13

A PAIR of young women slither past me on their way to the wine buffet. I turn to follow, moving with the casual grace that allows me to melt into large crowds. The venue for Lady Anne's French coming out party is cheek-by-jowl stuffed with people. In a crowd like this, which includes elite English and French luminaries, I can become unremarkable and utterly forgettable. These are perfect conditions for a little light thievery before the real party begins.

The girls are young, probably sixteen or seventeen years old, and have already learned the art of blending pouty-lipped flirtatiousness with the piety of vestal virgins. The quintessential Renaissance contradiction: Project the aura of being supremely fuckable while maintaining the purity required to obtain an advantageous marriage.

Men in the room swarm around them like honey bees to pollen-heavy flowers. While the noblemen's amorous pursuit of the girls is driven by knowing their rich daddies will pay handsome dowries, the girls' nubile bodies and Botticelli faces are a bonus no one with eyes could ignore.

They're not twins, but have worn matching outfits; celestial blue velvet gowns cut to highlight the delicate kirtles of ivory silk beneath their skirts and pulled through fashionable slashed sleeves. Also on display are their ample breasts, which look one deep breath away from a serious wardrobe malfunction. They look like they just stepped out of a Renaissance painting.

More germane to my interests than their clothes are their jewels. Ropes of perfect sapphires wrap around their throats and wrists, and the most glorious diamond earrings dangle from their dainty earlobes. The antiquated clasps of the necklaces look easy enough to manipulate, but the bracelets look easier. *Right. Bracelets it is, then.*

I stand behind the most flirtatious girl, close enough to smell both the pomander filled with fragrant herbs and spices that hangs from her waist and the pungent body odor it's meant to disguise. She's a giggling mass of energy aiming all her feminine charms at two men at the same time—one French, the other English—both seem equally enamored with her.

The crowded room provides precious little elbow room, and she's preoccupied enough with the men to be oblivious to my presence. This should be a breeze.

The girl leans in to whisper to the Frenchman and I lean into her; a discreet nudge into the middle of her back to knock her slightly off balance. The girl, no time to steady herself, stumbles forward. I grab her by the waist, an attempt to soften her landing as she falls.

"Pardon et moi." I pull her around to face me. Her cheeks are flushed with surprise and embarrassment. "Please forgive me."

I make a great fuss over her, smoothing the front of her puckered gown and the strands of hair that have tugged free from the front of her French hood with one hand while the other hand drifts down to her wrist.

A quick pop of my thumbnail under the edge of the clasp and the diamond bracelet falls into my cupped palm. I give the flustered girl a quick hug, and another apology, as I slip the bracelet into a hidden pocket in my gown and hustle myself to the opposite side of the room.

In. Out. Done.

"Give it back." Fagin's voice has a hard, sharp edge to it. She never used to treat me like a toddler caught raiding the sweets cupboard. From the day she recruited me, Fagin encouraged the prolific application of my thieving skills, and trusted I would get out of serious trouble before the shit rolled too far down the hill.

After the Benefactors descended on us like angry gods from Mount Olympus, she changed from the pragmatic entrepreneur who'd do anything to help me succeed to a puritanical, rule-following lackey. It makes for a tightly-wound Fagin. If I didn't love her so much, I'd spike her wine along with Trevor's.

It takes a few minutes of searching the banquet hall to find her; she stands near the buffet where the Vicomtess d'Auvergne zealously orchestrates the distribution of Madeira to the nobles gathered for the feast. There's a throng of courtiers crowded around her, but Fagin remains as calm as a buoy floating effortlessly on the frenzied wave of activity around her. She peers at me over the rim of her goblet as she drinks.

I look away. "I have no idea what you're talking about."

"Don't play games with me," she says, dryly. "Return the bracelet."

Merde. She saw it. "You're the one who said robbing the English blind could be my revenge. You said—"

"I know," Fagin interrupts. "But what Trevor might miss reporting to the Benefactors, hidden cameras could pick up. You must follow orders exactly, and that means anything not on the acquisition list is off limits."

"My skills are rusty. Gotta keep myself nimble for the real work." As rationalizations go, it's not a bad one. But Fagin sees right through it.

"Give it back or I will," she says. "Going off script is dangerous for all of us and you know it."

In a test of wills, it's almost an even draw between Fagin and me for who would win. We're both stubborn. Both can hold a grudge. But Fagin holds the purse strings, so she wins.

It takes numerous glares from Fagin to swallow my pride and work my way through the throng of courtiers between me and the

Botticelli girls. When I reach them, I slip the sapphire bracelet from my pocket, stopping to finger the perfect, smooth surface of the stones before letting it slide down my skirt to the floor.

I tap the girl on the shoulder. "Mademoiselle, I think you dropped something."

She follows my gaze to the floor and squeals in dismay. "My bracelet," she says. The Frenchman bends down to retrieve it, then fastens it on her wrist. "I would have walked away never knowing it was lost. It would devastate me to lose this; it's a gift from my father." She clasps my hand in hers and kisses one cheek, then the other. "How can I thank you?"

"No need to thank me," I say in a voice so syrupy and fake it makes my teeth hurt. "Knowing you're reunited with a cherished gift is reward enough."

If I had let her, the girl would've kept kissing my cheeks and expressing her gratitude long enough that I might have changed my mind and stolen the bracelet back. She wears stacks of identical bracelets, it's hard to believe she would have missed one. My stomach churns with too much anger and frustration as it is, so I take my leave as quickly as I can.

"That wasn't so bad, was it?" Fagin says, as she watched me stalk toward the wine steward. I shoot her a dark look and she brushes it off with an eye roll. "Take a walk around the room. You'll feel better."

It doesn't make me feel better. In fact, it makes me feel worse because it has been a long time since I've been hog-tied like this. To compensate, I can't resist slipping a bracelet off of another woman when Fagin's back is turned. Now, I feel better.

The great hall of the Staple Inn is bathed in the light of two thousand candles suspended from the ceiling by twenty enormous iron candelabras. Fires in twin hearths, one on each end of the room blaze in their grates making for a warm and cozy venue in contrast with the darkness outside and rain that falls like a curtain over the windows. Gold wreaths studded with diamonds, pearls, and rubies line the walls, and gold tissue is draped over every stationary object in the room and even a few non-stationary objects; several English ladies have co-opted sheets of tissue, wrapping them around their shoulders like fur capes.

It's a cheery venue. It's festive. It's disgusting.

Galling, actually, considering the wealth in this room is in stark contrast with the humbler dwellings of Calais a few streets away. Even more irritating than the decor is the necessity of strolling around this grand room, smiling and making polite conversation with enemies I'd just as soon gut as look at. I wish I could treat this like just another job, but my God...I feel dirty among them. I feel trapped.

I want to tear these golden walls down with my bare hands.

"Is it just me or is this decadence so extreme, it's vulgar?" Nico says, echoing my thoughts. "There's so much wealth in this room, I'll bet it could feed the people of Calais for a generation or more."

For all the vitriol in his tone, Nico's voice in my ear is comforting. At least I know I'm not alone in loathing this whole situation. "Two-hundred and fifty-six years, six months, and eight days until the barricades arise," I say.

Nico goes quiet for a moment, then adds, "Vive la révolution."

"Thank you for the social commentary," Fagin cuts in. "Can we nix the judgment and get back to our jobs, please? Any sign of Mary Boleyn?"

"Not yet," Nico replies, sounding like Fagin has just poured a bucket of cold water over his protest. "You'll know when the royals show up. Trumpets will sound and there'll be the sweet smell of greed and naked ambition in the air."

"Nico—" Fagin says.

"Yes, ma'am. Shutting up, ma'am," Nico snaps and the line goes silent.

"Speaking of greed and naked ambition, where is Trevor?" I say, scanning the room for the dimwitted lieutenant. If things went to plan, she's passed out in her crew quarters, sleeping off the effects of the sedative Nico slipped into her wine.

Nico's voice breaks over the CommLink. "I think Lieutenant Lightweight may have overdone the Miracle Madeira quality control checks, if you know what I mean. She passed out ninety minutes ago. I had to carry her to her quarters."

I'm tempted to shoot two enthusiastic thumbs up at him through one of the many camouflaged surveillance cameras installed in the room, but I'm sure the party is streaming live to the Benefactors back home. I envision the lot of them huddled around display screens, popcorn and red licorice in hand, watching our every move.

It sends a momentary shiver up my spine. I wish I could cut the communication just so I can work in peace, but I'm sure the assholes trying to ruin my life wouldn't believe the "oops, did I do that" excuse for why the transmission feed inexplicably died during one of the most critical points in the mission.

Likewise, being a little too happy about their spy's incapacitation would be equally hard to explain, especially if Trevor suspects her reaction to the Madeira was helped along by something a little stronger than alcohol.

"How long will she be out of commission?" Fagin asks. She casts a questioning glance in my direction, a clear sign she suspects some degree of underhandedness in the lieutenant's condition. I give her my best "who me" shrug.

"Don't know for sure," Nico replies. "I think she drank a lot."

"Let me know if her status changes," Fagin says.

"Acknowledged." Nico replies. "If Trevor so much as flutters a drunken eyelash, you'll know."

More courtiers, equally as bejeweled as the Botticelli girls, stream into the hall. I've been on high profile jobs where the bounty targets were worth as much as the entire Gross National Product of small countries, but this gig is in a class by itself. I should be giddy about plundering these people. Instead, it's torturing me to look and not touch.

"Dodger," Fagin says in a weary, admonishing tone.

"So unfair," I say, making eye contact with her. "We need a Plan B to line our pockets in case this thing goes sideways, and—"

"It can't go sideways." Fagin's expression constricts into a small, tight grimace. The fear on her face, visible from across the room, is palpable. "Do you hear me, Dodger? With Trevor here, we can't put a toe out of line. If we fail, we won't be the only ones. The Benefactors will target everyone we've ever known. Hunt everyone we've ever loved."

I swallow hard. From the moment she told me of this mission, she has loudly lamented the danger we're all in—self-preservation is always the foundation of humans' hierarchy of needs—but this is the first time she's mentioned concern for anyone else outside our team. It makes me wonder. Who else is there in her life that she needs to protect?

The idea that Fagin has kept someone she loves a secret from me widens the ever-growing gap between us into a chasm of doubt and distrust. How are we going to repair all the damage? A tiny voice inside me whispers that our version of normal is gone for good.

"Except for you, I have no family to threaten," I say. It's a lie. I'd risk my life to protect Nico, but admitting that on an open Comm chanel would put his head on the chopping block if it's not already there. A deeper dive into who Fagin loves must wait as well. I hate waiting.

"Do. You. Hear me?" The hard edge softens into an urgent, breathless plea for my compliance. "Please. Don't let me down."

Merde. I close my eyes. Take a breath. "I won't let you down," I say with more certainty than I feel.

"Thank you," Fagin says, softly.

A moment later, the courtiers burst into ecstatic applause as King Francois and King Henry enter, arm-in-arm. Lady Anne and her maids follow close behind. The French court's most important women are absent from the gathering in protest—even Louis' maîtresse-en-titre refuses to legitimize Anne with a meet-and-greet. Whether she provokes their jealousy or is a simple, devastating reminder that they're all expendable if their king so decides. There's no feminist solidarity where the Boleyn girl is concerned.

The newly minted Marquess of Pembroke may as well be a beggar in the streets for all the disrespect her enemies heap on her.

As the monarchs stroll like peacocks toward the head table, laid out with fine linens and expensive gold plate, the crowd parts before them like the damn Red Sea before Moses. King Henry is resplendent in clothing of purple silk embroidered with so much gold thread that the embellishments twinkle in the candlelight as he passes the candelabras. A string of fourteen enormous blood-red rubies, the smallest stone the size of a goose egg, are set in the collar. The king must've thought these embedded stones didn't quite do the job because he also wears a double strand of pearls that boasts yet another gigantic ruby.

Just one of these gems, with authenticated provenance of being worn by King Henry on this historic day, would be enough to fund my retirement a dozen times over—Nico's and Fagin's, too. With the risks involved, it's stupid not to leverage every chance to line our pockets. In the mania and chaos of packing to return to England, no one would miss one or two baubles if they went missing.

"Dodger, Mary Boleyn is at a table to your left," Nico says. "That's your cue to become her new best friend."

I sigh. "Got her."

Turns out to be easier said than done. Mary's table is filled with courtiers, so I'm forced to sit at a table across from her. Noticeable, even from a distance, is Mary's necklace. It's a ruby. It's not as large as the goose egg-sized stone King Henry wears, but it's close. The stone is square-cut and set in a gold mount. A pearl nearly the size of the ruby dangles from a cabochon positioned just above Mary's cleavage.

My palms itch again. *Dammit, Fagin.*

The feasting passes slowly; God, these people can eat. I spend most of the meal working my way closer to Mary, but every time I get close, the consummate social butterfly floats to another table.

As expected, our Miracle Madeira is the toast of the party. Everyone is wrangling for a cup. The Vicomtess d'Auvergne guards the wine supply like a prison planet death row guard; she has already threatened courtiers she has deemed unworthy of sampling the wares with severe maiming several times.

The unworthy designation seems to be reserved for anyone below the rank of duke or duchess. This goes over like a boulder in an avalanche when Lady Anne's father, the Earl of Wiltshire—not immediately recognized by the Vicomtess—is turned away like a commoner as he reaches for a goblet. Charles Brandon, the Duke of Suffolk, guffaws at the snub; he despises Thomas Boleyn.

"Heads up," I say as Lady Anne excuses herself from the head table, followed by her ladies, including Mary. "Looks like the real show is about to begin."

With a grand flourish, King Henry announces a special treat for the French king and, with a nod to the English musicians assembled on the far side of the banquet hall, music begins to play.

Seven masked female dancers, all clothed in crimson and gold, glide into the hall and begin to dance. The ladies choose male partners from the audience. Though masked, I can tell Lady Anne from the rest because she's the one who leads King Francois to the dance floor.

The French king is bewitched by the enchantress, but I can't tell if he is ignorant that it's Anne behind the mask or if he's just playing along. Their dance is seductive enough to elicit gasps from the pious courtiers in the crowd. In one move, Francois pulls Anne into his arms and, twirling, lifts her into the air. He buries his nose into her midsection before setting her down again.

Fagin, drink in hand, appears next to me. "The minute Mary Boleyn gets off the dance floor," she says, "put yourself in her path." She grips my forearm. I don't think she realizes how tightly she's holding me until I wince and glance down at my arm. She blinks, then releases me with a loud exhale. Her eyes look tired. Almost as an afterthought, she strokes my cheek. "We're all counting on you."

King Henry moves toward the dance floor. He steps behind Anne and, with a grand flourish, snatches her mask away, revealing her identity. Francois seems thoroughly surprised and throws his head back, roaring with a hearty laugh. He brings her gloved hand to his lips, then with a wave invites everyone to dance. As the floor fills with people, Mary Boleyn slips quietly away from the crowd, headed toward the windows at the other end of the hall. I grab two wine glasses filled with Miracle Madeira and follow.

Before I reach her, she's intercepted by three men who surround her like foxes circling a prize hen. They're as exquisitely dressed and bejeweled as the Botticelli girls, which means they're high-ranking and important. They're also supremely drunk and more than a little rowdy.

At first, Mary seems happy for the attention, enjoying their flirtatious overtures like a cat playing with a toy. They're polite enough at first, but they move to sandwich her between them and begin pawing at her.

The first man, clothed in a fur-trimmed cloak, smells of onions and beer. The second, a short and crusty fellow in a plumed hat nearly as tall as he is, presses himself against Mary. He must smell equally as bad because no matter which direction Mary turns, she looks barely able to control her gag reflex. A third man, a sinister-looking rogue with a wide, thick scar running the length of his right cheek has his nose buried in her hair.

Their hands are everywhere, seemingly intent on fondling as much of her as possible in the shortest amount of time, and nobody else in the room seems to notice. It triggers a sick flash of a long-buried memories, off being similarly ambushed by two of Captain Bartholomew's crew. Bartholomew had intervened before the assault progressed too far, but only because it would cost him money if he had to replace me.

Mary's eyes flash in helpless shock, confirmation she's not a willing participant in this affair. I discard the wine glasses on the nearest table, then press myself between her and the man in fur, slipping a hand beneath his cloak to stroke him. "Sir," I say, purring in my most alluring tone, "wouldn't you rather have me?"

He shudders in response. "Mademoiselle, you look ravishing tonight," he says. If he were any closer to me, he'd be inside my gown. "Perhaps you can join us as we entertain Mademoiselle Boleyn."

Sometimes I revel in the raw power that a single touch can have over a target. With every smile, every gesture and tilt of the head, or brush of my hand, I can usually get anyone to crave more of me. If I play my cards right, I control the room and can steal whatever I like with little interference.

My goal now isn't to seduce or tease. I want to send this asshole a message and make Mary Boleyn obliged to me. Two birds. One stone.

The gentle, tantalizing squeeze tightens into a vise grip on one testicle trapped in my right palm. The man groans, face contorted in agony. He trembles, and I release him as he drops to his knees. He remains on the floor, panting and cradling his balls like they're as fragile as glass.

Scar Face glowers at me and takes a menacing step forward. I stop him with a demure smile and a not so subtle threat. "It would be unwise to draw the English king's ire for abusing his future sister-in-law in such a disgusting manner. One scream from me and the full weight of the English court falls on you."

The man in the plumed hat gasps. Recognition dawning, he gazes at Mary Boleyn as though he's seeing her for the first time. He shoots rapid-fire glances between this Boleyn sister and the royal party on the dance floor. His chin quivers as he excuses himself in a flurry of contrite bows. The man I put on the floor has recovered enough to follow his friend. He gets as far as the closest table before collapsing into a chair.

Scar Face regards Mary with disdain. "Our king will never sanction the whore's elevation to queen. We'll see how far your king's petition gets with Spain's Emperor and the Holy See of Rome."

"Your ignorance is astounding, monsieur," I say, coolly. "King Francois despises the emperor. His great desire is to isolate the Spanish, then crush them into dust. After King Francois supports Lady Anne as King Henry's legitimate wife, not even the pope will deny her as England's legitimate queen." I bump into his chest, forcing him to take a step backward. "King Francois would be enraged if your actions frustrate his carefully laid plans. Are you so eager to spend what remains of your life in the Bastille."

"Get her out of there, Dodger." Nico's voice is urgent in my ear. "Starting a fight with the locals will attract the wrong attention."

"What the hell are you doing, Clémence?" Fagin says.

I ignore them both and continue to glare up into Scar Face's black eyes. Half of me wants this asshole to stand his ground so I can kick his ass into the next millennium. God knows I've got enough tension coiled in inside me to start a proper roadhouse brawl if he makes one more wrong move.

Scar Face considers me with a mix of suspicion and apprehension, like he's trying to figure out if I'm lying or just foolish. He seems to choose the latter opinion. "Women make terrible spies," he says with a smirk. "You always give too much away when you talk."

"That may be true, monsieur," I say with a nod. "Still, you don't deny the truth of the current political climate, so who has given away too much?"

The man's eyes narrow. He scratches his chin as he throws an anxious glance over my shoulder toward the dance floor. "The English mare isn't worth the trouble," he says. The comment is an undeniable reference to the crass gossip regarding King Francois' nickname for Mary, chosen as a reference for how frequently he has ridden her.

I wait until Scar Face is out of range before steering Mary toward the wine buffet. She clutches my hand, her breath coming in shallow pants of frustration and anger. I nod at the Vicomtess who obligingly provides two goblets. I take one and offer the other to Mary, who accepts it with trembling hands.

"Thank you, mademoiselle," she says, taking a deep, grateful draught from the goblet. "A gallant knight couldn't have defended me —and my sister—more perfectly than you. France is not as welcoming as it was the last time I was here."

"You must be careful, Mistress Boleyn," I say, "There are many in this room who would make sport damaging your reputation."

She takes a deep breath and lets it out slowly. "I am well-acquainted with court intrigues; I served in Queen Claude's court when I was young. What I am not accustomed to is the righteous indignation of those who should have no say in matters regarding my sister."

"Our king will do his best to dispel any ill wishes directed toward her. He has pledged his support of the union to King Henry."

"King Francois says he will publicly support their marriage, yes," she says. Her expression turns skeptical. "If true, why have both his queen and sister refused to receive Anne? Their denial is a terrible omen for the King keeping his promises."

"There are people in the French court who continue to remind our king that forging a strong alliance between France and England against the emperor in Spain will change the world."

"Good, Dodger. Make her believe you're an ally." Fagin says, in my ear. It's the first scrap of validation from her in what feels like forever. My heart leaps; I could run on this simple praise for the next month.

"There are days when I fear it's quite an ill-fated path my sister follows. It is well-known that our king can be..." she pauses, hesitant to speak the words she's mulling over. As most well-positioned courtiers with something to lose would do, she softens her tone with a diplomatic whitewash. "Well, he can be inconstant in his mood and appetites, moving easily from one liaison to the next, leaving a woman to contend with being a social pariah. I have much experience with this matter."

"Your king is well-known for his appetites," I say. When Mary frowns at the overly familiar and, slightly judgmental bent in my tone, I give her my warmest, most engaging smile. "But, you're a resourceful woman, and with your sister as queen, surely you have many suitors fighting to wed you."

"No, mademoiselle." Her eyes grow sad. "Having occupied too many royal beds, my value in the marketplace suffers. I'm afraid fate has utterly abandoned me."

"I don't believe in fate," I say. "We create our own destinies. Any royal court overflows with schemers. You can scarcely throw a stone, in any direction, without hitting someone who covets what you have. Material riches are shallow compared to true wealth."

"Riches and wealth are the same thing," she says, perplexed. "I don't know how long my father will support me without having a proper husband."

"Dear Mary, never confuse money with wealth." God, I sound like Fagin. "One is used to buy goods that decay with time. The other is the thing of higher value that you would abandon all of your earthly possessions to gain."

"You speak in riddles, Mademoiselle. What is true wealth?" She asks, earnestness brimming in her eyes.

"For some, it's good health or a clean conscience. For me, it's being the mistress of my own life. To owe allegiance to none but myself. To thumb my nose at the fates."

Mary's face opens up in an expression of incredulous disbelief. "Can any woman have such a life? These are bold words and dangerously close to treason," she whispers. "Even my sister owes her allegiance to the king, as her sovereign."

"Where I come from, Mistress Boleyn," I lower my voice to match hers, allowing the spark of a tantalizing, utopian desire to embed itself in Mary's psyche, "there are precious few who have not sacrificed their desires on the altar of convention and practicality. An independent life can be had if you want it enough."

There's a flicker of raw energy in her smile, and I sense an unexpected yearning begin to form within her. Mary Boleyn, feminist superhero. It could happen.

Mary loops her arm through mine and pulls me toward the dais where the King and Lady Anne now sit. "You should meet my sister and the king. They need to know how you saved me and—" She stops dead in her tracks and turns to give me a blushing smile. She shakes her head in a self-deprecating manner. "How silly of me. You saved me from those wretches, and yet I haven't been courteous enough in return to ask your name."

Gotcha. I smile and dip a little curtsey. "I'm Clémence Areseneau. My mother and I are wine merchants. We supplied the Madeira for this feast."

Mary curtsies in return and giggles. "All the more reason you should meet them. They have high praise for the quality of the entertainment and your Madeira, esteeming it above anything else they've tasted during our time in Calais."

"My mother will be glad to hear it," I say. "And if it's entertainment you seek, I write poetry and clever riddles. Perhaps I will perform something for you tonight." Fagin catches my attention as she dances, and I point her out to Mary. "My mother is the lady dancing with the tall gentleman in the blue velvet."

Mary gives Fagin an appraising once-over. "She looks more like your sister," she says in a conspiratorial tone.

"So I've been told," I say, motioning Fagin toward the head table.

"Your mother?" Fagin says when she catches up with me. "I should take you over my knee for that."

"Try it," I say, chuckling.

Mary ascends the dais and leans to whisper in Anne's ear. Anne's eyes lock on mine for a moment, then she turns to King Henry. They confer for a moment, and the English king gestures to us with an open hand. We stand before the dais, aware that all eyes are glued on us. Fagin and I offer our best curtsies in deference to both kings.

As I look up into King Henry's eyes, anger sends a scorching trail of bile up my throat.

"And you are...?" The king asks.

"Clémence Arseneau, Your Majesty." My mouth feels dry.

Reflexively, I lick my lips. "Allow me to introduce my mother, Madame Fagin Delacoix."

"Fagin is a curious name, Madame," Henry says. "How came you by it?"

"A pet name given by my father, Your Majesty."

I toss a curious glance over my shoulder at my mentor. Fagin knows everything about me and I know so very little about her; even her true name is a mystery to me. I talk and she pretends to listen, but never offers a glimpse of the real woman behind the austere, professional veneer. When asked something as simple and innocuous as the brand of her signature high-gloss crimson lipstick, the reply is usually, "I'd tell you, but then I'd have to kill you."

There's an awkward silence. King Henry commands her gaze, all but willing a truthful answer from her, but Fagin offers only a Cheshire cat smile. Clearly, she's in no mood to reveal any of her secrets.

"Well, Madame Fagin, if that is how you wish to be addressed," Henry says. "My sweetheart tells me that you are the purveyors of this Miracle Madeira." He holds his goblet aloft in salutation. "We commend you for providing such excellent drink for our feast."

"More importantly," Lady Anne cuts in, "my sister says you offered a great service in coming to her rescue, and my defense, when she was accosted earlier. We are grateful for your friendship."

"It was my pleasure, Your Majesties," I say, swallowing the bitterness sitting at the back of my throat. "My mother and I are humbled and grateful for the privilege of serving the wine tonight."

"It is a most exquisite drink. Its equal I have tasted nowhere before," King Henry says. "Truly one-of-a-kind."

"We would be most happy to bring our wine to your court, sir," I say. "A more perfect way to herald your new queen I cannot imagine."

Anne peers at me, barely suppressing the smirk playing at the corners of her mouth. She seems pleased we're acknowledging her as Henry's queen, but I know she's been privy to many backroom conversations questioning her legitimacy to trust anyone on a first meeting. There is hesitant skepticism behind her eyes.

"What do you say to this request, sweetheart?" Henry asks. "I know how fond you are of all things French. Would you enjoy having this mademoiselle as one of your ladies?"

Anne looks me over, head to toe, before speaking. "Mary tells me they are clever and have many artistic talents. Tell me, mademoiselle, what employment can you offer in return for an invitation to our court? Everyone who attends me has some talent to offer."

After dozens of Sim Lab etiquette and historical lessons—the endless chivalric games and politics simulations—I know the perfect, honeyed flattery Anne loves. "I offer all of myself to Your Majesty in whatever employment you think suitable."

She gives me a tolerant smile. "Yes, but what particular talents have you to offer in my service?"

"I can offer talents in many leisurely entertainments, my lady. Singing, dancing."

"My sister tells me you write poetry and compose riddles," Anne says. "I'm very good at riddles. Do you have one that would challenge me?"

"Yes," King Henry says. "Tell us a riddle. If it's clever enough, you shall have a position as lady-in-waiting."

He looks to Anne, who gives him a wide-eyed look in return. She whispers to the king. He whispers back and she nods what appears to be grudging approval.

Courtiers jostle for better positions in the crowd so they can hear and see. As a time traveler who has assimilated into dozens of cultures, in many time frames—not to mention a thief who's had to talk her way out of trouble after being caught in the act—I like to think my performances rival any classically trained actress. This should be a piece of cake. "Very well," I say. "Are you clever enough to solve this puzzle?"

. . .

"One lady conquers her foes on the board, her lord's life to secure;

A second plays her hand with her love on her sleeve 'til a suit of four be procured.

A third leads her fellows when they are abuzz, and their insults mightily sting;

Pray, what in common have each of these ladies when fortune kisses the ring?"

"Did I not tell you, sister?" Lady Mary says. "She is so clever, we must have her at court."

"We shouldn't be so hasty, *sister*," Anne says, admonishing Mary with a sober look. "We must first know the riddle's answer to see if it is, indeed, clever. What is the answer, Mademoiselle Clémence?"

"I'm sure a great mind such as Your Majesty's will unravel the mystery," I say, offering what I hope is my most flattering smile. "If not, then I shall tell you after you bring us to England."

A collective gasp ripples from one end of the room to the other. Out of the corner of my eye, I see Fagin glaring at me. If it were possible for steam to rise from a human head, Fagin would be a smokestack of frustration and irritation. The room exhales when both kings and the would-be queen roar with laughter.

"Methinks she has, indeed, offered a great challenge to you, my lady," King Henry says, kissing Anne on the cheek. "Come, sweetheart. Let's find the answer together."

"As you wish, Your Majesty." Anne says. She repeats the first line of the riddle. *"One lady conquers her foes on the board, her lord's life to secure."* She nibbles her lower lip as she thinks; her eyes sparkle. She lifts her chin and regards me with cool confidence. "In chess, which piece has the most power to protect her Lord, the king, from capture?"

Francois chuckles, then elbows Henry in the side. "The queen, of course."

"Very good, majesty," I say. "And *the second lady who plays her hand with her love on her sleeve 'til a suit of four be procured?"* I raise a questioning brow, eyes drifting from one royal patron to the next.

King Henry's eyes pop and he grasps Anne's hand. "Perhaps the queen of hearts in a deck of playing cards."

"Exactly." I reward the correct answer with a flashing smile.

"Then, the final piece of the puzzle," Anne juts her chin into the air, a self-satisfied smile on her lips. "*A third leads her fellows when they are abuzz, and their insults mightily sting."*

I nod, my eyes locked on Anne. "And the last line?" Several seconds pass. Fagin walks to my side and loops her arm through mine.

"Perhaps, the last line refers to..." Anne pauses, considering. Then chuckles. "All of these ladies have one thing in common when fortune kisses the ring." She lifts King Henry's hand to her lips and plants a light kiss on his signet ring. "They are each a queen."

"What a keen mind you have, Your Majesty," I say. "You have guessed exactly right on every count."

The room erupts in applause, as the royal party makes their way from the dais to the dance floor. Anne glows from the adulation. "You have won your prize, mademoiselle. You have a place with my ladies in our English court."

"Dancing!" King Francois says, with a wave to the musicians. "We shall have more dancing!"

The music begins anew, and the royals make their way to the dance floor. Before the dance begins, I overhear Anne conspiring with her sister. "At the very least, this French beauty may be a great challenge to our brother's wife, that little cur. It will be great entertainment to watch Jane squirm when we unleash Mademoiselle Clémence at court."

As the sisters laugh over plans for their sister-in-law's humiliation, Fagin hugs me tightly. "You did it, ma petit. *There's* the Dodger I know and adore!"

"Well done, kiddo," Nico says, echoing the sentiment.

I can't revel in this first victory. My mind is stuck on the Boleyn sisters using *me* as their weapon of mass destruction against their sister-in-law. Is this arrogant enjoyment of domination just another family heirloom to be passed down like money, titles, and land? There's no one here to stop them in their cruel games.

Well, that's not exactly true. There's me.

CHAPTER 14

I DIDN'T THINK it was possible for Becca Trevor to be more grating, more annoying, more Becca than before, but somehow she is. As she stares glassy-eyed into the half-empty mug of coffee in front of her, she punctuates guttural moans with curses.

"Shit," she says. "Shit. Shit. Shit."

Her eyes are red, puffy. She clamps her fists over her ears and throws a murderous glance at Nico as he ambles past on his way from the galley to the cockpit, coffee in hand, to perform the morning system checks. He whistles an effervescent rendition of Boogie Woogie Bugle Boy and gives me a mischievous wink as he whistles louder.

"He's a sadist," Becca says, her voice is a sandpaper rasp, the result of a morning spent retching into the toilet.

"You missed a helluva party last night," I say, raising my voice. I slide onto the booth and clank my coffee cup and bowl of cinnamon oatmeal down hard onto the table. "What happened?"

"You're both sadists," she says, flattening her palms against her ears, trying to muffle the noise.

"Are you ill? You were well enough at dinner last night." I lean across the table and place the back of my hand on her forehead in mock concern. "Maybe you just need an aspirin."

She slaps my hand away. "You know very well what happened to me. Either you or that asshole," she nods toward the cockpit, "put something in my drink last night."

At close range, her breath smells of vomit with overtones of coffee. I scoot back into the corner of the booth in self-defense. It doesn't help much. "For God's Sake, brush your teeth. If nothing else, you'll smell better."

I pull a data pad closer to me, plug my earbuds into the auxiliary port and tap the screen. A blueprint of a grand Tudor residence displays and the accompanying audio narration buzzes in my ear. "The following schematics are the blueprints of Greenwich Palace during the reign of King Henry the Eighth. The Tudor court was in residence at Greenwich from Twenty-Seven November of 1532 through early February of 1533. The first floor—"

The sound abruptly stops. My hands spring up to my face as the earbuds are ripped from my ears.

"What the hell is your problem?" I shout, snatching the dangling audio wires from Trevor's grasp. "I don't care who you are, don't you dare put hands on me like that again."

"I'm not done talking," Trevor says. "You think you're so bloody clever. Trying to derail this mission by knocking me out."

Fagin and Nico both emerge from the cockpit. Nico gives me a questioning look. Fagin just looks perturbed.

"What's the problem, ladies?" Fagin asks, her voice tinged with weary annoyance.

"She thinks we drugged her last night to keep her out of the action," I say. "I have no idea what she's talking about. Do you?"

"That's a pretty serious charge, Trevor," Fagin says. "We can do a blood test to see if you ingested any toxins in the last twenty-four hours."

"Excellent idea." Trevor face brightens, and she leans on her forearms on the table as she stares me down. Her gaze is pure panther.

"You're serious," I say, shooting Fagin an exasperated look. "Are you really going to indulge this fantasy?"

"Best way to put this accusation to rest is by testing her hypothesis. If there are illicit drugs in her system, blood tests will confirm it."

Fagin retrieves a medical kit. She dons a pair of latex gloves and sterilizes the area behind Trevor's left earlobe with a handheld sterilizer. Then, she presses a small blood and tissue sample extractor against her skin.

"Ow. Ow ow ow ow OW!" Becca says, whimpering like an exhausted toddler overdue for a nap.

"Christ," Nico mutters under his breath.

Fagin places the extractor on the table and we watch a series of abbreviations and numbers cycle through the panel of blood gas values. Nico shoots me a brief, wide-eyed look. *Fingers crossed that the drugs really are undetectable.* He seems to say. A sentiment I return with a discreet shrug. The numbers flash green on the display panel for several seconds before one of the test values hits red.

"See!" Trevor says, her voice drops into a dark I-Told-You-So tone. "There *is* something."

"Sure is," Fagin replies. "Your blood alcohol content is .07."

"So, Lieutenant Lightweight is still drunk," I say, allowing myself a satisfied smirk and a small sigh of relief. "Looks like she needs to learn how to hold her liquor a better."

"Screw you, *Dodger*," she replies, venomous. She turns to Fagin. "Someone on this crew drugged me. Run the test again and feed the report to the ship's main computer. Maybe there's something wrong with the extractor unit."

"All equipment was calibrated before we left base, per regulations, and we're very thorough in our work." Nico says. "There's nothing wrong with the extractor."

"I. Am not. DRUNK," Trevor bellows.

"You need a little more time to sober up after your bender last night," Fagin says. "Sleep it off and you'll be just fine."

"It wasn't a bender. There's been a mistake." Trevor snatches the unit from table and squints at the display panel as she scrolls through the test result list in clumsy, rapid-fire sweeps. She runs through the test results at least twice before shoving the panel across the table in frustration. Fagin catches it before it plummets to the floor.

"Careful with the equipment," Fagin says.

"The only thing those test results prove is that you gave me something that left my system fast or can't be traced at all."

"Why would we drug you?" I say. "Fucking with the Benefactors' informant would complicate our lives in a million different ways. We want to acquire the acquisition list items so we can finish this job and get home in one piece."

"Speaking of acquisitions," Trevor jumps to her feet and we stand nose-to-nose even though the stench of her breath is overpowering. She sways on the spot; it seems the sudden head rush of standing too quickly is making her woozy. She leans her backside against the table's edge and grips it with white-knuckled fingers. Her eyes cross and she blinks to refocus. "After I realized one of you is trying to sabotage me, I made two changes to the mission parameters beginning with the acquisitions list. You might want to take a look."

Nico pulls the file up on the Comm Panel and scrolls through the list. "What the hell?" he says, bristling. "You've added a full page of stuff to the inventory."

"Twenty-Five new items added, to be exact," Becca says. "For now."

"For now?" Fagin and I repeat, in unison.

"I have a rather extensive list of items that can be added at any time, depending on your level of cooperation. The more you fight me the longer the list gets."

"You've got to be fucking kidding-"

"You want more? That can be arranged."

We're toe-to-toe and as much as I want to remind her how much she reeks, the reality of her self-promotion is sinking in. Not wanting to blink or look away, I reluctantly take a small step backward.

"That's what I thought."

Her smugness is unbearable; beads of sweat pop up on the nape of my neck in response. Fagin places her hand at the small of my back and whispers in my ear: "Steady."

"You better get your asses in gear," Becca says, a smarmy smile plastered on her face. "I have a feeling it's going to take quite a bit of re-work on the mission strategy to fit all of these items into the schedule." She cocks her head to the side. "What happened to that smug little smile, Arseneau? Your plans to eliminate me from this mission not working out the way you expected?"

"Why would you extend the mission timeline by adding more shit to the list? Do you know how much longer we'll need to be here to finish this job, now?" An anxious pit forms in my belly; the thought of spending more time in England makes me want to hit something hard.

"The Benefactors knew you'd continue to be a problem. Redeeming yourself will require more than just stealing a trinket or two. I have full authority to modify the mission at any time to meet the Benefactors' goals." She pauses and gives me an ominous look that makes the hair on the back of my neck stand on end. "Which include not only obtaining the artefacts they desire, but to bring you to heel, dear girl."

She sways on her feet and belches; a sour, foul-smelling odor so thick it's almost visible hangs around her like a fog.

This gnat needs squashing. "You're not just hungover, you seem hangry, too, Trevor. You know what's good for a hangover? Food. Lots of food to soak up the greasy sick settled in your gut. Here," I reach over to the table and slide my bowl of oatmeal closer to her. "Have my breakfast. Or I can cook bacon and eggs, if you like. Or maybe pancakes loaded with butter and syrup. How about some hardtack biscuits and gravy? That's what the sailors I knew ate after drunken binges. Well, new sailors would vomit while the old-timers sat in the galley tucking into just about anything they wanted."

Color drains from Trevor's face, replaced by a look of queasy disgust at the mention of all that food. She bolts toward the narrow corridor leading to crew corridors, knocking Fagin into the wall as she races to her room.

"Happy now?" Fagin says, dryly. "You poked the bear, Dodger. We had her somewhat contained before, but now she's going to scrutinize everything more closely. We won't be able to take a piss without her permission."

"We got around her before. We can do it again," Nico says, leaning against the cockpit's doorframe. "We just have to be more cunning than she is."

"Shouldn't be too hard." I say, smiling at him. "We *are* pretty clever."

In unison, the three of us turn to stare at the acquisition list glowing green on the Comm Panel screen.

"Merde," Fagin says. "We better get busy. Trevor was right. We have to rework our entire plan."

"I'll make more coffee. It's gonna be a long night," Nico says.

It's the wee hours of the morning before we finish cataloguing every item on the new acquisition list, sorting them by owner, last known location, the royal party's residency at each location, and the risk factors for obtaining each item. Trevor has yet to reappear after fleeing the main cabin. I imagine she's probably passed out again.

With a swipe of his fingers, Nico highlights several items on the list—low-hanging fruit, he calls them. "Smaller jewels—rings, pins and bracelets—are easier to pocket. I recommend starting with these first." he says. "There are several gems the royal ladies-in-waiting seem to already have on this journey with them. Leeds Castle is the first stop on the road back to the king's London palaces."

Fagin positions her data pad in the middle of the conference table and taps the screen. "Remember the ruby necklace Mary Boleyn wore last night?" A three-dimensional hologram image of Mary Boleyn, wearing the necklace, springs up from the data pad. "I'm sure it caught Dodger's eye."

"What of it?" I ask, pretty sure the answer is going to piss me off.

"It's now on the list," she replies.

"Dammit, Fagin," I say. "I could've acquired it last night."

Fagin only shrugs. "Hindsight is a bitch sometimes."

Nico zooms the image until the Boleyn girl's neck and heaving cleavage is dead center. The necklace fits snugly in her décolletage. The hologram's realism makes her skin look warm and inviting and physically present; even the blood coursing through her carotid artery is palpable enough that you could take her pulse.

His head tilts to one side and with a quick intake of breath, realizes the zoom perspective is too close. Noticing that Fagin and I are staring curiously at him, he zooms out again, blushing as he mumbles a quick, "Sorry."

"The ruby wasn't the only asset on display." Fagin chuckles. "We could take advantage of the ship-board time to procure a few of the items we know are here in Calais if we can secure passage back to England on the King's ship. You're in pretty tight with Mary," she says to me. "Pop in over at the Exchequer and take Mary a bit more wine for her personal use. That gorgeous French courtier she marked for conquest last night seemed to really enjoy it. Mary could use the wine to coax him into a liaison."

"Too risky," I say, rubbing my eyes which, from the feel of them, must be bloodshot from ten hours of bouncing back-and-forth between computer files and hologram videos. Blinking against the dryness, the insides of my eyelids feel like sandpaper scraping across my corneas. "The Swallow is too small to comfortably pilfer anything from the passengers without risking detection. If we're caught, the whole mission would be over. We'd get shipped straight back to France as soon as we made port in Dover."

"If you're not thrown overboard on the way." Nico says. "Agreed. It's too risky." he leans back in his chair and stretches, the fabric of his T-shirt straining against his taut biceps and pectorals. Warmth spreads up my neck and pricks my earlobes as the longing to let my fingers explore Nico's terrain grows. When he smiles at me—eyes clear and bright and oh-so-damn-sexy—it takes every ounce of self-control not to drag him to my cabin. "Besides, you're not leaving me alone with Trevor."

"Speak of the devil," Fagin nods at the acquisition list. "She's adding more."

In the bottom-left corner of the screen, the total number of records in the data set begins ticking upward. *Twenty-six, twenty-seven, twenty-eight...*

The count paused at thirty new items, then continued its upward trend.

One by one, Fagin displays the holograms of each new addition and reads the descriptions. "None of these look like low-hanging fruit: A silver locket containing a miniature portrait of Anne Boleyn painted during her childhood at the French court; Mark Smeaton's violin and music sheets from the masque performed at Christmas of this year; BOTH goblets used by King Henry and Lady Anne at their wedding— "

"They married in secret," I say, pushing the hologram image to the left to get a better look at the other side of these jewel-encrusted gold goblets. "No Observers have attended that ceremony. We only have vague dates as to when the wedding actually took place."

"Looks like you might be the first, Dodger." Nico sighed. "You'll have to work that Mary Boleyn connection to make sure you get an invite."

"With everything on this list, we could be in England for an entire damn year. Some of these items are located in Scotland." My gut clenches at the thought of staying long enough to watch the birth of the English colonizer—Elizabeth Regina the First. Even as a squalling, red-faced infant, her entry into the world marks the beginning of everything that destroys Acadia.

Destroys my people. My family. I can't bear the thought.

"The mission takes as long as it takes, Clémence." Fagin regards me with a cool curiosity; her narrowed eyes convey the same suspicion when she knows I'm up to something that she hasn't approved.

"Also on the list is a letter from Queen Catherine of Aragon—dated in April 1533—smuggled by Spanish ambassador Chapuys to her nephew, the Emperor of Spain."

"I guess she didn't much care for your breakfast recommendations." Nico replied. "This list seems custom-made for exacting vengeance or, at the least, teaching us a lesson."

"April of next year? The letter to Spain is dated for next... year?" My breathing quickens into sharp, shallow breaths that make my chest tighten like someone is squeezing my heart and won't let go. "No. No, I can't stay until April. I can't stay—"

The claustrophobia I felt in the Sim Lab during the training exercises hits me with the force of a battering ram to the chest.

I don't remember standing up, don't remember clambering over the table in front of Fagin to get out of the dining booth, but I must've done because the bench sits flush against the wall, and the only way out—if you're sitting in the corner and someone is next to you— is if the other occupant stands up first.

Nico moves closer. He pulls me into an embrace and I'm surprised to feel wet spots bloom on his tee shirt as my forehead rests against him. Once I notice the tears, I can't stop them. Great, heaving, sobbing tears spill out onto his chest.

"Hey," he says softly against my hair. "Hey, come on. I know it's a pain, but—"

"There's so much you don't know, Nico." Fagin says. She sounds distant, like she's talking from the bottom of a well. The voice I hear louder than any of them is the narrator from the Tudor hologram files the Consigliere gave me.

"...*without Elizabeth on the throne in the sixteenth century, England would not have conquered what would ultimately become...*"

What if I'm still here when Lady Anne's conceives? What if I must watch as her belly swells like a watermelon? Can I watch her child come into this world, a squalling red-faced infant, knowing she is destined to destroy everything I love? I can't let her happen. I just can't.

THE PORTRAIT MINIATURE is my exact likeness. It's set in a sterling silver locket engraved with curlicue flourishes. There's a demure smile on my face—definitely not painted from life because nothing about me is demure—and every color used, even the royal blue background, complements my features in a perfect balance of highlights and shadows.

I wonder how the artist—infamously temperamental Hans Holbein the Younger—painted this image when I know I've never modeled for him. This painting is so breathtaking in its delicate lifelike perfection, it feels as though portrait-me could step out of the painting at any moment.

How much would a Benefactor pay for a Holbein original even if it's of me?

"Our artist is a genius," Anne says, peering over my fingertips at the portrait. She holds her hands, clasped in front of her. Draped over the top of one fist is a thin leather cord; whatever is attached to the other end is hidden inside her palm.

"I'm flattered, my Lady Marquess, and confess to being quite confused," I say. "I've done nothing to earn this gift."

"It was my suggestion," Mary Boleyn says, grinning from ear-to-ear. "My sister planned these gifts for her ladies to celebrate her triumph in Calais." She wraps her arms around Anne's shoulders and squeezes. "Since you have an honored position in our circle, I knew you should have one, too."

I feel the weight of the stares from the other ladies-in-waiting. They've not been warm and welcoming, but I'm not here to be their best friend. It's clear from their side-eye glares and subtle sighs of disgust, they don't consider me worthy of a gift from their queen. I don't care what they think. This Holbein original is worth bank to a collector back home.

"Mary was quite insistent that you be included," Anne says. "When storms over the channel delayed our return to England, I asked Master Holbein to make good use of the time to paint your likeness as discreetly as possible. He only finished his work yesterday."

I noticed the bearded, block-faced artist leering at me over the two weeks we spent waiting for the weather to clear so we could sail to England. His stalker behavior was creepy, and I intended to put a well-placed knee into his groin. Fagin nixed the idea since clobbering the king's favorite artist might get us banished from court.

"I'm surprised Master Holbein was agreeable in observing me under such conditions," I say, turning the exquisite necklace over in my palm. "He doesn't seem the kind of man who relinquishes control of his artistic environment."

"He did grumble about the circumstances. When we arrived at Dover Castle, he demanded that you either sit for him or he wouldn't complete the work," Lady Anne says. "As a compromise, we asked your mother's help in providing a reasonable likeness of you so Master Holbein could finish the painting by the time we arrived here at Greenwich."

I turn to Fagin who shrugs. "I remembered that beautiful charcoal rendering the Spanish artist drew for your birthday." She fidgets a bit. She knows how I feel about surprises.

"I don't recall that one," I reply, folding my arms in a tight knot across my chest.

When the hell did Nico have time to—

"I can draw every curve of you from memory." Nico's voice buzzes through the earpiece, answering my thoughts. "Don't worry. I filtered this transmission. You're the only one who can hear me."

"For your sake, mademoiselle, we shall forgive your mother's ill choice of patronage with a Spaniard." Anne wrinkles her nose and her dramatic black eyes flash. No doubt, her thoughts are on the Spaniard impeding her path to the throne which doesn't dispose her kindly toward any Spaniard.

"I would like to know the artist's name, so I can thank him for his part in this...surprise." *Actually, I'd like to throttle him. Did I mention that I hate surprises?*

Nico picks up on my annoyance and returns the volley, a laugh tucked inside his wry commentary. "I'm shaking in my boots. Remind me to faint when you get back."

I play along like a good soldier. "Offering a simple 'thank you' doesn't seem adequate for this treasure, but thank you both," I say, offering a curtsey. From the depths of this obeisance, I glimpse the item Lady Anne holds as it slips through her fingers. She catches the leather cord before the thing drops to the floor.

A ripple of adrenaline makes my breath catch in my chest, and I have the sudden urge to scratch the itch in my palms. It's Anne's portrait miniature, the one Trevor added to the acquisition list. Lady Anne's silver locket, when shut, forms a seamless closure beneath the lapis lazuli cabochon—so blue it's almost black—embedded in the locket in a way that allows it to straddle both sides of the locket wings when closed.

"Your locket is exquisite, my lady. Is there also a limning inside?"

"There is," she says as she slides her fingertips around the rim of the silver filigree edging and flips a tiny hidden latch. The locket opens to reveal the famous Anne Boleyn portrait—the red dress, pearls, and the "B" initial necklace she wears now.

The necklace is an intricate puzzle that mimics a solid piece of jewelry; one would never know there is a portrait miniature inside unless you knew how to open it.

"It's a present for the king," she says. "I'm giving it to him tonight at the banquet."

Anne's ladies-in-waiting squeal over their own limnings and plot which eligible bachelor will receive their portraits as precious tokens of courtly love. Some of the prospects elicit eager sighs, confirming the target's desirable status. Others induce lectures from the older women for their more rakish and questionable attributes. When Grace Parker jokingly suggests Will Somers — the King's fool — as the *only* acceptable choice of romantic suitor for a discerning noble-woman, visions of the jester in his parti-colored tunic, hose and floppy, three-horned hat, unleash gales of laughter.

Lady Margaret Douglas wipes tears from her eyes. "Take care that Master Somers doesn't aim his sharp tongue at you for those words, my dear."

"Nonsense. Being a merry and pleasant fellow, he may take liber-ties without offense." Grace selects a fig from a platter of dried fruits. "His humor is done with such goodwill that if the King himself is not displeased by his jests, it's impossible for anyone else to truly be injured by him. Except, perhaps, the Spanish ambassador." She frowns in disapproval. "He was quite churlish when Will teased him." She twists her face into an exaggerated impression of the comic — cheeks puffed out, eyes wide and wild — only inches from Madge Shelton's face. "Sir, what say ye with your fat face?"

Madge screeches and turns away, laughing. "I shall tell Master Somers that you swoon for him. You can give him your likeness so he may dream on it every night," she teases, and a spirited game of keep-away—with Grace's locket as the prize—begins. Madge tosses it to the other side of Lady Anne's temporary privy chamber. Anne Gainsford elbows a sullen Jane Rochford out of the way to catch it.

Grace dashes around the room in vain attempts to intercept the next throw as the locket flies from hand-to-hand. When it lands with

Jane Seymour, she takes pity on the poor victim and returns the necklace.

"My ladies." Anne pokes Madge Shelton in the ribs. "Give your treasure to one worthy of its value. Villains will only break your hearts and sully your reputations."

"Which treasure do you mean, madam?" Madge replies with a breathless giggle. "I can think of more than one."

"Virtue is the treasure you should protect," Lady Margaret cautions. "It's more valuable than any else you possess."

Eyes collectively roll, but no one dares contradict her. Cheekiness with this elder stateswoman of the court is cause for dreadful lectures and shorter leashes to curb bad behavior.

"Lady Douglas is a stern taskmaster, but she means well," Lady Anne shoots a teasing look at Lady Margaret, who exhales a soft *pffft* in response. "Master Holbein took so long with each painting, I worried these gifts for a job well done in France may become gifts on a more significant occasion." She makes a great show of selecting the perfect dried date from the silver tray and plops it into her mouth.

"Sister." Mary Boleyn's eyebrows fly up into her hairline. "Have you news to share? Do you speak of your coronation?"

Lady Anne notes that I still hold my necklace while everyone else wears theirs. She sweeps my hair to one side and secures my locket in place around my neck. I feel her breath on my skin as she whispers in my ear.

Fagin studies me intently; I can tell she's trying to work out whether I'm on my game or if she'll have to do damage control from whatever outburst might be coming.

My blood runs cold. It's not Anne's words that hit me with the force of a tsunami; it's the arrogance bleeding through them like a toxic red tide. Her hubris is overwhelming.

All eyes are on me and I have a choice: lose my shit and strangle her where she stands or play the trusted ally, keeper of secrets. Out of pure self-preservation, I choose the latter, forcing laughter so deep and raucous that I cry real tears. I wonder if they can tell it's all just an act.

"What is it?" several voices demand at once, laughing in earnest because I'm still cackling and the sound is infectious.

"Le falcon doit consommer le grenadier." I repeat Anne's words in sputtering gasps. That part—the wracked breathlessness stemming from disbelief mingled with grief—isn't an act, but everyone seems willing to think the mania is still laughter.

Fagin, still watching me, moves to stand at my side and digs her fingernails into my shoulder. A silent admonition to pull myself together.

Mouths drop open. There are blank stares. "The falcon shall consume the pomegranate," I say, translating for those whose French is weak.

Lady Anne smiles and settles into a chair upholstered in crimson and gold. When she asks for a footstool, Madge fetches a red velvet pouffe, and carefully arranges it under her feet. Among the ladies-in-waiting, flickers of recognition begin to spread.

"By the time the king and his lords finish their tour of the coastal fortifications the servants at Greenwich will be done replacing that Thin Old Woman's pomegranate and crown badge with my white falcon holding a scepter," Anne says.

Her message is clear: Change is coming. She will displace her rival as Queen of England. A mixture of confusion, shock, and excitement buzzes through the chamber as Anne defers any more questions.

"When the time comes, you'll know all there is to know." She smiles and I want to strangle her all the more.

"I think Lady Anne's pronouncements are a bit premature," Nico says. "Her coronation doesn't occur until the end of May next year. She must be talking about the wedding to King Henry or she's referencing when her child is conceived, which, according to historical holograms, both occur around Christmas."

"Christmas," I say, murmuring under my breath. "Doesn't give me much time."

There's a brief silence on the other end of the CommLink. "Enough time for what?" Nico asks.

"Nothing," I say, murmuring again.

"Dodger?" His voice is more urgent, more concerned.

"Shh. I'm thinking."

The door to Anne's privy chamber swings open and George, the eldest Boleyn sibling, sweeps into the room trailed by two servants bearing more food and wine. He's handsome enough, but the way he leers at the women attending his sister makes me feel like something slimy is dripping down my arm.

"Lord Rochford. Great. Watch his hands," Nico says. "I saw some footage of him with a few of the French girls in Calais and let's just say it's not family viewing."

I skirt around Anne and Mary, who move to greet their brother, but I'm not fast enough to escape him. He catches me around the waist and breathes into my ear. There's the strong smell of wine on his breath. It's not even noon yet."

"Mademoiselle Clémence, leaving so soon? Every time I seek your company, you run the other way. If you keep avoiding me, I shall take offense."

"You flatter me, Lord Rochford." I say, attempting to wriggle free of his vise grip. "I'm a simple maid and not worthy of your attention."

A tipsy laugh, ending in a high pitch squeal, escapes his throat as he buries his nose into my hair. George breathes heavily against my neck; the sickly sweetness of his breath makes me want to gag. Discreetly trying to free myself from his grasp isn't working, and no help is in the offing from anyone else in the room.

"But I do fancy *you*, my girl," he says. "Come, I'm sure my sister won't mind if I spirit you away and entertain you with my poetry. But I must warn you, spend much time in my presence, and you may not maintain your honor for very long."

"Fagin," Nico says, a note of alarm in his voice. "You gonna take care of this or do I need to pay him a visit later?"

"I've got her," Fagin says softly. She moves closer, keeping an eye on Boleyn's hands. She can't make any bold moves; it would risk flaring Anne's temper.

"It's fine. Everything's fine," I say, trying to calm Nico. Nico going rogue to defend my honor is the last thing we need.

"Our brother is quite handsome." Anne's flashes the kind of smile a bad influence gives as they talk you into doing something rash and stupid. "I think you would thoroughly enjoy his...poetry."

Mary goes wide-eyed and a delighted gasp gushes out of her. "I agree. George should share his 'poetry' with our new friend. Then, she can tell us how she likes it; whether his words are slow and soothing or wickedly hard and— "

"Husband," a stern voice chides from behind us. "Do you ever tire of making a public spectacle of yourself by molesting young maidens in full view of the entire court?"

George makes an awkward turn, with me still in his arms, to face his wife, Jane, Lady Rochford. "You forget yourself, madam. It's you who are the public spectacle. A public spectacle of an albatross around my neck."

Jane's expression contorts, as though he has slapped her in the face. She manages a smile, but her reply is filled with venom. "Seek pleasure with this trollop, then. Or your sister, for all I care. Any of them can be in your bed tonight, because it won't be me."

"Both Mademoiselle Clémence and my sister would be more pleasant company than you, good wife." His smile is a twisted, humorless thing devoid of any good will. He looks ready to spit in her face, but a more fitting verbal attack seems to have come to mind. "I will decide who is in my bed tonight. If I am feeling charitable enough, it may even be you."

"Jane, this is only innocent banter and no cause for a public outcry," Anne says. Whatever she had in mind about using me to make mischief between George and his wife, she apparently hadn't bargained on a public confrontation between the two.

There's cool determination in her eyes to get the scene under control before it escalates further. Anne steps closer so that only Jane, George, and I can hear. "George is only pursuing a friendship with Mademoiselle Clémence. Surely, you can see that."

"I see very clearly, madam," Jane says, indignation burning white-hot in her eyes. "It seems I am forever damned to mockery for your perverse entertainment. My position is unbearable and I have no stomach for it."

Anne pauses, her eyes searching Jane's for a sign she'll back down. Knowing that everyone in the room is watching and, not seeing an inch of ground being given by her brother's wife, she turns to her brother. "I think it's best if you retire to your chambers, sweetheart."

"Will you allow this cur to dictate—"

"It's unwise to further provoke this matter further. Please." Her eyes plead with him as she clutches his arm, "I will speak with you later."

George tries to shrug Anne off, but she grips him tighter. "George," she says firmly, accompanied by a severe look that brooks no further argument. "Now."

He stumbles slightly as he pushes me away. He bows with mock flourish to Jane, who turns on her heels in flushed embarrassment and retreats to a corner of the room near Jane Seymour and the other ladies.

Thankfully, drunks have short attention spans. Lord Rochford mumbles something about finding better company elsewhere and staggers out of the room.

Two boys bearing more wine and food catch my eye. One bustles throughout the room with precise efficiency; his actions and demeanor are the result of years of royal service. He's been all but invisible, carrying out his duties with minimal disruption.

The other servant, however, is conspicuous with his sloppy manners and inattention to detail. Moving at a snail's pace, this boy's orbit around the room is more languid than his peer's. There are furtive glances over his shoulder, but not long enough to allow me to get a good look at his face.

I'd lay odds this servant is soaking up every bit of gossip he can to take back to the kitchens. Still, there's something else. Something about the physical build that's softer and rounder than a teenage boy's body should be.

"Come," Lady Anne interrupts my thoughts, beckoning me to sit in a chair next to hers. "There's been enough upheaval today. Let's distract ourselves with another of Clémence's riddles."

"If you wish, Your Majesty." If flattery is the main currency of the court, then I'm intent on making Anne a billionaire. "I have a challenging one for you tonight. Let's see who is clever enough to answer this riddle."

"My dress is silver, shimmering gray,
    spun with a blaze of garnets.
    I craze most men, rash fools I run on a road of rage,
    and cage quiet determined men.
    Why they love me — lured from mind
    — stripped of strength, remains a riddle.
    If they still praise my sinuous power when
    they raise high the dearest treasure,
    They will find, through reckless habit,
    dark woe in the dregs of pleasure."

Settling back into my seat, I let my fingers dangle over the arm of the chair and survey the room. "Who's going to take the first guess?"

Madge chews a fingernail, her brows pinched in concentration. "Silver dress, shimmering gray, blaze of garnets," she repeats. "A jewel?"

"No. It does sparkle like one, but it isn't a jewel."

"Crazes most men, making them rash fools," Grace says, then

shrugs one shoulder. "What crazes men most?"

"War," says Lady Fitzwalter.

"Sport," says Anne Saville.

"We do." Lady Anne laughs, inducing giggling fits in the younger girls, and knowing nods from their elders.

"A woman, then." Madge jumps from her seat, certain it's the right answer.

"It sounds like our guest, doesn't it?" Lady Rochford's bloodshot eyes bore holes into me.

Of all the royal ladies, Jane Boleyn is the only one who hasn't joined in the evening's entertainment, choosing, instead, to continue sewing. She pulls her needle through the linen shirt, snapping the thread with the force of her last tug. She glances at the broken thread, then back at me. "I imagine *you* have run men's wives by the wayside as well. Did you enjoy having my husband's arms around you?"

"Jane," Lady Anne frowns. "That's quite enough."

"It is no matter, Your Majesty." I wave it off, trying to appear unfazed by the accusation. She doesn't know how close I came to defending her. The price of it would have been our mission. "And the answer is quite wrong, it's not a woman. Go to the next part of the riddle."

I repeat the second stanza.

"Why they love me — lured from mind

— stripped of strength, remains a riddle.

If they still praise my sinuous power when

they raise high the dearest treasure,"

"Lured from mind, stripped of strength," Anne says. A coy smile spreads across her face. "And you're certain the answer isn't a woman?"

"Silver dress, crazes most men. Reckless habits and dark woe." Madge ticks the clues off on one hand.

"In the dregs of pleasure," several voices finish the clue in unison.

There's a murmur of voices around the circle as the clues are dissected from every conceivable angle.

Silver dress...Crazes men...but, not a woman.
Whatever it is, it strips one's strength.
Dark woe in dregs of pleasure men love.
Raises high the dearest treasure.
Like a toast at a banquet, maybe?
Silver...garnet...powerful dregs.

"A cup of wine," Lady Anne says, her words coming in an excited rush of breath. "That's the answer: a cup of wine. The dress is a silver goblet. Drinking too much red wine is, indeed, a most reckless habit. Those who love it too much, find dark woes in its dregs."

There are furrowed brows and frowns, then gasps of delight as they realize Anne's answer is the only one that makes sense. Of course it's a cup of wine. It couldn't be anything else. We should have known it right away. The murmur around the circle grows into a buzz of excited chatter.

My eyes are glued to Lady Anne. She's charismatic—able to influence everyone in her world to give her exactly what she wants. Dangerously cunning. She's the kind of person who can convince you she has only your best interests at heart while she's digging your heart out of your chest with a dull spoon. She's a tormentor, content to cause destruction and death as long as she gets what she wants.

And her daughter will be just like her.

"Magnifique," I say, pretending to applaud the effort. My brain screams at my heart as I wrestle with vengeance. "It is, indeed, a cup of wine. Do you always have the perfect answer?"

"Yes. I do," she says, smugly, before calling out to the sluggish servant, "Boy, bring more wine. I've worked up a thirst solving our French friend's clever riddle."

The boy steps toward Lady Anne, pours a rich, crimson wine into her cup and, in a feigned baritone voice says, "Miracle Madeira, my lady. This is the wine from Calais you love so much."

I know that voice. My eyes drift up to the servant's face and I have to fight to control my body, my expressions. Disguised in men's clothes, and staring down at me with a piercing gaze, is Becca Trevor.

CHAPTER 15

"Shit," Nico says. "Trevor, what are you doing there?"

Trevor smiles and gestures toward my empty goblet with the wine carafe in her hands. "I brought wine, mademoiselle. Would you care for more or have you had enough?"

I shake my head, a gesture anyone, except Fagin, would interpret as declining the offer. I recognize the same sentiment burning in Fagin's eyes: *Don't do it. Don't go there.*

"You're wearing your CommLink, aren't you?" Nico says.

In response, Trevor smiles and throws a glance up to the hidden camera embedded in the corner.

"Get your scrawny ass back to the ship, now," Nico continues. "This isn't part of the plan."

Fagin extends her cup toward Trevor, facing her squarely, and then says to Anne. "Are your servants in the habit of addressing the ladies of your court in such a manner, Your Majesty? In France, such impertinence would be punishable by flogging."

It takes a minute to realize that I'm holding my breath, an action usually reserved for moments when I'm distracting my mark with some misdirection or another before picking their pocket. On the exhale, I'd have the wallet out of the pocket or the bracelet off of the arm and be on my merry way.

I'm not sure what will happen if I exhale now: Trevor's next move could bring the entire mission crashing down on us. If Becca's cover is blown, how the hell are we going to get her out of the Tudor court without risking our own exposure?

"Boy," Anne says, "What's your name?"

"Cesario, Your Grace."

"Cesario?" Anne looks perplexed, like the name doesn't fit the lanky youth standing in front of her. "Are you English or Italian?"

"Both, Your Grace," Trevor says. "My uncle lives near the River Avon, and he writes plays. He suggested the name to my mother, who has relations in Verona."

Nico breaks in. "You stole a name from Shakespeare for this bull-shit? Leave the classics alone. Maybe use Matahari or something else, next time you decide to scupper our operation. Or how about this?" He bites each word off like he's snapping clean through iron bars with his teeth. "There better not be a next time."

Lady Douglas steps forward, wringing her hands. "This is my responsibility, Your Grace. Young Cesario is here on my account. It was not until the boy arrived at court with a letter from my late, dear sister that I learned she left behind a ward in need of care upon her death. If it please, Your Grace, I gave him work in the kitchens so he could earn his keep." She pauses, her voice shakes. "If he distresses you, I can find another position for him."

Anne dismisses her concerns with a wave. "If the boy is now your ward, Lady Douglas, he is welcome at court as long as he remembers his position." She turns to Trevor. "Can you do that? Never speak to my ladies unless they address you first."

"Of course, Your Grace. My apologies. I seek only the health and safety of your guests while they're here." Trevor says. "And that they see this visit as a very...profitable one."

Trevor is like a splinter that works itself into you so deep that nothing dislodges it. It just sits there, below the skin, festering. "We don't need your help," I say. "Leave us to our own affairs."

"I am at your service, my ladies. My desire is your happiness." Her eyes have grown dark and dangerous. Like a shark's.

"Of course," Trevor continues, a sardonic grin pulls the corners of her mouth upward making her look sinister. She's enjoying this way too much. "I'm sure you're both capable of accomplishing all you set your mind to doing."

Lady Douglas wrings her hand and takes a tentative step toward us. She says to Lady Anne, "Madam, with your permission, I'll return Cesario to his duties. I'm sure the cooks need him to help serve at tonight's banquet."

I'll give Trevor credit for one thing: She reads the room rather than blundering ahead. As she studies my face—and Fagin's and Anne's—her expression flickers from steel-eyed smugness to something else. Realization that she's outnumbered, maybe? Whatever it is, it's enough to convince her this is not a hill to continue climbing, let alone die on.

"As you wish, my lady," Trevor says to Lady Douglas leaving behind an air of tension so thick, a one of King Henry's hunting knives couldn't hack through it.

Fagin and I have just enough time to exchange "what the fuck" looks when Trevor's voice breaks over the CommLink. "You think you're so smart, the three of you."

"Trevor, get your ass back to the ship, pronto, or this escapade is going in my own report to the Benefactors," Nico cuts in. "I'll make sure they know you nearly blew the whole deal to smithereens just now."

"They won't give two shits about your report, Garcia. I'm their proxy, so what I say goes. Remember that I said I changed two mission parameters after you sabotaged me the first time? Here's the second one: Dodger has until tomorrow morning to obtain Lady Anne's portrait miniature and bring it to me."

Fagin inhales sharply. A new deadline is a serious snag in our carefully laid plans. She looks like she's wracking her brain, with little success, for a way to compress the timeline in the meticulous plans we rehearsed. The current plan is as tight as it can be.

"If you're even a minute late, *Dodger*, Fagin and Nico will pay the price for your failure. Believe me when I say: I have punishments in mind that will make them cry for mommy."

"Melodrama isn't necessary to make a goddamn point!" Nico says in a rush of angry breath.

"While I do love good theater, this isn't melodrama. If Arseneau fails this task, I'll take it out of your ass. Fagin's, too. Fancy a long stretch in maximum security on a prison planet after we get home? I can arrange that."

A crowded room is the world's worst place to listen as to your world goes to shit and you've got to keep a straight face. Fagin and I trade looks and for a moment, I consider storming out of the room to chase Trevor down.

"Dear Clémence," Lady Anne says, her dark eyes flood with concern. Guess my poker face needs work. "What is it that troubles you so? The color is gone from your cheeks and you're trembling."

"The next shipment of our Madeira is late because of storm in the channel," Fagin says, putting a protective arm around me. "We're worried there won't be enough wine for the banquet tonight."

Trevor keeps yammering in my ear, continuing to argue with Nico. "You three clowns don't call the shots. I do. I can add time limits to deliver an item. I can add so many items to the list that you'll die of old age before this mission is done."

"This is crazy," Nico says. "Nothing you're doing makes sense if the goal is to acquire the objects on the list and get back home."

"You keep forgetting that stealing the artifacts is only half of the mission. The other is making our wayward Dodger a cooperative and obedient asset."

"Then why make it harder on her?" he asks, his voice filled with a lover's fierce protectiveness.

"Because obedience is forged in fire," Trevor snaps. "Besides, is payback for the three of you fucking with me in Calais. Don't blow this deadline or you won't like what comes next."

A gentle touch on my arm grounds me back into my surroundings. Lady Anne smiles at me, and her empathy and warm are as surprising as a burst of sunlight in a storm. Her comforting gesture makes me squirm in my seat; she's not supposed to be nice. She's supposed to be a bitch bent on world domination, or at least her little corner of it. I find myself liking her, a little bit, in spite of myself.

"If we don't have enough wine for the banquet tonight," she says. "We'll serve the best Madeira early, then offer lesser wine when the courtiers won't know the difference. Dear girl, don't worry. All will be well," Anne says, with a note of finality. She holds my hand. "I will welcome the king home and give him this token. All of you," she sweeps an arm around the room, "make yourselves beautiful. We have a feast to attend."

CHAPTER 16

Rain drives against the stained-glass windows at the far end of Greenwich Palace's great hall, making the images seem eerily animated when lightning strikes. It's mesmerizing. The colors flicker and fade in staccato rhythm against the fluid motion of the water as it cascades down the glass in sheets.

Another immutable gray day in England. There's not a window in the palace that permits more than a murky glimpse of the gardens. Even if the storm abated, there wouldn't be much to see. The landscape is withered. Dead. Autumn's color and crispness have been exiled by early winter's carrion of muted brown hedges and trees defrocked of their clothes.

Defrocked is exactly how I feel. I've been stripped bare of every shred of autonomy, every last ounce of freedom. Trevor might as well parade me around the palace on a fucking leash. It's a wonder she doesn't make me beg her permission to breathe.

Throngs of courtiers file into the Great Hall for the evening's festivities: another banquet celebrating Anne's triumph with King Francois. It's been the Party That Never Ends since we left Calais. King Henry has worked overtime ensuring the point of Anne's elevation to queen is driven home ad nauseam.

It has gotten pretty damn old, pretty damn fast.

"We've been in tougher spots," Fagin says as we survey the room and the courtier circus as the pecking order rears its ugly head.

For a moment, my mentor seems like the Fagin of old as she mulls over Trevor's deadline: She looks in control. Calm. Determined.

For all her Machiavellian traits, she has chinks in her emotional armor. All but imperceptible to others, they're as glaring and obvious to me as her tells when bluffing at cards.

Her fingernails are chewed down to the quick.

Dark circles lie in the hollows beneath her blue eyes.

She rubs the right side of her face where the lower jaw hinges; a sign she's been grinding her teeth nearly nonstop for the last few hours since the thorn in our collective sides put us on a clock.

"Nico," I say, "any luck finding references in the holograms about when Anne gives Henry limning?"

Nico's voice buzzes through the CommLink. "Nada. So far, the logs only reference sparse facts we already know: The mini-portrait was painted by Holbein and given to the king as a gift. Nothing more than that."

"Keep looking," Fagin says. "While you're at it, keep eyes on Trevor for the rest of the night and let us know if she gets anywhere near us. I don't want any more surprises like the one we got in Anne's chambers."

"Roger," comes the reply. "At the moment, the dear lieutenant is in the kitchen turning a pheasant on a spit over an open fire."

"Is she miserable?" I ask, and Fagin raises an eyebrow. I shrug in return.

"She's been a mosquito dive-bombing my ear for the last hour. I had to turn the volume down on her CommLink because I couldn't listen to her anymore." He pauses, then says with an expectant tone, "And... you're welcome."

"I'm sorry. What are we thanking you for?" Fagin asks.

"For keeping Trevor on another CommLink frequency so you don't have to listen to her."

"Keep us updated. If she's frustrated, she might let something important slip," Fagin replies.

"She's not likely to start screwing up now that she's got us all dancing to her beat," I say.

"Don't be so sure," Fagin shakes her head and gives me a knowing look. "Hubris like hers always costs something, and it's usually a big fat mistake that kicks your ass out of the frying pan and into the flames." She cranes her neck forward, peering around a gaggle of women clustered together just near a wide, floor-to-ceiling carved wood pillar at the room's entrance. She gives a subtle nod in their direction. "Madge Shelton and Grace Parker just joined those women. That means the rest of the royal circle probably aren't far behind."

"What's the plan?" I ask. The adrenaline is pumping. I love this juice that kicks up my heart rate and makes my blood race through my veins like wildfire. This time, though, it's tainted with a sickening jolt of fear: What happens if I fuck up?

If Trevor really does go gunning for Fagin or Nico, I'll—

"Work the plan," Fagin says, interrupting my thoughts. "Just like any other mission day. Glean as much information as we can and go from there. Lady Anne likes you, so maybe a simple, direct question about the limning will do the trick." Fagin says.

"Stranger things have happened," I say. "There was that time in the French Quarter working a job for the high-rolling pirate buff. Remember?"

Fagin saunters into the Great Hall—I follow close behind—and peruses the sweets table. "The Battle of New Orleans agreement between Jean Lafite and General Andrew Jackson."

I nodded "I thought it was going to be a lot of cloak and dagger stealth, but all I had to do was talk to that pirate, Reginald Hicks. He told me exactly where—and when—the two would meet. All I had to do was ask."

Fagin rolls her eyes and the look is unmistakable: She knows when I'm leaving something out of the story.

"Yeah, I know. I had to find him a priest to perform the ceremony so he could marry his sweetheart before the war started."

"The Pirate Reginald Hicks," Nico says, cackling with glee. "That gets me every time. It's like calling a pirate Larry. Or Bob. Or Walter. It doesn't exactly conjure images of fierce, leave-no-witnesses pillaging and plundering."

"I'm sure you remember Reggie's plundering skills were more than adequate," I say, dryly. "Didn't he pick your pocket at Laffite's mansion when you left the ship to check up on me?"

"You went dark for two hours. I was worried." He expels a rush of air in one large exasperated breath. "And, don't remind me about Reggie's skills." I can actually hear the air quotes he must be making around the last word. "That rat-bastard kept my money."

"Save it for later, you two," Fagin says, nodding toward Lady Anne as she, and the rest of her entourage, stroll into the Great Hall. "It's show time."

The party reminds me of the training sessions in the Sim Lab version of Greenwich. Same layout for the public spaces, same corridors and staircases and bedchambers. I'm assuming the guards posted outside Henry's rooms are already on duty, too. Aside from the difference in the item I'm going to acquire tonight—Henry's rosary will have to wait awhile—there's one other big difference between the Sim Lab training practice and this job: This time, we're going in blind.

No days or weeks of practice. No do-overs. Only one shot to get this right.

Fagin and I pick our way through the crowd. Trestle tables are placed end-to-end along the longest walls in the oblong room; this is where the invited guests will sit when they're not schmoozing and dancing. At the far end of the room is the head table where Lady Anne has joined the king.

"I'm going to check the Madeira and make sure a good amount makes its way to the head table," Fagin says, then nods toward Lady

Jane Seymour. "After that, I'll start interviewing sweet Jane. Maybe she knows something."

"I'll go make myself indispensable to What's-Her-Name. Maybe I'll peel her a grape or something," I say, jerking a thumb toward Anne.

Fagin throws a playful elbow jab to my ribs. "Get moving, kiddo."

Missions always have an element of déjà vu. Just like the days when I learned to be a pickpocket, it's all just muscle memory. Practice a series of repetitive steps enough times, it becomes part of you.

Beyond rehearsing the mission tasks—the meticulously choreographed steps of the action plan, critical to get the job done and get out alive—there's a been-there, done-that feeling from the Sim Lab sessions that bleeds over into reality when I'm finally immersed in the mission.

The taste of roast meats and jellied fruits served from silver platters with gilt edges are familiar, even comforting, because I've eaten them in the Sim Lab. The aromas floating through the room—everything from the acrid vapors of an extinguished tallow candle to the spicy-sweet citrus and herb pomanders people wear to stave off foul body odors—are familiar, too.

Legal Observers put their faith in the measure of comfort and security found in this familiar repetition. That view has always been foolish to me because there's one variable no time traveler can control: the actions and choices of real people. The locals—the term used by Observers for indigenous folks—aren't just study subjects, they're also the monkey wrenches thrown into the works.

I guess it's different for Observers who always color within the mission's boundary lines. They're note-takers, dispassionately recording events with a clinical eye for facts alone. They don't concern themselves with a local's unexpected actions that might throw a carefully crafted plan off track. There are three hundred meticulously dressed, jewelry-laden, half-drunk monkey wrenches in this room. It's going to be an interesting night.

The atmosphere in the Great Hall is an odd mix of celebration and funeral dirge. Lady Anne's supporters are giddy with their ascendancy into the political court stratosphere; those on Queen Katherine's side mourn as though she's already dead.

Before I reach the dais where Anne and Henry are seated, I hear a slight hiss as I pass a small cluster of disgruntled-looking courtiers.

"Jezebel." The woman's voice is faint, but I'd recognize that word —so pregnant with fully gestated, holier-than-thou judgment— whether it's shouted from the rooftops or whispered as softly as a prayer at Mass. Many refined, respectable matriarchs in polite New Orleans society hurled that—and worse—at wayward women in the French Quarter when I was a kid.

Then, as now, judgment makes my stomach churn.

"Hold your tongue, woman," a male voice says. "Lest you get us both thrown into the tower."

Stealing a glance over my shoulder, only the backs of two heads are visible as a bald man clutches a woman's arm as he steers her away toward the back of the room. At the front of the room, the king occupies the monarch's chair of estate beneath a crimson canopy with gold fringe. Lady Anne sits next to him in a smaller chair.

"We're missing some courtiers," Fagin's voice says.

I turn around and walk backward a few steps, searching for her tall, elegant frame. I spot her across the room, approaching Jane Seymour. She pauses and cranes her neck around as she surveys the gathering. "I don't see the Duke of Suffolk."

"How could Charles Brandon not be here? He's the King's best friend," I say.

"Good question. Guess who else isn't here?"

"Aside from Suffolk, everyone who's anyone seems to be here. The French and Venetian ambassadors are over to your left, gorging themselves on appetizers," I say. Fagin looks to her left and nods as she spots the pair helping themselves to candied fruit from one of dozens of gilded platters. "The ambassador from Flanders is chatting up the Dukes of Norfolk and Surrey over to your right. And the biggest threat in the room is Anne's brother. He's right behind you."

Fagin's shoulders sag at the prospect of fending off Mr. Hands. She sighs in relief as George Boleyn brushes past her and, his eyes locked on mine, saunters toward me. His curled upper lip — his exaggerated, gross idea of sexy — turns my stomach.

"Shit." I move toward the dais, hoping I can outpace him getting to Anne before he catches up to me.

"Chapuys," Fagin says, finishing her thought. "Ambassador Chapuys of Spain isn't here."

"He attended the same mass as Henry and Lady Anne this morning, but it was probably by accident and certainly more for his own devotions rather than a show of support for Anne. That's probably as much as he could stand for the day. He's thumbing his nose at the king by not being here, but Henry won't risk open war with the Emperor of Spain by banishing Chapuys from court over it. Given the circumstances, you can hardly blame the Emperor's man for not blasting a celebration trumpet."

"Just letting you know some important courtiers MIA. No telling how these slights will affect Henry and Anne's mood tonight, so proceed with caution."

"Roger."

Lady Anne laughs. It's a hearty, full-throated sound that resonates from deep within her chest. Everyone around her joins in. It doesn't seem manufactured or perfunctory. It's raucous, infectious, genuine joy for Team Anne.

She catches sight of me as I negotiate through several clusters of courtiers and smiles, beckoning me to her side. I pause in front of the table and offer a curtsey to both her and the king.

"Come here, mademoiselle," she says, waving me to join her on her side of the table. "I wish you nearer to me." She motions for her sister-in-law, who stands behind her left shoulder, to move.

Lady Rochford stands her ground and communicates her disapproval with a dismissive 'tsk.' Anne turns in her chair and looks Jane up and down; her dark eyes narrow. Jane blinks and takes several steps backward to make room for me.

"You look ravishing tonight, your grace. There isn't a woman here who can compare." Flattering Anne is an exercise in self-control: sound convincing without crossing the line into sycophant. At least I'm not lying about the dress. It is exquisite.

"What a jewel you are. Every day you become dearer to me." Anne grabs my hand and presses it against her cheek. "If only you could be another star in Constellation Boleyn, it would be a happy circumstance for my family. Alas," she glares over her shoulder at Jane, who stares at her feet, not willing to return the look. "I have but one brother and he already has a wife."

"You honor me, madam. The gift of Master Holbein's limning was generous enough." I run my fingers over the locket around my neck. Anne frowns at me. "Joining your family would be..." I'm trying to think of a better word than loathsome. "A greater honor than I deserve."

"It would also be quite scandalous," King Henry scoots his chair back a few inches, so he can see me. His smile is mischievous. He seems to enjoy stirring the pot. "Think of it. A French woman as my sister. Francois would be steeped in agony at the prospect of French blood so close to the throne of England and, yet, it's not his own."

"Don't tease sweet Clémence, my love. We must keep her as our friend even though she cannot be our sister. You still have your limning," Anne says, staring at my locket. "The portrait is not meant to keep, dear one. It's meant to give away. How can you do that if there is no one to give it to?"

"One day, I may find someone who is worthy of it. Does the king have your limning in his keeping?"

Before she can answer, King Henry distracts Anne with a conspiratorial stage whisper. "If we are to make her happy, and keep her at court, then she must have a husband."

"Oh... Ohhh. I thank your majesty, but it's not necessary." The king gapes at me like I've just thrown a rare diamond back in his face. *Think fast. Think fast. Think fast.* "Forgive me, sir. I have no thoughts for my own advancement, only desires to serve your majesties."

"Nice save," Nico says. "And, if I'm not mistaken, that was strike one on finding this damn portrait."

Slightly mollified that my profession of loyal servitude is the reason for the refusal, his face softens. He leans toward the other end of the table and whispers something to a steward who scuttles off to do whatever it is the king has commanded. He leans back in his seat and returns to me. "You would be the first in history to ignore your own elevation, mademoiselle." he says. "Still, you should not deny yourself the pleasures of our court whilst here."

"I find pleasure in my lady's company, sire," I say. "And in the company of other ladies who attend her."

"By Saint George," the king says, laughter crinkling the corners of his eyes. "Do you have the perfect answer for everything I say?"

His gaze flits over my body, lingering on my décolletage a few seconds longer than necessary. His lips part just a smidge before capturing his lower lip between his teeth. When he raises his attention to my face, there's a flash of lust.

Oh.

His greed dissolves as quickly as it sprang up—good thing, too, because Anne is sitting less than a foot away from him—but for a moment, it was there.

"Yes, Your Majesty," I smile back. "I do."

Across the room, a phantom violin begins to play a lively tune. The source of the music, hidden from view by the throngs of attendees, moves through the crowd, growing louder the closer it gets. In front of the dais, the crowd parts like Moses himself is commanding them. Through the gap, the musician appears.

Tall, lean, and scruffily bearded, he beams at Lady Anne, who squeals and claps in the time with the country dance rhythm.

"That's Mark Smeaton," Nico says. "Musician and Hang on, I'll pull up his file."

Lady Anne jumps to her feet, grabs me by the wrist, and pulls me onto the long, narrow dance floor space in the middle of the hall. Elegant courtiers dance around me in a rainbow swirl of damask, silk taffeta, and velvet. "You will enjoy yourself. I command it," she says, pushing me into a set of strong arms and, suddenly, I'm being whirled around the floor.

I look up into the face of my partner, and it's Anne's brother, George.

Merde. No easy way to get out of this without causing offense.

These English dance patterns are confusing. Boleyn turns left when he's supposed to turn right. He pulls me forward when it looks like he should circle around me. He causes me to stumble more than once.

Fagin joins the dance and maneuvers next to me. "What are you doing?" she asks with a tight smile. If she clenches her teeth any harder, she might snap a molar in two.

"What does it look like? I'm dancing."

"Smartass." She circles to the right with her partner, and on the next pass in my direction, she leans in again. "We don't have time for this."

"Can't do much without more intel," I say. It would be trouble to rummage through the royal apartments with zero idea of where the limning might be kept.

Mark changes tunes and tempos, and Lady Anne leads the revelers through the choreography filled with complicated kicks and skips and leaps. I kick George in the shins twice and he smiles through gritted teeth.

"You call that dancing?" Nico says with a snicker. "Looks like you're wrestling him for the best two out of three."

"Fuck off," I say under my breath.

"Is that an invitation, mademoiselle?" George says with his trademark sliminess. He pulls me into him, and gives my right boob a vigorous squeeze.

"Sir, you are too bold," I say, prying his fingers from my chest.

"But, you said—"

"I'm French. I say a lot of things."

"When this is all over," Nico says, his voice is rich and seductive in my ear. "We'll take a trip to 1943, and I'll teach you to Lindy Hop. I won a dance marathon at an officer's club once. If anyone can teach you to dance, it's me."

"My dancing isn't that bad."

"Yes, my love. It is."

A tall, elegant man with tousled, sandy-colored hair moves between us, forcing George to step back or be stepped on. "Mademoiselle Clémence, I believe you have promised this dance to me."

"Wyatt." George Boleyn says, "This dance is mine. Go back to your poetry."

"The lady has had quite enough of your charm," Sir Thomas Wyatt says with a thinly veiled smirk. He whisks me away from Boleyn with a smooth, graceful turn before the lecher can protest more.

An hour later, the dancers show no sign of slowing down, but Fagin's blood pressure has likely raised by twenty points waiting for Nico to give the green light to search the king's chambers.

Still emboldened by what he thought was an invitation to my bed, George tries to cut in on Sir Thomas Wyatt three more times. Luckily, Wyatt resists. I can't tell whether his unwillingness to part with me is because I'm captivating company or he just wants to frustrate Boleyn's efforts to get what he wants.

Fagin has extricated herself from the group by feigning breathlessness. She waves off her partner and retreats to one corner where she can see the whole room. Still panting from the exertion, Fagin says, "Nico, tell me you've got something. We can't be stuck here all night."

"Not yet. Still searching through the footage from the hidden cameras installed throughout the palace. We don't have a camera in the royal apartments. If Lady Anne gave him the portrait miniature in those rooms, we won't be able to see it." He pauses. "I don't suppose there's time for Dodger to search both rooms tonight."

"It would be tough," she replies. "The royals are night owls; retiring for the night usually occurs somewhere between eleven o'clock and midnight. I'm not sure there'd be enough time to get in and out of both royal apartments before everyone goes to bed."

Dodger would have a hell of a time explaining to Anne why she's in Henry's bedroom if she's caught there."

"It's well after nine o'clock now. I'll keep looking."

There's a muted voice on the periphery of my attention, like an echo in an empty, cavernous room. It's only when Thomas Wyatt pulls me out of the dance circle and leans in close, his eyes boring into me, that I realize he's talking to me.

"Mademoiselle. I asked if you require assistance. Rochford is, for lack of a more polite term, a libertine. If he harasses you further, I am at your disposal to—"

"Thank you for the kind offer, Sir Thomas. I can manage George Boleyn on my own. I am quite used to fending for myself."

He sighs. "Is it difficult for you here? A French woman in our court? Do you have many problems with my countrymen pressing their advantage?"

It would be a bad idea to tell him that Lady Anne, herself, is responsible for pushing me into her brother's arms. "For the most part, everyone has been welcoming, and Lady Anne has been very accommodating of me and my mother since we've arrived. She is a generous mistress."

"Aye. Generous," he says with a small laugh. "She is that."

"She gave me this locket. Isn't it beautiful?" I glance down at the ornament around my neck and open it to show the treasure within. "There's a portrait of me inside. Lady Anne wants me to find a lover so I can give it to him as a token of my undying love and affection."

"Master Holbein's work."

"It is. All of the ladies have one. I confess to being quite at odds over whether I want to fall in love or not. It seems quite a painful exercise for most women of my acquaintance."

With a small, sad smile, he looks askance at Lady Anne, who is entwined in Henry's arms. "It's often painful for men, too."

"Ah, well, the course of true love never did run smooth."

He looks back at me with wide-eyed appreciation. "That's rather good. Are you a poet, too, mademoiselle? I've heard you have a clever wit."

"Not a poet on the same level of skill and talent as you are, sir. Take it. It's yours."

"Are you certain, mademoiselle? There are one or two pieces of my current work where a sentiment such as that would fit well."

"I insist."

Nico cuts in. "I can't believe you just quoted the Bard to Thomas Wyatt. What if Shakespeare never writes anything because you gave his work to Wyatt?"

"Back to work, Garcia." Fagin says, countering the intrusion. "We're on a deadline, here."

Ignoring both of them, I keep my attention on Sir Thomas. "Poetry is the language of l'amour courtois. Had you stayed in France after the royal visit to Calais, you would have done very well with my countrywomen."

"The ladies of the French court are lovely. Alas, my home is here. I don't think I could leave it for long." His gaze flits, once again, to Anne.

"I think what you are saying is that you couldn't leave the one who gave you a limning as a token of undying love and affection. Perhaps it is someone you cannot have?"

He catches on that I'm looking in Anne's direction, and bristles at the implication. He diverts his attention to the dancers, clearing his throat several times before speaking. "I have no such token from anyone, not even from my wife. She and I are...well..." he pauses and gives me a similar sideways glance, "not on good terms."

"That is a shame, sir, because you seem to be a true and loyal friend any woman would be glad to have as a lover."

His muscles grow more tense, causing his shoulders to inch up further toward his ears. He takes a deep breath. "You are very kind, mademoiselle. The woman I love is lost to me now. Sometimes we must bear our longing and pain in silence, for there is nothing else to be done."

He still loves her. This could be useful.

"Perhaps, your lost love still longs for you, too?"

"I doubt it. She now occupies a station that is so far above me, that—" he catches himself, seemingly embarrassed—or maybe fearful —that he's said too much. "It's enough to say she is lost to me. I also have the consolation that loving her has inspired my work."

"Would this love of yours have given her own limning—her token of highest love and affection—to another?" I ask. "That seems rather cruel, if she loved you at all."

"She has most certainly given that token to another. She made sure I knew of it so I would abandon hope of ever regaining her favor," he says, looking me dead in the eye. "Caesar, after all, requires his tribute."

Fagin places a hand on my shoulder and smiles widely at Sir Thomas. "Pardon, monsieur, if I may have a word with my daughter, please. I require her assistance in a matter of some urgency."

"Of course, madam." He bows his head and then addresses me. "If you're certain you no longer require my services, then I will leave you in your mother's kind and beautiful hands." He kisses Fagin's hand and then mine. He hesitates before leaving and gives me a long, deliberate look. "Before I go in search of drunken oblivion, there is one thing. May I trust your discretion, mademoiselle, to not discuss what has passed between us with anyone? There are those who would—" he tilts his chin toward his chest and runs his tongue over his top lip, "misinterpret my meaning."

"Have no fear, Sir Thomas, you may count on my discretion."

He blinks several times, takes a deep breath and nods. With a quick bow, he leaves us in search of a bottle.

"That was an interesting conversation," Fagin says, taking my elbow. "Does it mean what I think it means?"

"I think so. If Anne really gave her portrait miniature to the king in Wyatt's presence, just to make sure he knew she's a lost cause, that means the locket which was in Anne's possession earlier this evening has changed hands. Since the king isn't wearing it, there's a strong possibility that it's in his chambers right now."

Nico's voice cuts in. "It's nine forty-five. If the king retires at eleven, it means you have a little over an hour to go through both his outer privy chamber and his bedchamber. That's a lot of ground to cover."

"How many guards outside his apartments?" I ask. I'm already nonchalantly moving toward the exit.

"Two guards posted. Both looking rather bored," he says.

"I need help with them. Get your Renaissance clothes on, Nico, and bring a couple of sedative hypos. We need to put these guys to sleep for a while."

"Trevor still slaving in the kitchen?" Fagin asks.

"Yep. In for a penny, in for a pound, I guess."

"Good. Send her a message to bring more food up to the great hall. I'll keep her here in the room with me so I can keep an eye on both her and the royals. I'll let you know when Anne and Henry are on their way back."

"Roger that," Nico says.

"You don't have much time." Fagin pulls me into a hug. "Be careful."

My arms wrap around her in a fierce, quick squeeze. It's the first time she's hugged me in months. When I pull out of the embrace, I flash her a beaming smile. "Hey. It's me."

CHAPTER 17

THE PARTY in the great hall fades into faint echoes as I stride through the long gallery. The corridor is empty except for a stray pair of lovers, their silhouettes visible in the shadows of an alcove. I doubt they're paying attention to me as I make my way to the rendezvous point with Nico. Still, I'm careful to survey my surroundings as I head to the stairs leading up to the king's privy chambers.

A figure in black clothing—the ubiquitous Tudor men's gown and hose—emerges from the circular tower that houses the privy stair. I slow my steps, waiting for the newcomer to reveal themselves.

"It's me," Nico says, waving me forward. "No guards on the staircase. There are two men playing cards in the page's chambers next to the king's apartments."

"Got the hypos?" I ask, quickly closing the gap between us.

He extends his arm and hands me a small silver-colored cylinder. It has a sleek, ergonomic shape, designed to fit the contours of a human hand, and it snaps into a square head. A phial of light blue liquid is inserted into the hollow of its base. A control button within thumb's reach initiates a blast of high-pressure air that penetrates skin, delivering the drug into subcutaneous tissues, arteries, and muscles.

"What's in this cocktail?" I ask.

"Diazepam with a midazolam chaser. Knocks the subject out fast with a bit of amnesia on the side to boot. They won't remember the truck that's about to hit them."

I nod. "How many doses do we have?"

"Couple dozen per hypo unit. Unless we have to knock out every courtier in the building, we're good to go."

"Let's get to it." I step ahead of him, but he pulls me back to his side.

"Hang on. There are no surveillance cameras in the king's private chambers. Once we dispose of the guards, we'll have to clear the rooms the old-fashioned way. Stay behind me, follow my directions, and once we know there's no one else inside, I'll be out of your way fast as I can."

I touch the tips of two fingers to the corner of my eyebrow in salute. "Aye, sir."

His mouth twists into an amused smirk. "Even salutes look sarcastic on you."

"Just my natural charm and appeal, I guess. Lead on."

Nico is smooth as silk ascending the staircase; I can't hear his footfalls and I'm right behind him. On the final turn at the top of the staircase is a small landing. The door to the page's chamber is open, allowing a narrow glimpse into the room. Firelight flickers against the part of the wall I can see, bathing the entryway in an orange glow.

I can't see the occupants, but there's laughter and the heavy *thunk* of pewter tankards against the card table.

Nico makes a small circle with his right hand before pointing to the side of the arched door frame where he wants me to move; it mirrors his position on the other side of the doorway. When I'm in place, he holds up a fist. *Freeze where you are.*

He points at the doorway, then cups his hand by his ear. *Listen.*

From my vantage point, the view of the room's interior is more limited than it was at the top of the stair; one short section of wall and the outermost edge of the mantle above the fireplace are visible. Nico seems to have a better view because he holds up two fingers, confirmation of the initial surveillance camera footage. Two men occupy the room.

Only one man is enjoying the card game; he barks out a triumphant laugh as he slaps his cards down on the table. His partner groans.

"Cheat!" the loser says. "On my life, with the cards I possess, you should not have won that hand."

The loser's tone is warm and collegial, holding an edge of mock indignation that their friendly banter engenders. It's a good thing these two seem to be friends. Accusations of cheating can go pear-shaped fast and end with bloodshed.

"Would I do such a thing to my friend?" The reply is teasing, playful. "If you wish to improve your card skills, I would be happy to teach you. Until then, I shall add these coins to my pocket, unless you want another chance to lose more of your purse tonight?" There's the sound of metal scraping across wood, and the jingle of coins as the winner pockets his money.

"Next time, we play dice. I'm good at that game," the Complainer says.

Nico points to me and holds up a palm. *Stay where you are.*

He points to himself, then points into the room. *Going in.*

I give him a thumbs-up.

The friendly banter stops, and chairs push across the wood floor as Nico enters the room.

"Sirs," he says to them. "they have sent me to fetch you. Master Secretary Cromwell requires your assistance in a matter of some urgency. And—"

"What assistance does Secretary Cromwell require that would convince us to abandon our post?" the Winner of the game says. "And who are you that we should obey?"

"Am I lord over my master that I should ask him to explain his business when he sends me on an errand? If you wish to ignore Master Cromwell's command, 'tis no skin off my nose. I'm certain he'll understand your refusal to comply."

There's a shuffling of footsteps, presumably Nico's, as he moves to leave the men to their disastrous choice of ignoring an order from the king's most influential advisor. His exit is interrupted by the loser of the card game.

"Hold, sir. We will obey Master Secretary Cromwell's order." Then, to his friend, "We must go see what this matter is, and quickly observe whether his request may be fulfilled by one of us. If so, the other may return to post."

There's a short back-and-forth between them before the more cautious of the two convinces his friend that ignoring this order could cost them their heads. I hear them rise from the table and move toward the hall.

"After you, good sirs," Nico says.

The first man steps out onto the stairwell landing. He's a bald, square-shouldered man, and the smell of ale enters the hallway before he does. He catches me out of the corner of his eye too late as I lean in and press the hypo against the exposed skin of his neck above the collar.

A small, pneumatic hiss of air confirms the drug has been administered. He sways on the spot, his unfocused eyes glaze over in a dreamy state. Stumbling to the side, his back hits the wood-paneled wall and slides down the length of it. His legs splay out in front of him as he slumps to the floor like a rag doll that's been propped up in the corner.

There's a heavy thud as the page I can't see hits the deck.

Nico drags the man who collapsed in the hallway back into the room. I help him lift each man into their chairs and arrange empty tankards to make it look as though they've passed out from too much drink.

"Let's check the upper level, next," he says, maneuvering back toward the staircase. "We can work our way back down to the bedchamber. Stick right behind me until we figure out who, or what, is up there."

On the upper floor, I tuck in close behind Nico, one hand rests on his shoulder. As my torso presses against him, I feel an oddly-shaped lump positioned at the small of his back. Attached to the belt fastened around his mid-section is a black leather pouch. I've got a good idea what's inside, but let my hand stray down his back to his waist.

"You're groping the wrong side, kid." He glances over his shoulder at me. "I'm not complaining, mind you, but we're a little busy at the moment."

"Keep being sexy and you might get lucky later." My fingers trace the outline of what I know is a phaser. "Better not let Fagin know you're packing. She'll lose it." Aside from the strict rule that she doesn't work with assassins, Fagin can't stomach blood and gore. Even when she was running small-time mercenary jobs herself, before she became a Thief Master, she couldn't stand physical violence on a job. I get the feeling something went very wrong on one of her own missions, but she won't talk about it. She has seen some shit and it changed her.

"Relax," Nico says. "It's just insurance in case we don't get a solid dose of sedative into a target. It's set to stun, anyway."

"Ok. It's your ass if she finds out. Let's get this going."

We move in tight lockstep, advancing to the next door as one person.

The door to the room—it looks to be a library of sorts—is open, perpendicular to the doorframe, leaving a No Man's Land behind the door to the left and in the corner to the right.

Nico holds up three fingers, the number of steps we'll take as we shuffle forward to the entrance. When we reach the door, he moves left, I go right.

There's a small alcove over to our right with window seat shelves. Instead of floor to ceiling bookcases, there's a series of low tables and chests scattered throughout the room with stacked papers and books.

. . .

We're half-finished clearing when a heavy thud echoes from the next room. We move quickly in the direction of the sound, and hear distinct footsteps walking toward the entrance. Nico sweeps his right arm behind him, catching my shoulder. Together, we side-step toward the wall so that when the door swings open toward us, we have brief cover behind it. As long as whoever is in the other room doesn't look behind the door.

My breathing thins into shallow inhales and exhales. Nico's jaw tightens, his body's automatic response to the adrenaline that must be pumping through his veins as it does through mine. There's a thick, phlegmy cough as a man clears this throat.

Nico holds up his right hand. *Wait.*

Balancing on the balls of my feet, ready to move on Nico's word, I redirect the energy coiling in my belly into taking slow, easy, inaudible breaths. We wait for whatever is going to happen next.

The room feels stagnant, like nothing is going to move for years to come. There's a moment where the silence is almost too much to bear. Finally, a man with an athletic build ambles through the door, a book tucked under one arm. He doesn't turn around. If he had paused for even a second to glance behind him, he would've spotted us in a second.

Nico gives the signal and again we follow our established pattern. We've worked together so long, our rhythm is anchored in muscle-memory: He moves left, I go right.

Sensing too late that he's not alone, the man spins toward Nico. Before he can speak, I push the hypo against the back of his neck. His muscles stiffen and there's a whimper before his legs give out. He falls into Nico, who catches him under the arms. The man is out cold before he hits the floor.

"Meet Sir Henry Norris," I say. "The Groom of King Henry's Stool."

"What's the guy who hands the king his toilet paper doing up here in the library? Shouldn't he be turning down the king's bed and leaving little mints on his pillows?"

I pick up the leather-bound volume lying beside Norris. *The Divine Comedy.* "Reading the classics. Apparently, he's a big Dante fan. What do we do? Leave him here or drag him downstairs?"

"He stays where he is. We've got to clear the downstairs rooms. Once we're sure there's nobody else in here, you can get to work."

We move down the stairs—noting the door to the page's chamber is still closed—and into the king's inner sanctum: the suite of rooms that comprise the king's study, bedchamber, and private bath.

Nico motions toward the door just to our left, the one leading into the outer most room of the king's private apartments. Tudor palaces are a maze of public rooms. A courtier's station in life determines whether or not entry into the king's private domain will be granted. The higher up in the food chain, the more access you have to the seat of power.

These rooms are heavily guarded when the king is in residence. During a grand occasion such as tonight, there's less traffic, but it doesn't mean we won't have more company. Given that Henry Norris was perusing the upstairs library instead of the king's bedchamber, it could mean he already prepared the room for the king to retire for the night. Or it could mean Norris is slacking in his duties and has someone else performing that task. Maybe we'll get lucky and it's the former and not the latter.

The door is ajar and Nico nudges it farther open with his foot and scoots just to the edge of the door frame. I come in right behind him.

The Withdrawing Room is a personal study used by the king to entertain the most favored courtiers in a more casual environment. I'd had a few training sessions in the Sim lab set in what was supposed to be a replica of Henry's apartments, but it seems the historical holograms aren't completely accurate. Since very few other Observers have been granted entry to the king's inner sanctum, the reality of the room setup differs from the imagined furnishings of the simulation.

I'll bet Nico and I are the first Observers to get this far inside to explore in more detail. There's no time to take a historical inventory. Instead, we sweep through the rooms—including the bath and a much smaller room that looks like a personal religious chapel—as we did upstairs: moving as one synchronized, cohesive unit.

All clear.

"It's all you now, Dodger," Nico says, squeezing my forearm. "The king could come back any minute, so be careful and be quick." He considers me for a moment and then takes my face in his hands, pulling me into a mind-melting kiss filled with longing and feral heat. My breath catches in my chest at the feel of his lips and the lingering taste of the wine on him. He pulls back, smiles a lopsided grin, and says, "That's for luck."

"Damn. How am I supposed to concentrate now?"

"I have every confidence in you," he says, heading toward the exit. "I can keep a better eye on things for you back on the ship. Besides, I have to check on our dear lieutenant to see where she is. Hopefully, Fagan still has her contained in the Great Hall."

He gives me a wink and takes his leave. One side of my brain wants to stay inside that beautiful kiss and drag him to the king's bed for a little more. The other side pulls me back to the task at hand. Damn it.

Once Nico is gone, I get to work analyzing where the king might keep his most precious things.

He's a romantic.

Obsessed with Anne.

The locket is a piece of her, so he'd keep it somewhere close to him, in his most private and unguarded moments.

The bed chamber is the most logical place to start.

Moving quickly through the study, I enter his bedroom and head straight for the enormous canopied, four-poster bed. The mattress sits on a platform and boasts intricate carvings along the edges of its frame are meticulously crafted. Wood carvings that resemble animal claws adorn each of the lower corners of the platform. A lion, perhaps? Or a bear?

The canopy is fashioned from royal blue velvet, trimmed with gold tassels and intricate gold embroidery of lions' faces, perhaps to match the clawed animal feet below. It stretches halfway up the wall of the cavernous room. The ceiling must be sixty feet high if it's an inch. The bedcoverings are red silk. There's a fireplace to the left of the bed; a fire blazes in the grate. A sleeping gown is laid out on the bed.

When people say something is fit for a king, this is the scale they imagine.

The rest of the room is sparsely furnished: two small chairs and stools, padded for the occupant's comfort, a small table beside the bed, and a large wooden chest sitting in one corner.

Henry might keep a piece of Anne close to him as he sleeps, so I start with the bed and the side table first. Unlike modern furniture, there are no drawers, just an upper shelf and a bottom shelf.

No luck.

I search down between the mattress and the platform. Under the pillows. Even under the bed, as far as I can see, in case the locket might have been knocked off the table.

Nothing.

Moving methodically through the room—thoroughly searching one quadrant before moving to the next—yields no results. I have to search the entire suite.

Merde.

Where's the next most private place the king might keep the portrait?

Aside from the carnal passions he holds for Anne, the king still—at least outwardly—goes through the rituals of religious devotions. Maybe the limning is in the private devotions closet.

Inside the room, there's an altar, lit from above by a clerestory window. Instead of sunlight, only the stars are visible through the glass. A padded kneeler, the king's private prie-dieu, sits beneath a canopy made of the same electric blue velvet and thread of gold trim used on the bed.

On a nearby stool, a prayer book lies open. Sitting in the center of the binding, like a bookmark, is a rosary.

A crucifix strung with ten wooden beads. The initials HE8 and Ka are carved into either side of the largest bead.

Holy shit. Henry's rosary.

The largest bead can be opened. Gingerly, I unclasp the hinge. Inside is an intricate miniature carving of a religious scene: holy men gathered for a service; a priest at an altar, and a sinner kneeling before him.

If the portrait miniature isn't readily at hand, the next best thing is another item on the acquisition list. I pocket the rosary and keep searching.

Lifting the prayer book from the stool—Anne's locket may lay beneath it—a specific passage catches my attention. I read it out loud. "Let him kiss me with the kisses of his mouth; for thy love is better than wine."

"Still thinking about that kiss, huh?" Nico's voice is filled with swagger as he apparently misinterprets the reading as my poetic reaction to his touch.

"As kisses go, it was okay," I tease, then hold the book up so he can magnify the text on the page through the contact lens cameras. "Zoom in on this."

"King Solomon was an old smoothie, wasn't he?" he says.

"Of much greater interest is that the king reads erotic literature during his private spiritual devotions. This raises the study of his obsessions to a whole new level."

"Sex is as much a spiritual connection as a physical one." Nico pauses. "Kinda like the first time we—"

"Dodger, status?" Fagin's voice breaks into the conversation.

"Nothing, yet," I say. "How are things progressing down there? Is Trevor still with you?"

"Nope. She just left the Great Hall. Nico, do you have eyes on her?"

"Yeah, and you're not gonna like it. She's not headed back to the kitchens. She's moving in Dodger's direction."

"Oh, fuck me," I breathe out in on one long breath. "Can't anyone stop her? I don't need help up here."

"I'm pinging her on every frequency, but she's ignoring me," Nico says.

"We've got another problem," Fagin says. "I overhead the king mention some new scientific instruments he received as a gift from the Flanders ambassador. He's on his way up to his apartments to fetch a Shepherd's Dial and an equinoctial dial."

"Time to go, kiddo. Get outta there." Nico says.

"I need more time," I say, hurrying through the rest of the devotions room. No portrait.

"I've got Trevor on another frequency," Nico says, "She knows we've been keeping her out of the communications loop, and she's... annoyed. Patching her through now."

"I need more time," I repeat. "I found Henry's rosary, but still looking for the portrait."

Trevor's annoyance would better be described as fury mixed with abject scorn. "What's this? The infamous Thief of the Century is coming up empty?" she says, unforgiveness thick as venom in her tone. "Aren't you supposed to be more clever and accomplished than anyone else on the Benefactors' payroll? I think they would be sorely disappointed in your lack success finding one simple act locket."

"Trevor, I swear to God, if you don't get out of my ear. I'll—

"You'll what? I'm beginning to think you're nothing more than the pettiest of thieves who ever lived. So far, I'm not impressed."

"Do you know how tempted I am to leave your ass here when this mission is done? How do you think you'd fare among the locals with no money, power, or position to call your own?"

Trevor laughs. "Don't worry. I have backup. As a reminder," she continues, "you must produce Lady Anne's limning by tomorrow morning. The rosary won't cut it. If you don't come through, both Nico's and Fagin's families are on the chopping block."

"Good luck with that. I don't have any family," Fagin says, sounding like she could reach through the CommLink and strangle Trevor with one hand.

"What about Isabella?" Trevor asks.

There's a brief silence on the line. When she speaks, Fagin's tone changes from fury to shock. "H-How do you—?"

"You should know by now there's nothing the Benefactors don't know about you."

My brain races through all of Fagin's recruits since I've known her. I've never heard that name before. *Who the hell is Isabella?*

"Dodger," Fagin says, her breaths coming in short, fast bursts. It sounds like she's running. "The king is on the privy stair."

Fuck. He will find the unconscious men in the pages' chamber. That could bring a swarm of guards upstairs if they think it's a security breach and not an open-and-shut case of dereliction of duty.

I make it as far as the door between the bedroom and the outer chamber, before the king's voice booms through the corridor outside. There's no choice, but to hide until the king returns to the party. And just like that, I'm trapped in the toilet. Again. At least this one has an upholstered red box—with a padded seat, no less—covering the piss pot hidden within.

"What is it with you and getting stuck in the bathroom?" Nico says. "You need to find better hiding spots. At least this one looks bigger than the one at the d'Medici villa. Is that a wood bathtub in front of a fireplace in the background?"

"Do something," I hiss. "Create a distraction. Get the king out of here."

There's muffled words and shoes scuffling on the wood floor out in the king's Waiting Room, and beyond. Then there's shouting. They've found the guards, presumably still slumped in their chairs at the gaming table.

Pressing my ear against the door of bathroom, I'm startled to hear King Henry's voice so close. He's in the bedchamber.

"Send them to the tower," Henry says, his voice a deep growl. "One hundred lashes minus one for each. Teach them what happens when they fail to protect their king."

"Yes, Your Majesty." Lady Anne's father is in the room. Footsteps retreat to the other room.

I'm not sure if the king exited the room with the Earl of Wiltshire or not, so I wait.

And listen.

The only voice I hear is Becca Trevor buzzing in my ear like a mosquito. "Poor, sad, pathetic little Clémence," she chuckles. "You think you're the only human to suffer trauma and heartache?"

Nico's voice cuts in. "Unless you want me to use this hypo on you, *Trevor*, you better shut the fuck up."

Once she learned the king returned to his chambers, Trevor must've changed her mind about joining me. From the sound of it, she's back on the ship and close enough to Nico for him to make good on the threat.

"You could incapacitate me. The question you should ask yourself is what I might do to your little girlfriend if you do." Trevor says. "Don't even think of cutting off this transmission. That's an order. Because if she doesn't hear everything I have to say, this mission will get a whole lot worse for all of you."

There's a grumble from Nico. With the king so close by, I can't risk answering her perverted rant, and she knows it. She has me muzzled, and knows I have to stand here and take the abuse.

"Poor daddy murdered by the English," she says in a sing-song voice, like she's reciting the beginning of a nursery rhyme. The tone turns colder, more cruel. "Bet the fact that you have to work this mission and make nice with the butchers who eventually slaughter your family sticks so far down your craw that you're choking on it."

Trevor is the second loathsome person who knows details about me that only Fagin is supposed to know. My stomach does a free fall to my toes.

"Clémence." Nico doesn't often use my given name. When he does it's because he seriously needs my attention or wants to make a point. With this single, calm utterance of my name, he let me know that even if he can't stop this full-scale assault, he's with me, and it's comforting. "Don't listen to her."

"Trevor...please." Fagin's voice is a wounded whisper. She's still gasping for breath. From what I can gather, she hasn't yet made it back to the ship.

The lieutenant mocks her with an exaggerated whine. "Trevor, please." Then, she unleashes on me again. "What happens next? Oh, yes. You and mommy get put on a ship for the colonies and it sinks from under you. How does it feel to be an orphan all alone in this big, bad world?"

"Fucking hell, Trevor," Nico says. "What are you doing? It sounds like," he pauses. His tone shifts from questioning to accusing. "Like you're purposely trying to shove Dodger off a cliff."

Bile burns the back of my throat as I fight to keep the tears locked inside. My knees give way. I lean against the wall. Close my eyes.

Faces flash through my memory. Papa in a pool of his own blood and the Redcoat standing over him. Mama's horrified face as she's swept over the rail of the ship by a monster wave. The grim face of the ship's captain as he drags me, screaming in terror, below deck.

Trevor sounds like she's just getting started; she speaks at a faster clip, hammering each word like the final nail in a coffin. "How does it feel to know you're powerless? Impotent? Forever trapped in the living the hell the world has created for you. Hell, you can't even get out of the toilet, can you? Say the words: I'm powerless. There's nothing I can do."

I don't answer. I'm afraid if I do, a primal scream will erupt like a volcano.

"Say it, now," she repeats, biting out each word.

No.

"You have to the count of three to say it: I'm powerless. There's nothing I can do."

No. I can't.

"One..."

"You fucking bitch," Nico says.

"Maybe if I turn the screws on Nico, you'll be able to say it."

"I'm a big boy. I can handle whatever you throw at me."

"Or maybe Fagin," Trevor says. "Two."

I believe her. I believe every fucking word she says. If I don't comply, she'll hurt Fagin and Nico out of irredeemable spite.

"Last chance."

Hoarse. Drained. Defeated. I whisper the words. "I'm powerless. There's nothing I can do."

Without warning, the lever of the bathroom door turns down, and I don't have the energy to hide as it swings open leaving me face-to-face with a dumbfounded King Henry the Eighth.

CHAPTER 18

THE SHOCK on King Henry's face tells me that finding a young woman hiding in his bathroom is not an everyday occurrence. For a moment, we're both immobilized, blinking at each other like idiots.

The king glances over his shoulder, but he doesn't call out for Wiltshire or any of his guards. He looks around the stool, then back at me. "Mademoiselle?" he says, extending a tentative hand. I must look a fright because he moves like he's approaching a wounded animal. "Are you well?"

"Wh-what?"

"You look unwell."

It takes every ounce of energy I have to rise to my feet. I wobble, reel backward on my heels. The king rushes forward and grabs my elbows. He leads to the bedroom and settles me on a low stool.

Kneeling beside me, he asks, "Why are you here, child?"

"Tell him you had a fight with your mother," Nico says, realizing my brain is still rebounding from Trevor's blows. "Tell him you had to get away from the crowd."

I inhale deeply, and let out a slow breath, focusing on the king's eyes. They're soft and concerned. His strong hand encloses my small one in a firm grasp.

Nico prompts again, "You had a fight with your mother."

"There was... um..." I stumble over the words, following Nico's voice to firmer emotional ground. "I fought with my mother. I was so distraught that I had to find a quiet place to think."

Henry's eyes narrow. "You thought you would find solace in my apartments?"

"This should be good," Trevor taunts.

My mind teeters on the edge of anxiety, again, when Nico counters her jab with a right cross. "You've had your fun. One more word from you and I'll pull Dodger from the palace right fucking now."

Trevor must believe Nico's threat because she actually shuts the hell up.

"I didn't plan to come here. Once I started walking, I found myself near the stairs, so I climbed them. I found those men asleep from all the ale they'd drunk, I could smell them from the corridor."

Henry grimaces. "My sentries slept at their post?"

"I didn't realize these are your rooms until I stepped inside. When I heard you ascending the stairs and I...I panicked. I didn't know what to do. I know I shouldn't be here, but I needed a quiet place to compose myself." I don't have to act unmoored and emotionally adrift. My heart is still pounding. "I'm sorry, Your Majesty. I don't mean to trouble you. I just feel so...lost."

I lean forward and rest my head on his shoulder. He startles and, after a moment's hesitation, puts his arms around me. He pats my shoulder in a paternal manner.

Powerless. Nothing I can do.

Nico, seeming to read my thoughts, says with quiet resolve, "You are who you choose to be, babe. All that shit Trevor said, it doesn't have power unless you allow it."

"Roger," I say softly, covering the word with a snuffle against the king's silk doublet. My nose is running, and it's left a small damp spot on his chest. Henry notices and I try wiping it dry with the fore-sleeve of my gown.

"Sorry," I mumble, looking up at him.

No matter how tender he seems, Trevor is right about one thing: This king's progeny will rain violence and bloodshed not just on my parents, but on millions.

Nico's right, too. I'm not powerless unless I choose to be. In this moment, sitting with the king of fucking England, I see opportunity in a new light. *What if I could change everything? What if I could change the whole bloody world?*

"You've been so kind, Your Majesty," I say, turning the grief in my eyes to coquettish desire. "Allow me to return the kindness." I lean forward and brush my lips against his.

"Hey!" Nico says, alarmed. "What the hell was that?"

Henry emits a small, muffled sound of protest, grasps my shoulders, and gently pushes me away. "Mademoiselle, please don't mistake gentle concern for romantic intent."

"Forgive me, Your Majesty, but there was a moment, downstairs, when a look passed between us. You wanted me."

He looks puzzled. Then there's a small, surprised. "Oh."

There it is. The memory of lust.

"No, Mademoiselle," he says, giving me a gentle smile. "You misunderstand."

I didn't, of course, because he's glossing over the leer he threw my way at the banquet table. I play along and shake my head, looking slightly distressed. "Your eyes tell me that I perfectly understood your intent, sire. 'Twas desire that I saw in you."

"There was a time when I would have plucked you out from among the many roses in my court," he says, tucking a stray lock of hair behind my ear. "You are beautiful and clever, the wittiest of any lady here in my court save my own sweet Anne." He tugs upward on a black cord fastened around his neck and, up from the neck of his shirt, pops a silver locket.

I'll be damned.

He unties the cord and pulls it from his neck so he can open the clasp. Inside is Lady Anne's limning. "You do know that my heart belongs wholly, completely to the future queen." The words are kindly said; he seems to think I'll be crushed by his rejection.

He lifts my chin and wipes the tear from my cheek. With the other hand, he drops the locket into a leather pouch, leaving it's flap unsecured. "You protested against needing a husband. After this encounter, I'm not swayed from the opinion that you do. A husband would soothe your melancholy and divert your mind to more pleasant things."

"I will look to your good graces in supplying everything I need, Your Majesty." *Including the trinket in your pocket.*

"Good girl," Henry says, brushing a finger across the tip of my nose. "Make peace with your mother and all will be well. I will speak to my sweetheart about finding you a husband."

"Again, Your Majesty is very kind."

"Come, let's rejoin the banquet, and I will find you as many handsome, virile dance partners as you can stand."

I let him lead me back to the Great Hall and before we enter, I stop and pull him to face me. "I'm grateful for your kindness and discretion. I am forever in your debt." Biting my lip like a schoolgirl, I throw an arm around his broad shoulder and kiss his cheek. He's thrown slightly off-balance against my inertia, and he laughs before extricating himself from the embrace. He bows and I curtsey in return.

"If you're done playing footsie with the king," Trevor says in a brittle tone, sounding galled that I wasn't tossed into the Tower with the sleeping guards. "Are you going to do something about the limning the king has in his pocket?"

Leisurely strolling into the great hall, right behind King Henry, I cast a discreet glance downward. The LensCam rest on the portrait miniature tucked securely in my palm before stowing it in the pocket sown into the side-seam of my kirtle.

Nico sighs. "Damn, you're good."

Trever offers a disgruntled snort in response.

"Now, if you'll excuse me," I say, "the king has commanded me to dance."

Sometime after midnight, I stroll back to the ship. Everyone has waited up for me. Nico, his athletic frame more relaxed than I've seen him in days—no doubt the result of smashing Trevor's deadline and releasing the tension of the last few hours—sits in the crew lounge with Fagin and Trevor. All have abandoned their Tudor clothing for more comfortable, utilitarian apparel.

Nico wears jeans and a black *QUEEN* t-shirt—the night we spent together after that concert in Budapest still makes my heart skip a beat. "We Will Rock You" indeed. Both Fagin and Trevor wear loose black athletic pants and long-sleeved hoodies.

Nico pulls me into a tight embrace, kisses my check, and whispers against my ear, "You're gonna give me a fucking heart attack one of these days. You know that, right?"

Nico doesn't immediately release me, so Fagin leans over and squeezes my shoulder, then sweeps a finger across my brow, like she did when I was little. "Good job, kiddo."

Only Trevor is caustic in the face of my triumph; she looks like she just swallowed battery acid. She leans a hip against an adjacent club chair and glares at me.

Nico, one arm still around my shoulder, points an accusatory finger at Trevor and, if his expression is any indication of his intent, looks ready to tear into her. I give him a quick squeeze and shake my head. Nico backs off, giving me room to run.

There's nothing sweeter than proving a douchebag wrong. I keep my eyes on the lieutenant as I pull the first item slowly out of my pocket, bead by fucking bead.

Henry's rosary.

I lower it slowly, letting it coil in a spiral on the melamine surface of the dining booth table. It is an ancient spiritual relic, after all. Or will be in a few hundred years. It deserves to be treated with care.

Trevor's eyelids flutter, perhaps in exhaustion—or irritation— and she tilts her head to one side. Her eyes narrow as her gaze flits down toward my pocket then back up to my eyes.

She doesn't wait well.

Pulling Lady Anne's limning from my pocket, I let the gleaming silver locket—adorned with the raised initials "AB"—dangle at the end of the black cord. Trevor reaches out for it, and I pull it back just out of her grasp.

"Let me make something clear: If you continue threatening Nico and Fagin, or ever talk about my family, again, I *will* kick your ass so hard they'll feel it back home. Then, I'll strand you here. I'll shove you so deep undercover that an Observer team could search for centuries and still not find you."

"Big words from a—"

"Look in my eyes and tell me if you think I'm bluffing."

She stares at me, wide-eyed, and finally blinks.

"Say it: I believe you'll kick my ass and strand me here."

She laughs, and I shove her into the wall so hard that her head hits the paneling with a solid *thunk*. For good measure, I put my knee into her groin and press my forearm into her windpipe just enough to get her attention. "You want war? Get ready because it'll be ugly and bloody, and you'll wish you'd never even heard my name. Keep threatening people I love, and I'll start fucking with people closest to you."

"Dodger," Fagin says. "Enough."

We stand toe-to-toe for a few moments longer before I step back. Trevor extends her arm, palm up—there's a slight tremor in her pinky finger.

"Not until you say it," I say, still dangling the necklace just out of reach. "Say: I believe you'll kick my ass and strand me here."

No answer.

I begin to count. "One."

She swallows and says in a low growl. "I believe you'll kick my ass and strand me here."

"Good," I say, in as patronizing a tone as I can manage. I drop the portrait miniature into her outstretched hand. "We understand each other. If you're smart, you'll agree there can only be mutually assured destruction in a private war between us. Detente is the best we can hope for, I guess."

"Next time—" Trevor begins, her voice thick with what sounds like either anger or humiliation. Probably both.

"If you're smart, there won't be a 'next time,'" I reply.

She snatches the rosary from the table and deposits both it and the limning into a velvet pouch. She turns on her heel and strides off in the direction of her quarters.

The tension rooted in my neck and shoulders feels excruciating. I roll my head from side to side, trying to release it. Fagin comes up behind me kisses me on the cheek.

"Crisis averted, this time. That was a helluva job, kid," she says. "And that was quite a your little speech was quite a bluff."

"I wasn't kidding." I say. "I'm not living through the rest of this mission with Trevor's brand of torture. I can't do it, Fagin."

She gives me a look. "I know." She nods at Nico, then drifts toward her own quarters. "Get some sleep. We've got a long way to go yet."

Nico settles on the small sofa catty-corner to the dining booth and gestures to the space on the floor in front of him. "I could help you get out of that costume if you want."

I give him a cock-eyed smile and plop myself down on the floor in front of him, my gown pooling around my crossed legs in ripples of green silk. "I'll settle for one of your infamous massages, if you don't mind."

His fingers are magic, and that's not an overstatement. Within minutes, he has worked his will on the knots in my shoulders and neck until they melt beneath the heat and pressure of his hands. I groan and roll my head forward, eager for this delicious release to flow further up the back of my neck.

"Not to spoil the mood, but," Nico says, the hesitation obvious in his voice, "what Trevor said. I'll listen if you want to talk about it."

"I know."

"It's just—and don't take this the wrong way, I'm not pressuring you into talking about what happened to your parents—but, I don't understand why she would go after you so vehemently about something so painful and personal from your past. I mean, that kind of fuck-with-your-head bullshit is more likely to make you screw up than encourage high performance. Why would she do something like that?"

"She a narcissistic freak who likes messing with people's heads." I say, leaning forward so he can reach further down my back. "She's not living rent-free in mine anymore."

"Just tell me there's nothing else going on here." He stops massaging, lets his fingertips rest on my shoulder blades. "There was a whole lot more beneath the surface of her tirade."

I glance back at him. "Like what?"

"I dunno. All that talk about not being able to save your parents. Just tell me you're not thinking anything crazy."

Oh God. Does he know something? "Define crazy."

"Crazy like, changing a fixed point in time that could impact the future."

Nervous, now, that he actually can read minds, I scoot forward out of his reach and struggle with my gown. "What the hell gave you that idea?"

"I don't know, it was weird how she kept pushing you to say there's nothing you can do. It sounded like she was goading you into something."

"That's ridiculous." I turn away, but he catches my arm and pulls me close to him.

"You know the penalty for meddling with history. At best, your memory is wiped, and you get a one-way ticket to the Hotel Prison

Planet. At worst, you're executed. Clémence, please." He takes my face in his hands, again, but this time instead of a kiss, I get eyes that are sober and pensive. "Promise me you're not going to fuck with the timeline."

I blow off his concern with a soft *pffft*, but he knows it's not agreement.

"Dodger!"

"I'm not going to fuck with the timeline," I say, more forcefully than intended. "Yes, I hate colonizers. I want them to pay for decimating my family two hundred years from now. But I'm not stupid enough to risk a memory wipe or death. I just want to finish this damn job and go home, okay?"

"Okay," he replies. He chews his lower lip, then gestures at my neck. "I can finish the massage."

"Later," I say, suddenly exhausted from the stress. I don't like lying to Nico about something between the two of us. It makes my stomach queasy.

"I'm gonna turn in, too."

Once in my cabin, I sit in the dark staring at a blinking cursor on a blank computer screen. The replicator will create the aged parchment and replicate quill strokes to perfection. My fingers tremble as I type the words that will change everything; an incantation that will speak into a different world into existence. It will restore what I've lost. It will set things right.

My Dearest Thomas,

I weep for our lost love as I prepare to marry the king. I beg you, do not exile me from your heart. I could not bear it if you do. Please, my dearest, do not abandon me in my hour of need.

Your Faithful and Loving Servant,

Anne

CHAPTER 19

LIKE LIVING in the pit of hell, Beelzebub's fire roasting my immortal soul for all eternity: That's the best way to describe every moment I've endured since the day this mission bomb dropped. After all of Fagin's scolding about keeping the tightest rein on my temper, I'm livid to discover that keeping even the tiniest embers of a revenge quest smoldering is a laborious, patience-defying task.

It's been several weeks since I stole the limning, which caused quite a commotion at court when Henry ordered an extensive search of courtiers' chambers. Given that the locket is safely stowed on our ship, it will remain an unsolved mystery. The king has already commissioned another limning of Anne from Master Holbein.

Things have settled somewhat since.

Except that I've been unable to plant the letter in the king's apartments.

Christmas is a few days away. With the flurry of activity, and the increase in courtiers arriving at court for the holiday, there has been time to sneak back into Henry's chambers.

It's risky. I got lucky the last time I snuck into Henry's apartments. I'm not so sure I'd get a merciful response from the king if I infiltrated his inner sanctum a second time.

Implementing Plan B—getting the fake letter into the hands of Anne's enemies, so one of them can deliver it to the king—is riskier. If it falls into the wrong hands and it's traced back to me, I could find myself locked up in the tower or worse.

Charles Brandon—a staunch supporter of Queen Katherine—could be trusted, but he has spent more time at his residences than with the king because he despises Lady Anne. Any way you look at it, once the letter is out of my hands, I lose control. There'd be no telling when—or even if— the letter might make its way to the king. Better to bide my time and figure out a way to plant the letter myself.

Waiting to deliver this damn letter is hard enough, but the prospect of sitting through one more sewing circle with these simpletons the pretender queen calls her royal ladies-in-waiting is maddening. If I'm forced to take part in that charade much longer, the only escape from the agony will be wrapping my fingers around each of their puny necks, squeezing until their eyes bulge, and the last of their pathetic, worthless breaths escapes their lips and—

Jesus. Where did that come from?

In the back of my mind, there's an uncomfortable twinge; a moment's tortuous hesitation as I let the warning bell in my brain stall the race toward the line I plan to cross. My patience, though thin as a silkworm's cache, must coalesce into stone-cold resolve to get this job done.

The war between my better and darker angels is in full swing:

You'll be on the run forever if you do this. What about Nico? And Fagin?

They killed your parents and sold you into servitude. Just plant the damn letter and be done with it. You'll be doing history a favor.

I run a finger back and forth around the outline of the folded page that's been tucked into my pocket for weeks. There's a sharp twinge on my index finger; I've run against the paper's edge at the perfect angle for a paper cut. When I withdraw my hand from my pocket, there's a tiny pearl of blood on my fingertip. I suck it clean and let the pain—insignificant compared with the pain in my gut—feed the revenge-rage like a wellspring.

Setting the scenario where Henry thinks she's in love with Wyatt should result in banishment to a nunnery. Even sending her home to Hever Castle, never to lay eyes on her again, would be enough to keep her from conceiving the queen who destroys my world.

I can't remember a time when I wasn't at war with the world. This act could soothe the Valkyrie riding me. If I'm lucky, peace will follow.

What if it doesn't? What if it costs you everything?

I can do this. I could save Papa and Maman and bring them into the future with Fagin, Nico, and me. The thought of my family restored and safe, as though their deaths never occurred, pulls a lump of emotion into my throat.

No time for sentimentality. I shake my head to clear the fog; there will be time for tears later, when I have them all together.

Resigned to the fate of yet another exhausting needlework circle, the ladies-in-waiting entourage—strutting through the corridors like peacocks—follow Lady Anne to her apartments. Fagin's skirts swish with the rhythm of her walk as she follows me. The rest of the ladies are close behind us.

Anne and her sister, Mary, lead the pack, chattering away like a couple of hens in a barnyard. They enter the staircase first. Coming down the staircase, carrying a tray of wine goblets, is Becca Trevor—again, dressed as a servant boy. Our eyes meet and she give me a smarmy smile.

Lady Anne pauses on the stair, one foot on the next tread, and tosses a bright smile over her shoulder at me as she massages her flat belly.

What an odd thing for her to do.

"I have such a furious hankering for apples," she says, laughing. "The king says—"

Like a lightning strike from a cloudless sky, a masked figure in a black cloak tears down the stairs. It moves so fast it's hard to imagine its feet are touching the ground at all. Lady Anne doesn't have time to look up.

Even for those of us who manipulate its fabric, time is a quirky, unsettled thing. It has a funny way of speeding up or slowing down when traumatic events snatch the rug out from under you. I'm not sure how much time passed. What felt like forever was probably only seconds.

The assailant tucks chin to chest as he drives a black-cloaked shoulder into Mary Boleyn's right side with enough force to make her teeter on the stair's edge before she spills backward, arms wind milling in a useless attempt to keep herself upright.

Mary crashes into Madge and there's a sickening crunch of bones as momentum and gravity tumble them down the stairs like a pair or dominoes. I push Grace Parker and Anne Saville, both rigid with shock, out of my way, trying to get to Fagin. Screams erupt as people realize what's was happening.

Fagin pushes Jane Seymour to the bannister and lunges forward, grabbing fistfuls of Anne's kirtle to keep her from taking a disastrous backwards nosedive over sprawled bodies. Lady Jane Rochford backpedals away from the scene. When she realizes I'm standing between her and safety, she shoves me with both hands.

I fall into the path of the would-be assassin, who vaults over me, and the last two stairs.

Scrambling to my feet, I look up at Fagin.

"I have her!" She cradles a whimpering Anne in her arms. "Go!"

Hiking my skirt to my knees, I bolt through the gallery after the retreating figure, who slams through several older women, knocking them to the ground. The attacker doesn't slow, but keeps on at full sprint, even in heavy black boots.

The figure deftly maneuvers around the next corner without sliding and bursts through the terrace doors leading to the gardens.

The slick checkerboard stone floors of the palace are the polar opposite of the cinder racetrack that Nico and I use for our training: no traction at all. I'd give anything to be wearing track shoes instead of these lame satin slippers that send me skidding past the corner when I reach it.

I stumble into more courtiers and disentangle myself before racing outside.

The broad-shouldered figure sprints through the gardens toward the large pond hosting a pair of swans, pausing briefly to look behind him several times as he goes. His cloak flaps around the ankle-length black pants he wears.

Pants *not* of this century.

"Nico, this guy is not a local. Did you see his pants?" I say, gasping as I dash toward the retreating figure. If not for the pre-mission physical training, running while costumed in thirty pounds of Tudor regalia would would border on impossible. "Any outside cameras in this area?"

"Dodger," Fagin's hoarse whisper breaks into the conversation. "Are you sure he's not a local?"

"His clothing isn't of this time period."

"Dodger," Nico says. "There here are two cameras in the rose garden to your right and several in the trees down the path toward the meadow."

"I lose sight of him every time he takes a turn through the gardens. You're likely to see him before I do if he tries to sneak around to the left."

"I don't know about that. He seems to slow down long enough to let you catch up to him a little bit."

True to Nico's assessment, the assailant pauses at the next corner of the terrace and glances back at me before continuing on.

"All right, asshole," I say. "Let's see what you've got."

By the time I land on the ground-level promenade, there isn't another person in sight except for the would-be assassin. Gasping for breath, I spin around and around, looking for the next direction, some clue as to the route Anne's failed executioner has taken.

"Nico, where is he?"

"He ducked behind that grove of bushes over to your left. I didn't see him come around the other side, so he could be waiting for you to move past him. Move around to your right and come up behind him on the other side."

A flash of multi-colored light streaks upward from behind the bushes.

"Is it me or did that flash of light look like a transporter beam?" I poke my head around the leading edge of the shrub.

Nothing.

"Maybe. I don't know," Nico says. "I don't have a camera on that side of the bushes. But, the long-range camera from the West side of the garden would've picked up anyone running out from behind that greenery, no matter which direction they were headed. And it should pick up a transport in progress, too."

There are voices shouting near the palace; the king's guards are joining the pursuit.

A multi-color beam of light—it looks like a rainbow filtering down through the barren tree branches—appears down a stone path a few dozen meters away. The light shifts between green and blue until a steady blue light comprised of all-too-familiar energy fractals emerges.

Merde.

"Definitely a transporter beam." I say, trying to steady my breathing.

"Yep, and it's not one of us. Both Fagin and Trevor are onsite with you," Nico says.

The dark-clad figure materializes from within the light and stands next to a knight-shaped topiary.

"Seems Trevor's not bullshitting about having backup," Nico says.

The failed slayer's arms are raised, stretched wide as though welcoming my pursuit.

A subtle gesture from the gloved hand urges me closer. My steps are slow as I scan the garden for anyone else who might also have seen the attacker appear out of thin air.

Judging from the volume of the shouting, the king's guards are closing in, but they're probably too far away to have witnessed what they would surely have deemed as witchcraft.

The figure stands, unmoving and silent. As I get closer, I get my first good look at the mask: a full-face black leather executioner's hood with slits for the eyes and mouth, making the features of the one beneath it undistinguishable.

The cloaked one stands as rigid as the stone statues lining the path on either side of me. I close more than half the distance between us when the transporter haze reappears like a halo emanating from within the figure itself.

The air vibrates with a faint hum, and the transporter light grows brighter. A sideways cock of the head, then the assassin waggles a few fingers at me in farewell.

Oh no, you fucking don't. A primitive snarl explodes into a howl as I sprint toward him. My fingertips brush the billowing cloak flapping in the breeze.

A final lunge forward and, instead of grappling with the attacker, I collide with thin air.

A patch of loose gravel pitches me headfirst into a half-frozen mud hole. My kirtle rips as my knees and hands plunge through the surface layer of ice and grind into the layer of rock beneath it. My chin hits the ground with a bone-jarring *thunk* that makes my ears ring.

I crawl out of the slurry. Splotches of blood stretch across the raw, shiny wounds on my palms, and I feel the sting of the same broken skin on my kneecaps.

We've been playing defense with Trevor for too long, and now there are more Observers on the ground as her backup. Who knows how many of them there are? Whatever else is going on with this shit show, one thing is painfully clear: This mission isn't just about teaching me a lesson for going rogue with the side jobs on other jobs.

My stomach churns as I march past the palace guards who are still searching the grounds for the attacker.

Courtiers gape at the sludge smeared on my torn clothes and dripping from my chin. I take the stairs two at a time, on my way to the queen's apartments where hysterical cries echo through the corridors.

Fagin spots me as I enter, ragged and bloody, into Anne's bedchamber. Her eyes go wide and she extricates herself from Anne's frantic grasp. I motion to the outer chamber and she follows.

"What the hell is going on?" Fagin asks. "We're supposed to be the only mercs here."

"Not anymore," I say. "Looks like the Benefactors sent Trevor reinforcements."

"Reinforcements to do what? We just watched an attempted assassination on Anne Boleyn by a time traveler," Fagin says. She paces, wild-eyed and on the verge of hyperventilating. "We've just entered a whole new realm of disastrous complications. We'll have government agents breathing down our necks before too long."

"That's probably a good bet," Nico says, in a chagrined tone. I picture him rubbing the back of his neck the way he does when he's embarrassed or flustered. "That data feed wasn't jammed. I'm sure we broadcast it back home."

"Can we trace the attacker back to his ship? They've got to have a transport around here somewhere," I say.

"I'm tracing the transporter's sub-space signature. It's very faint, so I don't know if I can pinpoint their location or not. Maybe I can get close enough that our geo-probes can pick up any other energy pulses that might indicate a camouflaged ship."

"This is bad," Fagin says, still pacing. "Really bad."

"Calm down," I say, still shaking from the encounter with the assassin. "You've told me a million times, getting flustered is a waste of energy."

Fagin looks at me like I have three heads. "Flustered? Someone tried to kill a key historical figure years before she's supposed to die.

I'm way past 'flustered,'" She stops pacing and glares at me. "Why aren't *you* more upset?"

In the last few months, I've seen sides of Fagin I never knew existed. My once-unflappable mentor is slipping into increasingly agitated and paranoid states. The Fagin before me now is terrified, bordering on unhinged.

"I am upset." I say. *Just not in the same way you are.* I want to say those words aloud. But if I do, the whole sorry mess will pour out of me.

CHAPTER 20

"I THOUGHT the government put a lid on intertemporal assassinations," Nico says when we return to the ship. "Once the GTC gets wind of this, there'll be so many Observers on the ground, we won't be able to tell the locals from the time travelers."

"Are you sure the data feed of the chase in the garden got through?" I ask.

"I filter as much as I can, especially when you guys are somewhere you shouldn't be. But if there are too many unexplained breeches in communication feeds and protocols, there's a metric fuckton of questions to answer when we get home. It's better to let the mundane feeds go through with no interference. Going up the stairs after dinner was supposed to be a mundane event."

"So no filter?" I ask.

"No filter," he confirms.

The best- and worst-case scenarios for swarms of Benefactor proxies sent to evaluate the situation plays in my head. Whether or not this staircase incident stays a curious blip on the radar or explodes into a full-blown investigation, the assault on Anne complicates things.

If the assassin wasn't Trevor, then who the hell was it?

I'm so caught up in my own head, I hear only part of Fagin's question. "—frame the attack as court intrigue by the anti-Boleyn faction?" She rubs her chin.

"Nope," Nico says. "The broadcast feed included the attacker's transporter sequence. The assassin is a time traveler."

Fagin blows out a sharp exhale. "Nico, keep a Comm channel open to see if you can pick up GTC's chatter. Let us know if you find anything on the transporter signal. Maybe we'll get lucky and pinpoint their location so we can figure out who the hell they are."

"Aye, sir."

"Got eyes on Trevor?"

"She's in the kitchens scrubbing pans."

There's a sharp cry from Anne's bedroom. Fagin and I rush into the room to find her ladies propping her up in a cloud of pillows. They arrange her like she'll break if they move her the wrong way. Mary Boleyn, busy stuffing a pillow behind Anne's head, catches sight of me. "Mademoiselle, has the doctor arrived? My sister's injuries must be treated."

"Not yet, my lady. I'm sure he will be here soon."

Anne pushes herself higher on the pillows, wincing from the effort. The pinched expression relaxes when she spots me. "Clémence, come."

My feet feel like they're encased in lead. The last place I want to be is anywhere near this bed. I take a full minute to drag myself to her side.

"How are you, my lady?" I ask.

Anne strokes her belly. "All will be well. I'm sure of it. I am forever grateful for your bravery. You and Madam Fagin saved my life."

Fuck me. Did I just become her hero?

Tears slide down Anne cheeks. The ladies-in-waiting huddle closer, their comforting tones mingling with Anne's whispered prayers for a male heir.

If I don't plant this letter fast, I'll lose my nerve and any chance of saving my family.

Extricating myself from Anne's grasp, I say, "My lady, allow me to fetch the doctor. He is too long in coming."

Anne keeps my hand in her grasp and pulls me toward her. She plants a kiss on my cheek. Reflexively, I pull back and brush my fingertips across the spot, still warm from her breath.

"Soon, I will bear the king an heir. He will be his father's son and sit on the throne one day." Her voice cracks with emotion. "We have you to thank for it."

Swallowing hard, I push myself to stand on quivering legs and somehow drop a curtsey without falling over. "Your servant, madam," I say, then gesture toward Fagin and the exit. "With your permission, I will fetch the doctor."

She nods, gratitude spilling down her cheeks.

By the time Fagin and I reach the corridor, the Wyatt letter feels as heavy in my pocket as a millstone around my neck. Its gravitational pull dragging me down. In my other pocket, a sedative hypo spray in case I run into guards in the king's apartments and a small data pad to send instructions to the ship's computer. One tap on the display and Betty will run the looped video file in my LensCam feed so Nico thinks I'm anywhere but in King Henry's chambers.

If I don't plant this letter today, I'll never do it.

By the time we reach the Great Hall, where lower-ranking courtiers linger over their meals, Fagin has quickly outpaced me. When she realizes I'm not behind her, she stops and turns back, joining me as I stand near the fireplace.

"Is there a problem?"

"I told Lady Anne I would fetch a doctor," I say, careful to keep my voice steady. Fagin looks me up and down, then tilts her head as she meets my eyes. *She's looking for something. Keep it together.* "Are you starting to like her?"

"Are you kidding?" I feign disgust. The truth is: I'm beginning to feel something warm towards Lady Anne. I wouldn't go so far as to label it liking her. "No. If the doctor doesn't show up, I don't want him telling the king or Lady Anne that I never spoke to him. I'll get to the ship as fast as I can."

Her eyes narrow and she considers me a moment longer. "Don't take long. Doesn't sound like whatever Nico wants us to see can keep." She pauses when she spots something over my shoulder. "Uh-oh."

When I turn to see the cause of her exasperation, I'm greeted by the sight of Becca Trevor clearing dishes from the tables. Trevor casts furtive, smirking glances in our direction like she has more nasty secrets she's just dying for us to find.

"Go on," I say. "Get back to the ship. I won't be long."

I wait until Fagin's out of sight, then slip from the room when Trevor's back is turned. Once in the corridor, I take the data pad out of my pocket and tap the video loop file.

"Dodger?" Nico's says, concerned. "Your LensCam feed just flickered off and back on. You okay?"

"Yeah. Probably just a glitch." Another lie to add to the first one.

"Get back to the ship and we'll have a look. You might need a new pair."

"Be there soon. I have to find the doctor."

"Roger," Nico replies.

Without another word, I mute the CommLink mic, too.

Two guards—both new to court—stand watch at the king's chamber door. I flash my most alluring smile. "Is this where they hide court's most handsome men? Sentry duty?"

They puff up their chests, reveling in my attention, yet somewhat wary of an unaccompanied woman's presence outside the king's apartments.

"I have a message for the king," I say. "From Lady Anne."

The beefier of the two narrows his eyes. "None but the king or his counselors are allowed in his chambers without permission. If you give the message to me, I will give it to the king."

Fat chance, buddy.

I slip the letter out of my pocket and hold it up. "Surely, we can make an exception for love's messenger. The letter bears Lady Anne's seal and she told me to place it in the king's prayer closet myself. If I can count on you to help complete this task, I would be ever so..." I walk my fingers up the beefy man's chest as I speak, and brush my index finger across the tip of his nose. "...grateful to you."

The men exchange wary looks. The skinnier of the two gives an apologetic shrug. "We have our orders, my lady. You cannot enter unaccompanied."

"Then, there is the way for me to complete my task and for you to obey your orders. If you escort me inside, then I won't be unaccompanied, will I?"

They still look hesitant, so I play the ace with my most doleful expression. "Our future queen will be displeased if I fail her, and it would be most unfortunate if they placed any blame on your shoulders for my failure."

The beefy man shakes his head and, just as I reach into my pocket for the hypo spray, he unlocks the king's door. "I will escort you, my lady. I am Cupid's most humble servant." He smiles at me and ushers me into the king's apartments.

Nico's warning rings in my ears. I could have philosophical conversations with myself for the next year about morality and the terrible responsibility we have to keep time in its place, and still come back to the same conclusion: Having my parents alive is worth the risk of a one-way ticket to a prison planet.

With trembling hands, I place the letter on the padded rail of the small kneeler in the king's prayer closet. "Gotcha," I say, softly.

"I beg your pardon, mademoiselle?" Beefy man says, confused.

"Nothing. Thank you for your help," I reply, and kiss his cheek before slipping into the corridor and down the privy stairs.

The whole thing took less time than I thought—who knew the guards would be willing accomplices in the name of love—but it was still too long an absence for Fagin.

Her voice booms in my ear. "Dodger?"

"On my way," I say, as I sprint down the corridor.

"Get a move on, kid. Nico found the transporter signature, and he's got a clip of the assailant, unmasked. You need to see this."

When I get to the ship, I find Fagin and Nico wound tighter than a three-day clock.

"Look. Right there," Nico says, projecting the three-dimensional hologram image onto the small conference table in the ready room.

A three-inch-tall image bolts through the winter-decayed landscape of Greenwich Palace's gardens. The figure is clad in black, head-to-toe. His face is visible, in profile, and is covered in black. Behind him, a swirl of russet-colored taffeta and me in hot pursuit.

"John Wilkes Booth, I presume?" I ask, feeling the same sense of frustration I did when I chased him through the gardens for real.

"Booth was a successful assassin," Fagin replies. "Our guy isn't." She pauses. "Can we increase the image quality?"

"A bit." Nico moves a spare window with sweep of his hand, then zooms the video footage screen with a reverse pinch motion and the image expands. "Magnifying image one hundred percent."

While the resolution is somewhat pixelated, the shape of the executioner's mask is identifiable. "That's our man," I say.

There's a shaft of brilliant multi-color light and a shot of me plowing through swirling mist just after the attacker disappears. The next shot is a flying blur that lands in a half-frozen mud puddle.

Nico air taps the rewind command and the scene backtracks to the frame where the figure disappears in a haze of light and I land in the mud puddle. He rewinds again and again until it's just me vaulting into the muck.

"Seriously?" My deadpan response must be hysterical because Nico belly laughs himself into tears.

Even Fagin cracks a smile. "It is entertaining to watch. You're quite graceful flying through the air." She tilts her head to one side and peers at the holographic version of me lying face-down in the mud. "Do you know how many credits a good mud bath costs back home? You're getting one for free."

Nico wipes tears from his cheeks. "Would you rather be known for always getting trapped in the toilet on missions or this heroic action shot of diving into the mud?"

"Can we stop relieving my blooper reel and get to the point? We know the assailant transported out of there, but where did he go?"

"Computer, trace the transporter signal embedded in hologram file 1532.SOL142," Nico says. "Display geographic visual in tabletop configuration." He glances up at me and taps out a few more commands on the display screen. "This camera is several miles from the location where the transporter signature ends. It's gonna be a little grainy and unfocused, but I'll dial the resolution in the best I can."

The hologram shifts scene to the middle of a barren field. Nico and Fagin exchange glances and give me expectant looks, like I'm supposed to know what I'm looking at.

"He transported to an empty cow pasture?" I ask, confused.

"Wait for it," Nico says.

A few seconds later, light flashes in the emptiness as vegetation the width of a narrow door slides open to the right. The image is more pixelated than the assassin's figure in the previous file, but visible inside what looks like a gaping wound in the countryside is the vestibule of a time pod.

Shadows move just inside the entryway of the other ship. A few seconds later, one shadow moves through the door and emerges into the sunlight. It's a male figure—light-haired, broad shouldered, walks with a bit of a swagger. He moves around the perimeter of the ship—

one of many physical camouflage-checks a time flight crew performs during the day—and Nico zooms in for a better look.

The backside of his head— a mop of curly blond hair—comes into sharp focus and I know exactly who it is before his gaze moves up toward the sky and back down again. The last time I saw this asshole was on the De Medici job when he ragged on me for screwing with his retirement with one breath and offered to be my father figure with the next.

Merde. Jackson Carter—the rat-bastard ex-commander who put me in this shitty situation in the first place—is on the scene and working with that psycho, Becca Trevor.

This is bad. Really fucking bad.

CHAPTER 21

"FAGIN. Dodger. Get up here now. We've got a big problem," Nico's voice booms over the CommLink speakers in my quarters, waking me from a dead sleep.

It takes a few minutes before I'm lucid enough to do anything more than groan at the intrusion. "Computer, time check," I say, croaking the words out. My throat feels like I've been walking in a desert all night. "And what the hell is wrong with Nico?"

"The time is Zero-Five-Thirty." The computer's soothing feminine tone is more sedative than energetic motivation to climb out from under my pillow. "Commander Garcia's heart rate and respiration are elevated, indicating he is—"

"Computer, shut up." I'm not looking for a laundry list of Nico's vital signs.

"Dodger!" Nico says again, his voice more urgent.

I groan. "On my way."

Last night, we spent several hours combing through the footage Nico had pieced together from several long-range cameras, to figure out how many backups Trevor has on the scene.

I couldn't concentrate. The emotional and physical exhaustion only intensified as the night wore on. Somewhere south of two o'clock, Fagin ordered me to bed—dozing at the conference table and drooling on the tabletop is a breach of etiquette she can't stomach—even though we still hadn't seen hide nor hair of Trevor in the surveillance footage.

If I dreamt at all, I don't remember, but it must've been a restless night. The sheets are twisted around me, and I feel as though the scant three hours of sleep have drained my energy more than not sleeping at all would have done.

There's a sharp rap on my door. "Dodger, let's go," Fagin says.

Five minutes later, both Fagin and I slouch in chairs in the Ready Room peering at a tabletop hologram image paused in mid-action: Lady Anne exiting the palace, flanked by two of King Henry's guards. "This better be good," I say. "I haven't even had coffee yet."

Nico paces the room. He chews the skin on the side of his thumb and his eyes never leave the hologram.

Fagin stares at the image. "What are we looking at?"

"Lady Anne on her way to the tower," he says in a dry, matter-of-fact tone.

"She's not supposed to move to the queen's apartments in the tower until her coronation," Fagin replies. She shoots Nico an annoyed look that asks: *You woke us up for this?*

"She's been checking the place out for the last few days. Henry's been refurbishing the rooms, and she wanted to get a good look at the progress," I reply.

"This footage is hot off the presses." Nico checks the time. "Like, fifteen-minutes-ago hot." He works the hologram control panel and the image springs to life again, this time in reverse; he rewinds back to the moment they roused Anne from her sleep.

Thomas Howard, the Duke of Norfolk and Anne's uncle, stands in her privy chamber waiting for the ladies-in-waiting to finish dressing her before she can receive him. When she emerges, still half-asleep and dazed, he wastes no time getting to the point. "My Lady Marquess, I am sent by the king to arrest you on the charge of seducing his royal majesty away from his lawful wife by means of witchcraft."

Fagin and I exchange wide-eyed looks and spring out of our seats. Norfolk's words are more effective in jolting us out of the sleep-deprived mental haze than a high-powered stimulant. Fagin opens her mouth to speak. Nico frowns and gives her a sharp wave, deferring the questions he sees in our eyes, and points at the hologram.

My stomach cramps. This is wrong. So very wrong.

We watch Anne's eyes dart around the room. She's fully awake now, too, and looks bewildered. "Uncle?" There's the hint of a smile on her face, as though she thinks this might be someone's idea of a tasteless prank—one which would surely cost the jokester their standing at court, if not their head. "What is your meaning? Surely, you can't believe—"

"I am entirely in earnest, Your Grace," he says in a tone that suggests this is anything but a joke. "Last evening, the king received information that you have been unfaithful to His Majesty. After questioning several witnesses, a talisman was found in the king's chambers under his bed, one that was seen in your possession by your ladies. Bishop Fisher has pronounced it cursed with a spell to tempt the king into your bed."

"Sir, I am no witch," Anne says, crying out in rage. "The king loves me of his own accord. He knows his own mind and my conscience, in any regard to the king, is clear."

"Have you no concern for your immortal soul that you lie so egregiously?" Norfolk tugs a piece of parchment free from its place tucked into his belt. He snaps the paper open with a flick of his wrist and reads:

. . .

*I weep for our lost love as I prepare to marry the king. I beg you, do not
exile me from your heart. I could not bear it, if you do. This child I
carry is yours, not his.*

My heart skips a beat. *No. Oh, no, no, no, NO!*

"What's going on?" Fagin cuts in, talking over the hologram
audio. "Anne Boleyn isn't arrested for treason, and executed, for four
more years. This isn't—"

"Sh!" Nico hushes her and points back to the hologram. "Listen."

"What letter is that you read?" Anne says. A wild and terrified look
washes over her face, and she leaps from her chair. "Do you think to
accuse me with this falsehood? The child I carry is the king's!" She
snatches the letter from her uncle and scans it, her lips moving as she
silently reads.

"This was delivered to the king last evening," Norfolk says. "We
have confirmed the charges with Lady Rochford, and many other
witnesses, that you dallied with Sir Thomas Wyatt in your private
quarters, and—"

"Falsehood!" Anne screams. She crumples the paper in her
hands and moves toward the fireplace.

Norfolk blocks her path and wrestles the letter away from her.
"We have Wyatt's confession."

Anne freezes in place, her face a mask of horror and disbelief.
"No. It isn't true. You must have tortured him to gain a false confession. Anything he said under the pain of torture is suspect. There is
nothing between him and me."

Out of patience, Norfolk glances at the two guards flanking him
on either side. With a quick jerk of his head, he gives the command
for the guards to take Anne into custody. "You have offended our
sovereign the king's grace in committing treason against his person,
and you are condemned to die for your crimes. You will be impris-

oned in the Tower of London until the king's pleasure is further known."

Lady Anne wails as the guards drag her from the room by her wrists.

Nico pauses the hologram. For a moment, we stand in stunned silence. My arms and legs feel like they're weighted down, and a surreal kaleidoscope of images swims through my head as the last twelve hours rewind themselves in my brain. I know the contents of that letter. Faking Anne's declaration of love for Thomas Wyatt should have resulted in banishment from court, not arrest. Tenterhooks of regret rake through my heart like scalding claws. *Did I so badly miscalculate the king's reaction? What have I done?*

Fagin explodes. "What the hell happened?"

"I don't know," Nico says. "I kept searching surveillance tapes after you both went to bed. The MicroCam in Lady Anne's chambers is motion-triggered and set to higher priority than cameras in the common areas. When Norfolk entered with the guards, the feed popped up on my auxiliary screens. When I realized what was happening, I called you."

"This isn't supposed to happen," Fagin continues, nervously. "She has to give birth to Elizabeth." She stops and looks at me. "What was the last thing you saw Anne doing? Did you see any of this going on? You've been with her more than any of the rest of us, surely, you must've seen something if these accusations are true."

The cramps in my stomach have migrated to my chest in a radiating, constricting band of spasms in my chest. It's suffocating me. *I have to get out of here.*

"Dodger!" Fagin grabs my shoulders and gives me a shake.

I run my tongue over my parched lips and try to focus. I must choose my words carefully; I can't give anything away. Not right now. "I've seen no evidence of witchcraft." Then, glancing at Nico. "Where's Trevor now?"

Nico taps the control panel. "Lieutenant Trevor, report in," he says. There's nothing, not even static, over the CommLink. He waits a few seconds and tries again. "Trevor, do you read me?"

Still nothing. Nico shakes his head and taps the panel again. He peers at the data onscreen and lets out a long breath. "She's not onboard. She must've removed both her LensCams and CommLink because I have no audio or image feeds from her for the last twelve hours. There's not even a bio-signature reading. She's gone completely off-grid." Nico's eyes widen in understanding. His eyes sear into mine and I can hardly stand the weight of them. "You think she had something to do with this?"

Until I find out exactly what happened, I'm not getting anywhere near a confessional booth. "Maybe." My tone is as noncommittal as I can manage. "Won't know for sure until we figure out where she's been all night, and what she's up to now." Willing my muscles to work, I move toward the door. "We need eyes and ears on the ground out there. I have to get dressed."

"I'm going with you." Fagin says, heading toward her own quarters to change out of her black sweats and into court-appropriate attire. "I'll start looking for Trevor in the kitchens; if she's still in disguise, she might show up there, first. You..." She points at me. "Talk with any of Anne's ladies-in-waiting that you can find, especially the ones who testified against her last night. And you..." She points back at Nico. "See what else you can find about these bogus charges and when they have scheduled the execution. She's being set up and you can bet whoever's behind this will want to see it done as fast as possible."

When I arrive at the palace, I find the outer chamber of Anne's apartments deserted. It also looks freshly ransacked. I wonder if the raiders found—or planted—any fake evidence to bolster the charges against her. *They didn't need much help in that regard. You did a fine fucking job of giving them a smoking gun letter to finish her off.*

Having a conscience can be a bitch.

"Someone was in a hurry," Nico says, deadpan. "Turn to your left and give me a view of the other side of the room." When I oblige, and he gets a glimpse of the detritus scattered everywhere, he lets out a long, low whistle. "Whoever it was, they were moving hard and fast looking for whatever it is they were looking for."

"They didn't bother tidying up when they were done tearing it apart, either."

A faint sob drifts out of Anne's bedroom.

"I think we've got a live one," I say, moving in the direction of the sound.

"Easy does it. Give me a good visual sweep of the room as you go in."

"Roger that."

The door is ajar and I nudge it farther open with one foot before peering around the edge. The moon has set, but the sun hasn't yet broken the horizon so there's no light in the room. I can't see much further past my extended hand until my eyes adjust.

"Easy," Nico repeats. "That's it, nice and easy."

The sob is soft, muffled. It's coming from the left side of the room. There's a hiccup and a sniffle before the sob builds. It's definitely a woman's cry.

"Hello?" I say, not too loud. I don't want whoever is in the corner to scream. "Hello, who's there?"

There's another snuffling sound, then a tentative question. "Mademoiselle Clémence? Is that you?"

"Yes. Who is there?"

"Anne," comes the reply. "Gainsford."

My eyes have adjusted enough to see the woman's silhouette as she crouches in the corner. I scan the rest of the room again to confirm there's no one else hiding in the shadows before I move over to her.

"Anne, tell me what happened." Kneeling next to her, I reach out my hand. When my fingers graze her knee, she lunges into my arms, nearly knocking me off-balance, and sobs into my shoulder. We collapse in a heap on the floor.

Though I make all the comforting sounds I can—a Herculean feat given that the agitation coursing through me still has me off-balance—it doesn't soothe her; she alternates between anguished howls and full-on blubbering. All of which makes intelligible speech an impossibility.

"Anne, I can't understand you. Slow down." It takes some convincing, but I finally get her to lock eyes with me and breathe together in a slow, smooth rhythm. When her breathing settles into gentler pattern, I question her again. "What happened?"

"How could they treat her thus?" Anne's eyes burn with intensity, a mixture of grief and anger and confusion. "The king seemed so in love. They both seemed so in love."

I don't have time for this. "Anne," I say, controlling my words in a gentle, measured tone. "Tell me every detail that happened from the time I left your company in Lady Anne's chamber last night and this morning when Anne's uncle arrived."

She chews her lower lip. "I served Lady Anne's dinner—she had little appetite and vomited halfway through the meal. No doubt from the horror of the vile attack on her person—then I helped her with the stool, and..."

"Perhaps, not that much detail," I say, cutting her off before she goes any further in-depth regarding Lady Anne's toilet habits. "Tell me what happened this morning."

"My lady is falsely accused," she says. Her eyes turn cold and hard. Sweet Anne Gainsford, perpetually kind, sincere, and unassuming, turns from meek lady-in-waiting to hellhound in the time it takes to snap your fingers. "I wish I could cross paths with the villain who has maligned my sweet lady in such a way. Whoever has cast such vile and deceitful accusations against her would be fortunate to spend eternity in hell for their lies rather than face my wrath."

From the look on her face and the venom in her voice, I'd be tempted to choose hell instead of facing her if that act of penitence were required to enter heaven.

"Calm yourself. Surely, the king will show her mercy and listen to her defense in these accusations. He loves her with his whole heart and soul, of that I am certain."

Anne wrinkles her nose and looks at me as if I'm talking nonsense. "Listen to her?" A sob hiccups, again, in her throat. "The trial is done and she is condemned. There will be no mercy for her."

"What about her father? Can't he speak to the king on her behalf?"

"All of the Boleyns have been banished from court. At least, they will be exiled after the execution today."

Oh, fuck.

Nico's voice breaks in, "Today?"

"When is the execution?" I ask, swallowing the bile that rises to the back of my throat.

Anne Gainsford's eyes well up again. Her shoulders heave and her whole body trembles so hard it seems ready to explode. She shakes her head, perhaps thinking that not answering might delay the inevitable.

"Anne, what time?" I grip her shoulders and give her a good shake.

She casts a glance toward the windows of the Eastward-facing window seat. There's a red-orange glow shimmering through the lead-paned glass and the room is growing brighter.

Anne swallows hard and, unable to keep the levy from rupturing, lets the tears fall again as she chokes out a single word: "Sunrise."

CHAPTER 22

A HANGMAN'S noose sways in a slow arc, nudged by a winter wind carrying the scent of wood smoke and horse dung. In front of the noose, a wooden plank balances across two trestles. Several yards to the right of the scaffold, a bonfire burns. I don't feel the fire. I don't feel the cold.

The sensation welling up inside me is the turbulence of too many emotions to compress into one neat little word, but "terror" comes the closest.

Lying on the makeshift table are several gruesome-looking knives; the first rays of today's sun gleam across the surface of the curved blades making them look even more ominous.

A carnival-like atmosphere grows as the village awakes and word of the impending executions spreads like the spark of a gunpowder trail. Clusters of people, mostly courtiers buzzing with curiosity turned excitement, swarm Tower Hill. From the snippets of conversation, I overhear, as I push my through the crowd, the identity of the condemned, and the specific charges against them, are mostly lost on the crowd-at-large.

All they know is: There's going to be a show and they want a good view.

Toward the front of the pack, Charles Brandon stands beside the king's chief minister, Thomas Cromwell. Their expressions are grim. Weary. They look like they've haven't slept at all.

I pull the hood of my cloak up over my head and move to stand behind them. They speak in hushed tones.

"By Saint George, I knew it would come to this, yet I didn't think it would happen so soon," Brandon says. He sounds confused, but not shocked. There was no love lost between him and Anne, and he wasn't cozy with Sir Thomas, either. "The king knew of my suspicions regarding his lady and the poet. I would have given anything to spare him this pain."

"The king knows his own desires. Once something is put into his mind, it's difficult to sway him from his course," Cromwell says. He pauses a moment. "Do you think he will bring Queen Katherine back to court?"

"The king is incensed, his spirit crushed. I don't know what he will do next."

Cromwell asks, "Do you believe she is with child and that Wyatt is the father?"

What? She's not supposed to be pregnant until January.

"It doesn't matter what I believe. After the trial last night, the only thing that matters is that the king believes it. Lady Anne wouldn't soon be a head shorter if he thought the child she says she carries is his."

Moving to the edge of the crowd, I hail Fagin. "Got eyes on Trevor yet?"

"Negative," she replies. "Nico, any movement on the Benefactor ship?"

"Not yet," he says. "I'll let you know when there's something to know."

"Nico," I say, my mouth feeling dry and thick, as though my body has forgotten how to make saliva. "When does Anne Boleyn know she's pregnant?"

"Why do you want to know *that?*"

"Just look it up," my reply is as anxious as his guarded answer. "Could she be pregnant now?"

There's a pause. "Elizabeth is born on the seventh of September. It's possible Lady Anne is already pregnant."

Fuck. Fuck, fuck, fuck!

The Constable of the Tower appears, leading the processional of the condemned as they approach the scaffold. Cheers erupt from the burgeoning crowd as a chestnut-colored horse trots through the gap between the front line of spectators and the execution platform dragging a muddy and blood-spattered Sir Thomas Wyatt behind it.

Gasps and murmurs ripple through the crowd as the assembled spectators recognize him. Some in the crowd jeer him and others genuflect and offer vocal prayers for a swift and painless death.

From the looks of things, the answer to their prayers will be: No.

Lady Anne follows, dressed in a simple black gown, her hair covered with a linen cap. Her face is ashen and her chest heaves in short, fast bursts as she walks. She passes within a few feet of me. She stops, glances back over her shoulder. When her gaze fixes on me, it is so piteous, a wave of regret washes over me like a bucket of ice water.

"I'm sorry." The apology is out before I even know I'm talking.

Missions usually feel like a game; a larcenous romp at breakneck speeds that end with a priceless treasure in my pocket and another nudge toward freedom. This is anything but a romp. This is a nightmare.

Anne tilts her head, puzzled. "Pray for my soul, mademoiselle. I am innocent."

I open my mouth to speak again, but nothing comes out.

Holy Jesus, what have I done?

There are shouts when the crowd recognizes Anne. Some are cries of shock and horror; others are jubilant cheers. Her personal chaplain embraces her with a steadying arm around her shoulder. Anne covers his large hand with her small one and nods. After a few deep breaths, she casts her eyes to the heavens.

Rotted vegetables and fruit litter the steps around the execution platform. Only the priest on the scaffold stops the gathered assembly from launching more consumable missiles at the condemned man as he mounts the platform.

The executioner, a black leather mask concealing his identity, binds Wyatt's hands behind him and places the rope around his neck before placing him on a small stool. A quick beheading is reserved for those of noble birth and is a manner of death considered too good for commoners. Having endured being drawn by the horse, Sir Thomas is about to be hanged and quartered, then beheaded.

Brandon said the king was incensed by the turn of events he never expected. Approving this gruesome death for Wyatt is proof positive of the depth of his fury. Who knows what manner of death he has chosen for the woman he believed was the love of his life? The prospects make me shudder.

"Guys," Nico says, breaking in over the CommLink. "I just picked up a transporter energy surge from the other Observer ship. Looks like you're gonna have company."

"Roger," I say.

Back on the scaffold, the chaplain stands beside Wyatt and asks if Wyatt has committed his soul to God. When the poet nods in response, the priest offers a prayer for his soul, then makes the sign of the cross in the air. As a last act, the condemned man is given leave to speak his last words.

Overcome with emotion, it takes several minutes for him to find the words. When he does, they're not what anyone expects.

I find no peace, and all my war is done. I fear and hope. I burn and freeze like ice.

I fly above the wind; yet can I not arise;

Bewildered whispers spread through the crowd. One woman asks, her mouth agape, "He recites his own poetry as he dies?"

Wyatt ignores the murmurs and continues.

And naught I have, and all the world I season.
  That loseth nor locketh holdeth me in prison
  And holdeth me not—yet can I scape no wise—
  Nor letteth me live nor die at my device,
  And yet of death it giveth me occasion.
  Without eyen I see, and without tongue I plain.
  I desire to perish, and yet I ask health.
  I love another, and thus I hate myself.

He chokes back a sob. His eyes are swollen, face bruised. Torture must have extracted his confession, whether it's fact or fiction.

I feed me in sorrow and laugh in all my pain;
  Likewise displeaseth me both life and death,
  And my delight is causer of this strife.

He stops again and looks out over the crowd. Somehow, he locks eyes with me. He gives me a small, weary smile and shakes his head.

"I had thought to live among you for much longer than these short, cruel years," he says, gazing at me as if I'm the only one on Tower Green. As if I'm the only one who can save him. I can't stand the weight of his pleading eyes.

"I beseech you all, for the love of God and his saints, to pray for my soul," he continues, his voice raspy and broken. "And pray for His Majesty the king because...though I confess that I am a sinner before God and man, I am innocent of the charges laid against me."

His eyes are still on me. I look away. My own tears begin to flow.

"Thus, I take my leave of you." He gives a short, curt nod indicating that he's done. The burly executioner wastes no time—there's a sharp kick against the stool and Wyatt is dangling at the end of the rope.

His body convulses as the rope pulls taut. His toes scrape across the platform's surface trying to gain purchase; he's a quarter-inch from being able to fully support his weight. It might as well be a mile.

His eyes bulge, legs thrash, and his face turns a mottled, purple hue.

The crowd erupts in a wall of noise, and some hot-tempered Neanderthal taunts him as he strains to breathe, but is interrupted by cooler heads. Just as Wyatt reaches the edge of unconsciousness, the executioner cuts the rope. The wretch falls to the floor. He coughs, chest heaving as life floods his lungs.

The executioner drags Wyatt—sputtering from lack of oxygen— to the trestle table positioned toward the front of the scaffold.

The executioner picks up a blade and slices through the lower abdomen; it wrings a shriek from Wyatt that I've never heard before. The sound is much higher-pitched that I expected; if Banshees were real, this wild and terrified keening wail is what I imagine they sound like.

I realize the sound isn't coming from Wyatt—it's Lady Anne giving voice to the horror playing out on stage.

"Dodger," Nico's voice is sober, measured. Like he's trying to talk me off a ledge. In a way, he's doing just that. "Don't watch. Do you hear me?"

I set this in motion. This is my punishment: bearing witness to the carnage I helped create.

The volume of blood is overwhelming. It spurts upward onto Wyatt's chest in several violent waves until it slows to gurgling crimson trickles. Wyatt's screams fade as the dissection continues. By the time they take his testicles, his voice is long-gone and his eyes are glazed over.

"Dodger. Get out of there." Nico says, the cadence of his voice shifting to urgency. "Whatever has gone bad in this timeline, we can't fix it. We've got to get back to base before things get worse."

"I can't," I reply. "Not yet."

Wyatt's organs are tossed into the bonfire; the putrid smell fills the air, causing those closest to the flames to retreat or attempt, in vain, to block the odor with silk handkerchiefs or embroidered velvet sleeves. Several spectators with more delicate constitutions stumble out of the crowd to vomit.

The executioner delivers the death blow, one swift strike to the neck.

The remaining blood in his body streams from the neck cavity, then cascades in a thin, uneven waterfall over the sides of the plank. The head hits the scaffold floor, then bounces down the wooden staircase with sickening thuds. It comes to rest at the feet of Sir Henry Norris, the Duke of Norfolk, who snatches the head up by the hair, and holds the bloody mass up to the crowd.

Some onlookers weep. A handful offer lukewarm cheers. Others stand silent as stone. Off to my left, a trio of ladies sob into each other's shoulders.

Fagin's voice breaks in; her voice is breathless "I found Trevor. She's running toward the stables. I'm in pursuit."

"Negative, get back to the ship," Nico says in an unyielding tone that brooks no argument. "I have two more huge, distinct energy signature readings popping up on the display panels. It's either more Benefactor ships arriving to back up Trevor or, they're government agents sent here to bring us back to base for questioning about timeline tampering." Nico shoots the next comment at me. "Last time I'm gonna say it, Dodger, get your ass back here or I'm coming to get you."

"I need more time," I have to shout over the growing din of the crowd. "They're moving Lady Anne to the scaffold."

Nico says something else, but his words are lost in the cacophony of shouts and screams around me as Anne mounts the execution platform.

The chaplain goes through the same motions with Anne that he did with Thomas Wyatt.

When given leave to speak, Anne takes a deep breath and looks around, shaking her head in disbelief, as though she still can't quite grasp the turn of events that have landed her at the end of her short life just as it's supposed to begin.

She takes a breath, then speaks in a halting voice. "Good Christian people, I am come here to die, for according to the law, and by the law I am judged to die for the sins of which I am accused. Yet, I say to you that I am innocent, having never betrayed my sovereign lord, the king. I have ever been a true, faithful, and loyal servant of his majesty."

She pauses, scans the crowd like she's looking for something—or someone. The king, perhaps? Or her father or her brother, George? For a moment, her expression is hopeful, like she expects a savior to appear. For a crazy moment, I consider fighting my way through the crowd and rescuing her myself.

Anne squares her shoulders and continues her farewell speech. "I pray God save the king and send him long to reign over you. He is a gentle and merciful prince, and I would have borne for my sovereign lord many sons." She places her hands on her still flat belly, and I wince.

The executioner steps closer to Anne, and she casts an anxious glance over her shoulder at him. Her voice shakes. "And if...if any person will meddle of my cause, I require them to judge the best. And thus I take my leave of the world and of you all, and I heartily desire you all to pray for me. O Lord have mercy on me, to God I commend my soul."

She kneels on the floor and gives one curt nod to the executioner. Where Wyatt's hands were bound, hers are unrestrained. In stark contrast to the brutal death of the poet, Lady Anne—because of her rank and station—is given the easier death by beheading.

It feels like the entire assembly is holding their collective breaths.

There's a warm, moist breath on my right ear, making the hairs on the back of my neck stand on end. Thinking it's just some louse trying to cop a feel, I spin to my right and come face-to-face with Commander Jackson Carter.

"At least you're not stuck in the toilet this time" Carter says with a smirk as he grabs my ,arm.

Merde!

The crowd presses forward toward the platform, jostling us back and forth enough to allow me to yank my arm from his grasp. Several larger men elbow their way forward, and I use them as leverage, pushing them backward so that they crash into Carter, sending them all tumbling to the ground.

There's a narrow gap between two groups of ladies and I dart through it, shouldering my way through people still moving forward toward Anne.

I glimpse Carter, who has disentangled himself from the sprawled bodies struggling to right themselves after the fall. His eyes sweep through the crowd, searching for me. I pull my hood up over my head and melt into the crowd.

At the corner of the scaffold, I stop. I have a direct line of sight to Lady Anne as she waits for her end. She turns her head and glimpses me. I get one more look at those dark, seductive eyes—now fearful and incredulous—before they fix a blindfold over them.

Holy God.

"I've lost Trevor." Fagin's voice is breathless. Frustrated. "She nabbed a horse and is headed East. Nico, monitor the MicroCams aimed at the Benefactor ship. I think she's headed in that direction."

It's astounding how a minute can drag on forever. Everything feels dreamlike as the executioner raises the ax.

"Nico!" Fagin says. "Do you copy?"

The sword swings upward into the air, then cuts a smooth, downward arc.

Mercy. Have mercy.

Then...

She's gone.

There are wails. Whimpers. Cheers.

And so much blood.

Someone bumps me. I barely register the hit until a pair of hands seize my shoulders. I feel myself pivot and, once again, stare up into Carter's face.

He peers at me and curiosity flickers in his eyes, but it's quickly replaced with skepticism. Carter says something, but the words don't register over the shouts of the crowd. He moves closer, his face mere inches from mine.

My hands instinctively raise and land on his chest, but before I can push him away, there's a burst of motion and Carter is jerked backward off of his feet.

It's Nico.

Surprise is his best leverage against Carter, who has a good four inches and thirty pounds on Nico's taut, trim frame.

There's a sideways scuffle, and then a flurry of fists until Nico lands a punch to the solar plexus followed by an uppercut that connects with Carter's jaw, sending the larger man tumbling to the ground.

Nico grabs my hand and we push our way through the mob. Once free of the constraints of the crowd, we hit a full sprint toward the gardens.

"If you had listened to me for one damn minute." Nico says, trying to breathe and talk while running at full speed. "Fagin, I've got her. Get to the ship."

"Be there as soon as I can. I've been...detained," comes the cool reply.

Shooting a glance over my shoulder as we race into the garden, I spot the commander—red faced and snorting like a raging bull—as he rounds the corner of a hedge. Nico glances back, too.

"Shit," he says in a huff.

Nico veers to the right, pulling me with him as he barrels toward a grove of trees. Once inside the grove, he drops my hand and skids around a large oak tree.

"This way," he calls out. "We have to get to the other side of the trees so can't see us transport."

Hitching my gown up to my knees, I pump my legs as hard as I can to keep up. The underbrush catches the hem on the back side of my dress and I hear the faint rip as the fabric tears.

On the other side of the trees, Nico reclaims my hand and pulls me closer as he slows, then stumbles to a stop. We can hear Carter's footfalls as he crashes through the brush.

"He's getting closer," I gasp.

"Betty," Nico says into the CommLink, equally breathless. "Two to transport. NOW!"

My body tingles as the transporter energy surges through me. There's a glimpse of Carter as he emerges from the trees a few hundred feet away, and his frustrated grimace when he realizes he won't catch up. The next moment, Nico and I collapse on the transporter pad on our ship.

"Arseneau!" Carter's voice booms over the ship's loudspeakers.

"How the hell..." I gulp air into my lungs. "...did he access our communication system?"

"Someone gave him the access codes." Nico scrambles off the pad, and heads toward the cockpit, shouting over his shoulder at me as he goes. "Three guesses who might have done that."

Trevor.

Once at the command console, Nico's fingers fly over the controls. "She could have given him access to every system on the ship." He squints at the display screen. "I don't see any evidence of recent system changes, so it doesn't look like there's been any tampering."

"No tampering, yet, Commander Garcia. I hope you'll both cooperate so I won't have to take control of your ship," Carter says. "I have access to your communication feeds and transporter system. I can also block you from taking off to parts unknown. After that sucker punch, maybe I should just take command of your ship right now."

"Carter, I thought you'd be retired by now. What the hell are you doing here?" I ask.

"Trying to fix what you've broken," he says in a dry tone.

Nico swivels in his seat and raises a questioning eyebrow. I look away.

"You should have taken me up on the offer to be your advisor, Arseneau. I could've kept you from getting stuck in this mess."

"Given that you're the Benefactors' bulldog now, I doubt that," I say.

There's an audible sigh. "You've got me all wrong, kiddo. There are things you don't know about how you were chosen for this mission."

"What do you mean 'chosen?'"

"You've been set up."

"Set up?" Nico's jaw drops. "Dodger, what's he talking about?"

"How am I supposed to know?" I say. Then, to Carter: "You have thirty seconds to explain that or I'm cutting the transmission feed."

Nico holds a finger to his lips, then taps the communications panel, switching to an alternate frequency. "Fagin?" Nico says. "Are you hearing this?"

No answer.

"I'm afraid Ms. Delacroix can't come to the communicator right now. She's in deep discussions with my compatriots, at the moment," Carter says. "And, yes, we have full control over all of your communication frequencies. We need to talk, Arseneau. You're trying to climb a slippery slope, and you know it."

Nico leans back in his chair and shoots me a loaded-for-bear look. "What in the hell is he talking about?"

Fuck. "It's...complicated." My mouth goes dry.

Carter makes an annoying tsk-tsk sound. "It sure sounds like you haven't kept your boyfriend in the loop regarding your extra-curricular activities."

"Dodger, one more time...what's he talking about?" Nico's eyes turn pleading, like he knows he's going to hate my answer, but he needs to hear it anyway.

I settle into the co-pilot's seat, and stare into my lap. I can't meet his gaze anymore. A few minutes pass in silence, until Carter's dangerously thin patience disappears.

"Enough playing around." His voice turns hard. "You have five minutes to surrender, and allow me onboard, or I'm coming in there after you. If I have to do that, I promise you won't like the outcome."

CHAPTER 23

"Four minutes left." Jackson Carter's voice blares over the speakers. "It'll go a lot easier for you if I can tell my bosses you voluntarily cooperated."

"I'll bet you didn't make that offer to Fagin as you hold her prisoner," I reply. "You playing good cop to get her to cooperate, too?"

"She's not a prisoner. Fagin is free to leave protective custody at any time."

"Protective custody. Is that what the kids are calling time traveler jail these days?" Usually sarcasm rolls off me like butter across warm toast. Right now, though, my stomach feels ready to turn cartwheels, making it hard to enjoy trading witty comebacks with Carter. "I have no freaking clue what's going on, but—"

"Don't you? This party is all because of you, Arseneau."

Nico leans forward in the commander's chair and rests his elbows on his knees. The expectant look on his face makes my stomach churn. It's all about to come spilling out and while I'm convinced I won't receive better treatment from the Benefactors by cooperating with their errand boy, I'm equally convinced the little toad is right about one thing: Bad things get worse when you don't face them head-on.

Because he's the kind who gets quieter the angrier he gets, Nico's silence as he shifts from annoyed curiosity to active agitation is alarming.

"Does your boyfriend know what you've done?" Carter says. "Was he in on your little scheme? I'm sure my superiors will want to interrogate him, too."

Nico continues to stare. After several long seconds, he takes a measured breath and says, "He's not talking about this disciplinary training mission, is he?"

It takes two hard swallows to force saliva down past the lump in my throat. "Do you believe someone can do the wrong thing, for the right reasons?" Desperation crowds into the edges of my voice. "Even if it's something horrible? I mean... sometimes you really don't have options when your only choice is between bad and worse."

"There's always a choice." Nico says, his voice quiet. Resolved.

"Three minutes." Carter says.

Fuck.

The corner of Nico's left eye twitches. He pushes himself out of the chair, hands clenched in fists at his side. "What. Did you. Do?"

"It wasn't supposed to happen this way. You have to believe that. Just..." I press my palms flat on his chest, hoping—for even a second—to keep his fury at bay. I swear I can feel his heart pounding. "Just tell me you believe I didn't intend for things to go down—"

"If you don't quit dancing around the issue and tell me what you did, I'll open that fucking door myself."

Everything tumbles out in a rush of words I hope make sense. "English soldiers murdered my parents. They killed Papa right in front of me. My maman died when our ship to the colonies sank in a storm. And then..." Nico tries to side-step around me; I clutch fistfuls of his shirt to keep him in place. I know it all sounds like pathetic excuses. He doesn't look me in the eye. Come to think of it, I wouldn't look me in the eye, either. Still, I hold tight to his shirt like it's a lifeline to his heart. "After that, I was sold into indentured servitude."

Tears stream down my cheeks. *He's got to see what they did to me. Why I had no choice.* "I was nine years old! It's like fate pointed her cruel, twisted fingers at me and cursed me with surviving alone. So, that's what I did: I survived."

A slow, rhythmic clap echoes through the cabin. "Brava, my dear," Carter says. "You should resurrect the Penny Dreadful tales of old. You're quite the storyteller. Dial it back a little bit, though, you're overacting."

"I swear to God, Carter," I say, clenching my teeth, "if you say one more word, I'll—"

Nico interrupts. "I know you're a survivor. That's not the point."

"I didn't mean for anyone to get hurt." *Why can't he fucking see that?*

"You're dancing around the question. What did you do that caused the king to execute Anne before she gives birth to Elizabeth?"

Carter's voice breaks in. "I can read him the letter, if you like. I've got it right here."

"What letter?" Nico says, folding his arms over his chest. His jawline is hard set, like marble.

"I forged a letter from Lady Anne to Sir Thomas Wyatt that made it look like she's still in love with him."

"Shit," Nico swears under his breath.

Carter reads part of the letter.

"My Dearest Thomas, I weep for our lost love as I prepare to marry the king. I beg you, do not exile me from your heart. I could not bear it if you do. Please, my dearest heart, do not abandon me in my greatest hour of need. The child I carry is yours, not the king's."

He pauses, then adds: "As love letters go, this is particularly poignant."

"I didn't write that," I say, shaking my head.

Nico sighs and his eyes narrow. "You said you wrote the letter."

"The one I wrote said nothing about Anne being pregnant because, I overheard her uncle and Charles Brandon at the scaffolds today, I wasn't sure she was with child." My shrug feels as helpless as it must look. "I guess it was easier to ignore the whole scenario."

"You're saying someone faked your fake letter?" Nico says.

"Someone changed the letter, yes. No wonder Henry went ballistic and executed them both. He thought Anne carried Wyatt's child."

"Who died and made you God? You think you can judge who is born and who isn't?" Nico says it softly, but it hits my heart like a neutron bomb. And his pained eyes tear me in half.

"Don't look at me like that." My eyes fall to the floor.

"Like what? Like I don't know you anymore? Like I can't fucking believe you would do something like this?"

"I saw a way to stop my parents' murders before they happened. I had to save them. I had to try."

Nico pushes past me. He interlaces his fingers and cups the back of his head with his hands as he stares at the ceiling. "Your actions killed Anne Boleyn and the future queen of England," he says, sounding exhausted.

"I didn't think anyone would die. I thought if I convinced the king that Lady Anne was still in love with Thomas Wyatt, he would just banish her from court. I didn't know—"

He turns and we lock eyes, and it's a glare that pushes my heart off a cliff. I open my mouth to apologize for the whole mess, but he holds up a trembling hand. A cascade of shifting emotions flickers across his face: anger, hurt, bewilderment, sadness, disappointment.

"You told me you wouldn't do anything stupid, but you were planning this all along." He lets out a long, ragged breath. "You lied to me."

"We lie all the time." I offer a half-hearted shrug. It's a shitty move, I know, but I feel like I'm hanging onto him with my fingertips and my grip is slipping. "It's what we do on every job. We lie all the time. To everyone."

Nico explodes, directing the force of his rage into his fist as he drives it into the cabin wall. "Not to each other! Never to each other."

"You don't know what it's like," I shoot back. My face feels flushed with heat. "You've never lost everyone you ever loved. Never lost--"

"How the hell do you know what I've lost? You push me away too much to know anything about my past." He licks his lips and squares off to face me head-on. "Revenge. Is that really what this is really all about?"

"What would you do to save your family?" I'm vaguely aware that what I intended to say with some semblance of calm has erupted as a primal howl.

"Not this." He wipes the back of his hand across his mouth. "Anything but this. I could have helped you. We could have worked through all of this together."

"Nico—" I say, but he cuts me off.

"You let her get to you. Goddamn it, Dodger, you let Trevor get in your head."

"Two minutes," comes the next countdown warning.

"Fuck off, Carter," Nico bellows.

"Do you know what you've done?" Nico rakes his hands through his hair. "You changed a fixed point in time. Do you know the impact of stopping the birth of a someone who is *supposed* to live?"

"No." I stop to consider the possibilities, and the first thought that comes to mind is--if I went looking for them--whether I could see my parents' faces again. *Merde. Are they still alive or did I fuck that up, too?* "Do you?"

He blinks and, for a moment, I'm distracted by a flurry of dark eyelashes. He's standing close enough for me to catch his scent: clean male with a hint of the wood smoke from the bonfire. It's a heady fragrance, and I wish we could fast forward through this mess and be okay again.

"No," he replies. "That's the whole fucking point, Dodger. No one knows the impact of this level of meddling, because no one has ever done it before. Actually," he lets out a snort, "What you've done can't be labeled simple 'meddling.' More like you've royally fucked the future. Who knows what we'll find when we get home. If there's a home to go back to at all."

"What if the future's not fucked up? What if things are better because of this?"

Hope is like a drug. It mollifies guilt and makes justifying insanity a tiny bit easier. I don't know if I believe whether this surreal turn of events could possibly change history for the better, but one thing is sure: We'll find out whether we like it or not.

"Time's up," Carter says. "Open the door so we can have a proper chat about the fine mess you've gotten us into, or I'll let myself in."

Nico pauses, a puzzled look flickers across his face. He moves to stand shoulder-to-shoulder with me and whispers: "Why doesn't he barge in here and take us into custody like they did with Fagin? Why is he so interested in helping us look better to the Benefactors?"

"No clue," I whisper back. "Maybe he doesn't want to attract any attention from the locals?"

"Something doesn't smell right. If Carter could get in the ship, he'd already be onboard. Keep him talking. I'm going to run a quick diagnostic to see if I can find which controls have been hacked. Could be they didn't get any farther in than the CommLink frequencies."

"I'm waiting," Carter says in an irritating sing-song voice.

I swipe two fingers across the Comm Panel, and an exterior video feed hologram pops up on a nearby table. Somehow, reducing Jackson Carter to a six-inch tall action figure takes some of the bite out of his bark. Flicking a fingernail through his holo-head several times and watching as the light fragments scatter and reassemble themselves is childish, but satisfying.

"Last time we saw each other, you threatened to sic your highly-placed friends on me. I didn't take you for a guy who does his own dirty work. Or are you still sore that I almost torpedoed your perfect mission history on the de Medici job?"

"Personal vendettas are a luxury I can't afford right now. I have a job to do."

"What, exactly, is your job?"

"You're tap dancin' on my last nerve, kid. Gotta hand it to you, though. When you fuck up, you do a whiz-bang job of it." He sighs. "I'm here to fix what you've broken."

"Fix it how?"

"Depends," Carter replies. "We don't know how much damage has been done. Our recovery team lost communication with the base back home the moment we arrived here. It's possible the fabric of everything we knew began unraveling the minute you sent history to hell in a hand cart." He pauses. "What we know for sure is that we can't sit around and do nothing."

"Okay," Nico replies, "there could be a wound in the time continuum, as you say. Or the communication channels could be jammed by the government so we can't talk to the Benefactors. It could be any number of things that screw with the frequencies, like solar flares."

"Put two and two together, Garcia, and I'll bet you still come up with four. What's that old saying: The simplest answer is often the correct one?"

Nico turns back to the command console. After a few minutes, he looks back at me. "We can't get through, either. No response from Command Ops back home."

"Told you," Carter's voice brims with weary annoyance.

"You're a manipulative son of a bitch," I say. "You could've sabotaged the communication frequencies, yourself, to convince us to cooperate. I'd like to know how much the Benefactors are paying you. Whatever it is, it must be a handsome sum for you to take this job on."

"Maybe I'm here just to watch you go down, Arseneau. That would be payment enough."

"That answer doesn't inspire confidence in your Kumbaya pretension."

"You want inspiration to cooperate? Envision this as your last breath as a free woman. That oughta perk you right up."

Nico, engrossed in running system diagnostics, holds one finger in the air. He needs a little more time.

"I need to talk to Fagin," I say.

"After you open the door," Carter snaps.

"Fuck off, Carter. Someone changed that letter to convince the king that Anne Boleyn got knocked up by another man. If anyone can help sort out this mess, it's Fagin."

There's a soft, humorless chuckle from Carter. "She can't help you. You have no leverage. If history has changed so much that time travel is never invented, we could all be stuck in this time. It's in everyone's best interest to get along and work together."

Nico beckons me into the cockpit and points at the holographic display screen. "Only thing they hacked is the communication channels," he says. "No other systems are compromised."

"Yet, Commander Garcia," Carter says. I glance back at the hologram image of him, still projecting in the middle of the tabletop behind us. He's wearing that dumb-ass smirk of his that I hate. "We haven't compromised the rest of your ship's systems, yet. Open the fucking door and cooperate with us or you won't like what comes next."

I shake my head at Nico and mouth: [Can't trust him.]

Nico mouths in return. [I know.]

Carter's voice breaks in again, "Guess we have to do it the hard way. Open the door right fucking now and we'll only wipe your memories and send you to a prison colony instead of executing you."

"You won't do anything of the sort." I say, spitting the words out. "You just said you need us."

"We want to get the job done faster, and it's easier with your cooperation. We could do it without you, if we must."

"Bullshit. If our cooperation weren't critical, you'd have stormed the ship by now."

"If you believe nothing else I say, believe this: If you don't help fix the timeline, you'll face a tribunal for your crimes. I'll be the government's star witness. Do you really want to stay on my bad side?"

The lump in my throat is back. Jackson Carter is no friend of mine—or Nico's—and he does have the power to make our lives shittier than they are right now.

"Commander Garcia," Carter continues, "We didn't hack all of your ship's systems as a gesture of good faith, proof we want to work together. But you leave me no choice," Carter pauses. "Retraction of that good faith gesture starts right...now."

Nico lifts his hands from the command console, frantically scanning the controls as they erupt in a flash of rapid-fire color. "Damn it to hell." His fingers fly across the display panel. "Those are unauthorized sub-routines trawling through the ship's systems. They have the computer access codes." He works the display panel feverishly, trying to slow the attack. "Betty, throw in more sub-net mask layers to slow them down.

"Acknowledged, Commander, honey," she replies.

The rhythm of the display screens shifts to a dance at breakneck speed between the hackers' attempts to breach our systems and Betty's smooth countermeasures. These assholes don't know what they're up against. She's going to wipe the circuit boards with their guts.

"C'mon, baby." I feel the need to offer moral support for the only sentient being on the ship who can keep our doors locked.

Nico grimaces. "It it's a temporary measure, at best. It won't keep them out forever."

"At the risk of stating the obvious," I say, jumping up to stand behind his commander's chair. "we have to do more than just delay them from breaking in."

"If you have a better idea, I'd love to hear it," Nico says through gritted teeth as he continues to pound on the control panel.

"Time jump."

Working frantically to trying to stem the tide of the cyber-attack, he only manages a quick glance over his shoulder. "The fuck you say?"

"How does a lifetime prison sentence with a side of amnesia sound to you?" I shout.

He grimaces, then shakes his head. "What if the time portals aren't working. Screwing history the way you did could mean time travel hasn't been invented in what is no longer our future. Carter's right. We could be stuck here."

"Only one way to find out." I reach past his shoulder and type the criteria into the computer. "Follow these geographic and temporal coordinates."

Nico squints at the data and moans. "You've got to be kidding me."

"Go, Nico. Do it!" I say, sliding into the co-pilot's seat and belting myself in.

Carter says, "In case you were wondering, I'm not the only one here. I have more Observers standing by to board your vessel once we break through the security codes."

Glancing back at the hologram of Carter, I count more than a dozen soldiers have joined him, and they're all waiting for the order to move. "Catch us first, asshole." I reply. Then, to Nico. "I know I screwed up, but listen to me: We need time and space to figure out what went wrong. If Carter gets in here, they'll find any excuse to kill or imprison us. If you ever trusted me before, trust me now."

Nico takes a deep breath and mutters under his breath. "Fuck me running. I'm gonna regret this."

"Tech team," Carter shouts at his subordinates as our ship lifts off. "Breach the transporter controls. Get me on that ship!"

Outside the windows, the English countryside streaks by in a blur of winter gray as we race toward our time portal.

"Shit." Nico breathes out, his eyes darting from the time portal coordinates to the display panel screen. "They're almost in. I need you to get down to the transport pads and manually take them offline in case they break through Betty's defenses."

"But I don't know—"

"I'll walk you through it. Go!"

I unlatch the buckle on my restraint system and stumble to the ladder leading down to the lower deck just as the ship veers starboard, tossing me into a wall.

"Sorry," Nico calls out. "Evasive maneuver. They're on our ass."

A quick slide down the ladder, a few stumbling steps to the right, and I'm at the transport pads. I tap the communication link on the wall panel.

"I'm in position. What now?"

"Open the control panel to the right of the pads. Tap the door release. It's a small, square glass screen in the lower right corner."

I open the panel door. "Got it. What's next?"

"Second row of data displays from the bottom, there are two blue slider controls on the left side, two green in the middle, and two brown chips on the far right end of the next row down."

My fingers float over the edges of the small chips; the chips are color-coded, just as he said. "Got 'em."

The ship pitches to the left, tossing me backward. I can't hold my balance and sprawling out on the floor. I have to crawl back to the control panel. "What the hell was that?" I ask.

"Goddamn it, they're chasing us!" Nico replies. "Hold on down there."

One of the transporter pads glows blue. "The transporter pad is activated." A faint outline of energy glimmers in the center of the transporter pad. "Someone's trying to board the ship. There's an energy signature on one pad."

"Drag the brown sliders first, one at a time. Then, the blue, one at a time. Do the same thing with the green sliders. In that order. Brown. Blue. Green."

"Brown first." I repeat, and slide the control to the off position. The display glow dims as each one gets shut off. "They're out," I say when it's done. The energy signature flickers and then dims, but doesn't disappear. "What's next?"

"Upper right quadrant of the panel. There's another set of

circuits. Both of them are red. Slide them to the off position. That should do it."

The ship tilts to the right, just as violently as the last maneuver. I crack my head on the corner of the wall console and fall to the ground again. A warm damp spot grows on my scalp. I put my hand up to feel it and it comes away bloody.

The circuits I just switched off—the brown, green, and blue—glow bright and incandescent as they spring to life. "They're over-riding the system," I say, struggling to regain my feet.

The energy signature glows bright on the pa once more and takes human form.

I lunge at the control panel and swipe my fingers over the circuits: brown, green, blue. Finally, red.

Before I can swipe the last red circuit, the lights in the transporter bay—including the lights on the transporter pads—blink out. It's so dark, I can't even see my hand in front of my face.

"Nico?" I call out. "What the hell—"

As quickly as they were extinguished, the lights flicker back on. All the lights except for the transporter pads, which pulsate several times before going dim.

"We're in the cavern. At the entrance to the time portal," Nico says. "Transporter offline?"

"Yeah," I reply. "It was touch-and-go there for a minute. Carter almost boarded us."

I climb the ladder up to the main deck and settle in the co-pilot's seat. Outside the windows, the gemstone-lined cave glistens. Ahead of us, the star points of the portal glow a ghostly white.

"You sure about this?" Nico nods towards the coordinates on the display panel.

"It's the one place they won't think to look for us." I reach over and put my hand on his. He stiffens, but doesn't push me away. "I know you're mad—"

He shoots me a look. "Mad doesn't begin to cover it."

"I know." I take a deep breath and let it out. "I fucked up big time. I don't know if I can make it right. What I know is that someone —probably Trevor—changed my letter and we have to figure out why. We can't go home because they'll be waiting for us."

"If there's a home to go back to." He shifts in his seat and peers out the windows, assessing the situation. "The portal doesn't look any different than it normally does, but I don't know enough about quantum mechanics, or the way the portal works, to assess if that means it's working or not."

"What's the worst that could happen?" I ask, leaning over to peer out the window with him. The walls of the cavern gleam with an unearthly light that radiates from inside the stone.

Nico shakes his head. "Either the portal doesn't let us through, if it's not working, or we get stuck in a temporal loop and never make it home."

"Or we could end up exactly where my coordinates say we'll land."

"Can't go back there." Nico jerks a thumb toward the direction we just left. "Can't go home because they'll arrest us."

"The only way out," I reply, pointing ahead of us, "is through."

"All right. Hang on." Nico sighs and taps the control panel, locking the coordinates into the navigation system. "Gonna be a bumpy ride."

There's the familiar deep hum of the engine as it spins up. Nico swipes the navigation control circuits up, and the ship vaults forward into the portal.

CHAPTER 24

I'M aware of my body floating. Aside from this, I feel no other physical sensations: I must be breathing—if I weren't I wouldn't be conscious of everything around me—but I can't feel the air exchange in my lungs. No inhales. No exhales.

There's no sound.

No scents.

It's pitch-black.

I don't even feel the weight of clothing on my skin.

Am I dreaming? Can you wonder if it's a dream if you're in the middle of one?

I can't feel the muscles in my arm as I bring my hand up in front of my face. In fact, I can't see my hand, though I know that it's there.

Out of the silence, a sound like top-volume feedback from an amplifier **blasts in my ears**. Out of the cacophony, a vibration streaks from my head down to my toes; I wonder if my body is being recalibrated from floating nothingness back into physical matter.

The vibe concentrates in my chest -- a warmth that spreads like someone's pulling a wool blanket around me as I'm sucked down into my body. The sensation isn't heavy. It's lighter than the air I must be breathing but still can't feel.

A voice calls out, so faint that I wonder if it's human. It sounds like an echo and it's growing louder with each iteration.

Yes, it *is* a voice. My name. Someone's calling me.

"Dodger."

The vibration in my core downshifts to the gentle pulse of my own heartbeat.

There's a rough shake of my shoulders and a loud gasp; I'm startled to realize the sound came from me.

I open my eyes to Nico standing over me, peering down into my face.

"God, I thought I lost you," he says with a relieved sigh. "Stay put while I get some water."

He disappears—presumably to fetch the water—and I take blurry stock of my surroundings: I'm in the ship's cockpit. The co-pilot's seat. Outside the windows, dense fog obscures whatever lies beyond it.

My head hurts, a dull throb in my forehead and behind my eyes. Nico returns with a cup. "Drink this."

The water hits the back of my throat with a hot metallic bite. "Did the replicator fill this thing with iron first? It tastes horrible. And it's scalding."

"No, it's room temperature." He takes a huge swig, something he wouldn't be able to do if it were as hot as I think it is. "It'll probably take a few more minutes before your body adjusts. There seem to be a few...side effects."

"Side effects to what?"

"The time jump."

"That makes no sense."

I try to push myself vertical, but a head rush drops me into his arms. He settles me back into the seat.

"Don't try to stand yet."

"Merde." I pinch the bridge of my nose between my fingers. "What happened?"

"Don't know. I woke up fifteen minutes before you came 'round.

You scared the hell out of me," he says, exhaling a loud breath. "I'm pretty sure we were knocked out when we hit the portal."

"Felt like I was floating."

He bends down on one knee, scrutinizing my face like a doctor examining a patient. He grabs a pen light and shines it into my eyes.

I cringe, squinting against the brightness. "Hey!"

"Everything go black?" he asks. "No sounds or smells?"

I nod. "There was a lot of buzzing, too. It was like—"

"Like your insides vibrated so hard they might bust through your skin?"

"Exactly."

He drops the pen light on the command console. "If your recovery is like mine, you'll be back to almost normal in a few minutes."

"How are *you* feeling?" I ask, leaning forward to search his face for lingering physical symptoms. His skin is a little flushed, but no dilated pupils.

"The headache is almost gone," he says, standing. "It took a few minutes to stay vertical without the head rush. I need to bring the transporter system back online. You sit and rest for a bit." He gives a command to the computer. "Betty, get our chameleon cloaking up and running."

"Chameleon cloaking up and running, Gorgeous," she replies.

Nico turns to leave the cockpit, and I grab his hand. This time, he doesn't pull away. Maybe because he was scared to death I was dead. I want to tell him, again, how I didn't mean for any of this to happen, but the look in his eyes talks me out of it: He's still pissed as hell.

I drop his hand and the idea of defending myself. "Any idea where we are?"

"Hopefully, we're exactly where your coordinates said we'd be: December 1755. One of the Acadian settlements just before..."

I pick up where he paused. "Just before The Expulsion. If we can find my parents—"

"We've impacting the timeline enough, don't you think? The only reason we're here is because it's marginally better than doing prison time."

"I'd say it's better than the options Carter gave us." Feeling brave enough, I push myself out of the co-pilot's seat and—wrestling with the Tudor gown I'm still wearing—elbow past Nico to head for the galley. Maybe caffeine will help the time jump jet lag lift quicker. "At least we have a little bit of time to figure out what to do next."

Nico follows me to the replicator. "I wouldn't count on having time to do anything. The physical effects of this trip through the portal are singular. Unprecedented. To my knowledge, nothing like this has never happened before because, if it had, we'd have heard about it during training briefs. Something has changed." He watches me make two cups of Nico's chicory coffee blend. "Not to mention, if Carter follows us into the portal, he can pick up our energy signature through T-Jump Ops and get our location. For all we know, they could already be here."

I hand a mug to him. He barely glances at it before setting it down with a *thunk* on the counter. I drink the liquid down, but can tell it will take at least a dozen cupfuls to clear the haze clouding my brain.

"That fog out there?" He points out the window. "I haven't had time to run tests, yet. If we're not where we're supposed to be, that stuff could be anything. Who knows if we're even still on Earth and whether it's breathable out there."

"Or it could be just fog off the Bay of Fundy. That stuff rolls in off of the ocean all the time."

He doesn't seem to appreciate the tone in my voice. He puts his fists on his hips, then gives me a smirk and a raised eyebrow. I roll my eyes. "Betty, can we breathe the air outside? Also...confirm current coordinates."

"External atmospheric composition supports human life," Betty says. "Current coordinates: Earth, 5.2733 degrees North, 66.0633 West. What is now Saint John, New Barcelona. Would you like to hear how the area was colonized by the Spanish in the late Sixteenth century or the weather report?"

"The Spanish?" My stomach churns and it's not because of time travel jet lag. "So, it's not a French-settled colony, then?"

"There are humans of French descent settled in the area, but they are the minority," Betty says.

I haven't worked missions in Spanish-colonized eras, but I know Observers who have. When I was a pint-sized recruit—Fagin had plucked me from Eighteenth Century New Orleans only weeks before—a first year Observer made it thirty-six hours into a month-long Spanish Inquisition mission before returning in a catatonic state. The experience so traumatized him, the agency created the Hot Zone policy: No First Years assigned to missions set in historically merciless, overly volatile, and brutal times.

Poor guy never recovered.

Trauma would be easier to manage if memory wipes were an exact science; if they could be targeted and selective enough to erase only the bad and leave the good. It doesn't work that way. Wiping a mind is an all-or-nothing proposition. All Observers carry the burden of memory. Some better at it than others, and if they're not, they at least hide the pain behind a believable mask.

All time travelers undergo regular psychological testing, especially after psychologically scarring work events, but there are ways to get around those tests. Self-medication is the most popular option Observers employ, to some degree or another, to manage the memories. As long as the situation doesn't get out of hand, superiors usually turn a blind eye.

"Could be worse." I offer a half-hearted shrug.

Nico must be thinking about the same unlucky Observer. "Whether things are worse because of your meddling, or not, is a matter of perspective. Depending on who's telling the story, the Spanish were among the more brutal colonizers. I'm sure the Aztecs would agree. And the ones who endured the inquisition."

"You're Spanish," I say. "Do you really have so little affection for your own people?

"I'm a lot of things," he says in dry, patient tone. "This time travel gig opens your world up, doesn't it? Or at least it should. You know the rules: You can't go back to your own time unless your memory is wiped. I have too many incredible memories to lose. You, for instance." From the look on his face, that bit of information wasn't supposed to make it out into the open. His eyes lock on mine as he runs his tongue across his bottom lip. He holds the gaze for a long minute and then, flustered, turns toward the nearest computer control panel. "You're such a pain in the ass."

A sliver of hope that Nico doesn't hate me sparks my heart. Still, humility is probably the best approach. "I know."

He huffs out a big breath and shakes his head. He taps a sequence of commands on the control pad. "I could do without all this bullshit, just so you know."

"At least we're still on Earth and the air is breathable. In case, you know, we wanted to—"

"Oh, no you don't." He spins around and points a finger at me. "You. Stay. Put."

"Just hear me out."

"No. There's nothing to hear." He shimmies down ladder, headed toward the transporter pads. I follow close behind. "We're here because we were minutes away from that maniac boarding the ship and arresting us."

"Carter said we can fix this mess," I shout down to him.

"Could've been a trick to get in the door."

"On the off chance he wasn't, wouldn't it make sense to get a good look at the environment out there and see what has changed, so we can figure out what we're dealing with?"

"First, you have a nasty habit of going off-script. The de Medici job is a good example. Pretty much every job is a damn good example." Nico works through the sequence to activate the transporters.

He frowns when the device doesn't come back online, then pops the composite panel off of the display panel to work. "Second, you don't listen. I screamed at you to leave Tower Hill and you ignored me. Which meant I had to rescue your ass when Carter nearly snagged you the first time."

"I didn't know he was here."

"I did. Which is what I was trying to tell you while you ignored me."

"Sorry."

He glances over his shoulder, and asks softly. "How long did you plan it?"

Merde. He wants to do this now? "It's...complicated."

"Did you plan it from the beginning or was it a spur-of-the-moment thing?"

"Like I said. Complicated."

His shoulders sag and he lets out a ragged breath. "Aside from the obvious cosmic implications, did you stop for a nanosecond to think about Fagin and me?" His voice is soft, wounded.

I move toward him and place a hand in the middle of his back. The warmth of his skin radiates through his shirt—he still wears the linen blouse of his Tudor costume, but the coat, doublet, and hose have been replaced by black sweatpants, wool socks, and athletic shoes.

"I couldn't think about anything except saving Papa and Maman." I feel his breathing change; it's deep, controlled. Like he's trying to contain an explosion. "I know I fucked up, but I need you to believe me." I turn him around to face me. The pain in his voice pierces me, but I'm unprepared for the devastation in his eyes. "Someone added the part about Anne being pregnant to that letter. Henry wouldn't have killed her if it were a matter of being in love with Wyatt. I think it was the thought of her carrying another man's child that pushed him over the edge."

His lips purse as he considers my words. "Who has a vested

interest in keeping the king and his lady apart? Trevor may be the easy answer, but it has to be bigger than her."

"Isn't it obvious? She's working with Carter. They probably planned this whole thing."

"It has to be bigger than both of them. Why risk execution or a mindless exile to a prison planet for changing something so big in the timeline?" Nico steps back, shakes his head. "No. A fish stinks from the head and this has upper-echelon Benefactor stench all over it."

I have no answer, so I change the subject. "Any idea what we do now? Like you said: Can't go back. Can't go home."

"Only way out is through." he says, echoing my earlier words. He nods his head toward the display panel on the wall. "Go on. I know you're dying to find out, so why don't you just ask?"

"Ask... what?" I say, slowly, not quite sure what he's getting at.

"Run a query about your parents. See if Betty can find anything on them."

Now that I face finally knowing the answer to the question, I'm not at all sure I want to ask it. *What if they're both still dead? Even worse, what if they never lived at all? What if—*

"Go on. The sooner you know, the sooner we can focus on finding a way out of this mess."

Deep breath. *Here we go.* "Betty, search historical records for Louis Arseneau, born 1727 in Saint John. Cross reference search: Mariette Longpré Arseneau, born 1730, also in Saint John."

"Searching," she replies.

My heart beats like a dozen hummingbirds' wings in flight; each passing second feels like an hour. I sense Nico's gaze on me, and glance over my shoulder. *He is looking at me.* I can't quite decipher his mood. Is it curiosity in his eyes? Apprehension? Maybe both. He bites his lower lip then returns to his work.

"Records related to Louis Arseneau and Mariette Longpré Arseneau are inaccessible," the computer says. "Try again later, honey."

"What does that mean, inaccessible?" I say, typing the search criteria into the search field on the display panel. Historical records are recorded in multiple formats—holographic, written, and audio only. Still, my search returns no results. The error message displayed reads: *Database offline*. "Where are the historical records? No files display even through manual search."

This gets Nico's attention. He scrambles to his feet and rushes to peer over my shoulder. We stare at the blinking cursor where the database sub-folder list should be. "Damn. Who knows how man systems have been affected by whatever that energy pulse was." he says. "Betty, modify diagnostic parameters to analyze all ship's systems, priority on critical systems first. I want to know what's malfunctioning, the suspected cause of the damage, how widespread the impact is, and recommended resolutions."

"Just because she didn't find anything doesn't mean my parents aren't out there," I say. Now that the door has been opened, even just a crack, I need to run through it to see what's on the other side.

Nico senses the urgency in my voice and gives me a look. He backs away, both hands held up to stop further conversation. It doesn't work.

"Aren't you the least bit curious to see what, exactly, has changed?"

"We're not going outside until I get a handle on how much damage we've sustained."

"Betty," I say, as Nico places his diagnostic tools back into the open toolbox on the floor. "How long will it take to run the system tests?"

"The entire diagnostic array will take six hours to complete," Betty says.

"Sounds like more than enough time for a quick recon mission into the village. Unless you just want to sit here and twiddle your thumbs while Betty works," I say, smiling.

Nico sighs and looks me over head-to-toe. My gown is still damp with mud from the race to the ship from Tower Hill. He looks at his own clothes -- not exactly eighteenth-century attire. "We need to get cleaned up. Do we have the right clothes in storage? We can't go out there looking like holdovers from a Ren Faire."

"There are a few pieces we can put together to blend in. It's winter, so long, heavy coats will cover a multitude of fashion sins."

I move toward the ladder, but Nico pulls me back. "Before I agree to anything, I have a few conditions: First, you do exactly what I say, the second I give you an order. We can't lose track of each other for an instant; who knows whether our external communication will be online from one moment to the next?"

I salute and he responds with a smirk. "I'm not kidding, Dodger. I need eyes on you at all times."

"Aye, Cap'n. And second condition?"

"If we find either of your parents..." His eyes go dark and serious. "No contact. Not a word. Not a gesture. Nothing."

"But—"

He grips both of my shoulders and pulls me close. For a breathless moment, I hope for a kiss to get lost in. Instead, I get more grim reality.

"You've unraveled a damn big thread in the timeline." His voice turns pleading. "Whatever you see, whatever you hear, don't interfere. You'll have to be satisfied with just knowing whether or not they're here."

My slight hesitation is enough to set his jaw in stone. "Do you want to make things worse? Either you agree to these conditions or I swear I'll throw you over my shoulder and lock you in your quarters for however long it takes to get the hell out of here."

I consider throwing a "you wouldn't dare" at him, but I know—without a doubt—that he *would* dare if I don't follow through with his conditions. "Fine. Agreed."

His fingers dig into my shoulders. "Once more with feeling, please."

I narrow my eyes at him, cross my heart, then raise my hand in a three-fingered oath that's practically genuflection. "I solemnly fucking swear that I will obey your fucking orders until the fucking recon patrol is over."

He relaxes his grip on me. "If nothing else, I trust it when you swear. I'm gonna hold you to your word. Take anything back and there will be hell to pay."

CHAPTER 25

"REMEMBER WHERE WE PARKED," I say, trying to lighten the mood as we trudge through the ice-mud on the beaten path into Saint John.

A sideways glance at Nico confirms my suspicions: his pensive expression suggests he's regretting giving permission for this venture into town.

He turns around and walks backward, peering toward the stone barn that hides our ship. If it weren't cloaked, the nose of the ship would be visible for fifteen or twenty feet past the corner of the structure. For now, we can see only a gray winter sky and barren fields.

Nico adjusts the buckskin bag slung around his shoulders and turns his attention back to the road. "Better pray to every god you might believe in that the chameleon cloak doesn't go on the fritz. If it does, our cover is blown."

"You said we have at least enough power to finish running the diagnostic tests and maintain critical systems. Doesn't that include the cloaking program?"

"It does, but only because I configured the critical systems list to include the cloaking program and life support and security systems. What worries me is having consistent power. It there's a fluctuation in the power grid, it could impact which systems come online and how long they stay intact. The cloaking program could cause the chameleon shield to flicker from invisible to visible. If the power goes out completely while the cloaking is unstable, the ship could stay noticeable. That would be...bad."

"The Master of Understatement." I chuckle. "Succinct way to say we'd be screwed more than we are if the power grid fails."

We walk for a quarter mile more in silence, surveying the terrain on the route toward Saint John, which lays two or three miles further down the road; we can see the first few buildings at the edge of town, standing like sentinels on either side of the path. There's also a pillar of dark smoke stretching into the sky just beyond the northern-most border.

A bonfire of some sort, maybe?

We'd found passable eighteenth-century garb in the costume storage compartments: a chemise, long skirt, jacket, linen cap and neckerchief—covered by a long wool cloak—for me, and for Nico: synthetic buckskin breeches, linen shirt, and a thick hooded hunting frock that falls just to his knees.

The wind gusts as it rolls in off the sea, blowing my hem up several inches. We pull our woolen outer garments closer around our now shivering bodies, but it doesn't seem to make much difference; the temperature feels like it's dropped at least ten degrees since we left the ship. On the eastern horizon, a line of low, gray clouds stretches like a sheet for several miles north and south of us.

"Snow clouds," I say. I pull my cloak's hood up over my head. "If we're lucky, we've got a couple of hours before that system moves in."

Nico turns to check the ship's visibility status again, and I point out the obvious: "You can go back to the ship if it makes you feel better. I can handle a simple recon mission."

He laughs. "Like you did at Tower Hill? Nope. Thanks for playing. I'm not taking a risk that you'll go off script on this one." He chews his bottom lip as he considers me with a long sideways glance. "Where you go, I go."

"Suit yourself." I pause, glancing over my shoulder with Nico as he looks one more time. Still invisible. I take it as a good omen.

Instead of the quaint cottages and gray-shingled business establishments I remember, the main street is a hodge-podge of ramshackle apartments shoved together in a discombobulated stack that reminds me of a toddler's clumsy, haphazardly built block tower. The edifices aren't flush along their front—some are set several feet deeper than the unit right next door—and each door is painted a different color, making the whole structure look like a disorganized rainbow.

The apartment structure reaches skyscraper-esque height in some areas, and they butt up against each other so close, there isn't a sliver of daylight through one building and the next.

"Not what you remember?" Nico says.

"Not even close."

As jarring as Main Street's aesthetic is, the most unnerving and noticeable detail about the town is the empty streets: There's not a soul in sight. There are no animals around, either; no horses tied at hitching posts outside places of business, no dogs sniffing for food.

The only thing keeping me from thinking we've just dropped into a ghost town is the muted drone of a crowd—like the one at Lady Anne's execution—coming from the East.

"This is weird," I say, still scanning buildings on both side of the road. "Are they all on holiday?"

"I've got a bad feeling," Nico says, fidgeting with the strap of the leather rucksack slung across his body. Inside the bag are two phasers. He opens the flap and digs them out, handing one to me. "Just in case."

Nico tucks his phaser into the waistband of his breeches and conceals it with his hunting frock. I do the same with mine.

I nod toward the East. "Sound is coming from that way."

"I'll take point. You cover our backs."

The streetscape changes when we turn right and head down the next avenue. The domiciles on this street are a dramatic change from the compact conditions we'd just seen. This street screams affluence:

Stately homes feature Arabesque iron lace balconies, covered passageways, and repeating arches from one building to the next. If I didn't know better, I'd say New Orleans' French Quarter, during the years of Spanish influence, had been transplanted here.

Childhood memories are imperfect, but there isn't a single familiar sight. Acadia of 1755—the year the Great Expulsion began and my childhood ended—doesn't exist anymore; this place is definitely not my home.

Even the ocean, its brine coating my lips as the wind hits my face, smells different, tastes different. The air is also tinged with soot, the result—no doubt—of that smoke cloud rising in gradient plumes of silvered gray and black.

The smoke pillar looks bigger, more ominous, and I'm not altogether convinced it's due to the point of view I have here compared to our view on the outer edge of town.

Nico seems to notice it, too. "Is it just me or does that smoke look worse?"

"Not just you," I say.

"Can we take a short cut through there?" He points to a narrow alleyway on our right.

"Your guess is as good as mine. I recognize nothing here."

He gives me a quick, sympathetic look, but doesn't slow his gait as we move into position at the entrance to the backstreet. We pull our phasers and advance down the alley, settling into our ingrained recon patrol patterns. Nico checks everything on the left, I check the right side, both of us careful to spot-check sections of roof we can see.

When the top crate in a pyramid of boxes stacked against the left wall topples into our path, we swing around to lock phasers on whoever—or whatever—is moving around inside the pile. Out of the splintered wood, several streaks of gray scurry past and disappear around the corner behind us.

Nico lets out a slow breath. "Rats."

My skin crawls. "I hate rats!"

It takes several more turns down other streets and alleys to find the wharf. The docks are an explosion of noise and heat, the latter emanating from a burning ship in the harbor—the light of the fire slices through the fog like a hot knife through butter. To the right of the ship that's engulfed in flames—and minutes away from sinking into the bay—sits a smaller ship.

I'm so transfixed by the fire that I don't realize Nico has moved until his hand stretches down into my face from above me. When I look up, I realize he's standing on a stack of crates to get a better view of the situation. He pulls me up next to him and I get a panoramic view of the crowd.

Everyone in town must be standing on the docks watching the ships burn. There are hundreds of people.

At the front of the crowd, a platoon of Spanish soldiers guards three men, all of them bound. The prisoners are wrestled into a rowboat and taken to the second ship. One soldier, who looks to be in command, addresses the crowd. Because we're at the back of the throng, we can't hear a word.

"My kingdom for a megaphone," Nico says, looking out over the crowd.

Soon enough, the commander's words drift back to us in a series of comments passed from congregants nearest the action to the rows behind them. By the time the content of the speech reaches our section of the crowd, I'm left wondering if this is just a high-stakes version of the telephone game.

"What news, sir?" Nico asks one man dressed in a mishmash of clothing styles. I've seen frontiersmen before and with his eclectic style choices of buckskins and furs, he certainly fits the bill.

He also smells like he's been camping for the last millennia and is dire need of a good washing.

"Pirates." The man replies, in Spanish, as he jerks a thumb at the burning ship. "Them and the sorry fuckers in Dante's Inferno."

"How many people were saved from the ship before it caught fire?" I ask. My stomach knots. Papa didn't talk about it in front of me, but I'd once overheard his account of being a helpless eyewitness to another ship burning into the sea. He talked of men screaming and jumping overboard hoping to escape death, but instead were swamped by a churning sea that swallowed them down.

Memories of losing Maman at sea wash over me. I feel the swell of the waves battering the ship's hull and the biting cold of the North Atlantic sea. I shudder.

The frontiersman laughs like I've asked the most ridiculous question. "Saved? That's the punishment for their crimes: burning with their ships. 'Tis a warning for all pirates that may follow that their brand of skullduggery will meet swift and merciless justice in Saint John. There are handsome rewards when scum like them are brought to the garrison. I'd wager whoever turned them in can now feed their family like kings for at least the next month."

Given that my current profession is a peg leg and pet parrot away from those miserable bastards—though it's a few hundred light years ahead of these wood vessels, I've got a ship, too—my heart skips a beat in terrified empathy.

"Is everyone in town here?" Nico asks. "This is the largest crowd at an execution I've ever seen."

"It's obligatory," Frontiersman says with a grim smile. He nods toward the sentries posted behind us. A line of soldiers stretches from one end of the docks to the other. "The garrison commanders like to remind us regular folk not to put a toe very far outside the lines."

We watch as the dinghy reaches the second ship and they haul the men up on deck. Within minutes, the executioners return to their boat and begin the journey back to shore, leaving me to wonder how the condemned are kept from jumping over the rails on the other side of the ship. *Are they in the cargo hold or tied to the masts?* I can't see them from where I stand.

From a third boat, archers shoot flaming arrows onto the deck of what is about to become their funeral pyre.

I've learned that public execution is a better window into a human soul than most anything else. Read the bystanders' faces and three types of people will stand out in the crowd: the Morbidly Curious, the Sports Fans, the Justice Seekers.

The Morbidly Curious seem to be the most benign. They're not rowdy or conspicuous; they're the ones closest to the action, watching every detail from beginning to end, with ghoulish fascination.

Sports Fans are the bloodsport spectators; the celebratory mood can usually be traced to these people. For them, executions provide a release from the soul-sucking grind of daily life. They're the party-goers out to have a have a good time, and they usually bring picnic lunches.

Then, there are the Justice Seekers; these are the ones who unnerve me. They watch death with cold, holy judgment, certain they've helped mete out the Lord's justice for that day simply by bearing witness. Exacting payment for sins is their highest concern.

I have no illusions about who and what I am. I steal things and do my best to survive when the universe pitches me, headfirst, into purgatory. This alternate reality version of what I hoped would still be home is looking more like purgatory every minute.

A dark-haired man standing fifty feet away catches my attention; in this sea of strangers, there's something familiar about him. The build of his body. The slope of his nose and strong jawline as he stands in profile. His dark hair. He reminds me of...

What did Papa look like?

My breath catches in my chest. I grab Nico's arm and point in the direction of the hooded figure. "Nico, that man. I think it's...he looks like Papa."

"You know this is a needle and haystack situation, right? I think you see what you want to see, cariña."

The dark-haired man elbows past a group of women huddled together against the cold; space between one body and the next seems to be little more than the width of a hairline crack. I can measure his progress through the crowd in inches, not feet, as the gargantuan physical effort to maintain forward momentum slows his advancement to a crawl.

My gaze snaps from the retreating figure to Nico and back again. I must look more desperate with each repeated glance because Nico sighs and waves a hand, conceding defeat.

"Fine. Let's go," he says. "You stay right behind me and, I swear, if you take off, I'll kick your ass all the way home."

"Fair enough." A beat. "Is now an appropriate time to remind you how much I enjoy spankings?"

It's meant as a joke—kinda—but Nico maintains a steadfast seriousness. "You won't be crazy about *this* spanking."

From ground-level, it's impossible to see over the wall of people in front of us—we're enveloped so quickly by the crowd it's claustrophobic. Even Nico—all six feet, two inches of him—has trouble seeing over some of the taller members of the mob.

"We can't wade through all these people fast enough to catch up with whoever you think you saw." He nods toward another narrow alley, identical to the one we'd emerged from twenty minutes prior. "This way."

"We have to figure out a way past the guards," I say, noting that each exit toward the center of town has soldiers posted to ensure no one leaves the party early.

"We'll think of a distraction. Just keep moving."

Before I learn what Nico has in mind to divert the soldiers' attention, the wind changes, shifting the billowing smoke toward shore. The crowd shuffles toward the alleys to escape the noxious fumes; their hive mind apparently wagers the authorities will also be concerned about avoiding the acrid cloud as it rolls in.

Seems the crowd won their bet: The guards, recognizing the crowd's mood turning anxious, abandon any attempts to stop the townsfolk from dispersing.

Nico pulls me closer and we melt into the crowd as it funnels into the choked artery leading to the next street. Though the air is frigid with ice particles, the cramped space turns into a slow heating oven with the body heat of several hundred bodies crammed into it.

Nico positions me in front of him. His hands go to my waist and he steers me like a rudder on a ship as we push our way to the right side of the crowd. "Don't get your hopes up," he says. "In this crowd, it would be a miracle if we catch up with him."

We exit onto the next street and nudge through several clusters of people trying to maneuver around us. We settle on the long porch of a mercantile store shaded by a balcony and watch the throng pass. There are droves of raven-haired, athletic men who look like they could have sired me.

What did Papa look like?

None of the women look like my mother.

Ten minutes more pass before Nico ventures a question.

"Anything?"

I shake my head; tears sting my eyes. Nothing feels like home.

I knew this was a long shot. I didn't expect the search to feel so...

Hopeless.

Nico puts his arm around my waist and we stand in silence watching the towns' people slide back into their daily lives.

Betty's voice buzzes through our CommLinks. "Intruder alert, Commander Garcia, darling. Security system breach is imminent. Unknown entities attempting to access transporter system."

"Fuck." Nico says. "Betty, divert power from non-essential programs to the security system. Lock everyone out of the transporter system except me. Authentication: Garcia 022358."

We pick our way through the crowd, but it hasn't thinned enough to make getting out of town a speedy process. The snow that sat on the horizon as we entered town arrives in a flurry of fat flakes that will lay a thick blanket of white over the town within the hour.

Betty broadcasts another alert: "Security system breach in progress. Intruders have boarded the vessel."

Nico said very little as we raced—as much as anyone can race in a burgeoning snowstorm—back to where we'd left the ship. We maintained radio silence since the last of Betty's transmissions; further transmissions would help whoever broke into the ship to trace the signal to our coordinates.

For all we know, they've already tagged our location as we sit, shivering, in the stone barn less than a football field's distance from the ship. While the barn offers protection enough from the wind, it's almost as freezing inside as it is out. The storm creeps closer to blizzard conditions, and our options for finding another sanctuary are few.

"The ship is still here." Nico stares down at the micro-control panel in his hand. "We're locked out."

Nico alternates between burying his nose in the data streaming from the ship's computer into his Comm Panel and peering out the narrow barn window at the field where the cloaked ship is parked.

"Did you think it wouldn't be?" I stamp my feet on the straw, more to generate some heat than from impatience to know what's going on.

"Why are they still allowing access to the ship's systems?" he says, muttering more to himself than to me.

"I think the answer to that depends on who broke into our ship. What are the odds of our visitors being anyone other than Carter and his goons?"

"Fifty-fifty. If it's not him, the Benefactors could have sent another recovery team to clean up this mess. If we're seriously unlucky, our guests are government agents and we can expect to either be marooned in this time or taken back to a prison planet."

"Would they do that? Strand us here, I mean."

"Let's assume that both the government and the Benefactors are capable of doing whatever the hell they want, whenever the hell they want," Nico says. "Just in case the intent of our guests is to make us permanent residents in 1755, we need to find out who has taken control of our ship and what their game is. I'm trying to hack into Betty's internal video feeds without being detected. If we can get a remote look inside, we may at least have the element of surprise on our side."

Having witnessed executions in two separate centuries, I'm not keen to attend a third any time soon, especially if it means I'm on the chopping block. I'm not crazy about the possibility of a memory wipe and a prison sentence, either.

How hard would it be to melt into 1755 again?

"Any way we can hack the transporter system to sneak back on the ship?" I say, pacing the floor.

Nico rolls his eyes and shoots me a pointed look. "Did you sleep through Emergency Ship Procedures class when you were in training? Even non-mechanics and commanders are required to pass it to prepare for emergencies. You know... like the one we're in right now." He huffs out a big breath of air that contains a hint of an impatient growl. "You must have because if you'd paid any attention, at all, you'd know one of the first actions after taking emergency command of a time travel ship is to change the security codes to prevent unauthorized ship transports."

"First, yes, I slept through Intro to Ship Maintenance because it was boring. Second, how the hell are we supposed to get on the ship if those assholes changed the security codes?"

He waggles the handheld at me. "Which is why I'm trying to hack my way in through the backdoor of Betty's systems. So far, they've done a damn good job of blocking all paths to bypassing the encryption for system access authentication to even get to the backdoor."

Outside the barn, the wind howls.

My stomach rumbles and a few seconds later, so does Nico's; neither of us have eaten all day. Before I can ask about the plan to scrounge up our next meal, the wood doors on both ends of the barn fling open.

Figures in winter camouflage uniforms and masks swarm through the entrances.

I hear clicks; the sound of weapons with silencers.

I dive at the bag where we stashed the phasers, but there's a penetrating sting as whatever they're firing hits my ass.

Tranquilizer darts.

I stumble, reach behind me in a failed attempt to pull the damn thing out.

Nico lies sprawled on the ground, a tranq dart lodged in his shoulder.

Legs numb.

Head swims.

Nothingness swallows me whole.

CHAPTER 26

CONSCIOUSNESS RISES up through the murky gray. There's vague awareness of warm air blowing on my face.

Purple splotches swell over the dark background of my still closed eyes as light soaks through the skin. I watch the shifting patterns with detached curiosity as they flow and ebb in fluid patterns.

Several things hit me at once: A dull ache fills my head and works its way down my body. My eyelids feel heavy, weighted; it takes effort to force open them. When I finally do, everything is hazy, like someone smeared an opaque glaze over my corneas while I slept.

I force my eyes to focus. A ventilation duct sits above me. I'm lying on a cot in a corner of a cargo bay. To my right, a row of costume racks stretches down the wall.

I'm on our ship.

Groaning, I push myself to sitting position. Footsteps echo above me, then there's the *ping* of boots on metal rungs as someone descends the ladder at the other end of the room.

With not much time to find a place hide, I bolt out of the bed and within three steps run smack into an invisible wall. The aborted inertia throws me backward onto the floor.

Commander Jackson Carter strides toward me, flanked by four armed guards.

"Merde," I sigh, not caring that I'm still sprawled on the floor.

"Good. You're awake," he says, as he stops a few inches from the force field. "I was hoping the tranquilizer wasn't too strong. We had to base the dosage on your recorded body weight at your last physical. But that was six months ago, so who knows if that's still accurate."

"Where's Nico?"

He gestures at the transparent space between him and me. "I regret that the dramatics at the barn were necessary, and the temporary restraints." He grabs a metal chair propped up against a nearby wall and turns it around so he can straddle it while resting his forearms on top of the chair back. "With our previous history, I didn't think you'd agree to meet for tea."

The four men stand in a line behind him and I wonder which one of them fired the dart that got me. Figuring that I'm stuck 'in this makeshift jail cell unless I can talk Carter into releasing me, I crawl back onto the bed.

"You couldn't have used phasers?" I say. "Tranq darts are so old school."

"As imprecise as tranquilizers are, there were locals in the area. Strange flashing lights inside the barn might have attracted the attention."

"Where's Nico?" I ask.

"We talk first. Then we'll discuss Commander Garcia."

"I'm not gonna talk to you about anything until I know Nico's okay."

"Garcia is fine. He woke up thirty minutes ago."

"You'll understand if I don't take your word for it."

"Dodger, you wound me," he says with a smirk.

I'm not sure which annoys me more: his tone of feigned outrage or his use of my nickname. I scoot backward and sit cross-legged against the wall and wait.

He contemplates me for a moment, then groans with reluctance.

"Computer, enable audio channels so we can speak to Commander Garcia."

"Screw you," Betty replies. The juxtaposition between the snark and her synthesized voice makes me chuckle. "You hurt Commander Garcia. I do not like you."

"Your computer has an attitude," Carter says, sounding irritated. "She's been fighting me since I boarded the ship."

"She hates assholes." I give him an eat-shit-and-die look. "Betty, please enable audio channel access. I want to talk to Nico."

There's a pause before she answers. "I will connect you for thirty seconds. The commander needs his rest."

"Thanks, Betty," I reply. "Nico, are you there?"

"Dodger!" Nico says, relieved. "You okay?"

"Little sore. Got a massive headache, but no major damage. You?"

"Same." He pauses for a moment. "I'm confined to quarters."

I glare at him. "I'm not. They stuck me in a corner of the cargo hold behind a restraining force field."

"You're okay. That's what matters."

"Yeah. You, too."

Carter makes a slashing motion across his throat and one of his goons taps a control pad.

"Nico?" I say.

Silence.

"I've muted the speakers, so even if your ship's computer left the channel open, you won't hear anything else he says. I've proven Commander Garcia is fine. Let's talk," Carter says.

"You must be terrified of me."

He chuckles. "How d'you figure that?"

"Do you need that much help to subdue one tiny thief inside a force field?"

Carter glances at his reinforcements before giving me a squint-eyed appraisal. "I've seen you wriggle out of tricky situations. I'm being cautious while we chat."

"Why don't we braid each other's hair and paint our nails, too?"

"There's that Arseneau sass I know so well." His face hardens. "It's time you appreciate the gravity of your situation."

"I don't appreciate anything about this. Your word choice sucks." The throbbing in my head shifts forward, settling in my temples. I press a palm against the right side of my head.

"Show some gratitude." he says. "Both you and Garcia are breathing. Those tranquilizer darts could've been bullets."

"The only reason we're alive is because the Benefactors need us for something. Otherwise, we would've been dead, or memory wiped, the second you captured us. Tell me I'm wrong."

"You're half-wrong." He raises one eyebrow in response to my confused scowl. "If you're done pouting, I have questions."

"You can ask. Doesn't mean I'll answer."

Carter rises from the chair and paces in front of the force field. My eyes follow his movements. He's two feet away, but it might as well be a hundred miles with this invisible wall between us. Glancing down at the portable force field generator, I see the power light is solid green. *If I can just find a weak spot in the field somewhere.*

He notes the flick of my eyes from the force field generator back to his face with an inquisitive tilt of the head. "I can always electrify it if that will remove temptation for you."

I blink and look away.

Carter's opening question is less than impressive. "You've accepted the freelance mercenary jobs from the greedier Benefactors for a while now, haven't you?"

I barely contain my laughter. He folds his arms over his chest and waits for my giggles to fade.

"Interrogation 101: Questions work better when you don't already know the answer," I say.

"Before you make your next smartass remark, remember this: I control your food, drink, and bathroom privileges. I can also blare noise over the ship's speakers, twenty-four seven, and keep you awake for the next three nights in a row. Sleep deprivation is an excellent way to motivate answers to questions."

"That's torture."

"Whatever."

I wonder if there's a bluff buried beneath his poker face. While I'm certain—*mostly* certain—that I'm important to the Benefactors, I don't know how far he's authorized to go to extract information.

Merde. Better not push too much further.

"I've been doing side jobs for Benefactors for a while," I say.

"Do you know the names of the individuals who pay for your services?"

"No one knows who the Benefactors are, they—"

"Are anonymous. Yes, I know." He folds his arms over his chest. His eyes narrow. "I'm asking if *you* know the names of the individuals who hired you?"

"I've never met any of them. It's safer that way."

Carter nods. "Why take jobs that you know will land you on a prison planet for life if you're caught?"

Surely, he can't be that clueless. I stare at him for a long moment, trying to determine if he is, in fact, dim-witted. "Have you ever been an indentured servant, Commander Carter?"

He doesn't seem surprised by my question. In fact, he takes it in stride with a smooth, denial. "No. I haven't."

"I have. A long time ago, I decided that having lots and lots of money is the best way to prevent anyone from ever owning me—in any way—ever again."

He purses his lips and gives a perfunctory nod. "Fair enough. Tell me how you got this particular job in the court of King Henry the Eighth."

"You're kidding, right?"

"I thought we agreed there would be no more smartass questions."

"I'm not being a smartass. You've been around a long time. Do I have to tell you how mercenaries work? You reported me to the Benefactors after the de Medici job. You put me in this position, and you have the *gall*—"

"I didn't report you to the Benefactors," he says in a tone as sincere and matter-of-fact as though he'd just told me that crabs can't sing.

I vault off the bed. If not for the force field between us, we'd be standing nose-to-nose. "Liar."

He doesn't blink. We glare at each other for an interminable minute.

"I'll ask it one more time: How did you get the assignment to King Henry's court?"

"You want honest answers from me, then you be honest. I was told that you reported me."

"Whoever made that claim is a bald-faced liar."

Thinking back to the first conversation about this disciplinary assignment, I'm certain Fagin told me Carter's report started this whole mess. "I want to talk to Nico again. And to Fagin. Until that happens, I'm done."

"I say when you're done."

"Go fuck yourself."

"You first, sweetheart." His upper lip curls in a sneer. There's a momentary struggle of conflicting emotions on his face, and I see the moment he decides that whatever he's thinking of doing to me likely isn't worth the consequences. He probably doesn't have authority to torture me.

He takes several steps back from the force field and composes himself, locking away the rage—or whatever it is—that seems to simmer inside him. He nods at a subordinate, who turns his back to us and speaks in a low voice into his CommLink.

"You don't want to talk to me? Fine. Maybe you'll have different answers for a familiar face."

Minutes later, there are footsteps pinging against the metal ladder as someone descends into the cargo hold. Thinking it's Nico, I feel a sense of smug satisfaction at winning at least a small battle with Carter.

Five minutes ago, I would've given almost anything to talk to

Fagin and brainstorm a way out of this mess. Now that she's standing next to Carter, an enigmatic expression on her face, I'm questioning my own perceptions. She glances at him and he nods in return.

What the fuck is going on?

Carter turns the metal chair around and gestures for her to sit. She follows the order with no hesitation. He stands behind her, a confident look in his eyes.

"Hey, kiddo," Fagin says. She sounds tired.

"Hey yourself."

"Wouldn't you be more comfortable sitting down?" She glances at the bed behind me.

"I'm fine right here."

She nods. "Recovering from the tranquilizer okay?"

"He told you about that?"

"I watched it go down."

"Oh," I say, raising an eyebrow. I wait for more, something that sounds like the Fagin who would be incensed over this whole situation, but it doesn't come. She doesn't say that they forced her to watch, that it was difficult or upsetting or rage-inducing to see her protégé—her child—drugged and captured. She doesn't offer empathy or sorrow. I get the distinct impression that she's free to roam the ship at will.

She just sits there like a stone with a stupid, blank expression on her face. "Was it entertaining? Because I can't tell you it sure as hell wasn't fun for me."

She leans forward in the chair. "Clémence, listen carefully. I know you're confused and scared. But—"

"You forgot angry as fuck and more than a little sick because you *watched* them shoot me and you're talking about it like it's the goddamn weather report."

She exhales a ragged breath. "Do you remember the conversation in my office before we began training for England?"

She doesn't flinch when I level a steady gaze at her. "Every damn word. You said the Benefactors designed this punishment mission because he—" I point at Carter. "—reported me for fucking with his retirement."

"Carter didn't report you." She runs her tongue over her bottom lip. "I was...mistaken."

"No, you weren't. You don't make mistakes like that. Your network is so wide, your contacts so trustworthy, you would *never* be mistaken like that."

"No one's perfect," Carter says with a loathsome smirk.

Fagin raises a hand and casts a furtive look over her shoulder at him. He falls silent again.

What the actual fuck is going on?

"More importantly," she continues, "do you remember the part about the Benefactors' judgment if we failed?"

"Prison or death. Pretty dramatic stuff. Hard to forget." Reality hits me between the eyes and anger turns to sick fear in the pit of my stomach. "We didn't get everything on the list."

"No. We didn't. Because you changed the historical timeline, we didn't even get close to completing the mission," she says. "This means if we don't work with Carter, we have no help. No protection. How long do you think we'd last being in the wind before the Benefactors caught up to us?"

"He works for the Benefactors," I say. "How is working with him going to protect us?" I turn to Carter. "I'll bet you were the hooded guy who attacked Anne on the staircase, too."

"Remember when I said you were half-wrong?" Carter says, folding his arms. "I work for the GTC. I'm in deep cover working to infiltrate the Benefactors. I wasn't involved in the attack on Lady Anne. That was all Trevor's team. We haven't caught up with them yet."

"Trevor has a team? So, the government knows we're mercenaries and will protect us because we didn't steal all of the shit we were supposed to steal?" I laugh. "That makes no sense. If you work for the government, you'd have us on an execution block or on our way to a prison planet right now."

"There's more to the story," Fagin says. "Listen to Carter. If you don't, our lives won't be the only ones on the line. Nico's life—and many others—will be in danger, too. Please, Dodger. Stop being so damn stubborn and listen."

"Listening is easy. Believing either of you at this point...not so much," I say.

"Infuriating. Obstinate kid." Fagin mutters as she jumps up to pace a short line between the chair and the force field.

Carter moves past Fagin and places a portable hologram display device on the floor. "Computer, play surveillance hologram Trevor215. The time stamp is ten minutes after Arseneau planted her letter in the king's chambers."

A scaled-down hologram recording springs to life in mid-air. We watch as Becca Trevor, disguised as Cesario, sneaks up the privy stairs to King Henry's chambers.

"Computer, zoom in on Trevor's right hand." Carter says.

She carries a piece of parchment, folded and sealed. She steps over the two unconscious sentries I hypo sprayed and slips into the king's chambers. The surveillance images fade, and Carter says, "I'll bet you know at least part of what the letter in her hand says." He steps closer to the force field barrier and swipes his fingers over the screen of a portable computer display. He holds it up so I can see. It's a list of Trevor's computer files.

He taps a file and shows me its contents. "Look familiar?"

My Dearest Thomas,
I weep for our lost love as I prepare to marry the king.

"That bitch," I interrupt. "She hacked my files."

"Indeed," Carter says. "Lieutenant Trevor has been under

surveillance for over a year," She's a Benefactor mole, groomed for years to infiltrate the GTC."

"This is bigger than the Benefactors flogging me for going out of bounds." I shuffle my feet; there's not much room in this cell for me to walk while I think. "We didn't get half the stuff on the acquisition list."

"Carter doesn't think punishing you was the point of the mission," Fagin says grimly.

"They wanted me to change history." Panic hits hard; my heart threatens to beat out of my chest. "I didn't mean for Anne to die."

"I believe you," Carter says. "The Benefactors lit this fuse, not you."

It takes a minute to realize Carter isn't blaming me for the entire shit show. "You're defending me?"

"Simply acknowledging you've been the Benefactors' useful idiot in this scenario," he says, with a dead serious look. "We knew an extreme Benefactor cell planned to interfere in the historical time-line. How, where, and when," he spreads his hands wide, "we could only guess until you jumped in with both feet. It's clear they played you like a fucking Stradivarius until you frog-marched to their tune."

"Why me?"

"You're clever and skilled and emotionally unhinged enough to go off half-cocked to save your family. Fagin gave us the date and time of your father's death. We bet the house on your inability to tame that legendary stubbornness and curiosity." Carter spreads his hands wide. "We triangulated that data with a trace on your ship's energy signature as it entered the portal. And here you are, just as we predicted."

My eyes dart to Fagin who offers a one-shouldered shrug, a shitty way to tell me she didn't think she had a choice in keeping her mouth shut.

"Did you stop to consider changing history could mean your parents might never exist at all?" she asks.

"No," I reply. Emptiness blooms in my chest like there's a

vacuum sucking the remnants of my hope into oblivion. My legs feel like rubber. I back-pedal to the bed just before they give out. "I don't know what happened to my parents. Betty couldn't find them."

"In the mess you created, the odds of your parents being born, meeting and falling in love, were astronomical," Fagin says, anger swelling in her voice. "Millions were never born because of you."

Lingering tranquilizer aftereffects mix with stone cold reality. The sick sensation in my gut intensifies. I wrap my arms around my midsection, but it does little to calm the feeling that I could fly apart at any moment. *What have I done?*

"Tell her what happens next," Fagin says, giving Carter a knowing look.

"A second chance to do the right thing," he replies.

I search Carter's face for signs it's a bait-and-switch where he offers hope, but instead only wants to see my eyes as he lowers the boom. He notes my skepticism and takes it in stride.

"I'm serious. I have an offer you shouldn't refuse," he says.

"Do I have to sell my soul?"

"No, but you do have a choice to make: Help us fix what's been broken and find the head of the snake. Do these two things, and you'll win your freedom. If you refuse, your memory will be wiped and you'll spend the rest of your life in a prison planet mineral mine."

"It's not just *you on the line*, Dodger," Fagin says, "It's Nico and me, too."

"You three are a package deal," Carter agrees. "If you say no, everyone goes to prison. You won't remember they're your friends." He offers a gruesome smile and a shrug. "But, hey, misery loves company."

"How long is the contract?" I ask.

"As long we think it necessary. Can't give you a timetable."

"I need to talk to Nico," I say firmly. If anyone can cut through the bullshit, it's him.

"We talked to him before we approached you," Fagin says. "Garcia is already on board."

"We?" I know we're in a life or death situation, and Fagin needs to toe Carter's line to avoid the government's wrath. But Sycophant Fagin is a little unnerving. It's not like her to give up an ounce of control and right now, she's totally Team Carter.

Again, she shrugs.

"Fine." I walk to the edge of my confinement and gesture at the force field. "Let me out of here and he can tell me himself."

Carter plants his fists on his hips and chuckles. "Not so fast. I need your agreement to work with us. You refuse, the conversation ends here."

"Like I have a choice? Just let me talk to Nico. Open the communication channel, at least."

"There's always a choice, Arseneau," he says. "You have to make this one all on your own. No help from Garcia."

I shouldn't struggle with this decision, but I do. The only thing worse than death or having every memory I have dissolve like a sand castle in tide wash is being owned again, and that's the whole nut in this shell: The government will own me for however long they choose.

I lock eyes with Carter. "I agree."

Fagin closes her eyes and sighs in relief.

Carter doesn't deactivate the force field. I'm not sure if he's stunned that I agreed or if he's waiting for something else.

"There is one more thing," he says.

"What else could you possibly need that my total obedience doesn't cover?"

He gives me what I think is a chagrined look. "Bypass the computer's personality profile and give me full control of this ship. It's being a pain in the ass and won't obey commands without a fight."

I allow myself the luxury of a chuckle. "You'll have to ask Nico about Betty. She's his girl."

"Surprisingly enough, the computer refused to give full cooperation without your consent, too." Carter folds his arms over his chest and glowers at me.

"Huh," I say, more than a little surprised. "I thought she hated me."

"Talk to the computer."

"Let me out."

He sighs and deactivates the force field, then strides off to climb the ladder to the upper deck. For a long moment, I'm rooted to the spot. I have to follow through, but somehow the act of taking this step into another indentured servant life feels huge. It feels permanent.

Fagin nods and gives me a faint smile, then strides toward the ladder, too.

I follow her.

CHAPTER 27

SQUEAMISH IS NOT a word that describes me. Life on a merchant ship with dozens of hardscrabble, seafaring men introduced me to the frailties of the human condition at a tender age. Three months into indentured service to Captain Bartholomew, I'd cleaned an incalculable number of vomit-splattered cot blankets, tended festering wounds accrued from shipboard accidents and bloody tavern fights, and sewn three disease-riddled corpses into burial shrouds.

It was enough gore to anesthetize me to all but the most putrid of bodily trauma.

Yet, watching Jackson Carter chew his food with sloppy, open-mouthed abandon disgusts me to the point that I want nothing more than to throw his dinner plate across the cabin just to stop the spectacle.

To be fair, he could sneeze too loud, cough too hard, or breathe too much, and I would hate it all the more because it's him.

"One more time," he says between bites of a super-size calzone dripping with stringy cheese. "We're going to run through the plan until you can recite it in your sleep."

"Already there," Nico says, shoving his dinner plate into the middle of the table.

Carter looks down at the barely touched paella and raises an eyebrow. "I don't mean to act all parental, but the next twenty-four hours will be insane. Who knows when we'll get another meal?"

Fagin glances at my barely touched cassoulet and her own full plate. "Looks like you're the only one with an appetite, Carter."

"And likely to regret it," Nico says. "Re-entry was a little rough last time we jumped. Doing it on a full stomach might have you reliving that meal a few times."

Carter wipes his mouth with a napkin—at least he didn't use his sleeve—and says, "Tell me again what happened. You were knocked unconscious? Serious time travel side-effects were eliminated generations ago. Why would they hit you out of the blue like that?"

"It was more than just passing out," I say. "It felt like floating outside my body and then being stuffed back into my skin. Pretty freaky."

"The nausea after you regain consciousness is where you might regret having dinner," Nico says.

"Like Carter said, time travel side effects were eliminated decades ago," Fagin says. "What could cause them to resurface?" Fagin asks.

"Let's find out," Nico says. "Betty, are the safety protocol reports done yet?"

"Yes, Commander, honey." the computer answers. "My analysis is complete and the reports are ready for display."

"Honey?" Carter laughs at the AI's term of endearment. "You need a real girl, Garcia."

Blushing, Nico's gaze flits toward me. "Fuck off, Carter." He grabs a data pad and swipes a finger across the display screen. "Tell me what you've got, Betty."

"The time portal's dark matter and energy have become highly unstable. Energy spikes outside the portal's normal operating parameters occurred on several star dates in your query," she replies.

"Are the spikes before or after the premature death of Anne Boleyn?" Carter asks.

"They occurred after the fixed point in history changed," she replies. "In each of the three time events in question, one or more algorithms established to ensure safe time jumps were insufficient to buffer the energy's impact on humans."

"Hypothesis?" Nico asks.

"Comparison of correlating historical documents with the available quantum data suggest the anomalies exist because Drs Joseph Pesce and Katherine Johnson--the physicists who developed safety protocols that eliminate time travel side effects—do not exist."

"What does she mean they don't exist?" Fagin asks.

Carter exhales an exasperated huff and motions to Nico to surrender the handheld tablet. Nico glances at him, settles back in his chair, and takes his sweet time scrolling through the results. Nico finally puts the device on the table in front of him, requiring an irritated Carter to rise from his seat to retrieve it.

"It means safe time jumps are now crap shoots because those scientists were never born," Nico says, not looking at me.

Frowning as he reviews the data, Carter agrees. "Because they were never born, the GTC hasn't perfected the safety protocols time portals use to protect us. Wild energy fluctuations in the portals can exceed the stress load of our ships' bio-filters and safety protocols."

"Betty," I say, "if ship safety mechanisms are compromised, what are the current statistical odds of injury during time jump?" Cosmic changes to both the universe and my boobs weren't something I bargained for when I shoved my better angels in a closet and barricaded the door.

"Current odds of time travel-related injury occurring are approximately one in three time travel events. Minor symptoms such as nausea, vomiting, and migraines, and potentially serious adverse side effects such as blindness, paralysis, or lack of reunification can occur."

"Define lack of reunification." Nico's voice is anxious, like he knows exactly what she means but doesn't want to know the answer.

"Lack of reunification occur when a travelers' consciousness does not integrate with the physical body. This results in a permanent vegetative state."

Fagin gasps. I nod slowly, trying to absorb the information. *A living death. Maybe that's what Nico meant when he thought he'd lost me.*

"Anyone on your ship get sick?" I say to Carter.

"After we touched down, three out of twelve crew members experienced flu-like symptoms" he says.

"Dodger experienced more serious side-effects. Took her a while to come around," Nico said.

"Computer," Carter says. "Are there physical variances between the two Timeships that may account for differences in physical side-effects between our two crews?"

The computer remains silent long enough for Carter to roll his eyes. "For fuck's sake," he grumbles, throwing both hands in the air in frustration.

"Betty, answer the question, please," Nico says.

"Four temporal filter settings in my programming differ from Commander Carter's ship," she says. "This may account for symptom severity variations if the temporal protection buffer is drastically compromised."

Carter fires a blazing look at me. "We have to set the timeline straight before this gets worse."

I can't look him in the eye. I know there are other Observers, other travelers, risking comas and death trying to get home from their missions. *For a moment, I could swear I had a river of blood running off my hands.*

"Arseneau? You with us?" Carter snaps his fingers in front of me. When I look up, he must see the anguish in my eyes. Whether it's pity or pragmatism, his expression softens. "You look like you need a break," he says. "Garcia and I will analyze, and adjust, the temporal filters to align them for both ships. That might improve our odds of getting everyone to 1532 in one piece."

"My team will work with you to modify both ships' programming. How long do you need?" Carter says to Nico.

"Depends. Check back with us in an hour and we'll have a better estimate."

Carter turns his attention to me. "Catch a nap, if you can. Make sure whatever's going on in that noggin of yours gets sorted and you're ready to go when I give the word."

"Check back in an hour," I say with a grim smile, knowing it will take a hell of a lot longer than that to sort out the guilty noise in my head.

As I suspect, sleep is impossible. I settle for rehearsing my part of the plan to stop Trevor from planting her version of the letter—which takes sixty seconds. For all Carter's insistence on my involvement in repairing the timeline, my part is inexplicably small. I'll be stuck in the kitchen, disguised as a servant boy, waiting for Becca Trevor to show her traitorous little face. I'm not supposed to engage her. Instead, I'm to call Carter's men to come haul her away.

Is this the sum-total of the GTC's use for me? Carter could have one of his flunkies do this job. Yet, he insists my participation is crucial to mission success.

There's a soft rap on my door. "Dodger, are you awake?" Fagin asks.

I swipe the lock on the remote control panel and the door to my quarters opens with a soft *swoosh*.

She enters, looks around my cramped, Spartan berth and shakes her head with a smile. "You've never been one for girly decorations. You were all business, even when you were small." She settles on the edge of my bed and looks at me with that keen awareness I've been accustomed to since I met her. "Why didn't you tell me? I could have helped you."

"You're on the GTC's side," I say. "Or the Benefactors' side. Hard to tell which sometimes."

"I'm on your side," she whispers hoarsely. "Always have been."

"They made you my keeper. I knew they had more on you—that you had more to lose— than you were saying. So, who's withholding information now?"

She emits a tiny, laughing snort. "How much more is there to lose than your mind or your life? I'm not sure which I prefer: the blank nothingness of a memory wipe or to just blink out of existence altogether." She snaps her fingers for emphasis. "Gone and forgotten."

"I'm not talking about *your* life." I pause, waiting to see how long it takes her to acknowledge the Benefactors' leverage. She doesn't take the bait, so I fix it on the hook a little more solidly. "Isabella."

Fagin usually controls her body language, but I catch the small wince at the name. I've hit a nerve. "Who is she? Your kid? Your sister? She's someone important to you or Trevor wouldn't have mentioned her when I was trapped in King Henry's toilet."

Fagin stands, forces her posture into ramrod straightness from shoulders to feet; she looks more like a puppet with a stick up its ass than I've ever seen her. "She's none of your business, that's what she is."

The lack of trust stings. "Who has her? Benefactors or the GTC?"

"You don't know what you're talking about." Fagin says, angrily swiping the control panel to open the door.

I jump up, reach past her shoulder and close it again. "You're not leaving until you tell me about Isabella."

"I can't."

"Yes, you can."

"The more you know, the more danger you're in."

"I can handle my shit."

"This time, you're in over your head and the consequences will be deadly," she says, trembling. Tears stream down her cheeks and the raw emotion shakes me to the core. "Isabella will die."

"I can't help you if you don't tell me what's going on," I say, measuring my words into calm, steady beats, hoping to settle her frantic emotions. "Secrets are bad. Let's have no more of them."

We sit together, on the bed, holding hands tight, an attempt to keep our world from flying completely apart. She sniffles and I hand her a handkerchief from bedside table. She runs a thumb over the Vicomte's embroidered initials and quirks an eyebrow at me.

"Old habits," I say with a dismissive wave. I could be eighty years old and I'd still nick a gentleman's handkerchief just to see if I could.

"Isabella?" I ask, again.

Fagin nods. "My god-daughter."

"I didn't know you believed in that sort of thing. Religion. Being a godparent. Raising a child in the way they should go and all of that."

"When you owe a life for a life, you have little choice over how, and when, markers are called in. When I was an Observer, before crawling my way up the ladder to Thief Master, another a woman named Andreen—another Observer—saved my life. She said I owed her a blood debt and, one day, she may need my help. I figured it was a small price to pay: a future favor in return for my life."

"Blood debts aren't small," I say, stroking her knuckles with my thumbs. "They're huge, hairy, life-changing deals."

"Isabella was certainly life-changing," she says, nodding in agreement. "Social worker showed up at my door one day with the four-year-old girl in tow."

"What happened to Andreen."

She shrugs. "Disappeared. A neighbor found Isabella sitting on her doorstep with nothing but the clothes on her back and notarized documents naming me as her legal guardian."

"Wow."

"Yeah." Fagin blows out a huff of air. "And me, not the maternal sort."

"That's not true. You mothered every kid who passed through your doors."

"Ah. That was good for business." She smiles.

"You're not as tough as you think you are, and whoever is using Isabella as leverage knows it," I say.

Her smile fades as she presses her lips into a tight, thin line. She takes a breath and rises from the bed, extricating her hands from mine.

"That's all you get," she says. "You know who she is and why she's important. I can't risk telling you anymore."

"Fagin, together, we can fix—"

"Enough," she says. The set of her jawline confirms that I could take a sledgehammer to that infamous stubbornness and never do more than surface damage. "I can't lose both of you, and that's what will happen if I keep talking." She glances around the room, once more. "You should at least change the wall color. Gray is so depressing."

An hour later, with the temporal filters modified to mitigate the more serious time travel side-effects, Carter gathers everyone on the bridge and lays out the departure plan.

"We have the arrival set for the date, time, and geographic coordinates. Since Becca Trevor plants the bogus letter in King Henry's chambers at eleven-thirty in the morning of December 23, 1532, we need to be in position by sunrise of that same day to intercept her."

"That's cutting it close, isn't it?" Fagin asks, her brow furrowed. "Why not go back earlier than the day she screws everything up? It gives us more time to kick her skinny ass."

"To give the Benefactors less time to throw counterattacks at us," I say. "If they're as brilliant as we think they are, they'll understand the more the timeline changes, the more the future may not be what they wanted."

"You're damn smart, kid," Carter says. "If only you used your powers for good."

"Where's the fun in being good?" I give him a sly smile and a wink.

Playful banter with Commander Carter. Will wonders never cease?

"We'll leave a small crew behind," Carter continues, "to protect the timeline from more manipulation. As I was saying," he nods at me. "Arseneau will take position, disguised as a servant, in the kitchen, and once she has eyes on the target, our security detail—dressed as the king's guard—" He gestures toward the four soldiers to his left. "will arrest her on charges of stealing jewelry. Easy enough to convince everyone she's a common thief." He grins at me and I smirk in return.

"There's nothing common about me," I say. "And you know it."

"What happens if she spots Clémence first and high-tails it out of the palace?" Nico asks. The nearness of him, the smell of soap on his skin, is distracting. I have to force myself to focus on Carter again.

One of the security detail leaders, a giant of a man whose muscles have muscles, says, "You'll be coordinating all of the security cameras installed from the command center on your ship. As we worked through in our strategy sessions, we'll have sentries posted at various points outside and inside the palace. Once she steps foot on the grounds, we'll track her movement through human and cameras observation. She won't get far if she bolts."

"Unless you guys were able to track the other ship and identify how many other Observers are on the ground, that's a risk." I point out what I think is the fatal flaw in their plans.

"We have elite special forces on this mission, Mademoiselle Areseneau," the security chief says. "Our boys will scout the grounds while it's dark to neutralize suspected targets. No one gets by us."

"What about the other versions of ourselves?" Nico asks. "Seeing our duplicates on that day presents certain paradoxical problems, right?"

Fagin leans into the conversation. "We avoid those problems by staying out of our own way. You," she points at Nico. "Remain on the ship, monitoring data feeds and providing intel. Since we know that Dodger went to the king's chambers after Original Timeline Me left her in the great hall, Current Timeline Me," she points at herself, "can step in after that and steal OT Clémence's letter before she gets to the king's apartments."

I roll my eyes at her. "Please. I'll see that coming a mile away. Do you have a backup plan?"

"Darling girl," she chuckles. "Remember who taught you to pick pockets."

I'm not sure what kind of paradoxical fuckery would happen if I came face-to-face with myself, even in this shitty disguise. I'd prefer not to mess with that.

"Regarding the time jump," Carter continues, "which will occur as soon as this briefing session is done, we'll caravan through the time portal. Since only one vessel can go through at a time, the other ship will go through first and wait—using the cloaking shield to obscure their presence—for us to complete our jump." He makes an inclusive circular gesture of himself, Nico, and me.

"Us?" I ask, hoping he's not suggesting what I think he is.

"You don't think I'm gonna let you jump all on your own. Look what happened last time. You wound up in hell. I'm here to keep you from wandering off. I'll also have a few of my boys along for the ride to make sure things go smoothly."

Three of the security team, all of them looking like professional wrestlers, nod at me. I'm not sure if it was a congenial, let's-be-friends acknowledgement or a try-anything-funny-and-you're-toast warning. To be on the safe side, I'll assume they're looking at Nico and me as potential toast.

"I can buckle into one of the jump seats in the ready room," Fagin says.

"Oh, no." Carter smiles and takes Fagin by the elbow. He steps her over to the security team leader. "Lieutenant George, here, will see that you're settled on the first ship. First class all the way."

Fagin and I exchange looks. *First class, my ass.*

Her smile is more nervous than appreciative. "That would be lovely. Thank you."

"Any questions?" Carter asks.

I raise my hand and the simple act of asking permission to speak instead of blustering forward startles him. "Areseneau," he says.

"What happens after we catch Trevor? We all go home and live happily ever after?"

Carter cocks his head and offers a smile. "That depends on your version of 'happily ever after', doesn't it?"

CHAPTER 28

"This is ridiculous." I push the brim of the twice-too-large cap up for what seems like the hundredth time. "Trevor gets an eyeful of me, she's going to see right through this disguise."

Carter gives me a hard look, up and down, inspecting my clothes. "You look like a servant boy to me. All you need to do is fire a flare when she shows up in the kitchens, and—" He stops, mid-sentence, and stares at the bulge under my shirt, right in front of my left shoulder. "What's that?"

I give him my most innocent look, but he's not buying it. He pulls me to a stop and pats down my upper body. He steps back and makes a "give it here" gesture. I sigh and pull the phaser from the shoulder holster.

"I confiscated all of the weapons. Where'd you get this one?"

"I didn't like the idea of going into this situation unarmed."

"Nuh-uh. No weapon for you," Carter tugs the phaser out of my hand. "I wouldn't want to tempt you to take matters into your own hands and have anyone wind up dead on the ground as you make your escape."

"I'm a thief, not a murderer," I seethe.

"We'll let historians debate that point," he says with a crooked grin. Then he speaks into the CommLink. "Someone check Garcia and Delacroix. Make sure they don't have weapons on them."

"We confiscated all phasers on their ship," comes the reply.

"Check again," Carter says. He turns back to me. "Alert me the moment you get eyes on Trevor. Understood?"

I hate feeling useless. On every job since I was fifteen years old, if I wasn't the one in control of the mission objectives, I was at least up to my eyebrows in the action. This time, I'll be up to my eyebrows in vegetable scraps and chicken gizzards waiting for the action to happen.

Given that I've been relegated to the sidelines and relieved of my only weapon, I'm ready to spit nails by the time Carter—posing as a visiting nobleman insisting on his own servant preparing his food—leaves me in the hands of the master cook.

Turns out the kitchen isn't just one room, it's a suite of rooms each dedicated to a specific part of a meal: bake houses for baking bread, pastry rooms for pie-making and cakes, the roasting room where dozens of chickens, pigeons or other fowl and meat, are roasted on open-fire spits. There are the boil houses for cooking soups and stews, a confectionary room for creating sweets both grand and humble, and various larders for storing all of the foodstuffs.

Because Henry's court feeds several hundred people a day—nearly a thousand during holidays— it takes an army of people to prepare and serve the food for several meals each day.

The master cook assigns me to the boil house, preparing onions and other sundry vegetables for a stew. The boil house, while large and open, is closed off from the outside world. The windows are too high to see out, and there isn't a direct line of sight into any other rooms of the kitchen suite. Of all the rooms I could've been assigned to, it looks like I'm in the blind spot.

"You've got to be kidding," I hiss into the CommLink. "Carter, how am I supposed to keep my eyes open for Trevor if I'm stuck in here? She could come through one of the other rooms and I would never see her. She could be halfway up the king's privy stairs by the time we realize she got through the palace door."

"She won't get by us, Arseneau. Relax."

"Relax, my ass. How am I supposed to redeem myself if I'm not actively involved in catching Trevor?"

"Don't leave your post unless you're given the word, Arseneau" Carter says. "And keep this line clear for mission commands."

The CommLink fills with other chatter: orders from Carter to Nico to modulate the encryption codes on the live audio and video feeds so the Benefactors can't hack into our feeds; orders to the security details to get into position in the gardens and inside the palace; another command for me to stay put.

Fagin confirms she stopped Original Timeline Me and picked her pocket. Fagin has my fake letter.

"You didn't feel a thing," Fagin says over the CommLink. It makes me smile. *God, she's good.*

One letter down, one to go. Things are going according to plan. As long as we stop Trevor, the timeline changes should heal themselves.

Chopping potatoes and onions would be cathartic in exorcising my tension and anger if it weren't welling up inside me with the bludgeoning force of a firehose.

Incremental changes to the angle of sunlight streaming through the windows is the only indication of the time passing; several hours, at least, since I've been holed up in here.

Finally, a perimeter sentry in the gardens breaks in: "I've got Trevor," he says. "North side of the palace. Looks like she's headed to the king's privy garden, not the kitchens."

Fuck Carter's orders. I'll be damned if I let things happen to me without a fight.

I carefully place the chopping knife—a seven-inch blade with a smooth wood handle—into my boot. I slip out of the kitchen, stride down the hallway leading to the kitchen gardens. Once outside, I sprint toward the location where Trevor was seen.

As I approach the North corner of the palace, closest to the king's apartments, I spot her: Dressed as Cesario, she strides toward the privy gardens. We're separated by little more than a hundred yards and some tall topiaries lining the path leading to the privy stairs. Moving parallel to her, I work my way around the spiral-sculpted shrubs, hoping to cut her off before she gets anywhere near the king's door.

Her head is on a swivel, perpetually scanning her surroundings. Her gaze stops on me. She slows, watches me for several moments. I keep moving, and hope I look like a palace servant on an errand, and she will relax and move on.

She stops. Studies the cast of characters milling around the gardens. She settles on a man casually inspecting the contents of a merchant's loaded cart—he's one of our team in disguise and occasionally casts discreet glances over his shoulder at her. Trevor's gaze drifts back to me.

Our eyes lock long enough for suspicion to firmly lodge itself in her brain. Whether or not she knows it's me, wariness changes her trajectory.

She turns away from the palace and heads in the opposite direction, her gait set at casual stroll.

I follow.

"Arseneau," Carter's voice says in my ear. "What the hell are you doing? Get back to the kitchen."

"This is my life, Carter. I'm going in and you can't stop me."

"Got your six, Dodger," Nico cuts in, "Keep your eyes open." Then to the commander: "Carter, she knows these palace grounds. Since she's already in pursuit. You could waste resources sending your men after her, or let Clémence in the hunt for real."

I smile. *There's my boy.*

"Murdock," Carter says, ignoring Nico. "Get Mademoiselle Arseneau back to the kitchen."

The man inspecting the carts moves towards me.

Trevor tosses a quick look over her shoulder and, noting that I'm following her and Murdock is right behind me, takes off at a run.

"Goddamn it, Arseneau!" Carter says.

In for a penny, in for a pound. If I'm gonna be crucified for stepping out of line, I might as well make it worth the pain.

"Got two plays here," I say, forcing the words out as I run, fullbore in Trevor's direction with Murdock hot on my heels. "Deal with me or chase her. What's it gonna be, Murdock?"

Carter swears again. "Murdock, stay locked on Trevor. She's the objective." He pauses. "Arseneau, I swear, if you fuck this up, you're done."

"No shit," is all I have time to say.

Trevor races through the palace grounds like an Olympic sprinter; she's so much faster than I would ever give her credit for. I'm pretty fast, but I won't be able to keep up if she's able to sustains this pace.

She enters a stand of trees, crisscrossing through them like it's a slalom course. We lose sight of her as she ducks behind a large oak on the far perimeter of the tree line. When we emerge from the trees, we're greeted by an empty wide-open field.

"Where the hell did she go?" Murdock huffs.

"If she's within transporter range, she might be back on her own ship by now." Carter's speculation is accompanied by a terse tone.

Something darts through the trees on our left. "Nope. She doubled back into the woods," I say, then follow her into the dense copse of trees. I catch glimpses of Murdock to my right as he runs even with me on the meadow-side of the trees in case she reemerges from the woods.

Trevor veers to the right, clearing the grove of trees once more. As I swerve in that direction, there's a flash of brilliant light.

"Their transporters got a lock on her," Murdock says.

Nico's voice breaks in, "I've pegged Trevor outside the stables."

"Get a lock on our guys farther east and transport them to the stables," Carter says.

I run as fast as I can. Trevor has a big head-start on me and reaches the stables just as a boy, leading two horses by their reins, rounds the corner of the building.

Trevor wrestles with a stable boy, who goes down screaming, and swings herself up onto the larger horse's back in one smooth movement.

She points her mount North and they take off at a gallop. Minutes later, when I get to the stable, the attendant lies writhing on the ground, screaming as he grasps his thigh just above his disjointed knee. A second stable hand, having heard the screams, races outside and kneels beside his friend.

I scramble onto the second horse's back; he snorts and paws at the ground, clearly not in the mood to be ridden by anyone who isn't his master. The gray Barbary stallion isn't huge, but still powerful. He shuffles sideways and tosses his head up and down, neighing in frustration.

"Whoa. Easy, boy, say, trying to calm him and settle myself in the saddle.

He doesn't want to take it easy. He continues to shuffle and stamp his hooves and shake his head. I grip the reins and pull back, bringing the horse's nose toward my knee. He settles, just a bit.

"Oi! That's Governatore, the King's favorite stallion!" The second man yells. "You can't steal the king's horse."

"Watch me." As soon as I nudge him, he bolts toward the open field where Trevor's figure is shrinking in the distance. She disappears over the ridge of a small hill.

The Barb's front quarters are filled with explosive power; he sprints through the meadow at a much faster clip than I expect; he may just be happy for the opportunity to run. We skirt the tree grove that clings to the Northward curve of the riverbank to our left and head toward the spot on the ridge where I last saw Trevor.

· · ·

We crest the hill; nothing but open fields to the North and East for the next five miles, at least. There's more trees and another ridge a little farther to my left. That's the only direction she could have gone.

Pointing my mount toward the west, I follow the tree line again and come upon a gristmill, its massive waterwheel pirouetting in the currents of an offshoot of the Thames. I take in the surroundings as I catch my breath from the work of riding the king's horse: A loose, riderless horse grazes on the tender marsh grass on the lee side of the mill. There's no one else in sight.

I slip from the saddle and loop Governatore's reins on a fence post at the edge of a well-traveled muddy path that leads to the lowest level of the mill. There are footprints in the mud, leading to a door which stands slightly ajar.

Why go into the mill just to transport to her ship when she could've made that jump once she was over the ridge and out of sight of any locals?

Because she's probably inside waiting for you. To finish things on her terms.

I ease the door open a little further and slip inside.

Wheat chaff swirls down from the rafters. The sun, what there is of it, filters through one small west-facing window, and illuminates only the bottom step of a stone staircase at the far end of the cellar. Muted gray shadows drip down the wall and spill across the floor.

I pause to listen. Outside, the river churns against the water wheel. Above me, there's the *ka-thunk, ka-thunk* rhythm of millstones turning on their grindstone. I feel my way across the room, moving inches at a time until I trip and land on a substantial, fleshy mass.

There are arms. And a torso. And a face covered with a slick, pungent substance. Shifting my weight off the body, my fingers fumble to find the carotid artery. I put my ear close to the mouth.

No soft, stirring tickles of breath on my cheek. No blood coursing through the veins beneath my touch. I leave my fingers in place longer than necessary, hoping for the blip that would signal life. I rock back on my heels and exhale.

Is killing really so easy for her? Does she think about it for even a moment before snuffing out that light?

I move toward the half-lit steps and stumble again, this time on something that jumps up and smacks me in the face. My right cheek throbs. I feel down the length of a wooden shaft with both hands.

A fucking rake.

I don't fancy using the knife nestled inside my boot. Knife fighting is so much more intimate than other types of combat, requiring eye-to-eye contact at close range. I'm not sure I can be eye-to-eye with an opponent—even Trevor—and feel the knife's edge pop the delicate skin in surrender. A weapon with a longer reach would be better.

For now.

I hold the rake into my body to keep it from bumping and thumping against the wall as I make my way up the stairs. There's no door at the top, only a wide, rectangular opening to the next level. I poke my head up to peer over the threshold.

Sturdy ropes loop themselves around and through hoists and pulleys used to raise filled bags to the floor above. Various milling tools are strewn on nearby workbenches or tucked into corners: wooden shovels and scoops, more winnowing rakes, hammers and chisels for working on the cog wheels of the gears.

Two sets of enormous round stones used to pulverize grain into meal take up most of space on the far side of the room. With all the machinery and stacks of flour bags, there are several places where a skinny girl like Trevor could lurk unseen.

Planks set in the rafters far enough below the ceiling that she could hide there, too. On the floor, sticking out from behind the grinding stones are a pair of motionless legs. I ease into position, next to the body, and check the man's pulse.

Trevor's body count is up to four, counting Lady Anne and Thomas Wyatt.

A voice drifts down from the rafters. "Just can't leave well enough alone, can you? I have things all planned and you go and screw them up."

I walk the perimeter of the room, eyes on the ceiling, and hold the head of the rake forward, ready to deflect the first strike when it comes.

"Something didn't go according to plan, Trevor? How disappointing for you," I say.

"Were you born with that remarkable sarcastic streak or is that a skill you learned on the streets?" Her voice moves; now it's coming from my left.

"Both," I say, looking upward for some hint of movement that might reveal her position. I nudge a set of pulleys out of my way and hear the metal squeak as they swing behind me.

Carter breaks into the conversation. "Trevor, we have reinforcements converging on that mill as we speak. Giving yourself up now would be the wiser move."

"Let's discuss wise moves for a moment, shall we?" Her tone doesn't sound defeated or even slightly concerned. In fact, she speaks in a victor's tone, like she believes it's all over but the crying. "There's a trained assassin with his eye on Lady Anne. If your men spoil my party, she'll be dead before you can say 'Shakespearean tragedy.'"

For a long moment, no one moves. No one speaks.

Carter says, "Delacroix, are you in position?"

"I'm with Lady Anne and the King in the Great Hall," Fagin replies.

"Anyone suspicious-looking?" Carter asks.

"They're all suspicious-looking. They're all back-stabbing courtiers working to advance their own interests." She snorts. "If there's are assassins here, they're blending in too well for me to spot them."

"You've been at court for months and you still can't tell the players without a scorecard?" Carter says, in a skeptical tone.

"It's fucking Christmas," Fagin replies. "More people here for the holiday, so that means a lot of new faces."

"Until we find Trevor's people, you stay glued to Lady Anne. You're her new knight in shining armor."

I smile. "Lucky me."

"Are we agreed, then?" Trevor says. "Your boys stay out or your precious timeline still goes to hell. This is between The Dodger and me."

Silence.

"Carter," Trevor says. "My patience is thin."

"Fine, we'll play it your way for now," Carter says, grudgingly. "Don't think for a second that you're walking out of there unscathed."

"Yes, my dear commander," she says, a lilt in her voice. "I am."

"We all know you can transport out of here any time you want," I say, taking a few hesitant steps forward. Eyes still aimed at the rafters. "What kind of game are you playing?"

"I want the opportunity to kick your ass. Call it my own personal vendetta."

"Have you cleared this cage match with your bosses? From what I hear, they had a very specific purpose for me."

"They did, yes." Her voice comes from ten feet further ahead of me and off to the right.

She moves almost as silently as I do.

"I'm all ears. I'd love to hear more about it."

"I won't light myself on fire to keep you warm." The voice moves again. "You could have been content with saving your parents and lived happily ever after. Isn't that what you wanted?"

"It's true. My parents were never murdered. But the only 'ever after' I saw was a future where they probably never lived at all. Turns out, changing shit that's supposed to happen creates all kinds of... other complications."

"See." She draws one syllable out into at least four. "Your dizzying intellect has revealed a cosmic truth: Be careful what you wish because it might come true." The echo of her soft laugh reverberates off the timbers. "They say fate is a fickle temptress, but what about people who don't believe in fate? Just because you don't believe in something doesn't mean it's not true."

Ahead of me, dust drifts down from the rafters. I freeze, listening for the groaning squeaks of floorboard joists from the weight of her footfalls. No sound comes.

"If I wanted an existential philosophical conversation, I'd go climb a fucking mountain and find a holy man. I'll stick to science, thanks." I say. "Elizabeth's reign is a fixed point in history and changing it fucked up everything that was supposed to come after on just about every level."

"That's what I'm talking about. That's your truth...your perspective. Just one of many possible realities. You think your truth is more valid than anyone else's?"

"The historical timeline isn't a judgment call to make. It just... is."

"Only for those who lack the courage to change it."

A surge of energy takes root in my chest. All the anger, sorrow, mourning, frustration, and helplessness of my life compresses into this single match strike. The fuse lit and it has nowhere else to go but into a powder keg of wrath. The Benefactors used me like a thermonuclear bomb they programmed for maximum destruction and then set off in the middle of King Henry's court.

"Brave words for someone who won't come out of the shadows," I say.

"I thought you loved mystery games and riddles." Her voice is an echo. The acoustics make it seem she's everywhere at once; I can no longer pin down where she is.

A few more steps and I'm standing in a large gap in the wood beams above.

"Come out and we'll discuss this face-to-face."

"As you wish." Her voice is right bloody behind me.

I turn toward the sound just as Trevor swings down from the rafters and plants her feet squarely in my shoulder.

The blow knocks me sideways. The rake head scraps the floor

catching in the seam of a loose board, causing me to lose both the implement and my balance. I scuttle backward like a crab, using my hands and feet, trying to put as much distance between us as I can.

She picks up the rake and swings it over her head like an ax, bringing it down hard and fast on a narrow sliver of floor between my legs.

I send a feeble kick at the rake, but it's enough force to knock it out from under her. I roll to the left just out of her stumbling path as her weight pitches forward.

She chuckles, regaining her footing. "It seems I must put some effort into killing you." Her eyes gleam and she twirls the rake from one hand to the other over and over like a martial arts master wielding a staff.

"You talk too much." I jump backward into the edge of a tool bench shoved up against the wall.

She swings the staff again, this time toward my lower legs, trying to sweep them out from under me. It's a narrow miss.

Stumbling backward down the bench, sweeping my hands along its splintered surface as I go, I search for anything I can use to block the blows so I can get to the knife in my boot. Lunging, I grasp a wooden shovel propped against the wall.

It's barely in my hands when the rake lands with a solid *thwump* on the table leg just in front of me.

"You're playing with me," I say. "Won't your superiors be angry that you're taking so long to kill me?"

"As long as you're dead, they won't care how long it takes. You've outlived your usefulness." She circles to the right, balancing her weapon first in one hand, then the other. "I'll be rewarded for dispatching you. I might even get a medal."

"Dodger," Nico says. "That shovel isn't gonna do the job by itself."

I take in his meaning: the knife. I swallow hard, knowing that I'm not likely to get out of here in one piece if I'm not willing to take her life before she takes mine.

"Your boyfriend's right. That shovel is useless." Trevor sweeps the rake down and then quickly up, catching the metal binding behind the bowl of the shovel between two of the rake's tines. One quick tug and she snatches the implement out of my hands.

It's enough time for me to get to the knife and rush her. The instant Trevor spots the blade, she flips the rake around and swings it at my head.

The corner glances off the spot just above my right ear and I feel the blood gush. My head throbs.

She cocks her weapon back, preparing for another attack, but leaves just enough of an opening that I can slip under her arms and thrust the blade upward.

We're nose-to-nose as I feel it slide into her and it's nothing like I expect it to be. It moves through her skin with so little resistance, it's like she's made of soft butter.

I feel her blood on my skin.

She staggers back, eyes wide, then falls.

Carter, having seen the whole thing through the LensCam, jumps into action, barking orders to everyone. "Team One, get in that mill and secure the prisoner. Team Two, get Fagin and Lady Anne to safety."

Nico follows up with a command of his own. "Team One, get Dodger back to the ship fast. She's hurt."

"Both of me," I say. "Don't forget the version lying outside the stable."

"She's been found by one of the grooms of the stable and taken to the castle. She...you will be fine," Nico replies.

The blow to my head isn't as serious as it could have been, but a light-headedness sweeps over me that drops me to my knees. Murdock places a steadying hand on my shoulder, then pulls me to my feet.

"I can't believe you're still alive," he says with a grudging sense of admiration in his voice.

"Neither can I," I say, still gasping for breath.

Becca Trevor, weak but still alert, meets my eyes; she's still lying on the floor allowing one of our guys to field dress her wound as we prepare to transport back to the ship. She really doesn't have a choice in the matter. She has six phasers pointed at her head.

"I know where Isabella is." Her voice is raspy with the effort to speak through pain. "When I escape, I'll pay her a little visit."

CHAPTER 29

I WAKE to Nico's arm draped over me and the feel of his slow, deep breath, warm on the nape of my neck. The weight of him is comforting; it's like being a child cocooned in swaddling clothes. Protected. Safe. Cherished.

I don't want to move. It might break this spell. *Could this be for real with him? A forever thing?* I've never really thought in those terms before, never thought of myself as the marrying or settling-down one-man woman type.

We've been home for two weeks and I still don't trust this happiness we have. A cosmos-changing switch in time blasted humanity's future to the brink of destruction and here we are playing house.

Is it real? Has he forgiven me?

I take a deep breath and let the possibilities wash over me. Nico stirs and when I move to face him, he holds me tighter.

"Please stay. I like you right where you are," he says, his voice still thick with sleep.

I can't help but chuckle. "Okay, I'll stay, but remember we're at my place."

He grunts, lifts his head and does a quick survey of the surroundings. "Oh...yeah." He plops down on the pillow again. "In that case, please let me stay. I like being here."

He kisses my shoulder and I feel his need growing apace with wakefulness. The nuzzling turns insistent. Explorative and hungry. I feel my own desire rising to match his.

He flips me onto my back and settles between my thighs as his lips move from my neck to my breasts. He brushes a thumb across my nipple and my body shudders in response.

"Just think: We could have done this last night," I say, teasingly, because my own appetite is now as ravenous as if I haven't eaten—metaphorically speaking—in years.

His eyes hold all the hesitancy and concern that had postponed our intimacy the night before. "The doctor just cleared you from the concussion from the rake to the head you took a few weeks ago. I want to be careful," he replies. One arm cradles my neck, his free hand drifting down between my legs. It's slick, warm, and ready. He plants a soft kiss on my lips and smiles. "I do like how you rise to the occasion, though."

"I think that's my line," I say, and we laugh. It feels as good as the moment we join. It has been months since we've laughed without wondering what fresh hell was around the next corner.

When we join, the rhythm is gentle, slow; I feel his caution, still not wanting to push too hard in case any overzealous jostling causes a concussion flare up.

"I really am fine, you know," I say as he brushes his nose against mine.

Our eyes lock and we share a near-kissing breath as we continue to move together.

He feels so damn good. I could stay here forever.

"I know," he says.

"So don't hold back. Love me like you used to." I cup his buttocks and pull him in closer, lifting my hips, matching his movements to encourage the coupling I want. He gasps.

"No, not like we used to. This is something new." The sweet and tender kisses turn fierce as gentleness yields to a deeper, rougher drive.

"That was..." Nico says, after, searching for the right word. "What's a stronger word than earth-moving?"

Depending on the situation, the after-play is usually one of two things: euphoric or awkward. The latter usually motivates me to escape as quickly as possible. For the first time, ever, I'm euphoric. I yearn to slow time and stay right where I am.

"Gloriously perfect." I finish his thought. I feel his head raise off his pillow. Unused to effusive praise where our sexual arrangement is concerned, he gazes at me a measure of uncertainty.

As I nestle into the crook of his arm, I place my fingers on his lips. "Hush. Let's just enjoy what we have right now. This moment. Who knows how long we get to keep it?"

He wraps his arms around me, settling into the embrace. "Roger that."

The CommLink panel on the bedside table buzzes. "Merde." I say. "Did you time that?"

"Yep," Nico replies with a sigh. "Duration of post-coitus total bliss: two minutes, tops."

Home Computer announces: Fagin Delacroix calling.

"On speaker," I reply. "No visual."

Fagin's voice comes over the line. "Dodger? Something wrong with your camera?"

"Nope. I have company."

"Hey, Fagin," Nico says.

"Nico," Fagin says. There's a brief pause. "I'm glad you're there, too. it saves me a call. I'm going out of town. I'll check messages as I can, but I'll be unavailable a while."

"You have permission to travel?" Nico asks, confused. He pushes up onto one elbow, listening more intently. The three of us have been on judicial lockdown, confined to base, since we got home. Tidying up the loose ends of our agreement with Commander Carter—and debriefing the Temporal Agency on the minutiae of our misadventures manifested itself in a shitload of post-mission mandatory meetings.

"You must be done with your obligations here. Good to know there's light at the end of that tunnel that isn't a fucking freight train," I say. "You going to see Isabella?"

There's a lengthier pause on the other end of the CommLink. "I'll let you know when I'm back. I just didn't want you to worry if you don't hear from me for a while."

"*She ignored my question*," I mouth to Nico.

His eyebrows lift, and he mouths in reply. "Not good."

"Fagin—" I say, wanting to question more, but she cuts me off.

"Look, I have to go. I just wanted to talk to you before I...before I left."

"Why don't you stop by for coffee," Nico says, trying to keep her on the line. "I'll even make breakfast. Bacon. Eggs. Whatever you want."

"I can't," she replies, her voice sounding strained. "You two just take care of each other. I'll see you when I get back. And Dodger," she pauses, "I love you."

"End of transmission," the computer announces.

"What the hell was that?" Nico asks, as I jump out of bed, and grab my robe.

I shake my head. "Computer, call Fagin back."

The line rings numerous times before going to voicemail.

"Redial Fagin's number."

This time, the phone goes to voicemail without ringing at all.

"Something's not right." Reconsidering the robe, I pull undergarments, jeans, and a crew neck T-shirt out of the wardrobe.

Nico's already half-dressed in the clothes he brought with him. "Carter should know what's going on. Fagin can't leave base without his permission, and he wouldn't let her stray too far without knowing exactly where she's going."

. . .

Thirty minutes later, we're pounding on Carter's apartment door. While he's not surprised to see us, he's not thrilled at the intrusion.

"You better have a damn good reason to wake me before..." he checks the time on the personal CommLink panel on the wall, "before seven-thirty in the fucking morning on a Saturday.

"Tell us where Fagin is going and we'll be on our way," Nico says, leaning his forearm against the door frame.

"Ah, she called you." He takes a deep breath and lets it out. He nods his head a few times. "Fagin is going out of town for a few weeks. She won't be in communication while she's gone. She'll check in with you upon her return. All better? Good." He waves us toward the door, a stupid grin on his face. "I'm going back to bed."

He tries shutting the door, but Nico blocks the closing door with his shoulder. "Yeah, we got that from Fagin."

"Great, so you know all you need to know. She's gone. She'll call you when she gets back. What more do you want?"

"More than that," I say. "Where's she going? Who is she going to see? Will she be safe out there on her own? It's only been two weeks since we almost died."

Nico and I trade glances. "We'll stand here all day, if we have to," Nico says. "I'm sure your neighbors will love the sound of us pounding your door down for the next eight hours."

He sighs and beckons us to follow. "This is not a hallway conversation."

Once inside the apartment, he doesn't waste time with niceties or play the gracious host. The place is almost barren—if architectural magazines had a template for 'disorganized, sparsely-furnished bachelor pad,' this would be it. "Ms. Delacroix is on assignment."

"What kind of assignment?" I ask.

"Classified," Carter replies.

"Where's she going?"

"Also classified." He yawns and crosses his arms over his chest.

"Is she going to see Isabella?"

Carter's eyes narrow, he looks genuinely confused. "Who?"

I cock an eyebrow at him. "You don't know who Isabella is?"

"Should I?"

I gape at him, then turn to Nico, who also stands with his mouth open.

Either Carter is lying or he really doesn't know about Fagin's goddaughter. Nico puts a hand on my arm.

"Is Fagin safe out there on her own?" Nico asks.

"Safe is a relative term these days, isn't it?"

"Carter, if you get her killed—" I say, trying to keep the panic rising in my chest from choking me.

"Relax," Carter waves a dismissive hand. "She has a security detail traveling with her. She's in capable hands."

"We're a team, Fagin and me and Nico. From now on, you don't send one of us out without the others." My tone is as authoritative as I can make it, but I know the implied warning is bullshit. From the expression on Carter's face, he knows it, too.

"You've forgotten that the Agency owns your life until it sees fit to release you from the contract. Until that time, you have no say in who goes where," he says.

"We're stronger together," Nico replies. "You've seen it. Don't break up the band."

"That's true for you and Arseneau," Carter agrees. "Where Fagin is concerned, there are extenuating circumstances."

"Such as?" I say, holding on to the demanding tone.

"Such as none of your fucking business," he replies, tersely. "This is degenerating into a whiny little bitch-fest and I haven't had coffee yet. Time for you to get the hell out of here."

He moves to the door, but I have one more question for him before he tosses us out on our asses.

"Why did you dump me in the kitchens at Greenwich in the first place?"

He stops, turns to gawk at me with a quizzical look.

"Let me recover from that stunning non-sequitur you've thrown at me before I answer." He holds up a finger, shuts his eyes briefly and then opens them again. "There. Okay, ready for the answer? Also none of your fucking business." He leans forward and smiles like he's just delivered the punchline to a joke only he finds hilarious.

"Contract or no contract," I say, "these are our lives on the line. If you're not painfully transparent with us, there's no telling what kind of mischief you'll have to contend with. So pay now or pay later. Your choice."

"You're in no position to demand anything," Carter says, his voice a low growl as he advances on me. Nico steps into the gap between us.

"Do you want to babysit us every minute of every day from here on out? Because I'm sure that's exactly what your bosses expect of you, right? To keep us in line...under control? We could go to war with each other starting right now, or you can answer our questions when we ask them."

Carter rubs his chin. I can see the wheels turning in his brain, weighing the choice before him: answers now or hell later.

"Okay. I'll give it to you, this time. But next time I may not be able to answer your questions and you're going to have a hard choice to make about what you do in that situation." He nods, purses his lips, then speaks. "Command headquarters thought you might be too emotionally distraught to think clearly if you came face-to-face with Trevor. They wanted to give you time to see if you—"

"To see if I was on your side or if I had really gone dark-side with the Benefactors." I say, flatly. *How could I be so stupid not to see it? It was a test. They wanted to see if I would work with them to catch Trevor or work with her.*

"That's about the size of it," he says.

"I'm getting really fucking tired of being set up. Your purity test was bullshit."

"We got our girl, that's all that matters."

"I guess my injuries were enough to convince them that I'm not one of the bad guys?"

"Something like that. You'll be interested to know that Trevor was transferred to a secret maximum-security location. As far as the Benefactors know, she's gone missing."

"What about her crew?"

"Along with jamming transmissions from 1532 back to our time, we jammed her transmissions to her ship. They believe she died at the grist mill."

"Are we sure the LensCam transmissions from those two days were scrambled enough to keep the Benefactors in the dark about what really happened?"

"There's no way to be one-hundred-percent certain, of course. But the chatter we've heard leans in that direction. They currently believe Trevor is MIA." He rocks back on his heels. "They will, of course, have questions for you about the incident. Our hope is that they'll approach you sooner rather than later with a recruitment offer."

Bile backs up into my throat as Carter's earlier words echo in my head: *Everything's special about you: you're clever and skilled enough to get the job done and emotional enough to go off half-cocked and step over that ethical line if it meant saving your family.*

"What does the chatter say?" Nico asks.

Carter wags a finger at us. "Most of the answer to that very broad question is classified. Upshot is: It's been fairly quiet since we got home. If it were imminent, as in the next few days, we'd give you a heads-up. Get some surveillance set up at your place to catch ingoing and outgoing transmissions. Trevor notwithstanding, the Benefactors are not usually careless or stupid. They'll find an unconventional way to contact to avoid getting on our radar." His posture changes and he herds us toward the door. "Enough soul-baring. You want to know more than that, talk my boss into giving you his job and the security clearance that goes with it. Bottom line is this: You just be ready to go when we call out the next mission. You tell us the second any Benefactor—or one of their Consiglieres—tries to recruit you. For now, get the fuck outta here. I'm going back to bed."

· · ·

When we return to my apartment, Nico cooks breakfast. Eggs. Bacon. Pancakes. Fresh New Orleans Style coffee. I swallow without tasting; my mind is stuck on Fagin.

Nico runs his fingers over the section of my hair that hides the bald patch, the spot where the doctors shaved so they could stitch up my head wound. Beneath the gauze patch, the stitches are almost gone.

"There's gonna be a scar," I say, brushing his hand away in a sudden swell of self-consciousness. "Good thing my hair will hide it."

Nico tilts his head and considers me with a cock-eyed smile. "Scars are sexy." He leans forward and kisses my forehead.

"Fagin said 'I love you.'" I fiddle with a piece of bacon, trying to focus my swirling thoughts.

"Yeah. Guess she wanted you to know. I mean, after the wringer we've all been through, it's good to say what you're feeling, right?"

"Guess when she said those words to me for the first time,"

He shrugs. "Haven't a clue. After she brought you to the future, maybe? On your birthday? My madre use to say 'I love you' a hundred times on every birthday. She said it brought good luck."

"Today," I drop the bacon back onto the plate and brush the crumbs from my hands. "The first time Fagin ever said that she loves me was on that call."

Nico nods in understanding and places a warm, comforting hand over mine. "I'm sorry," he says.

"Don't be sorry. Be worried. She could have said those words at any time, especially in the two weeks we've been home. But, she chose to say it for the first time as she leaves on some super-secret mission? She's still scared and this whole situation stinks to high heaven."

Nico moves to stand next to me, leaning his athletic frame against the solid surface of the counter, one foot perched on the bottom ring of my stool. "Carter's not going to give us any more information. We don't have a tracer on Fagin and she's not answering her phone. All we can do is wait."

"In case you haven't noticed, waiting isn't exactly my best skill."

"Good thing you don't have to wait by yourself." He leans in for a kiss.

It's sweet and soft and I wish I could forget everything but this.

I wish.

I pull back and look him in the eyes. "Nico, I'm not so sure this is a good idea. After Fagin's call, and everything coming at us in the next God-knows-how-long, being together could make us vulnerable. People have a way to hurt us."

He nods. "They had a way to hurt us before. Carter figured that one out when he used us as leverage against each other to seal this deal-with-the-devil crap. It's too late, Dodger. They know we're a thing." He moves closer, snakes his fingers gently into my hair and rests his forehead against mine. "If you're gonna pull this 'I'm no good for you, you have to stay away from me' bullshit, it's going to annoy the hell out of me. So just don't, okay?"

Pulling him closer, I breathe him in: He smells more of delicious morning sex than bacon and coffee. Maybe it's because I want that scent, need that scent. Maybe it's because I know he's right.

"The way I see it," he continues, "we've got two choices until Fagin gets back: Let the bastards divide and weaken us or stick together and get stronger so they can't break us. You're not stupid, Dodger. Neither am I." He pulls me off the bar stool, kisses my forehead. "I know which one I choose." He kisses my eyelids and my cheeks. Finally, tilting my chin up, he kisses my lips. "Maybe pick a side?"

He gives me a wink—damn him—and heads for the bedroom, stripping off his clothing as he goes. By the time he reaches the door, he's down to his skivvies.

What does freedom look like? Is it having enough wealth to carve my own path, control of my destiny? Is it revenge or justice or simply accepting the past for what it is, as damaged and painful as it may be?

I spent so long searching for the family I lost in the ashes of that burnt Acadian village that I almost missed the family that's right in front of me: Fagin. Nico.

Now there's a new choice, one of hundreds—big and small—to come: Run and let dark forces divide and conquer us or stay and let love mend my soul into something stronger than it was before.

I can see freedom. I know my choice.

I follow Nico.

The End

ACKNOWLEDGMENTS

Bringing a finished novel into the world— polished and ready for public consumption—is not a solitary process. It's true that writers sit alone at their desks, open a vein and spill their souls onto an empty page, hoping to have an impact on the world, one reader at a time. But if an author is lucky—and smart—they assemble an army of experienced publishing professionals who provide expertise, and have a network of family and friends who cheer and support the birth a tiny miracle that the writer can, one day, lift to the heavens from Pride Rock and proclaim: "I made this! Behold the glory of my creation!"

I have been incredibly lucky. I am occasionally smart, too, because I have an army.

First, I owe everlasting thanks, and profound gratitude, to the amazing and dedicated Indie publishing professionals who provided expertise, and a good kick in the pants to jump start my motivation (when needed):

Thank you, Dawn Ius—my book coach through Author Accelerator—for your guidance, encouragement, and for setting deadlines as I tore the original story—told from the wrong character's perspective —down to the studs and rebuilt it. I couldn't have gotten the book done without your expertise and support. Love you, girl! (And a huge thank you to Author Accelerator for connecting me with Dawn. Your book coaches are awesome!)

Thank you to editor, Ryan Boyd, who helped tighten the story in its final revision stage. You always provides concise, actionable feedback in a life-giving way that makes me want to be a better human, not just a better writer. I don't say this because I'm your mother, although giving birth to you was one of the great joys of my life (ok, maybe not the birth itself because...pain). I love working with you, and the experience yielded one of the funniest bits of feedback I've ever received ("Mom! The em-dashes!").

Many thanks to Dr. Joe Pesce, astrophysics expert with George Mason University and the National Science Foundation, who provided invaluable assistance with the time travel science pieces of the book. Up for another book project, Joe? (Psst... writers: If you don't know about the Science and Entertainment Exchange, a program of the National Academy of Sciences that connects content creators with scientists for all types of creative endeavors, you should!)

Finally, a huge thank you to the talented people who provided a myriad of Indie publishing services to get the book ready to publish: Chrissy at Damonza.com for the KICK ASS book cover design. It's fabulous; Bryan Cohen of Best Page Forward for the fantastic book blurb; Mark Dawson and James Blatch of The Self-Publishing Show podcast and Self-Publishing 101/Advertising for Authors training courses); Michael Anderle, Craig Martelle, and the entire 20Books-To50k® community for your storytelling passion and publishing expertise in the Indie publishing community.

Beyond the professional relationships, I'm lucky and grateful to have family and friends who support and encourage me in all things (except for the unfortunate crunchy perm phase in the 80s. I mean, what the hell, guys... you just let me go out like that without saying a word?)

To my family: Jason (my amazing first-born and a talented writer in his own right), daughter-in-law, Sami, and kids — Serenity, Kieran,

Sahara, Chloe, Kayley, and Alex (and the aforementioned Ryan). Thank you for loving me and being the support system I need even when my coffee isn't strong enough, I'm hangry or haven't had enough sleep. You're the best of me and I love you.

THANK YOU to my writing brainstorming group in Chicago: Hollie Smurthwaite, Llewella Forgie, Susan Levi, Lyssa Menard, and Danielle Baron. I've learned so much about writing, and the art of creative brainstorming, from each of you. When I was stuck, you helped unstick me. When I needed beta readers, you were there. THIEVES would've been much harder to write without you. I'm proud to call you my friends and fellow authors.

Thank you to Linda Rodriguez, Sally Tyler (for signal boosting the book cover voting on your Facebook page), Michael Kampf, Jen Batson, Andrea Surovek, Sharon Dillon, Erin Leavell, Susan Wade, Tyler Risk, Mary Canada, Maggie Kujawa, and Maria Perez, and so many others (you know who you are. I see and love you) for the support and enthusiasm.

Finally, a massive THANK YOU to you, the readers, for coming on this journey with me. I hope you enjoyed reading THIEVES as much as I loved writing it. There's more Clémence and Nico to come.

Lyn South
July 2020

ABOUT THE AUTHOR

Lyn South is a Chicago-based Science Fiction and Paranormal Romance author. Her favorite characters to write are fierce women who rise from the ashes to overcome impossible odds. She loves dogs —especially her Goldendoodle, Indy—motorcycles, outdoor adventures, and all things British. Her first book, THIEVES, is a Science Fiction Time Travel adventure.

Read more at https://lynsouth.com.

 facebook.com/LynSouthWrites

 twitter.com/lynsouth

 instagram.com/lynsouthwrites

THANK YOU FOR READING!

Please consider leaving a review at the retailer where you purchased this book. Reviews help Indie authors, like me, connect with other readers who may also enjoy our books.
If you enjoyed this novel, please tell your friends.

Join Lyn South's author newsletter for new book release news and other bonus content:
https://www.lynsouth.com

CITATIONS

Boyd, Ryan and South, Lyn. "The Queen's Riddle" Copyright 2020.
Anonymous Anglo-Saxon poet. "Riddle #9: My Dress is Silver".
Beowulf Longman Cultural Edition, pg 171, Riddle 9. 2004.
Wyatt, Sir Thomas. "I Find No Peace." Poems of Sir Thomas
Wyatt, the Elder. 1635-1653. Public Domain

Made in the USA
Middletown, DE
16 September 2020